The One *That* Matters

ELLE LINDER

OCEAN DREAMS
PUBLISHING

Minnesota

Ocean Dreams Publishing
17976 120th Ave NE
Thief River Falls, MN 56701
www.oceandreamspublishing.com
email: oceandreamspublishing@gmail.com

Publisher's Note: This is a work of fiction. Names, characters, places, and incidents are a product of the author's imagination. Locales and public names are sometimes used for atmospheric purposes. Any resemblance to actual people, living or dead, or to businesses, companies, events, institutions, or locales is completely coincidental.

Book Layout © 2017 (http://www.BookDesignTemplates.com)
Cover Design by James Smith (http://www.goonwrite.com)

The One That Matters/ Elle Linder. -- 1st ed.
ISBN 978-1-7324944-0-4 (softcover); ISBN 978-1-7324944-1-1 (ebook)

Our books may be purchased in bulk for promotional, educational, or business use. Please contact your local bookseller or Ocean Dreams Publishing via email at oceandreamspublishing@gmail.com.

For the women who loved, and tried, but couldn't make it work. I carry you in my heart, there is light.

"BE FEARLESS, BE BRAVE, BE BOLD,
LOVE YOURSELF."

—HARUKI MURAKAMI

ACKNOWLEDGEMENTS

My deepest gratitude and love goes out to so many who believed in me from day one. The creation of this labor of love was not a solo trip; there have been many, many people along for this ride.

My editor, Judith, thank you for coming through for me, editing this book during a very difficult and trying time in your life. I appreciate you dearly and have learned so much from you.

My social media content manager, Brittany. I stand in awe of all that you do for me. Not only are you fantastic with words, you are also tech savvy. You have blessed me greatly!

My proofreaders, Jennie and Beth. It was with your keen eyes for details and finding errors that this book is polished and ready for the reader's enjoyment. You both rock!

My beta readers: Maryann, Alyssa, Judith, Yvonne, Rita, Lilia, Judy, Katherine, Aurora, Jennie, Carrie, and Shelley. Your genuine excitement and encouragement motivated me through this journey. Without your honest feedback, this book may have never seen the light of day.

My awesome children; Brittany, Matthew, Sarah, Christian, Avery, Emma, Annemarie, and my daughter-in-love, Sydney. Thank you from the bottom of my heart for your patience as I talked about my writing constantly, and while I locked myself away to get the words put onto paper. You're all priceless to me.

My dearest bestie, Maryann. Thank you for hearing me out each time we talked on the phone. If I irritated you while I gabbed incessantly about the book, you never let it show. Your encouragement and enthusiasm about my story and me as a writer was next to none. You have been my loudest cheerleader. You are my rockstar of a best friend. I love you.

My support system, Kristi and Alyssa who, over drinks once a month at the Legion, let me talk about my newest story and pushed me to reach for the stars. Kim and Lisa, just knowing I had you two in my back pocket, ready to jump into action if the call came, meant the world to me. I love all of you!

My parents, Robert and Mel, there has never been a time you didn't believe in me. Your love and support has been the fuel that has made me who I am. I've learned how hard work and dedication produces success from the very best. You are my role models in life and I have been blessed beyond measure being your daughter.

Michael, my husband, you were with me when this idea was conceived, and throughout the process of writing this book, you have cheered me and challenged me. Knowing you were in my corner every step of the way was a crucial piece in this accomplishment of mine. Thank you, honey. I love you.

Lastly, my muses. My heart is filled with your stories and my soul has wept with you. You are strong and beautiful, and I believe in you. Follow your path with confidence and faith, there is peace beyond the chaos and pain.

The One That Matters

Chapter 1

Okay, *Abuelita*

Craig's aggravating voice droned on and on, with excuse after excuse. She had heard it all before, dozens of times. And yet his nonchalant attitude as he canceled his weekend with their son always felt like a punch in her gut. Try as she might, she couldn't remember a time when Craig had put her or the kids first. It wasn't that he didn't know how to be devoted to anything. He did. In fact, Craig's loyalties were to his parents and his family's construction business—and himself.

"Marie! Are you listening to me?!" His bombastic voice shook her from her reverie. The man had to have been a drill sergeant in a previous life, the way his voice boomed at the slightest frustration.

"Yes, I'm listening. You're going to Vegas with Sasha."

"Just tell Jackson 'another time'. I have to go. Our flight leaves in a couple of hours."

"You make it sound like being a parent is an option. He picks up on that, you know."

"You wanted full custody; now you're going to complain?"

"Huh-uh, don't twist this around. I'd love never to see you again, but you're still Jackson's father." Marie braced herself against the kitchen counter, gripped by the weight of her emotions threatening to pull her to the ground.

"Dammit! Don't do this!"

"What, hold you accountable to your children?"

"Shit. I'm doing you a favor canceling, so you won't be alone." *Alone.* The singular word had the power of a thousand to tear her down, and he knew it. She winced through the stretching and twisting of her innards. "I'll just email from now on."

"Perfect."

The hot water poured over the breakfast dishes while Marie stared out the window, transfixed on a tattered fence, trying to calm herself. Numb with nostalgia, she recalled her old view of a sparkling pool with strategically placed palm trees. The tranquil setting had been a lovely substitution for her ocean and made washing dishes bearable. If she tried hard enough, she could hear the roar and swoosh of the breaking waves and smell the seaweed. She could even feel the slithery vines snake around her ankles while she jumped into the frigid water.

A day at the beach with her *abuelita* was one of her fondest times. Once Marie had children, she took them to her favorite spot along the shore and created new memories with them while they splashed around in the Pacific. Giggle after silly giggle transported Marie back to her youth and to her dear grandma. Those short-lived days were a thing of the past. Now the old, weathered wooden fence in her view mirrored her lowly state.

You're pathetic, she thought as she turned off the hot water. This was what her life had become post-divorce: one ordinary, trivial task after another, with no one to hold her at night.

Her *abuelita's* words invaded her thoughts as they often did during times of distress. "Marie, *no estar solo*. Do not be alone," she had told Marie on the day she had joined Marie's *abuelo*, Pancho, in heaven. All her life, Marie had believed her dear sweet grandmother had spiritual powers, and that day when she took her last breath and said *"no estar solo,"* Marie had rolled her eyes. But now, Marie was alone.

Well, *this* weekend she wouldn't be alone. There was a silver lining in all of this. Jackson wouldn't be disappointed Craig canceled their weekend. He would be relieved. And Marie wouldn't be left in a puddle of tears after she coaxed Jackson out the door to go with a man he was invisible to. Perhaps if Jackson felt loved...wanted...and made a priority, he might want to go to Craig's of his own free will.

But Craig didn't see it that way and believed relationships didn't need nurturing. Nor did they have to be a priority unless you were a swimsuit model. Her mother had told her as much when she started dating him. She saw things Marie didn't see in her star football player.

"He's not like us," her mother would say in broken English.

To that Marie would reply, "I thought love conquers all, Mamá."

"*No siempre, mi amor,*" (not always, my love) her mother would tell her.

"But *Abuelita* used to say, 'All you need is love.'"

Her mother laughed. "A Beatles song? No, no, *Abuelita* is a romantic. *Tu corazón*...your heart is delicate. Choose wisely, *mija*," she had advised.

Perhaps Marie should have taken her mother's cautions more seriously. But then she wouldn't have Lexi or Jackson, and they meant everything to her. If nothing else, Marie would teach her children *family is everything.* It was the Valdez family motto: *"Familia es todo."* Aunts and uncles would throw those three words around like a hex if you didn't put your family first. Children grew up knowing their number one priority was family. As a child, Marie understood what her *abuelita* and elders had chanted on a daily basis. It showed in their actions. Everyone helped each other, even in the most mundane tasks, like doing the dishes. Someone always had your back, and they believed in the whole "it takes a village" mantra, something Marie would fully embrace now that she was alone. Her family always kept their word and they wouldn't dream of letting each other down. They loved big—*family is everything.*

Marie loaded the dishwasher and wiped down the counters. Craig's unexpected call had thrown her off her normal routine, and now she was running late. Still, her thoughts for the weekend were at the forefront of her mind.

Maybe Lexi will come over for dinner, she thought, now that Jackson would be home.

It had been a few weeks since she last saw Lexi. During that visit, Lexi had said her second year of college was ten times more difficult than she expected, requiring more of her time. Marie was so proud of her. She was doing things Marie didn't get to do at twenty years old, living life to the fullest, free and independent. Lexi was her own woman; no one controlled her. Marie couldn't be more grateful.

Looking up at the ceiling, Marie took a deep breath, her jaw set for the ritual of getting Jackson out the door. It was time to face off. "Jackson, we gotta go. I'll be late for work," Marie hollered from the base of the stairs. He was his typical uncooperative, angry eleven-year-old self. If their relationship didn't change in a significant way, Marie feared what the teenage Jackson would be like.

"I'm coming! Geez!" he screamed back.

Marie took a deep breath and shook her head. "Every stinkin' morning he *has* to be like this." She grabbed her keys and handbag off the entry table. She cringed, looking up at the second floor. The creaky ceiling made the cheap, nothing-special dome light shake especially hard beneath his rapid, heavy-footed steps. Her eyes followed the sounds as he moved from his room to the bathroom, then back to his room. Finally, he stomped down the stairs in a huff. It took all she had not to lose it. This same scene had played each day like a broken record since the divorce. She would wake him up, he'd grumble, drag his feet, and then switch gears, stomping around the house before they left. Not once would he have a civilized conversation with her. Two years ago, he never would have raised his voice or rolled his eyes in disrespect. But now he looked at her with disdain, and only spoke to her in anger. It pierced her heart over and over again. He had been the sweetest boy since the day he was born, and she had thought their bond was unbreakable. Her tender, funny, smart-as-a-whip boy had changed so much. Worse yet, their relationship was breakable now.

"All right, buddy, let's hit the road," she said playfully to lighten the mood. Her efforts received silence. She didn't know why she tried so hard when all he ever did was ignore her. But Marie held on to hope with a death grip that one day he would come around and have a relationship with her again. She would die before giving up on her son.

Jackson peered out the window as he always did on the drive to school. There was never a right time to talk to him, so Marie just went for it and braced for the backlash. "Looks like you'll be able to go to Ricky's birthday party after all." Jackson flinched with a slight twist of his head toward her, and she knew he was listening.

"Your dad and Sasha are going to Vegas this weekend. It was last minute. He said to tell you he'd make it up to you another time, and he's sorry." She embellished it to soften the blow. The slightest curl in the corner of his mouth reflected in the window. No backlash. Just silence.

When Jackson slammed the car door shut, Marie's tension dissipated. Now she would have fifteen minutes of peace and tranquility on her drive to work. It was just enough time for her to relax and prepare for a busy day, which she welcomed. Marie loved her job, her co-workers, and the law. As an IP paralegal for Malcolm-Bower and Associates, she had found her specialty with copyrights and trademarks. Work was the only place she felt appreciated, respected, and whole. And she wouldn't be alone.

Her tension returned at the sound of her phone buzzing. She picked it up to see who was calling, then sighed.

Chapter 2

Girls Night

There was only one reason Tessa called in the morning…on a Friday morning: to convince Marie to go out with the girls. It was a crapshoot. Answer and deal with Tessa, or let it go to voicemail and deal with her best friend, Ann, later. Marie answered the phone. Tessa was the lesser of the two evils.

"Good morning, Tessa."

"Morning. How are you on this beautiful SoCal Friday?"

"I'm good. Just dropped Jackson off at school and I *was* enjoying a quiet drive to work."

"Did I interrupt your meditation?" she teased.

"Look, let's cut to the chase…I can't go out tonight."

"Oh, come on! You didn't even let me give you the details," Tessa whined.

"That's because I don't need to hear them. I'm not going."

"Well, I'm going to tell you, anyway. We're going out dancing. To a Latin club—your specialty, if you recall. And it's been forever since you went dancing."

"Tessa, I can't leave Jackson tonight. We had a rough morning. Maybe another time."

"Oh stop! Don't let that little stinker ruin your weekend. It's been two years, Marie. The time has come for you to stop herming and hang out with your girlfriends," Tessa insisted.

"Herm-ing? Stop talking like you're a high schooler." Marie laughed. "Seriously though, Jackson's been a handful...more than usual. I don't want him to feel abandoned if I go out."

"What about tomorrow night? Call Lexi to sit with him. They need some brother-sister bonding," Tessa countered. "Wait! I thought it was Craig's weekend to have him?"

"Yeah, well *Sasha* wanted to go to Vegas, so he canceled his weekend with Jackson. Canceled, not even rescheduled."

"That son-of-a-bitch! He sees his son four fucking days a month and he can't schedule his sex trip for a weekend he doesn't have him?"

Marie smirked. She admired how Tessa had no qualms about using profanity. Marie never cursed. Her *abuelita* would have come unglued, along with her mother. "Nice girls don't have filthy mouths," they'd say. She took their words to heart. But something was liberating about profanity, though she could never bring herself to spout off curse words like her friends. However, their melodic use of obscenities strangely energized her.

"I agree with you, Tessa. Craig is awful. And every time he does something like this it hurts Jackson. But if I'm honest, I'm afraid to go out dancing or clubbing or whatever you girls usually do. Why don't we go to a movie?" A boring suggestion to be sure, but one she was open to entertaining. Except the girls were all single, and looking for love, which she knew they wouldn't find in a theater.

"A movie? Yeah, that sounds thrilling," Tessa mocked. "What are you afraid of? You're a fun, sexy Latina with brains, and nobody can dance like you. Come on… It'll be fun!"

"I'll think about it. I'm at work now. You have a good day herm-ing with your homies and hearing about their plans for the weekend." Marie giggled, *herm-ing*.

Tessa laughed. "Now there's the playful Marie I love so much. I'll talk to you later."

It was fast approaching noon, and Marie sat focused on the documents spread over her desk. The copyright for a song was the furthest thing from her mind. Tessa's call occupied her thoughts. She knew her girls would be relentless in getting her to go out with them. Knowing them as she did, they would be pushing harder than ever to break her out of the fortress she had built around herself. The gnawing in the pit of her stomach told her she needed to prepare.

Then a flash of panic hit. "Oh, I'm an idiot! I should know by now how those crazy girls work." She sighed. "Tessa's call was on behalf of Ann to test the waters. Crap!" It was true. Tessa was sent in to canvass Marie's mental state before Ann swooped in with the big guns. And she had fallen for it, giving Tessa the intel Ann sought…and she was afraid. Goosebumps covered Marie's arms while her palms grew sweaty. There was nothing to be done now but wait for Ann to call.

As four o'clock rolled around, Marie's dread turned to confusion. It wasn't like Ann not to have called by this time. Ann was the most punctual person she knew, and she always called by three to set up plans for the evening. The girls' Friday routine never changed. Dinner at seven, and then they'd hit up a club.

So why hadn't Ann called yet? Marie wouldn't dwell on it or let her thoughts run away with her. Maybe, just maybe, Tessa had convinced Ann to let her off the hook one more time. It was possible. When Tessa turned on her sweet, charming self, she could get even the hard-as-steel Ann to cave.

Marie shifted mental gears. She couldn't worry about the girls anymore. It was time to send Jackson his daily text, to touch base and make sure he arrived home okay.

> Marie: Hi buddy, how's it going?
> Jackson: same as always
> Marie: Do you want pizza for dinner?
> Jackson: whatev
> Marie: Ok, see you soon.

Even his responses were apathetic. At this point, Marie would do just about anything to restore their relationship. But what? What could she possibly do to make him happy? There was no way she'd take Craig back, not that he'd want her back with Sasha Hill in his life. How her forty-year-old ex had snagged her, Marie would never know. He was a lousy lover and an even lousier husband and father. Surely, he pulled the wool over Sasha. For a brief moment—a very brief moment—Marie actually felt sorry for the young twenty-nine-year-old swimsuit model.

After work, Marie stopped at Sonny's Pizza and then headed home. Sasha had remained on her mind. At thirty-eight, there was no way Marie could compete with the slender, blonde-haired, blue-eyed model with legs for miles…or any woman like her for that matter. Marie was softer in some areas, and her breasts weren't as perky as they once were, not to mention what pregnancy does to a woman's body—leaving her with wider hips and faded stretch marks. Marie had done her best to take care of herself, eating right and staying fit. The Latina had aged gracefully, like her mother and *abuelita* before her. Her tan skin, exotic features, and curvaceous body were envied by many, although Marie didn't have a clue what others saw.

A couple of years after she had married Craig, he began controlling most of what she did, from the way Marie dressed, to the amount of alcohol she drank, to dancing and music…right down to her very thoughts. The years with him had been unkind; she'd lost herself and her fight. Craig took on the role of "head of the household" with a firm grasp. Her *gringo* star football player outplayed her and her wits. As a child, she was raised to be obedient, but somewhere along the way, she didn't get the memo that she had a choice as an adult.

Marie put the car in park just as Lexi's car pulled in beside her. She quickly got out, excited to see her daughter. The sight of Lexi took Marie's breath away. It was like looking at herself in a mirror, circa 1998. Lexi looked like a younger version of Marie, with her long dark hair, piercing dark-brown eyes, a golden tan, and full lips. Marie's Latin attributes ran strong in both her kids, dominating Craig's Caucasian traits. Craig argued that the kids had dark hair and eyes like him, but they truly favored Marie, both inside and out.

"Hi, Mom," Lexi said as she exited her car.

"I didn't think I'd see you this evening."

Lexi only shrugged, pulling her backpack out of the backseat of her white Jetta. Perplexed, Marie grabbed the pizza and her handbag, closing the car door with her hip. It didn't matter why

Lexi had come home. Marie would have someone other than Jackson to spend the evening with. Her weekend had just improved tenfold.

"Jackson, I'm home," she called, entering the kitchen. No response. "Jackson, where are you, buddy?"

"Mom, I think I can hear the TV coming from the living room. I'll go check on him," Lexi offered.

"Thanks." She grabbed a paper plate, a few napkins, and a can of root beer. The doorbell chimed.

"I got it," Lexi called.

Marie slipped her pumps off, flexing her toes up and down after keeping them cramped in heels all day. As much as she liked dressing up for work, there was nothing better than taking off her heels and bra at the end of the day. However, the bra would have to wait a little while longer. She turned to exit the kitchen just as Ann walked in, stopping Marie in her tracks.

"Ann! What are you doing here?" Marie's incredulous stare must have been priceless the way Ann's obnoxious smirk radiated off her face.

"I'm here to see you," Ann said with a sly grin.

"Oh? Would you like some pizza?" Marie deflected as the goosebumps returned.

"Thanks, but no. We're having dinner out, but then you knew that." Ann cocked her head.

"You could think of it as an appetizer," Marie replied as she fought the internal panic taking root inside her. She picked up the plate of pizza and the soda, and carried them to Jackson. "Hey buddy, I have your pizza and root beer. What are you watching?" She stroked his hair, but he jerked away.

"Stop! It's *Pierce*," he protested. Marie sighed at his tone and walked out of the living room.

"Oh, I like this show. That Professor Pierce is pretty hot." Ann nudged him playfully.

"He's awesome." Jackson smiled up at her.

Marie's stomach twisted into a wicked knot as she selected a bottle of wine from the wine rack. She needed a drink of liquid courage for the battle that was to come with Ann. She searched in the kitchen drawer for the wine opener, but it wasn't there. Then she dug through another drawer. To her relief, she found it just as Ann returned to the kitchen.

"Don't open that bottle!" Ann ordered.

"What? Why not?" Marie froze with her hands in the air, bottle in one hand, the opener in the other.

"Cause we're going out. Let's go get you ready," Ann directed.

"I am not going anywhere. I can't leave Jackson. I told Tessa, and I know she told you." Marie leaned towards Ann and whispered, "Craig canceled his weekend with Jackson."

"Yes, I know what the bastard did. That's why I called Lexi to have her babysit. Now, let's get you ready."

Marie's mouth gaped open as Ann headed upstairs to her bedroom. Marie stormed up after her.

"You called Lexi? Why would you do that? She has her own life, you know. She doesn't need to be babysitting her eleven-year-old brother!"

Ann walked into Marie's bedroom and marched straight for the walk-in closet, completely ignoring Marie. She sifted through her wardrobe for a suitable dress. "Good god woman, your wardrobe is pathetic. I could have brought a dress from my closet. Well, not a problem. We have time to run by my house," she hollered from within the closet.

"No! I'm not going out." Marie crossed her arms over her chest in protest.

"Don't be ridiculous. You're going and that's final," Ann said as she exited the closet. Her calm, confident gait elevated Marie's heart rate. This was happening.

"You can't make me! Stop trying to bully me." Marie stiffened like a concrete wall.

Ann tilted her head, connecting her stern gaze with Marie's. There was nothing worse than Ann's death stare. She could make a WWF wrestler the likes of John Cena squirm in their seat. Marie closed her eyes to avoid the intimidating stare as she shook her head no.

"You're coming. I'm not taking no for an answer," Ann said, matter-of-factly.

In a last-ditch effort to win the battle, Marie grasped the smallest bit of fight in her to regain control of the situation. "So, this was your plan? Your little covert plan to pressure me—force me—manipulate me—KIDNAP me into going out with you? That's so wrong! Friends don't do that to friends!" Marie paced the room, her hands flying through the air in indignation. All the while Ann remained stoic. Marie knew she had lost the battle with every word that left her mouth.

"What are you afraid of, Marie, having fun with your girlfriends? Having a good dinner and some yummy cocktails with us? Laughing? Dancing? Living?" She arched her brow at Marie. "Maybe what you're afraid of is being rejected? Ignored? Passed over for a younger woman?"

"I don't know," her voice cracked. "I'm just afraid, of all of it." Marie collapsed onto the bed in defeat, her gaze dropped to her feet.

"Oh honey, I hate how that bastard screwed you up." Ann sat beside Marie and wrapped her arm around her back. "You're too goddamn beautiful and vibrant to waste away in your little home alone. It's time you re-entered the world of the living."

Marie stared off into the distance. Everything Ann said was true…so much so, it scared the bejeezus out of her. One thing was for sure—her girlfriends were the very best, but they were bossy as hell, too.

After her divorce was finalized, they had given her a year to regroup and adjust to being a single parent. They loved her and weren't going to rush her, knowing her emotional struggles after Craig walked out on her and the kids. But then they started inviting her out with them twice a month. Now, the invites were extended every Friday to wear her down…all part of the plan. Their determination to get her out of her sad little home had been ramped up, and they would not let her pity party go on any longer. Yes, they were the very best girlfriends a girl could ever have.

"I appreciate all that you girls are trying to do. But…"

"Stop right there." Ann raised her hand. "Do you have a dress in that deplorable closet of yours or do we need to swing by my house? I don't want to hear another word about not going."

"Wow, do you have to be such a…control-freak?!"

"Yes," Ann shot back.

"I'm not like you. I don't bounce back so easily."

"I know that, but it's been two years, Marie. Nobody says you have to laugh, dance, or talk. You can just sit on your ass and look like a mannequin if you want. But you're going out with us."

Marie sat shell-shocked. On the one hand, she was lonely and bored at home most nights, and too young to not enjoy life. On the other hand, the thought of being hurt again terrified her. The storm that had blown through the loving home she had worked so hard to create had destroyed everyone in its path. The damage left for her to clean up had been taxing, and she was tired. Tired of doing it all on her own—alone.

"How can a man be so selfish and not think of anyone else but himself?" Marie's eyes welled up. "I don't understand it."

"Craig…he's that man. A selfish prick. But not every man is like him," Ann comforted. "Go out tonight with *us*—your girls who love you to pieces. This will be the first step in taking back your life. Fuck Craig! Don't let him keep you down. Rise above this, start living and find happiness again. And that doesn't mean with a man. You need to do *you* first."

"How can I do me first when I don't even know who 'me' is?"

"Well, you start by saying 'yes' when you want something and 'no' when you don't. Except, tonight…you're going tonight," Ann said definitively.

"But I still feel like I was just hit by a Mack truck."

"I have the perfect remedy for that—tequila." Ann grinned with a mischievous glint in her eye. "Now, I'm gonna text the girls to meet us at the cantina at eight since we're running a little behind. Go grab your favorite nude sling-backs because I have the perfect dress for you to wear."

Biting her lower lip, Marie grabbed her shoes and her makeup bag. There was no fighting Ann—only surrender. *Abuelita's* words flooded back: "Do not be alone." She rapidly blinked, pushing back her emotions. *Okay, Abuelita.*

Marie went downstairs to find Lexi. "Now if there's anything you need, please call or text me. Don't be afraid to bother me," she stressed.

"Mom, we'll be fine. He's eleven years old. I'll make sure he doesn't drink the bleach or put thumbtacks in his mouth," Lexi teased. Marie's expression soured. She didn't find her funny one bit. "Seriously, Mom, it'll be okay. Have fun. You deserve it, and if you meet someone, don't worry about coming home. I can handle everything." Marie gasped while Ann laughed loudly.

"I love you, Lexi," Ann said, hugging her tightly. "Thank you for coming when I called." She handed her a hundred dollar bill. "Go buy yourself something pretty."

"Great, now you're bribing my kid with money."

"I'll do whatever it takes," Ann said with resolve.

"Money works just fine." Lexi giggled.

"You two, geez. Let me go say goodbye to my little angel." Marie found Jackson still watching *Pierce* in the living room. "Hey Jackson, how many episodes of that show are you going to watch?"

"I don't know," he grumbled.

"I'm going out with Ann and the girls tonight. Lexi is staying with you. I'll see you in the morning, okay?" He looked up at her, eyes wide with uncertainty. She stroked his hair and leaned down to kiss his forehead. He didn't pull away. "Call me if you need anything."

"Okay," he responded as his eyes went back to the show; there was a battle going on that drew his attention. But for two seconds, Marie had his attention again, and a brief glance reinforced the hope she held onto.

Chapter 3

Familial Feelings

Marie stared out the window of Ann's Honda Pilot as they drove south on the 405. "Where did you say we're going?"

"Océanos Latin Cantina in Santa Monica, across the street from the beach. I've heard good things about it. The Latin vibe is what we're after for you, honey." Ann smiled at Marie.

"Well, I hope I don't ruin your fun. I'm feeling exposed in this dress you made me wear." She looked down at the white, fitted spaghetti-strap dress with the magenta fade along the bottom edge.

"Not at all. It looks amazing with your gorgeous tan and hourglass shape. Shit, it fits you better than me." Her flattery was genuine, but Marie blew it off. It was just Ann being cute.

"What about my hair? I never leave it down. A French twist, or a ponytail?"

"Neither; a French twist screams uptight. For a Latin club wear your hair down. Be fun and sexy." Ann winked as she kept her eyes on the road.

"This ombre print, is it too young for a woman my age?"

"Seriously?"

"Seriously."

"We're the same damn age." Ann pinched her lips together. "Enough already. You're bringing me down."

"Sorry," Marie said in a quiet voice.

"You're sexy, freakin' hot...what more can I say?" Ann gripped the steering wheel. "First thing I'm doing is ordering up a round of shots...maybe two rounds."

"Wait! I don't want to get drunk. I haven't done shots in a long time. I refuse to get drunk."

"Marie, loosen up. Nobody is talking about getting drunk. Don't be so paranoid. Craig's not around to control you any-more."

Marie clutched her purse against her chest. "I'll try to relax."

"Good. We will have a great time, promise."

Marie nodded, pulling down the visor for the mirror. She wore a little more eye makeup than she would normally, but she rather liked it. She didn't care for lipstick, so she applied a tinted lip gloss instead. It was all her full lips needed.

"Now, do you remember how to dance?" Ann teased.

"I do, but I will not be dancing." Marie rolled her eyes.

"Here we go...round two with my sweet, irritating girl being stubborn as hell. Surely you've been taking lessons from Jackson." Ann scratched the back of her hair, fluffing it.

Marie pressed her lips together. Ann's comment was well-taken. Her nerves were making her act ridiculous. She was usual-ly calm and collected. At work, she was on top of everything—professional, intelligent, and never silly. Yup, she needed to get a grip, and quick.

Thinking back to her youth, she remembered being confi-dent...strong, sassy, and fun. School had been easy for her, and she had a lot of friends. The take-charge girl had her life all planned out: college, marriage, and kids. Her plan took an unexpected turn when she got pregnant with Lexi at eighteen. Craig had told her "pulling out" was all he needed to do, because he didn't want to wear a condom, and she had believed him. How could she be so naïve? But Marie was, and it had cost her big. Sure, she loved her kids more than anything, but her life didn't turn out the way she thought it would. A divorcée and mother of two, what was she supposed to do now? She took a deep breath as Ann pulled into a parking spot.

"Ann," she began, "I'll try to have a good time, but I need you to be patient with me. It's been a long time since I've been single. In my head, I'm still a wife." She grimaced.

"I know, honey. I get it. I won't let anything happen to you. Now let's go have good food, yummy drinks, and fun with our girls."

When Marie and Ann walked into the cantina, the packed entryway had people lined up for a table. Fortunately for them, they had reservations. Tessa and Brooke had already arrived and were at a table near the dance floor. The waitress led the women to the half-moon booth, and the girls gushed over Marie.

"Damn woman, you clean up well," Tessa said. "I'm so glad you came."

"Shit, I almost didn't recognize you with your hair down," Brooke added. "Is that cleavage?" Brooke's eyes bulged as she stared at Marie's chest.

"Um, wow…thanks." Marie self-consciously covered what little cleavage showed as she slid into the booth next to Tessa. Ann sat on the other end next to Brooke. She winked and motioned for Marie to lower her hand.

"What can I get you ladies, to drink?" the cute, young waitress asked.

"We'll have a round of tequila shots…Patrón," Ann answered for the table. The waitress nodded and left.

Marie scanned the club, the vibe electrifying, with people eating, drinking and talking with exaggerated facial expressions and hand gestures. She couldn't recall the last time *happy people* surrounded her. The Latin decor was bright and festive with hues of crimson, gold, and emerald. Terracotta tiles lined the walkway leading to a bamboo dance floor. Enticing energy rippled off the spirited dancers as they shook every part of their bodies to "Conmigo," a familiar salsa beat that brought a smile to her face.

It was like she was back home, a teenager at a family fiesta, minus the wild kids running around. Their gatherings were the best, especially the music. How she'd missed Latin melodies…mambo, salsa, mariachi. Then there was "Cherry Pink and Apple Blossom White," her grandparents' song. At every Valdez family gathering, the song played just for Pancho and Carmelita. Marie always admired their love and commitment to each other. It's what she always wanted in her marriage. Dancing with her love to a romantic Latin melody would have completed her dream.

After her parents, Henry and Rosa had moved to Miami, the Valdez family get-togethers decreased. Relatives scattered around the world and the once tight-knit Valdez community dwindled down to only a few in Southern California, one being Marie. The hardest part was being with Craig's family all the time instead of her own. Just like Craig, they didn't care for her traditions and culture. Little by little her Latin roots disappeared, and it had started with the music.

Now surrounded by her heritage once again, she was over-whelmed with excitement—and the awakening of her soul. Its dormant slumber had begun seventeen years ago when Craig took control of every aspect of her life. She smiled at Ann and mouthed, "Thank you," just as the waitress returned with their tequila shots.

"All right, ladies, lift your glasses. To Marie! May this be the first step in reinventing yourself. Self-discovery is a wonderful thing sweetheart. Enjoy the journey." Ann smiled. "*Salúd!*" The table of girls cheered "*Salúd*" then pushed back their shots.

"Whoa!" Marie gasped from the burn of the alcohol. She was glossy-eyed and breathing heavily; it had been a long time since her last shot of tequila.

An hour had passed since the girls' first round of drinks. Marie was the most relaxed she'd been in years. The waitress had just removed all their plates and taken their drink orders for the third time. Marie had just ordered a second margarita when a guy approached their table, his eyes locked on Brooke.

"Hi, would you like to dance?" he asked Brooke.

"Sure." She smiled, nudging Ann to let her out of the booth. The three women watched them walk to the dance floor with interest. Marie fidgeted with her cocktail napkin, wondering who would dance next. *Ann, maybe?*

"Isn't he cute?" Ann said as she slid back into the booth.

"Meh, he's okay," Tessa replied, unimpressed. "You know Brooke never declines an invite to dance. Cute isn't a prerequisite."

Marie chewed on her lower lip, taking it all in. "I'll be back." She pointed to the bathroom.

"I'll go with you," Ann said.

"I'll guard the drinks." Tessa laughed as she lifted her sangria to her lips.

"Well, you didn't seem impressed by Brooke's dance partner," Ann said as they approached the ladies' room.

"Everybody is different. She's such a pretty girl, and he's average-looking, I guess. Not my type. The beer belly is a turnoff." She preferred an athletic, muscular physique. Craig had worked out hardcore while playing football, and he never let himself go after becoming a husband and father. Then again, he also preferred a fit woman, but Marie struggled to stay in shape. Between being a wife, mother, and working, it was a challenge to hit the gym. She often wondered if her softer body was part of the reason he cheated on her with such a young, toned woman. After the divorce, she had managed to squeeze in a few workouts during the week. She liked her body mostly—when it was only her seeing it. But her boobs were a different story. Nothing would make her happier than getting a breast lift and her stretch marks erased.

"Oh, come on, you can't be so picky straight out the gate. If this is your attitude, you will never accept a man's invite to dance," Ann said, interrupting her thoughts.

"I told you, I don't plan to dance."

"You will dance with the first man that asks you," Ann said as they entered the busy ladies' lounge.

"Ha! Are you bossing me around again?"

"Nope, I'm making sure you have an awesome night."

"Well, I'm not making any promises, but I have one requirement—Latino."

Ann looked at her, surprised. "Latino? That's your requirement? A Latino man?"

Marie didn't respond as she walked into the bathroom stall. She didn't know what had possessed her to say a Latino man was her requirement. Maybe her subconscious spoke for her? After the way Craig dominated and controlled every area of her life, why would she risk a repeat with another white guy? No, a Latino man would understand and appreciate their culture. He'd be like her.

Two bubbly women walked out of the stalls while Marie washed her hands. She couldn't help but stare. Both women sparkled with vitality. They were young, attractive twenty-somethings with firm bodies and perky breasts. She glanced at herself in the mirror and glowered.

Ann followed behind them, unfazed, but Marie envied their youth and apparent freedom. Such liberties she never experienced in her twenties. The women talked and laughed without a care in the world. Did they know how lucky they were?

"I heard Parker is coming tonight," the cute blonde said to her friend. She was reapplying lipstick that matched her taut scarlet dress perfectly. What a dress it was—it showed every curve of her body and stopped mid-thigh.

"I doubt it. Isn't he filming right now?" the sassy redhead said, scrunching her natural curls. "Did you see last week's episode?" She fanned herself.

Marie listened to the women, and whoever this Parker was, they seemed to like him. Ann jerked her chin for Marie to follow her out. She complied, thrilled to escape the torture of the young duo.

On their way back to the booth, an average-looking Latino stopped Marie and asked her to dance.

"No, thank you. I'm here with friends," she answered.

"Oh, it'll be fine." Ann took her clutch and nudged her along.

Marie froze as the man took her hand, leading her to the dance floor with a cocky swagger that was not off-putting. However, her nerves didn't care if he was a stranger or her favorite uncle Louie who had taught her to dance the cumbia. At this very moment, she wanted to sit her ass down and make like a mannequin until she could resume her normal, boring and lonely life. *Get a grip, Marie,* she thought. *It's just a dance.*

Right away, Marie located Brooke in the crowd. The elation on Brooke's face seeing her forced a sheepish grin out of Marie. The music encircled her, and in an instant, her worries dissipated. "Adrenalina," an up-tempo song with a thumping beat by Wisin distracted her. She had never heard the song before but recognized Jennifer Lopez and Ricky Martin's voices. *I need to brush up on my Spanish.*

Lexi sat engrossed in Jackson's favorite TV show, *Pierce.* Unlike her mom who wasn't interested in what Jackson watched just as long as it was appropriate, Lexi used the show to bond with him. "So, this professor, how did he get his special powers?" she asked him.

"Stung by an eel in Asia, snorkeling. The eel was radioactive." Jackson grinned, bobbing his eyebrows up and down. "He's the coolest superhero ever. And he never kills any of the bad guys. His powers turn them good."

"Wow, I can see why you think he's awesome. He's not bad-looking either." She nudged him when he made a gagging face. They both laughed, then stopped when Darth Vader's theme song sounded on Jackson's phone. "Who's calling?" Lexi asked.

"Dad." Jackson frowned.

"'The Imperial March' is Dad's ringtone?"

Jackson nodded as he answered the phone. "Hi, Dad."

"Hey, Jackson. How've you been?" His dad asked as if he hadn't just canceled his weekend with him to take a trip to Vegas with his girlfriend.

"Fine."

"I want you to spend the night tomorrow, and we'll have dinner with Sasha. What do you say?"

"Um, I don't know. I have Ricky's birthday party tomorrow night at the bowling alley. It's a sleepover," Jackson said.

"Who's Ricky?"

"My best friend," Jackson snapped with a scowl on his face.

"Yeah well, there will be other birthdays. It's my weekend, and I want you tomorrow. Go ask your mom."

"She's not here."

"It's after nine, where is she?"

"Out with the girls. Lexi's here," Jackson said.

"Put her on the phone."

Jackson turned toward Lexi and pushed the phone at her. "Here."

"Hell-o."

"Hey Lexi, where's your mother?" he asked abruptly.

"Geez…I'm great, how are you, Dad?" She heard him huff. "Never mind. She's with Ann and the girls. They went out to a club. Why?"

"A club? She doesn't go to clubs." He scoffed. "I'm calling about Jackson. I want him tomorrow night. I would've emailed, but I thought it better to call since it was last minute," Craig explained.

"Well, she's not here," Lexi repeated.

"Call and ask her, then text me. I'm sure she'll say yes. It's stupid I have to ask to see my son," he snapped.

"Should've thought about that before you cheated," she said under her breath.

"What did you say?"

"I'll call her and let you know what she says."

"Tell her not to be out late. A woman her age has no business being at a club."

"Wow, that's insulting. Did you mean to say that?"

"Watch yourself," he returned.

"I could say the same to you. I'll text you her answer. Bye." And with that Lexi ended the call. "Grrr, he's rude!" Jackson faced forward, eyes on the TV. "Hey, you okay?"

"Now I can't go to Ricky's birthday party," he said, deflated.

"Aww, maybe Mom will say no since Dad had canceled originally."

"She won't, she never does. I thought he was going to be in Vegas all weekend." He huffed.

"It *is* strange that he'll be back and wants to see you."

The rush of adrenaline Marie had coursing through her body while she danced overpowered her thoughts. The song was a perfect introduction to living. The Latino dancing before her wasn't bad-looking. And *familial.* He had coarse, wavy black hair, slicked back, dark eyes that could pass for black marbles, and he wasn't much taller than her. A tattoo of the Virgin Mary on his forearm stared back at her—a little unnerving. Her eyes traveled up to his head, and a broad grin stretched across his face. She blushed and looked away.

The salsa moves Uncle Louie had taught her returned by the end of the first song, just like riding a bike. Actually, being Latino didn't mean anything; plenty of people in her family couldn't dance. However, the dancing gods had blessed her, and to her surprise, her partner could hold his own.

Marie didn't see celebrity Parker Nichols off to the side of the dance floor, doing his best to not draw attention to himself. Beside him stood his manager, Victor Medina, and close friend Dave Sumner. In the sea of dark, gyrating silhouettes, Marie stood out in her white and magenta dress. She had more than relaxed on the dance floor with Brooke and the Latino. Hips in a full-blown shake, her arms swayed above her head as she spun around in a tight circle in front of her partner. Her long, dark hair flowed around her shining face.

Parker eyed Marie working the floor around her partner. He couldn't remember if there was ever a time someone had mesmerized him. It was her carefree vibe…and that gorgeous body. Her tan arms moved with ease to the beat of the music; her shapely hips shifted from side to side, showing their experience. Parker imagined her lovely, provocative moves against him, but he didn't want to imagine. He wanted to experience. The sight of her sent his heart-rate skyrocketing with each shake and shimmy she performed. Then his eyes moved to the man dancing with her. Who was he?

"Sir, your table is ready," a star-struck waitress announced. He nodded, taking his eyes off Marie, and followed the waitress to his table. The gentlemen sat down and placed their drink orders—Patrón for Victor, Hennessy for Parker and Dave.

"Hey man, who's caught your eye?" Dave asked, jerking his chin toward the dance floor.

"Nobody. I'm just checking everything out," Parker said.

"Yeah right. You have that look you get when you're interested." Dave smirked, though his teasing did not affect Parker.

When the gentlemen had sat down in the half-moon booth, Parker stayed on the end, in case he needed to exit the club quickly. The waitress returned with their drinks and a seductive smile for Parker. "Thank you," he said, ignoring the flirting looks from the waitress. He turned his gaze back to Marie, eating up her dance moves—and her.

When the song ended, Parker watched as she grabbed the cute brunette's hand and pulled her off the floor, leaving both men standing there. He observed Marie with great interest and was elated to see her booth across from his, and that her dance partner did not join her.

Chapter 4

Just A Dance

Oh my gosh, that was great!" Marie announced, taking her seat.
"I told you," Ann said with a roll of her eyes. "Now drink your
margarita before it gets watered down."

"Yes, I'm parched." Marie took a large gulp and the powerful
punch of tequila hit her. "Whoa, that was a little much." She
checked her phone and saw she had a missed call from Lexi.
"Oh crap, Lexi called. I'll be right back." Marie went to the lobby, where it was quieter and hovered in a corner to return the
call.

"Hi, Mom."

"Lexi, is everything okay? I freaked when I saw your missed
call."

"Mom, it's fine. Dad called asking to have Jackson tomorrow
night, but Jackson said he had Ricky's party. So, Dad wanted me
to call you. Can he have Jackson?"

"Um, if Jackson wants to, it's fine with me. But he was excited about Ricky's birthday. Why is he coming back a day early
from Vegas? Ugh, it's so like him to flip-flop. I don't know what
to do."

The irritation in Marie's voice was loud and clear. Who could blame her? Lexi's call had interrupted her evening out—her first evening out since the divorce. But it was typical Craig being controlling, having to know *right now*. Especially after Lexi told him Marie was out for the evening with the girls; that was Lexi's first mistake. Her second mistake was calling him rude.

Marie knew Lexi had her own irritation with her dad. The strain on their father-daughter relationship had begun ten years earlier, once Lexi was old enough to understand his controlling, manipulative treatment of her mom. Marie had tried to shield Lexi as much as possible from the hurtful, ugly words Craig would say, but she couldn't. Time and time again, Lexi was a witness to her mom's tears, and it broke Marie's heart. When Craig left their home for good, Marie saw the enormous relief Lexi felt. Even so, Craig still controlled Marie, and Lexi had no way of helping her mother.

"Okay, Mom, I'll handle it, no worries. Are you having fun? You kinda sound relaxed. I can hear the music...you're dancing, right?" Lexi prodded.

"I am relaxed. And yes, I've danced to two songs."

"Well the night is still young, so I expect another dozen dances from you, missy," Lexi teased.

"You're an awesome daughter. Have a good night."

"You too, Mom. Bye."

Marie ended the call and paced, gripping her phone tightly. She couldn't believe Craig called Jackson after canceling his weekend with him. He was the world's biggest jerk, in her book. She took a deep breath and did a little shake to release her frustration. More than ever, she wanted to forget about her boring life and her ex. The call fueled her determination to have a good time with her girls.

When Parker saw the woman walk to the front of the club with her phone in hand, he assumed she'd be back, but his curiosity got the better of him. He excused himself from the table and followed her. He stopped several feet back to observe the delicious dress that hugged her curves just right. Her tan skin stood out against the white of her dress, begging to be touched by him. There was no question he found her attractive, and he hadn't even spoken to her yet...but he planned to.

Parker had watched the expression on her face change throughout the call—worried, then smiling, then frustrated with her hands balled up, then smiling again. The sight of her was magnificent, and more than anything, Parker wanted to dance with her.

As she walked toward him, he stepped in front of her. Their eyes locked and an unfamiliar surge move between them as her face flushed.

"Excuse me," she said.

"Would you like to dance?" She stared up at him, stunned. "I watched you dancing with the other guy. Your moves are pretty great. What do you say?" Just inches away from her, he could smell the soft scent of her intoxicating perfume, her eyes darting around with a look of uncertainty.

"Sure."

Parker nodded with a slight raise of his brows, then put his hand on the small of her back, escorting her to the dance floor.

Marie stiffened at the light touch of his hand as if hot coals burned through the fabric of her dress. The sensations put her on alert, instantly hyper-aware of his touch. She avoided looking in the direction of her table. The girls would for sure see the anxiety on her face and would likely give her crap about it.

This guy was gorgeous, in his black slacks and white button-down shirt that enhanced his muscular build and trim waist. She guessed he was several years younger than her, judging by his dirty-blonde hair that looked to be styled by a top-rated stylist— one of *those* Hollywood stylists. Then she remembered her Latino requirement; Latino he was not. However, this gringo had slate-blue eyes that were calm and safe, not at all like Craig's hard stare. *Why on earth did he ask me to dance? No matter, it's just a dance,* she told herself. *Just one dance.*

Marie turned to face him, his intense eyes consumed her with their intrigue and desire. A tremble radiated through her body; she needed to dance to get her mind off him. The song, "Me Enamoré" by Shakira, did the job. It was a sexy song she could get lost in as she danced with her handsome partner. All she had to do was pretend she was dancing in her kitchen, wiping down the counters and loading the dishwasher. *It's just one dance.*

Enthralled, Parker couldn't get enough of this dancing beauty. She made little eye contact with him, but when she did, her dark, piercing eyes stirred him up. All he wanted was to pull her close and feel her curvy body against him. When she whirled around and whipped her hair back, her perfume about knocked him off his feet. Then a flash from behind her caught his eye; a woman had her phone out taking pictures of him. It was crappy timing. He wanted to dance and be normal, not pose for selfies with his encroaching fans.

Just as the song neared the end, the Latino returned and cut in. "Can I have the next dance?" he asked Parker's partner.

"Sure." She smiled. "Thanks for the dance," she said to Parker as she turned to dance with the other man.

Deflated, Parker walked back to his table with a few women following him. He took a large gulp of his drink, then proceeded to take selfies with the women, but his gaze remained on Marie.

"Nice move on the free publicity," Victor praised. "You always surprise me with what you know how to do." Parker sighed with a slight shake of his head; his manager never quite understood him.

"She has you bent out of shape," Dave said, jerking his chin toward the woman who captured Parker's attention.

"Yeah."

"Did you get her name?"

"No. We didn't talk much. Damn, she's beautiful." He finished his drink, keeping his eyes on her.

"You let the dude cut in and steal her away. What's up with that? You never back off," Dave said.

"Because she wanted to dance with him." He shrugged.

Parker watched Marie through two more songs before she returned to her table. He called over the waitress. In a whisper, Parker requested an order of rounds for her and her party. By this time, he had already taken a dozen photos with fans.

While Marie danced with the persistent Latino, she watched Mr. Blue-eyes with curiosity. She didn't understand why women were lining up to take pictures with him.

"Well, well, well...joining us are you?" Tessa teased. "After all the complaining, now you're acting like a pro."

"Oh stop. I forgot how much I like to dance." Marie smiled.

"Only one dance with the hottie?" Ann asked with a raise of her brow. "Because he's not…Latino?"

"No. The other guy asked. I said 'sure.' Isn't that what I'm supposed to do?"

"Not if you like the hottie better," Ann said.

"That's a no-brainer, she has to like Parker Nichols better." Brooke snorted.

"Who's Parker Nichols?" Marie asked.

"The hottie you were dancing with just now. The guy with all the moves," Ann said.

"That tells me nothing," Marie said.

"Hi ladies," a waitress interrupted. "The gentleman over there ordered these drinks for your table." She grinned, tilting her head toward Parker's table.

"Well, how nice." Ann smiled and gave a little wave to Parker. Marie looked over, and his gaze was on her. She pulled back.

"Ann, I think it's time we leave," Marie suggested.

"I don't think so. He's coming over here." She raised her eyebrows with a smirk on her face.

"Yay!" Brooke cheered, bouncing in her seat.

"Hi ladies," Parker said. "Can I join you?"

"Please do," Ann answered for the table. Brooke stared, star-struck. He moved to sit next to Marie, and Tessa pulled her arm, making her scoot over.

"Thank you for the drinks," Tessa said.

"It's my pleasure." He smiled, turning his attention to Marie. "I'm Parker Nichols," he said putting his hand out to her. Marie stared at him, then at his hand. Tessa kicked her foot under the table, waking her from her trance.

"Nice to meet you," Marie said as she shook his hand. His eyes were locked on her when the two women from the bathroom walked up to Parker. They swooned like lovesick groupies at a U2 concert. Marie sunk into her seat, trapped in the booth.

In unison, they gushed over him. "Mr. Nichols, it would make our lifetime if you'd take a selfie with us. Pleeease!" Their tacky script appeared rehearsed.

Marie kept her eyes on her empty margarita glass. Embarrassment filled her, but what did she care who this *Parker Nichols* took pictures with or who he was? He was nobody to her, yet it annoyed her to see him smile while making the gushing duo's "lifetime." She rolled her eyes, then shot an aggravated look at Ann. "Let's go," she mouthed. Ann shook her head no.

The Latin man approached the table before Marie could have choice words with Ann, and she was relieved to see him. "Would you like to dance?" he asked her, and she nodded. Two seconds later she was out of the booth, clutch in hand.

"Enjoy the rest of your evening," she whispered to Ann. "I'll call Uber for a ride." Ann's mouth fell open.

Parker watched his evasive dance partner leave, burned by her swift exit. When his fans finally left, he rejoined the awestruck ladies, but the one person he hoped to talk to was on the dance floor without him...again.

"So, your friend," he began, "what's her name? What can you tell me about her?"

"Absolutely nothing," Ann answered. He furrowed his brow. "If we gave you any information about her, she would lose her trust in us. Sorry."

"Seriously? Can't you at least tell me her name?"

"Nope, Ann's right," Tessa agreed. "She didn't give you her name when you introduced yourself, so we can't either."

Parker took a deep breath, "O-kay. I'll stay here and wait for her." He turned his attention back to the dance floor while the women took great pleasure in gawking at him.

Marie remained on the dance floor for a second dance with the Latino, who had introduced himself as Juan. The longer Parker sat in her spot, the more frustrated she became. He couldn't be waiting for her, could he? It unnerved her every time their eyes connected, and butterflies fluttered about in her stomach. The flummoxed look on Parker's face was gratifying for Marie. Now, she wasn't the only person irritated. But she wondered why he was still there.

When the song ended, Juan asked her to join him for a drink. Without giving it a second thought, she accepted. The bright lights and hot, sweaty dancers around her sucked her dry, leaving her parched. She had no other choice but to accept Juan's offer. When she glanced over at her table, it amused her to see Parker's head drop in defeat when she took a seat with Juan.

"Ladies, it's been enjoyable," Parker said, forcing a smile. "I can see your friend won't be returning while I'm here, so I'll leave. I hope I didn't ruin your evening. I only wanted to get to know her."

"Mr. Nichols," Ann started.

"Call me Parker," he interrupted.

"Parker...she's complicated."

"Clearly." He looked over at her.

"Your instincts are spot on with her. She's terrific," Ann assured him.

"The very best," Tessa added, nodding.

"But she's screwed up," Brooke blurted. Ann and Tessa shot her a stern look. "Sorry," she mouthed.

"What's that supposed to mean?" He stared at Brooke.

"She's not screwed up," Ann corrected. "That's all I can tell you."

"Which is nothing." He winked. "Can you tell me this: is she a druggy, alcoholic, a gambler in debt to the mob, psychotic…married?" All their eyes turned to him. "She's married?"

"No, divorced," Brooke blurted again. The stern looks from Ann and Tessa were back. "Sorry, you know I have a big mouth."

"I can do divorced. Unless her ex is psychotic?" Parker asked.

"Parker, the bottom line is she's a private person. I assume you figured that out during this conversation." He nodded. "And you're a celebrity. Your fans took her picture out on the dance floor. If those photos pop up everywhere she's gonna come unglued," Ann warned.

"She didn't seem *that* bothered by it," he said.

"That's because she doesn't have a clue who you are. Once she finds out, she'll shoot you down. She's a 'no drama' kind of person." Tessa shrugged.

"I like that. So, you're telling me to walk away?" They all nodded. He looked over at her and her eyes connected with his, turning his stomach inside out. "Can you give her my business card?" He handed it to Ann.

"Sure. I'll put in a good word for you tonight when I drive her back to Sherman Oaks. And if that doesn't go well, I'll call her Monday while she's working on copyrights and trademarks." She winked.

Parker paused, she had just told him the city her friend lives in and what she does for a living. He stared at Ann for a few beats. "She's a lawyer?"

Ann shook her head no. "She works for two lawyers."

"Mhmm."

"Malcolm-Bower," Brooke blurted out. She covered her mouth, appearing horrified by her indiscretion.

Tessa and Ann laughed.

"I'm glad you have a big mouth." Parker laughed. "I'll be seeing you ladies around," he said with certainty as he left the table.

Chapter 5

A New Mom

Marie was in a trance, lacking the motivation to work. It had been a year since she had last visited the dark abyss; she'd hoped it was her last time. Lost in her self-loathing thoughts, not even her cell phone buzzing fazed her. Seconds later came another buzz...and another.

The last three days had been awful. Friday night at the Latin club had been fun…and exciting. The music, the dancing, her girlfriends, the incredibly handsome man vying for her attention—it had been intoxicating. It had awakened her from her slumber. Life appeared to be taking a positive turn. Then Sunday night happened. Her world imploded, sending her brief joy into a tailspin of despair.

"He hates me. No, he wants to destroy me. But why? What did I do to deserve this?" Her tears flowed down her face, dotting the keyboard. It was hard to believe she had any left. Since Craig dropped Jackson off at home Sunday evening, she'd cried an ocean's worth.

The knock at her door jolted her. Wiping her face, she exhaled. "Yes?"

The door crept open; it was Natalie, the office receptionist. Instead of calling from her desk, she checked on her in person. Over the last two days, Marie had secluded herself, much like she had done during her divorce. "Marie, Ann's on line two."

"Can you please take a message? Tell her I'm in a meeting or something. I'll call her later." Marie remained slumped over her desk.

Natalie studied her. "Okay. She said you're not answering her texts," she said.

"I saw them. Thanks," Marie mumbled.

After Natalie closed the door, Marie returned to the dark, depressing hole that was her life. Sunday had been a pleasant day until Jackson returned from Craig's, then it turned into the worst day ever—worse than the day Craig had announced his affair and that he was moving out.

Marie struggled to hold her tears back. The words had cut like a knife to her heart, ripping it to shreds. *"I'm getting a new mom."*

New mom hung in the air, sucking the life out of her. A declaration no mother ever wanted to hear from her child. Jackson couldn't have known the magnitude of his excited announcement. *New mom.* Like she was disposable. Replaceable. A robot without feelings. Not a second thought was given, trading old mom for *a new mom.* Her chest tightened, her sobs fighting hard to be free. No work was getting done today. She collected her things and walked out of her office, stopping at Natalie's desk with a vacant expression.

"I'm leaving for the day. Tell the bosses to call me if they need anything."

"Okay...I hope you feel better," Natalie replied in a warm, sympathetic tone as Marie walked out the large, smoked-glass door.

When she opened her front door, the quiet stillness inside sent an icy chill down her spine. Jackson wouldn't be home for several hours. She was alone—just her and her small, drab townhouse. It was nothing like the home she had lived in for fifteen years while married to Craig. Her lip quivered, remembering the beautiful 3500 square-foot custom-built home. It had top-of-the-line *everything* and only a sought-after designer would do for Craig. He wouldn't settle for anything less. Now, she lived in a 1200 square-foot townhouse with low-grade, subpar *everything*. A mishmash of furnishings bought at a local consignment store filled the small space.

They had sold the house and divided the money, along with all their assets, during the divorce. Marie had taken her portion of the money and put it towards a down payment on the townhouse. The comfortable life she had once lived was now a painful memory. Her salary at work paid the bills with a little extra leftover, but gone were the trips to Hawaii and Mexico. She couldn't even afford one day at Disneyland.

Craig had been ruthless throughout the entire divorce. He told her she could have full custody of Jackson if she gave up spousal maintenance. It was a crushing blow. Still, she didn't think twice accepting his offer on the spot. She agreed to all his demands to get the divorce over with as fast as possible. Ann had reminded her repeatedly that it was only money. Getting out from under Craig's thumb and verbal abuse was vital to her emotional well-being. Ann had been right. After Marie had signed the divorce papers, she was free.

Free from a physical standpoint, anyway. Marie's mental state was a life sentence in prison. She had failed, and she rehashed her failures each week. Although her marriage was empty and loveless, she had tried to make the most of it. She believed her love could sustain them. And it did for a while, as she believed in the phrase, "all you need is love." She had created a warm, loving home for her kids, and did her best to make Craig happy. Her countless efforts didn't matter because nothing pleased Craig. Dinner should be made from scratch and was never good enough; the house needed to be "white glove" clean; she needed to be thinner, and she needed to be more grateful for the privilege of being on the receiving end of his *massive, oversized cock*.

Not a day went by that Craig didn't brag about his buddies' wives—how Charlie was a lucky son-of-a-bitch because his wife blows him whenever he wants. Or how Tim's woman had the body of a Greek goddess with perfectly sculpted tits. "Why don't you give blow jobs like Charlie's wife?" he'd ask. His was relentless in hounding Marie about getting work done on her boobs daily. And there was Craig's favorite statement: "I got a reject in the spicy Latina department. What a fucking disappointment." She had heard it all *and believed every word*.

Marie poured a glass of wine and sat down on the barstool. It was one o'clock, and if she didn't respond to Ann's text, she might show up at work; or worse yet, at her house. So, she dug her cell phone out of her bag. There were three unread messages.

> Ann: Happy Hump day!
> Ann: Are you alive???

Ann: Did you call Parker???!!!

"Ugh, why on earth would she think I'd call Parker? It's obvious she's out of her mind." She typed out a reply.

Marie: I'm alive. It's been a busy day. TTYL
Ann: Something is wrong with you, what is it???
Marie: Nothing, I'm busy.
Ann: I don't believe you, I'll be over after work!

"Well crap, I don't want her coming over." Now what was she supposed to do? Jackson would be home in two hours, and Ann would be over sometime after that. "This day keeps getting worse," she mumbled. She decided to try lying.

Marie: No, I won't be home. Call me later tonight.

After she sent the text, she was over it. Leaving the phone on the counter, she grabbed her glass and went up to her bathroom. A long soak in the bathtub was what she needed to relax, to regroup; she would get lost in the wine, along with her Latin tunes. It was the perfect time to try out the bath bomb Ann had given her. She dropped it in the steaming water and watched it fizz.

The smell of vanilla and cherry filled the room as she undressed. "Mmm." She stepped into the tub and sank down in the soothing, spa-like water. Her eyes closed, and Parker's face was there. They burst open in shock. In a frenzy, she blinked to erase him.

Just no. He's a celebrity. A gringo. There will be drama. But damn, he's handsome.

She remembered dancing with him and how his rhythm shocked her. The fact that he could Latin dance scored big with her. But it was the intense gaze of his slate-blue eyes on her that stirred latent desires within. He had made her feel wanted and sexy...all with a look.

Any possibility with him had ended when she found out he was a celebrity—a celebrity who acted like he was interested in her...*her*. Impossible.

All she could do was laugh when Ann gave her his business card as if that would help his case. It was comical. Call a man? Never, let alone a celebrity. He's only after one thing...a one-night stand. The thought of having sex with him filled her stomach with butterflies again. It had been a long time since flutters or tingles coursed through her body. Experiencing the sensations again amazed her; she had forgotten how good they felt. But none of that mattered. Parker Nichols was all wrong for her.

Her eyes closed once again as her hands moved over her breasts. She cringed. There was no way she could be with a man, not with her body. In particular, not with a sexy celebrity who could have his pick of perfect women. Her hands continued down to her stomach. It was flat, but she knew where every stretch mark was.

Marie inhaled the vanilla and cherry scent. It brought a mischievous smile to her face. "Mmm... Well, I may not be with him for a dozen different reasons, but that doesn't mean I can't imagine being with him. I so need this...*gringo*, celebrity be damned." Her hand moved further down as Parker re-entered her mind, and she allowed herself to get lost in the moment.

Parker walked through the smoked-glass door of the law office of Malcolm-Bower & Associates. It was obvious Natalie recognized him by the wide grin on her face.

"Good afternoon, Mr. Nichols. How may I help you?"

"Hi," he greeted. "I'm looking for a woman who...um...specializes in copyrights." The questioning expression on Natalie's face made him feel like a fool. But he didn't care; he had to find her.

"None of our lawyers are women, only a few paralegals. I could schedule an appointment with Mr. Malcolm or Mr. Bower?"

"No, I don't need an appointment. I'm looking for the woman." Natalie stared at him, perplexed while chewing on the end of her pen. Parker could hear himself sounding like an idiot. He took a deep breath and continued. "I'm sure this seems odd. But, I'm just looking for a woman I danced with Friday night and I didn't get her name. I heard she works here. Can you help me?"

Before Natalie could respond, the phone rang. "Um, just a moment, Mr. Nichols." He nodded. "Malcolm-Bower and Associates, how may I help you?" she answered. "Hi, Ann. Sorry, Marie left a while ago. She seemed upset or maybe sick." She paused. "Well, you know how private she is, so she didn't give me any details."

Parker's ears perked up when he heard how *private* this Marie person was. So, he tuned in with interest to the one-sided conversation about...*Marie*. While eavesdropping, he looked around the waiting area of the law office. Black leather contemporary chairs with steel arms were in front of the floor to ceiling windows. White walls bounced the natural light off the white marble floors. On the walls hung large black and white photographs that showcased epic waves and surfers. It was modern decor of the finest quality—simple and understated.

"I assume she'll be in tomorrow." Natalie paused. "Not sure. I think she went home. She hasn't been herself the last few days." Her voice lowered. "I think it's her ex." Then there was silence. "Will do. Have a good day, Ann." Natalie hung the receiver up and turned her attention back to Parker.

"I'm thinking the person I'm looking for might be *Marie*. And I don't want to invade her privacy, so I'll leave now. But I'll be back." He turned to leave.

"Mr. Nichols," Natalie called. He stopped and walked back to her desk. "You said you danced with her?" He nodded. "And you're interested in her?" He nodded again. "You seem like a nice guy, and I've seen your show. It's really great." She smiled. "Without giving you specific details about this woman, I'll only say this, be kind to her. If you can't treat her well and with respect—just leave her alone." Natalie's steadfast devotion to Marie was admirable and telling. Marie must be an exceptional woman. Natalie looked young, and in her early twenties, but behind her blue-framed glasses were the soft hazel eyes of an old soul.

"I appreciate your candor. The woman I'm looking for has the most beautiful dark piercing eyes, tan skin, and let me tell you: she's an amazing dancer."

Natalie blushed. "You're looking for Marie."

"Thank you. I'll be back." Parker walked out to his black Range Rover, hopped in the driver's seat and smiled. "Marie..."

Frustrated, Marie grabbed a towel. No doubt, she was more relaxed and refreshed after her invigorating bath. Still, Marie felt pathetic masturbating out of necessity. If she wanted an orgasm, she needed to do it herself because Craig—the misogynist pig—didn't care about her satisfaction. He'd only need to stick in his humongous dick, grope her, and cum. Sweet success—all her sexual desires and dreams realized. Or so he thought. There was nothing passionate, sensual, or tender about the act. It was never making love. It was sex. And sex was only about him. Five minutes later he'd climb off her, beat his chest, and walk around like a primal beast whose latest conquest was mind-blowing. She laughed to herself. "And he thought *I* was a fucking disappointment." She froze. Had she thrown out an F-bomb? She giggled. Yes, and it was liberating.

The grin on her face was short-lived when she glimpsed her naked body in the mirror. *Could a man desire me?* Parker reentered her mind. He had piqued her curiosity on the dance floor. Just seeing his face while pleasuring herself had brought a new level of arousal. Was it her imagination, or might he be a good lover? She swallowed hard. *I have needs, too.*

After she put her clothes on, she pulled her hair into a ponytail and looked at her reflection. The woman staring back was attractive, intelligent, fun, and she had captured Parker Nichols' attention. A celebrity—a *popular* celebrity! That was saying something. Confident and determined, with a new perspective on life, she would not question where the confidence was coming from; she would embrace it.

"It's time I took control of my life," she told herself. "Every part of my life. First and foremost, I'm Jackson's mother. No way in hell will a swimsuit model take my place." She took a deep breath and marched herself downstairs, determined to do everything possible to be a better mom and win him back…starting with cookies.

Before the divorce, she had baked several times a week. The kids loved her homemade desserts, and so did her thighs. After the divorce, she stopped baking altogether, and the only cookies the kids ate were store-bought. So much had changed in two years for her and the kids, and none of it was good. She had crawled into a dark, lonely hole and did just enough to survive, but not live. Marie was done, over it. She was tired of failing as a woman and mother. It was time things changed. *No more pity parties, no more fear, and no more self-loathing. Only acceptance, respect, and love for myself.*

Already she felt empowered. The timer buzzed, and she pulled the second tray of chocolate chip cookies out of the oven just as Jackson walked through the front door. He suddenly stopped and stared at her.

"Hi, buddy."

"Why are you home? You made cookies?" A smile appeared on his face but disappeared just as fast.

"I came home early today and wanted to bake you cookies. How about some milk to go with them?" He nodded and hopped up on the barstool. She poured him a glass of milk and set a plate filled with cookies in front of him.

"Mmm…your chocolate chip cookies are always the best," he said with a full mouth. The praise caught her by surprise, and a lump formed in her throat as she remembered the closeness they had once had. Marie watched him gobble up the cookie and smiled. Then out of nowhere, Ann blasted into the kitchen from the entry, startling them.

"Marie, what's going on?" Ann demanded. Jackson's eyes widened. "Sorry, buddy. Something's going on with your mom and she won't tell me what it is." Floored by the intrusion Marie glared at her. "I called your office. Natalie said you left. Does this have to do with Parker? Or is it Craig?"

"Ann, not now," she said firmly. Ann's gaze shifted to Jackson, eating his cookies.

"Dad's getting married," he mumbled. "I'm getting a new mom." Marie's eyes stung at the sudden declaration, and she whipped around to face the sink. "Who's Parker?"

"Oh buddy, you're not getting a new mom. You have a mom," Ann corrected, touching his shoulder. Marie gripped the counter. "Just because your dad is getting married again doesn't make his new wife your mom. Just like if your mom remarried, her new husband doesn't become your new dad. You already have a dad. Does that make sense?" Ann asked, her voice tinged with an emotion she rarely displayed.

"Yeah, it makes sense. So, who's Parker?" Jackson asked again, as he reached for some milk.

"Nobody," Marie was quick to answer. "Why don't you take your cookies and milk into the living room to watch TV."

"Okay." Jackson left the kitchen, and now Marie was the one with the death stare.

"You bitch." Marie glowered. "Next time you have an issue with me, keep your damn mouth shut in front Jackson," she whispered. "We'll talk about whatever's on your mind in private, do you understand me? And never storm into my house like a lunatic again."

Ann stared at Marie, flabbergasted, and with her mouth ajar. "Marie…you cursed."

"That's all you have to say?"

"I'm sorry. Why didn't you call me? How am I supposed to help you if you don't call me?"

"Because I needed time to process. It killed me to hear Jackson say he was getting a new mom." She took a deep breath. "And I knew you'd bring up Parker."

"Okay, I get it. I'm a pushy bitch. But honey, you seem stronger. What's changed in you?"

"I'm tired of getting walked on and pushed around. I'm ready to fight."

"Well, it's about damn time." Ann pulled her into a hug. "You're rising above this."

Marie started the day with a bounce in her step. It was a new day, and she was filled with hope for the future. As Marie sauntered to the stairs to call Jackson, she hummed a tune. Had she paid attention, she would have recognized the song from the club and her dance with the hot gringo. "Jackson, we're leaving in five minutes," she called up to him.

"Okay," Jackson said running downstairs. "I need ten dollars for a t-shirt."

"Sure thing, in my wallet. I forgot my iPad upstairs. I'll be right back."

Jackson pulled her wallet out, removing several bills. As he counted out ten dollars, Parker's business card fell out between the bills. Jackson picked it up and read it. "Moooommm!" he yelled.

"What Jackson? What's the matter?" she said running down the stairs, iPad pressed against her chest.

"Why do you have Parker Nichols's business card? Do you know him? Is that who Ann was asking about? Mom, tell me!!!" His face was bright with excitement, a look she hadn't seen since before Craig moved out. Her heart melted. It was the little boy she'd been missing the last two years.

"We need to go buddy, or I'll be late for work."

"Okay, you can tell me in the car!" He grabbed his stuff and ran out to the garage.

The car ride was the most enjoyable time they'd had in…forever. Marie explained to Jackson that she didn't know Parker, but she had met him when she was out with the girls. He was beyond thrilled. You'd think he had just met Parker Nichols.

"Have a good day, buddy."

"Yeah, you too Mom, and we'll talk more about Parker later today!" He slammed the door shut and ran over to Ricky. Marie watched his mouth move at rapid speed, accompanied by animated gestures. One could only imagine what fantastical story he told Ricky. It was the perfect start to both their days.

At noon Parker walked through the smoked-glass door and smiled at Natalie as if they were old friends. "Good afternoon, Natalie."

"Mr. Nichols, I didn't expect to see you so soon."

"Is she here?"

"She is."

"Excellent, can I see her?"

Natalie held up one finger, and with the other hand picked up her phone and dialed Marie's extension. "Hi Marie, I have a Mr. Nichols asking to see you." She paused. "Um, Parker Nichols." Parker watched as Natalie's eyes roamed the lobby. "But…but he's…"

Parker frowned. It didn't sound like Marie wanted to see him, so he took control of the situation by reaching his hand towards Natalie for the phone. With hesitation, she handed it over to him. "Marie, it's Parker. Please come out to the lobby." There was silence. "Marie, please." He waited for her answer, and when she gave it, a broad grin stretched across his face. "Thank you." He handed the phone back to Natalie and winked.

Marie paced in her office. "What the hell? He's *here*! What does he want? How did he find me?" She squeezed her hands into fists, making them sweaty. Then she stopped when it hit her. "Those damn girls!"

He's just a man, she told herself. That didn't help calm her racing heart. She could be professional and in charge in her place of work. She fixed her grey pencil skirt and re-tucked her white button-down blouse, and with an air of confidence walked out to the lobby. At first sight of him, butterflies awoke in her stomach. It was the face she had held captive during her bath. Her cheeks warmed.

"Mr. Nichols."

"Hi, *Marie*," Parker greeted. She watched his eyes danced over her—up to her hair in a French twist, her crisp white V-neck button-down shirt, and grey fitted skirt that hugged her curves. "I was wondering if I could take you to lunch?"

Out of the corner of her eye, she noticed Natalie eavesdropping. "This way," she said walking to the door and jerked her chin for him to follow.

The afternoon sun shone brightly, sending off a heat that matched her intensity. Now more than ever she had to keep control of the situation. "Let me be straight with you. I'm not interested." Her matter-of-fact attitude stonewalled him, and she hoped it gave her the upper hand.

He stared at her confidently. "You aren't interested in lunch?"

She cocked her head to the side, holding his gaze. The sun shining behind him forced her to squint. When he smiled, she could tell he liked her sassy attitude. "Come on...Why are you here? Am I being punked?" By this time, she had her arms crossed over her chest and her hip pushed out. She wasn't up for playing games.

"Marie, let me assure you, nobody is punking you. You're a beautiful woman and I enjoyed dancing with you. Have lunch with me...please?"

Marie liked how he tried his best to charm the pants off her with his sexy grin. But she didn't cave like the other women who fell at his feet. She wouldn't crumble into a puddle of goo despite his charm and good looks. This *thing* wasn't going to happen. "You seem like a nice guy, but you're also a celebrity, or so my friends tell me." He laughed out loud, and she liked it. "I'm sorry, I can't." But she wanted to tell him, "You are a sexy gringo actor who will only break my heart."

"So, you have something against actors? It's just lunch." He flashed his best celebrity grin; it melted her, but she would maintain control.

"Yes, I have something against actors. It's not personal. I don't want my face plastered all over the internet. I like my privacy." She shrugged.

"It's kind of hard not to take it personally." He looked away from her, disappointed. "Do you have my business card?"

"I do," she said with a guilty smile.

"Good. Call me, Marie. Marie...what's your last name?"

She rolled her eyes.

"Ah, right. There's that privacy thing again," he teased.

"Ramsey." She shook her head and smiled. "Marie Ramsey. It's on the Malcolm-Bower website; it's public knowledge." She laughed as she tossed her head back.

"Are you *sure* I can't buy you lunch, or dinner?"

The butterflies danced in her stomach, his persistence endearing. More than anything she wanted to say *yes*, but they'd never work. How did he not see that? "Parker, I'm sure that I can't. I'd rather not start anything," she said with a hint of regret in her voice.

"Okay." He stood unmoved, staring at her as if willing her to change her mind.

"You have a good day." She waved as she turned back to the office.

Parker remained on Marie's mind the rest of the workday. It wasn't easy turning him down. And seeing him again reignited the feelings she had had at the club...not to mention the feelings she had in the bathtub. To make matters worse, Craig had never looked at her the way Parker did, like he was happy to see her, with those slate-blue eyes, sparkling like the ocean. *Did he have to be so sweet? And his charming grin... Ugh.*

But it was the look on Natalie's face when she walked back into the office she wanted to avoid—the star-struck, swoony, melt-at-your-feet look. The same look Brooke had had at the club. In fact, they all had it, including every fan that asked him for a picture. *I wish he wasn't a celebrity.*

Chapter 6

The Call

Saturday night, Marie was soaking in her tub when Ann called. She let out a heavy sigh as she answered. "You're interrupting my bath."

"Why are you taking a bath at ten o'clock at night?"

"Why are you calling at ten o'clock? I could be in bed."

"Because it's a Saturday night, and I knew you'd be up. You should be with Parker. I can't believe you declined lunch. Who rejects Parker Nichols?" Ann said in disbelief.

"Parker seems like a nice guy and yeah, he's very handsome. God, the way my stomach gets butterflies when I'm around him...but I can't. I have to think of Jackson. And if I'm honest, I couldn't handle love-struck fans falling at his feet. Besides, as I sit here in my bath...honey, he wouldn't want any of this." Her face soured, looking down at her breasts and stomach.

"Give me a break! I've seen your body. It's better than half the twenty-somethings I see out at the beach."

"Well, at least they have firm, perky breasts. Craig always pushed me to get a boob job. I should've listened. Now I can't afford one on my own."

"Jesus, Marie, stop it! Some men like soft breasts; they fit in their mouths easier. You need to get laid and all your worries will be over." She giggled.

"Man, you're vulgar," Marie chided, laughing at the same time. "But you're right. I need to get laid. It's been so long since a man has touched me, and lord knows, Craig was a horrible lover," she admitted. "But at least there was physical contact."

"Oh honey, I'm willing to bet Parker is a terrific lover. Call him! Call him for a booty call!" Ann rallied.

"Now *you* stop! I would never call Parker, let alone for a booty call. I'm not that kind of girl! And even if I was, I've given up on gringos."

"What's gotten into you? Now you're rejecting white guys?"

"My mother had reservations about Craig because he was different from us. Maybe she was right. Maybe it's better to stick with your own kind."

"That's a load of crap. You know that isn't true. Craig was wrong from the get-go! We established that years ago. I think you're just trying to talk yourself out of the sexy Parker Nichols…'cause you're scared."

"Yeah, I'm scared! You think I want a repeat of Craig? And being sexy doesn't mean good in bed. Or a good match for me. I know that from personal experience. My only O's happened in the tub." Marie had never been with anyone other than Craig. Fit, muscular, and attractive didn't mean a damn thing in bed. Craig had been a lousy lover, and he wasn't sexy. But Parker was, and from the vibe she got from him she'd wager he was a fantastic lover too.

"Wait! Why didn't you tell me you were getting off in the tub?! That's what you meant when you said I was 'interrupting.' Girl, you should have hung up on me!"

"Oh sure, if I said, 'I'm masturbating in the tub,' you wouldn't have gotten off the phone."

"Damn straight! I wouldn't have believed you knew how." Ann chuckled, always the wise-ass. "Well then, I'll let you get back to your fun. But if you called Parker, it would be more enjoyable."

"Enough about Parker!"

Marie didn't know it, but Jackson was eavesdropping and heard the entire one-sided conversation. The second he heard Parker's name, he stayed put, catching every word. From what Jackson could understand, his mom liked Parker. Maybe he could help her. He dug through her wallet for Parker's business card and ran to his room to put the number in his phone. He ran back into her room returning the card before she got out of the tub.

Back in his room, he paced back and forth, taking deep breaths. He shook his head and worked the kinks out of his neck, like a boxer right before entering the ring, working up the courage to call his favorite superhero. Seconds later the determined eleven-year-old pushed the call button. It rang and rang, and it went to voicemail. "Dang it!" He took a deep breath, "Hi, Professor Pierce, er I mean, Mr. Nichols. My name is Jackson Ramsey. Can you call me back? It's about my mom...Marie."

Parker had screened the call, unfamiliar with the number. When he listened to the message, he nearly dropped his phone. "She has a son? And he's calling me about her. Hmm..." He wasn't sure if he should return the call, but it wasn't like he could call

Marie to let her know her son was calling him. He was intrigued, and he liked Marie, so he returned Jackson's call.

"Hello, Mr. Nichols?"

"Hi Jackson, call me Parker. Is everything okay? You mentioned your mom."

"Wow, I can't believe I'm talking to you! You're my favorite actor."

Parker laughed. "How old are you, Jackson? Does your mom know you called me?"

"I'm almost twelve, and no, she doesn't know. She's in the bathtub."

"Oh," Parker said surprised. The thought of Marie in a hot, steamy bath made him smile while a sensation in his athletic shorts jolted him out of his chair. "So why did you call me? I assume you got my number from the business card I gave her?"

"Yeah, I found it in her wallet. Are you angry?"

"No, I'm not angry. Just curious. Why did you call?" Parker walked to his refrigerator, took out a beer and made his way out to the patio. Maybe the cool ocean breeze would keep his thoughts off of Marie, naked in the tub, but it wasn't likely. He twisted off the cap and took a few swallows.

"My mom likes you; do you like her?"

Parker coughed.

"Are you okay?"

Parker coughed more and cleared his throat several times.

"Yeah, I was drinking something, and it went down the wrong pipe." He cleared his throat again, composing himself for the most interesting conversation he'd ever had with a kid. "How do you know your mom likes me?"

"I heard her talking to her best friend Ann on the phone. She said you were sexy, but she wouldn't like fans falling at your feet. And something about a boob job and my dad was a horrible lover, and O's. Girls are strange. Half of what she said I didn't understand."

"Whoa, sounds like you heard a lot." He paused; this kid was something else. "Yeah, girls might be strange, but they're also great."

"Do you like my mom? Like, do you want to date her?" Jackson asked in an innocent voice.

"Yes—she's very pretty. I like her, and I would like to take her out to lunch sometime."

"That would be awesome!!!"

"Jackson, are you on the phone? It's late," Marie asked.

Parker's ears perked up hearing Marie's voice. The rapid beating of his heart was not normal for him. She stirred him up in more ways than one.

"I'm just talking to my friend. I told him you know Parker Nichols," Jackson said.

"Jackson, that's not true. I don't know Parker Nichols, and neither do you. Don't be lying to your friends."

"But you met him, so you know him. You have his business card. You could call him if you wanted." The excitement in Jackson's voice made him sound hopeful.

"I'm not doing this with you, buddy. I won't be calling Parker. Now I want you off the phone in ten minutes, okay?"

"Okay," Jackson agreed, pausing a few beats. "Sorry about that Parker."

"It's okay. I'm not sure I should talk to you on the phone. It sounds like your mom wants nothing to do with me."

"But, since I found your business card we've been better," Jackson blurted.

"What do you mean?"

"Since my parents divorced I haven't been very nice to my mom. I've been mean to her," he admitted.

"Why would you be mean to her? Is she mean to you?" Parker asked with concern.

"No. Mom's never even yelled at me. I was angry at her because my dad left us. She didn't make him happy, so he left."

"Jackson, your mom seems great. You should be nice to her. Divorce is hard on the parents too, you know."

"Yeah, she's cried a lot. She used to be fun until she turned into a zombie. Last week was the first time she went out with her friends in two years. She seemed happy after that, but she got sad again."

"What made her sad?"

"My dad is getting married, and I told her I was getting a new mom."

"Oh, I can see why that would make her sad. You only have one mom, Jackson."

"I know, but I want my old mom back. She used to laugh, be silly, and dance around the house. And she makes the best chocolate chip cookies."

"She sounds great. But now that your dad is getting married again, she might cry more…because she loves him and it takes time to get over someone."

"No, she doesn't love him. He was mean to her. He always made her feel bad. I think she cries because she's alone and thinks nobody wants her. That's what she said in the tub. And something about you 'not wanting any of this.' But, I'm not sure what she meant."

Parker laughed to himself. He definitely wanted some of *that*.

"I better go before she comes back and takes my phone away. Thanks for calling me, Parker. You're cool in real life, too."

"Thanks, Jackson. I've enjoyed talking to you, too. Maybe we'll get to meet sometime."

"That would be awesome! Except she said she'd never call you."

"I'll see what I can do. Goodnight."

Chapter 7

Summer Begins

Like clockwork, Parker received his first text of the day from Jackson. Several weeks had passed and following the unexpected call, Parker had left town to film in Budapest. The two became texting buddies while he was on location since he was unable to talk on the phone. Parker knew Jackson was pleased as punch that he, aka Professor Pierce, was his friend. A dream most superhero fans would never experience. And Jackson didn't hide his elation, the young lad was on top of the world.

> Jackson: Will Professor Pierce defeat the mutant squid that's roaming around San Diego disguised as a zookeeper????
> Parker: Are you doubting Professor Pierce's powers or intelligence?
> Jackson: Never!!! Have fun filming.
> Parker: Thanks. Have a good day. Watch out for the redhead!!!
> Jackson: I knew it!!!

Budapest used to be a location Parker enjoyed when they filmed on location. The change of scenery did wonders for clearing his head of the hustle and bustle in Hollywood. He worked with a different crew and spent time in the city with the locals. It re-energized him. Except for this time, Marie had entered his life and he wanted to see her again. Now all his hopes were on hold for three weeks. The crappy timing allowed his friendship with Jackson to develop more than he thought possible. As he learned about Jackson, he also learned about Marie. His desire to know her grew, with a longing unfamiliar to him.

Over the passing weeks, Jackson's attitude had changed in a big way, and Marie never questioned why. In her mind, the reasons didn't matter, but in her heart, she hoped her positive changes were rubbing off on him. Not only did she bake more, but she also watched TV with him, and started a new Friday night routine of pizza and a movie. Spending extra time with him allowed her to learn about his interests. She hadn't realized how much he'd changed over the last couple of years. Why it had taken her so long to pull herself together, she hadn't a clue. Ann had told her she was still reeling from the divorce and needed to give herself time to be ready. Marie agreed, however, her son needed to come before herself. He needed her, and now she wanted to make it up to him. The rebuilding of their relationship had begun.

The school year ended with everyone excited for summer, but nobody was more thrilled than Lexi. She had made it through her second year of college. She was attending CSU Long Beach to be an elementary school teacher. The one-hour distance was just far enough from home to give her the independence she wanted. Not only did she resemble Marie physically, she kept herself busy with friends and attending sporting events, just as Marie had done in school. Lexi had settled into her college life well over the last couple of years, so much so that she wasn't moving back home for the summer. Luck was on Lexi's side, and she snagged a campus job in the library. It was the absolute ideal situation in maintaining her independence and allowed her to stay on campus during the summer. When Marie heard the news, it was a major letdown, as it hindered her plans of restoring the weak bonds in their relationship. Now she needed to find a way to get some quality time with her over the summer.

The next blow hit Marie in the form of Lexi's new boyfriend, Isaac, when she announced she'd be spending all of her available time with her 'surfer' at the beach. The news did not go over well with Marie. She had heard very little about him, and now her plans to strengthen her relationship with Lexi would be more challenging than she had thought. But it was a challenge Marie was up for, with the added goal to win over Isaac so he would want to spend time with Lexi's family, and not hog her all to himself.

Operation *Win over Isaac* was in place, and Marie planned a barbecue so she could meet the new man in her daughter's life. With a confident smile, she called Lexi.

"Hi Lexi, I'm calling to see if Saturday works for you to come over for dinner? I would love to meet Isaac."

"Mom, is this going to be one of those weird dinners where you play twenty-questions with my boyfriend? If so, no thanks. We'll pass."

"I promise I'll only ask ten questions," Marie teased. "I'll even invite the girls to buffer."

"Oh that sounds tempting; they're worse than you. Isaac will run scared from this family."

"Please Lexi, unless you want to do a one-on-one dinner date? It's up to you."

Jackson walked into the kitchen and Marie noticed him listening to the conversation. She smiled at him when a glint appeared in his eyes.

"If we're having a party can I invite two friends?" he asked, interrupting her.

"Quiet, I'm on the phone."

"Please...can I invite two friends?" he begged.

She sighed. "Yes, now let me talk to Lexi."

"Yes!" He pumped his fist in the air as he ran out of the kitchen.

"Lexi, what do you say? I promise we'll be on our best behavior."

"Fine, Saturday works. What time?"

"Four o'clock. That gives us an hour for cocktails, and then we'll grill. It'll be fun, I promise."

"Mom you don't know how to grill."

Marie was silent. Craig had done all the grilling.

"Mom?"

"I think Tessa knows how. I'll buy hotdogs just in case I char the steaks." She forced out a small laugh. "It'll be fine. I'll figure something out."

"Okay, I'll see you Saturday," Lexi agreed.

"I'm looking forward to it. Bye, hon."

Marie sat at her desk watching the clock. It was pushing noon, and she was eager to check in with Jackson. During summer break he was home while she was at work. She hated leaving him alone for nine hours a day, but what could she do? So, she'd call or text him throughout the day to check in and to ease her mind. Every time it was the same; he was watching *Pierce*. By this time, she knew it was Parker's show and had learned what a huge fan Jackson was of "Professor Pierce." He talked about Parker as if he knew him. Little did she know, he *did* know him, albeit only through texting, and a friendship had developed.

Jackson's fanaticism with the show and Parker overwhelmed her. She didn't understand the whole superhero fandom. Although it was adorable seeing Jackson spellbound every time the show was on, still the guilt would set in. She could have at least introduced them. Then his little superhero fantasy would be fulfilled. *Hindsight's always 20/20.*

But superhero fantasies were the least of her worries. An even bigger problem had occupied her mind the last two weeks. If she so much as glimpsed Parker on the show, she'd have the most vivid dream about him in the tub with her. Startled and panting, she'd wake from her erotic dream, leaving her horny the rest of day. So, she avoided *Professor Pierce* like the plague. Even so, her avoidance didn't diminish the frequency of her nighttime baths. It increased them to several times a week.

What had come over her? Loneliness? Maybe. Was she desperate? Possibly. Whatever it was, it was bringing her back to life, and everyone around her noticed the changes. A relaxed and playful Marie replaced her sad, stressed self. She said "yes" to the girls and wore her hair down occasionally... "just to mix things up," she would say. Marie felt attractive and sexy. But she also wondered if her feelings were awful. Parker wasn't around to quench her desires, nor was any other man. It was just her, and not even close to how she wanted to spend the rest of her life. She and her baths could not be a permanent arrangement. It was then she finally admitted she wanted a man in her life. Her *abuelita's* words echoed in her head—*Do not be alone.*

Jackson bolted into the kitchen with his face beaming, catching Marie by surprise as she was chopping vegetables. "Hey, buddy, what's up?"

"What time is the barbecue?"

"Four o'clock. How many friends are you inviting? I want to have enough food."

"Just two, thanks!" And just like that, he left Marie to finish preparing dinner.

Saturday morning was like every other morning. Marie was awake at six. On the weekends she'd hit the gym for an hour, attempting to reshape her aging body. With forty staring her in the face, Marie would do anything to slow down time. While she was running on the treadmill, a man she had never seen before stepped onto the vacant treadmill next to her.

"Good morning," he said.

Marie nodded, staying focused on her running.

"I'm Seth; I'm new to the complex."

"Nice to meet you, and welcome," she returned. She had fifteen minutes left on her run. *Might as well be nice.* "I'm Marie," she said, keeping her eyes forward while feeling his eyes bore through her sweaty t-shirt.

"Good to meet you, Marie."

For the next ten minutes, they didn't speak, both focused on their running. Each time she'd peer out the corner of her eye at

Seth, Parker would pop into her head. It frustrated her. Why was he occupying her every thought? It was crazy; he was out of her league. And besides that, he was a celebrity. Not that any of that mattered. It had been weeks since she last saw him. Time to put him out of her mind and focus on "real life" prospects.

Seth wasn't bad-looking. Early forties with the athletic build she liked. Dark hair cut short, emphasizing his receding hairline. And he had rather small ice-blue eyes, but they weren't unpleasant to look at. They were friendly, just as he appeared to be. He was no Parker Nichols—just an average, everyday guy.

Marie took a deep breath. Five minutes left on her run and she could get out of the gym. The new visitor could not keep his eyes off her. Aware of his apparent interest, she was unsure of how she felt and needed time to process yet another *gringo*.

"Are you here this time every day?" He broke the silence, and the question caught her by surprise. "I mean, I'm new here, and it would be nice to know someone."

"Um, the time can vary along with the day of the week," she answered with a non-answer.

"Ah, so if I'd like a workout partner I have to hang out here every morning?"

Her cheeks warmed. "I guess so."

She slowed to a stop while he continued running. His flexed biceps caught her attention. Testosterone dripped from his body, and she liked it. She flashed her dark eyes his way. "Enjoy your workout."

"Thanks. I'll see you tomorrow morning," Seth said, keeping his eyes forward.

"Maybe," Marie said, but before she turned around Seth grinned, showing off his perfect white teeth. Soft flutters spurred to life in her stomach, and they followed her home.

Marie whipped around her kitchen with adrenaline coursing through her body, and it wasn't because she had completed an hour-long workout. No, his name was *Seth*. She grinned as she flipped pancakes on the griddle, sausage next. Did she meet a man? He came out of nowhere. He said he'd like to work out with her. The thought sent chills down her spine, and her mind went into the gutter. She might be open to him working out *on* her. A girlish giggle filled the kitchen, and she covered her mouth to muffle the sounds. "Is this about getting laid? Damn Ann for putting these thoughts in my head. I can't do this." But, it was too late; all the dirty thoughts flooded her mind. She redirected herself. "Jackson, breakfast is ready."

"Coming," he hollered down to her.

She watched in awe as he hoovered his pancakes in record time. Why was he eating so fast? Had she made him angry? It's like he was trying to get away from her. It made little sense. Weren't they past this? The last few weeks Jackson had been chatty and in a happy mood. This behavior was reminiscent of previous years.

"Jackson, is everything all right? I feel like you're trying to avoid me. If there's a problem, let's talk about it."

"No problem; everything's fine. I wanna clean my room before my friends come over."

Her eyes widened in surprise. "You're gonna clean your room?"

"Uh-huh."

Jackson hadn't cleaned his room once since they moved into the townhouse. Twice a year she would do a deep cleaning and would collect his dirty clothes once a week. His bedroom was always in constant disarray, with toys thrown about and books spread over the floor instead of on the bookshelf. Clothes were everywhere as if he'd tossed them into the air and wherever they landed they stayed. The day after Marie had put fresh sheets on his bed; it would have a mountain of blankets on it. To deal with the mess, she'd usually close the door to his room and ignore it. Nobody, especially her, wanted to see the pigsty he lived in. And now he's going to clean it?

"You're going to clean it?" she asked again.

"Uh-huh."

"You're not angry about anything?"

"Nope, just in a hurry."

The smile on his face filled her with relief. "Wow, then get to it." She smiled back, and he was off at lightning speed, leaving her at the table with her coffee.

In the quiet kitchen, Parker re-entered Marie's mind. "Why didn't he come to see me again?" She assumed he had moved on. If he were interested, he would have tried harder to change her mind, right? "It's whatever." She shrugged, but the ball was in her court, whether she wanted to admit it or not. Ann re-minded her often he had put it there. "Call me, Marie," he had told her. The thought pained her. She could never call him. As much as she found Parker attractive, she knew she didn't fit in his world, not with the hordes of women around him wanting selfies left and right. She'd go crazy with jealousy. Now, Seth— he was normal, just like her. She stood to clear off the dishes and prepare for her gathering. *I'll think about Seth later.*

Chapter 8

The Barbecue

The doorbell rang at three, and the door immediately flung open with Ann entering just as Marie stepped into the foyer. Such was their relationship for the past thirty years—Ann the bossy, controlling extrovert who never waited for anything or anyone and would take what she needed at the drop of a hat. Yes, she was the perfect best friend for Marie, who was the direct opposite in almost every way. Dancing was the one area in which Marie outshined Ann. In the end, both women needed the other to balance their shortcomings. Joined at the hip since the third grade when Marie had moved into Ann's neighborhood, the two women were each other's family.

"So, I'm here." Ann announced. "Take the pasta salad and I'll get the baked beans from the car."

"Thanks. Where are the girls?"

"They're right behind me," Ann hollered, walking out. Marie leaned out the door and sure enough Brooke and Tessa were piling out of Ann's car with bags in hand.

Ann returned within seconds leaving the stragglers in the dust. Everything she did was fast; she never strolled anywhere.

"I made a double batch, so you could freeze some for another time. Now tell me how great I am." Ann said.

"You're the best." Marie lifted the lid on the pot. "I love your beans. Mmm." She sniffed the amazing aroma.

"I know you do." Ann smiled. "I'll put the crockpot near the stove."

Tessa and Brooke followed behind Ann, chatting among themselves. Marie squeezed both their shoulders in acknowledgement as they walked into the small kitchen. It was a tight squeeze with all four of them gathered in it at once. The second Marie bumped into Tessa, all that she had lost in the divorce suddenly surfaced, souring her mood.

"This kitchen is so tiny. It's a wonder I can cook anything in it," Marie complained. Her eyes scanned the narrow kitchen, and she was reminded of her old kitchen with a Sub-Zero refrigerator and a Viking six-burner gas stove. Then there were the granite countertops she loved and a large island. She had taken it all for granted, even the moments spent with the kids while they ate their snacks at the island. Now she had a galley kitchen with laminate countertops and an electric stove. No island, just a small eating area and a single barstool at the end of the counter. "I can't believe what my life has become since the divorce." She glowered, looking around her dated home.

"Oh hon, think of it as temporary. One day you'll return to the lap of luxury." Ann patted her shoulder.

Marie laughed and shook her head. "Now that's a pipe dream if I ever heard one."

Ann scowled at her.

"Since I don't cook, kitchens don't matter to me," Brooke interrupted. "I just bring booze wherever I go. Ann, will you do the honors?" Brooke handed her the sack of alcohol.

"I'd be happy to." Ann curtsied, then displayed a saucy little shimmy.

"Hey, we all love it when you bring booze." Marie laughed. "I have some freshly made salsa and guacamole in the fridge, and I'm marinating steaks. Except, I don't know how to work the grill. Do you know how, Tessa? I know Brooke and Ann don't."

"Sorry babe, I haven't a clue about gas grills. Do you have the owner's manual?" Marie looked at her, confused. "It's the little booklet that comes with just about every appliance or machine you'll ever buy. This way you can learn how it works." Tessa winked.

"Crap, I'm sure I tossed it out when we brought it home. Well, how hard can it be?" Marie shrugged.

"Right. How *hard* can it be? With four intelligent women to play around with it, one of us is sure to light its fire." Tessa stuck out her tongue.

Marie's mouth fell open.

"I love it." Brooke giggled.

"What in the hell was that?" Ann said, shocked.

"I need a man. That's what that was about," Tessa grumbled. "I also need a shot. Bartender, serve 'em up!"

"I'm on it." Ann saluted.

"So, tell us about this Isaac?" Tessa asked, intrigued.

"Well first and foremost, Lexi doesn't want him getting bombarded with a gazillion questions so you all better be on your best behavior. I don't want her getting angry with me." The girls let out a frustrated sigh. "Now Isaac surfs and plays guitar, and according to Lexi is the hottest guy ever. That's all I know."

"That's so sweet. And where's the little turd?" Tessa scrunched her nose.

"He's upstairs with his friend, Ricky. I let him invite two friends. The other one will be here later. I gotta tell you guys, he's like a changed boy. I don't know what happened, but I am so grateful."

"What about you?" Ann said as she passed a tequila shot to each one of the women. "Look at you. Your hair is down and you have a glow about you." Ann waggled her brows. "If I didn't know better I'd suspect you had a man in your life," she teased.

Tessa and Brooke's head whipped around to stare at Marie with suspicious eyes.

"Stop it you three. Baths are a wonderful thing." Marie lifted her glass. "*Salúd.*"

"Woohoo!! *Salúd!*" The women cheered and pushed back their shots.

Marie ushered the girls out to the patio, which was her outdoor living space. It was more accommodating than Marie's kitchen, plus it was nicer than the rest of her home. She had turned the patio into a welcoming, tropical paradise. Even Ann and the girls loved it. Many of their evenings were spent on the patio drinking, eating, laughing, and listening to music while Marie refused to leave her house. It took her a month to turn the plain, boring concrete pad with pergola atop into her dream escape. The time and money she had invested had paid off, giving her a tranquil retreat to relax in at the end of the day.

Stylistically, the patio didn't match the rest of her house, or the complex for that matter. But her goal had been achieved. When she was on her patio, it transported her to a luxury resort. The colorful outdoor rug that lay beneath the teak patio set, and the two chaise loungers with striped cushions that complemented the rug, all contributed to the tropical feel of the space.

There were clay pots filled with flowers that changed with the seasons, courtesy of Brooke, who was part-owner of a flower shop, along with a couple of potted dwarf lemon trees placed along the fence. Strands of lights were hung from the pergola and draped along the fencing with various outdoor plaques and signs.

In the evening, the warm glow from the lighting and flickering candles on the table provided a romantic ambience. Her patio was her pride and joy. It's where she spent most of her free time at home, cozied up with a glass of Merlot and a good book. It was her little hideaway from her boring, sub-par life. And a perfect reflection of her.

"All right ladies, drink requests?" Ann asked. The saucy, fair-skinned blonde with a vulgar mouth was the mixologist among the women. There wasn't a drink she couldn't make, provided the ingredients were available. What made her the best at mixing cocktails? She liked to add extra liquor. But by day, she was an office manager for an accounting firm where she had to keep her mouth in check.

Outside of work, Ann was the F-bomb Queen, and Marie's oldest and dearest friend. Nobody knew Marie better than Ann. After they graduated from high school, they had remained best friends, but their friendship deepened through each of their divorces. Ann married several years after Marie, but her marriage only lasted three years. It ended when she caught her ex in bed with the neighbor. Although in hindsight, it was actually the best thing to happen to her. Who wants to be married to a man who won't make love to you because he's not attracted to you, or any woman, for that matter? As shocked as she was, Ann bounced back rather quickly. Over the years she'd had boyfriends, but she'd been hesitant to commit to another man, on the off-chance he didn't really know if he liked women or men.

One after another the women shouted out their drink requests, "Tequila sunrise!" "Margarita on the rocks!" "Rum and coke!" In her element, Ann went straight to work preparing the drinks.

With drinks in hand, the women relaxed and were in a constant state of laughter as they munched on chips, salsa, and guacamole. Marie turned on Latin music, with "Oye Como Va" first on the playlist. The girls squealed and jumped out of their chairs. Hips gyrated rhythmically, shoulders shimmied, hands flew through the air, and the occasional provocative pelvic thrust was performed, followed by giggles.

"We'll have to get a conga line started later," Marie shouted. Her comment was met with clapping and cheering. She turned her attention to the grill and was stumped seconds later, unable to start it. She threw her hands up in frustration, grabbed her tequila sunrise, and went back to dancing.

Once the song ended, the girls settled back in their seats. Marie plopped down with a ridiculous grin on her face.

"What's with the stupid grin?" Ann asked.

"Do I have a stupid grin on my face?" All three women nodded. "Well, I'm not sure…the tequila?"

"I don't think so. That's the look only a man can bring to a woman's face." Ann snorted.

"Did you call Parker?" Brooke asked, bouncing in her seat excitedly. She was the youngest of the four friends. At thirty-three, she was coddled by the older women; she was their little "Brookie." Despite her age, she acted more like a teenager, flying through life by the seat of her pants and her head in the clouds. To Brooke, life was meant to be lived to the fullest and her number one priority was love.

"No, I met a guy in the gym this morning. He's new to the complex. His name is Seth," Marie informed the group.

"Well…do tell." Ann sat forward in her chair.

"There's not much to tell. We ran alongside each other on the treadmills and he said he'd see me tomorrow morning." Marie shrugged.

"No, no, no…we want the good stuff. What does he look like?" Tessa demanded.

"Let's see… He's tall with dark brown hair and icy-blue eyes. They really jump out at you. And he has an amazing set of biceps." She shivered just thinking about what they'd feel like wrapped around her, holding her close.

"But was he cute? Handsome? Sexy?" Brooke asked, clearly exasperated.

"Yeah, how does he compare to Parker?" Tessa asked.

"Parker who?" Lexi asked as she walked out the sliding glass door, holding hands with Isaac. "I see the party started without us." She flashed a bright, full smile and kissed Marie on the cheek.

"No, baby, this is just the pre-party. Now that you're here the real party can start. Now let's meet your guy," she whispered.

"Isaac, these are my mom's best friends, Ann, Brooke, and Tessa. You might remember Tessa from high school—she's the art teacher. And this beautiful lady is my mom, Marie," Lexi said proudly.

"It's nice to meet you all," Isaac said. "Ms. Romero, I wanted to take your art class. I had heard you were awesome, but it was at the same time as music, so I had to go with that. Music's my passion," Isaac said.

"Totally understandable. So, I hear you play guitar?" Tessa asked.

"Yes, and piano, but guitar is it for me," he said.

Isaac easily fell into conversation with Tessa and Brooke, so Lexi went inside with Marie to assist her. "Well, what do you think?" Lexi asked.

"He's adorable. And very polite, and you know how I like that."

"Yes, he is polite *and* respectful."

"I'm so glad," Marie said while she assembled a veggie tray. "Can you grab the bowl of berries out of the fridge, please?"

"Sure. Where's Jackson?"

"Oh, he's upstairs with Ricky. They're keeping watch for another friend."

"What other friend? I thought Ricky was his only friend." Lexi placed the bowl of berries on the counter.

"You know, I don't actually know. I guess we'll find out when he gets here. Now, I better figure out how to work this grill or we won't be having any steak." Marie rolled her eyes, trying not to let her inadequacies ruin her evening. "Grab the berries, will you?" she asked, walking out to the patio, veggie tray in hand.

"Yup, but first I'll go check on the boys," Lexi said.

Lexi was headed up the stairs when the doorbell rang. "Must be the other little boy." She bounced back down the stairs and swung the door wide open. Not a little boy, but the furthest thing from a little boy. Her jaw hit the ground.

"Hi," Parker greeted.

"Oh my gosh, Parker Nichols... Are you lost?"

"No, not lost. Lexi, right?"

Her eyes bulged in disbelief. "Yeah, how do you know my name?"

"Your brother Jackson said he had a sister named Lexi. I assumed you were her. Can I come in? I don't want to draw any attention."

"Yes, of course." She moved out of the doorway for him to enter the townhouse, then quickly closed the door behind him. Speechless and star-struck, she stared at him.

"I'm a little concerned by your reaction that you weren't expecting me. That would mean your mother isn't expecting me either?" Parker furrowed his brow.

"I don't think she knows."

Just then the rumble of footsteps roared down the stairs. "Parker! Oh my gosh! Ricky, I told you he was coming," Jackson yelled, "and you didn't believe me."

"Hey Jackson, it's great to finally meet you." Parker put his hand out just as Jackson's face fell. Parker followed his gaze to Marie, and their eyes connected.

"Mom, don't be angry," Jackson pleaded, walking to her. He rubbed her arm up and down. "Please, Mom. I called him." Her eyes were locked on Parker. "Mom...?"

Marie took a deep breath. "Parker, it's nice to see you. Please, come in." However amicable it may have sounded, there was a serious, stern tone in her voice, the kind most mothers mastered.

"I don't understand what's going on," Lexi interrupted.

"Parker's my friend," Jackson declared. Anyone could see how proud he was with a cheesy grin stretched across his face.

"How? How would *you* meet Parker Nichols? You never go anywhere." Her mouth gaped open, shocked by Jackson's announcement.

"Let's move this onto the patio." Marie managed to keep her face devoid of expression. Lexi nodded and ushered the boys along. When Marie turned to follow, Parker startled her by grabbing her hand. She stopped instantly. Slowly she turned to face him.

"Marie, I'm sorry. When he invited me, he said it was okay with you."

Speechless, she looked down at his hand holding hers, as the fluttering began in her belly. He let go and her eyes traveled up to meet his. They were genuine...safe. All she could do was stare at him. He was in her house and knew her son... How?

"Parker, I don't understand how all this happened. I never expected to see you again. We'll talk about this later. Right now, I have guests out on the patio. You're welcome to stay since you're apparently friends with my son."

"Marie, he said he got my number from your wallet. I was a little confused when he called."

Her mouth gaped open.

"Yes, he called me, and I talked to him. I didn't know you had a son, but once I knew, I couldn't turn him away. He's a great kid. Don't be angry with him...or me."

Marie's stomach was in knots. Parker Nichols...he was more handsome than she remembered, and his intense gaze sent a surge of desire through her, just like in her dreams. How could she be angry? "I'm not angry. I'm surprised...very surprised."

"I can see that. I brought you a bottle of Patrón." He lifted the gift bag. "We could do a few shots to take the edge off." He winked at her and flashed that sexy grin. "Or, I can leave if that's what you want."

Why did he have to be a celebrity? Marie scanned her house—it was not worthy of a celebrity. Then she looked down at herself and cringed. Parker looked like a million-bucks, and she looked like she had been cleaning house in the grey cotton romper she was wearing. What could be done now when she was actually happy to see him? But here in her home... *Roll with it, Marie.*

"Do you know how to work a gas grill?"

He nodded and raised an eyebrow.

"Good, because I don't. In fact, I can't even start the darn thing. So, I'm going to use you—to grill." Her eyes smoldered up at him.

"Use me. You have my permission." Parker wasn't joking and that made her feel tingly inside. "Now point me in the direction of the grill." His warm, strong voice melted her like butter.

"I'll do better than that, and take you to it myself," she said, taking hold of his hand. But she stopped again to look up at him. "Thank you for the tequila."

"You're welcome. Thank you for letting me stay." He stared at her...she could tell he wanted to kiss her, and the sparks she felt went off like fireworks.

Once the excitement settled down from having a celebrity in the house, Marie put Parker to work. Whatever he asked for, she retrieved. They worked well together. In fact, she enjoyed assisting him. She relaxed as the awkwardness of having him in her home faded, and then she noticed Ann's eagle eye on her. She knew she was analyzing their interaction. Every flirting look, whisper, and occasional touch between them was filed away in Ann's brain. Her smug expression told Marie as much, in typical Ann fashion. Their chemistry wasn't hard to miss even—Marie couldn't deny it.

Not only was Parker Nichols a master griller—the compliments abounded—he was also a captivating storyteller. During dinner he shared stories about his adventures in acting. Everyone at the table hung on his every word. He was animated with his gestures, and even did voices, which the boys loved. Marie was seduced by his warm gaze and the light touch of his hand on her knee. Electric surges would shoot through her each time he touched her, and she grew more nervous as the evening went on.

What was she going to do about Parker Nichols? When she excused herself from the table to put the food away, Ann volunteered to help.

"What an interesting evening this turned out to be. I'm so glad I decided to come," Ann teased.

"Oh, I bet you're glad." Marie laughed. As if Ann would ever decline an invite. In the last thirty years, Ann had attended every party or gathering Marie had planned.

"That man out there..." She jerked her chin towards the patio. "He has it bad for you."

"And what do I do about that?" Marie whispered.

"What do you mean? You run with it." Ann busied herself, putting plastic wrap on the platter.

Marie leaned in close to her. "I'm afraid. The way I feel when I'm around him…it scares the shit out of me."

Ann's eyes shot to hers.

"It just seems easier…safer…if I never see him again."

"Don't do that," Parker said.

Marie whipped around, startled. Parker stood before her with empty glasses in his hands. Flustered, she took the glasses from him and put them in the sink. Marie shot a pleading look at Ann.

"I'm gonna go check on the…on the others," Ann said with a glint of mischief in her eyes as she left the kitchen. Marie was on her own this time.

"Marie, I've had a really great time tonight. It looked like you were, too." As Parker touched the tips of her fingers and ran them between his, she turned to goo. "Give me a chance."

"Mom," Jackson interrupted, and Marie pulled her hand away from Parker.

"What is it, buddy?"

"Ricky has to go home now." Ricky came up behind him and grinned at Parker.

"Yeah, I have to be home by nine. My sister isn't going to believe I met Parker Nichols. Can I get a picture with you?" Ricky asked.

"Of course. Can you take a picture of us?" Parker asked Marie.

"Yes, let me grab my phone."

Parker and the boys huddled together for a group picture.

"Okay…say cheese."

The boys grinned widely while Parker did his serious look…his *Professor Pierce* look. His eyes never left Marie's, and those dang butterflies were in a full-on frenzy.

"Now, let's have just Parker and Ricky together." She snapped the picture. "I'll send these to your mom right away." She smiled at Ricky.

"Thanks for having me to dinner. This was the best night of my life." Ricky beamed, with a Professor Pierce autographed t-shirt and ball cap in hand that Parker had given him.

"You're welcome, sweetie." Marie patted his shoulder.

"You're the luckiest kid ever. Parker Nichols is your mom's boyfriend," Ricky exclaimed as the boys walked out the front door.

Marie blushed, looking at Parker. He walked over to her and took her fingers back into his hands. A chill shot down her spine. "See me again."

"Parker, you've been great…"

"Marie…" he interrupted. His voice strong—commanding, yet gentle. "See me again…tomorrow?"

Nervously, she inhaled and nodded "yes" just as Brooke walked into the kitchen.

"Oops, sorry. I didn't mean to interrupt." Brooke quickly turned around.

"No, that's okay. I got what I wanted." Parker smiled at Marie and walked back out to the patio. Marie turned around fanning herself.

"He got what he wanted? What does that mean?" Brooke asked.

"I agreed to see him tomorrow."

Brooke's face brightened with excitement. "This has been the most amazing evening. He's so freakin' sexy!"

"I know…I need Ann."

"I'm right here. I figured you'd need me after Parker came out looking victorious."

"Great! I'm going back out with the celebrity." Brooke grinned and hustled out the sliding glass door.

"So, what happened? You're not going to stay in here all evening with him out there are you?" Ann teased.

"He got me to agree to see him tomorrow. I swear my heart is going to burst out of my chest." She gasped.

"Good for him...and you. Now let's go back out. He's telling another story."

"Wait! I can't go out with him tomorrow. Look at me. I look like a frumpy mom of two. While he looks like... Jesus, he looks like..."

"A hot steamy bowl of sex. Grab a spoon and take your time, honey. That man looks like he can go for hours."

"Ann!"

"Honestly, I don't see the problem." Ann nudged her elbow.

"Will you be serious for once. I'm falling apart here," Marie said, aghast.

"Stop panicking and enjoy the ride. You need this, and I don't think any woman in her right mind would pass up a chance with Parker Nichols."

"Ann, I'm not like most women."

"I know, and that's why you've snagged him." Ann smiled her most sincere smile. "Now let's go back out."

Marie and Ann rejoined the group and Marie took her seat next to Parker. For the remainder of the evening she was mesmerized by him, as was everyone else. The soft glow of the flickering candles created a sensual atmosphere, or maybe it was the Patrón. Either way, Marie was transfixed by Parker. She couldn't fight it—no one else existed.

At eleven o'clock, Parker announced he needed to leave. A celebrity through and through, he had taken pictures with everyone…except Marie. Every time someone asked for a picture she'd become uncomfortable. Though it wasn't like she never took pictures or selfies. It was just different—Parker was a celebrity.

"It was a pleasure meeting all of you," he said, smiling as he scanned the group.

"Yes, we hope to see you again," Ann returned. He nodded in a "me too" sort of way.

He went over to Jackson and squatted next to him. "I'm glad we were able to finally meet. Make sure you watch the new episode. It will blow your mind." He patted Jackson's back.

"Really? Oh man, I'm not gonna miss it," Jackson said. "Will you come over again?"

Parker stood and looked at Marie. "I hope to."

She rose from her seat, and he took her hand. With a final wave to the group, the charming Parker Nichols had won everyone over. And the whispers behind him brought a smile to his face as he, and Marie went inside the house.

At the door he faced Marie. "How's eleven?"

She looked at him, perplexed.

"For tomorrow…you said you'd see me tomorrow," he reminded her.

"Yes, I know. But why so early? I thought you meant dinner."

"No, we'll do lunch and dinner. Let's make up for you rejecting me when I asked you out to lunch way back when."

"I didn't reject you." She shook her head, knowing full well she had.

"Yeah, you did," he teased. "So, eleven, then we'll just see how the day unfolds. But for the sake of planning, for Jackson, just assume you won't be home until late."

She bit her lower lip as he stroked her cheek with his thumb. "Okay, I'll see you tomorrow." His touch made her heart pound. She had never felt such a strong connection to anyone before.

"I'm looking forward to it. Goodnight." He gave her hand a squeeze and left.

She closed the door and leaned her back against it, like a swoony, love-struck girl who had just met her teen idol. What in the hell was she going to do now?

Chapter 9

Like A Dream

I can't believe it. Best. Day. Ever!" Jackson exclaimed. "So, where's Parker taking you?"

Marie wasn't paying attention as she dug through her closet for something nice to wear.

"Mom, did you hear me?"

"My wardrobe sucks," she hollered from inside the closet.

Jackson's eyes widened.

"Sorry…" She stuck her head out of the closet with a guilty grimace. "I shouldn't have said that."

He laughed at her.

"I don't know where we're going or what we'll be doing. I know lunch. What do I wear to lunch with Parker Nichols?" She went back to searching in her closet for anything that wouldn't scream, "Boring; mom of two."

"Something sexy," Jackson shouted.

"What do you know about *sexy*?" Marie asked, walking out of the closet with her hands on her hips.

"Mom, I'm almost twelve. I hear stuff, I see stuff, and guys like sexy." She rolled her eyes.

"Jackson, you're making me nervous. This is just crazy." She threw her hands up in the air. "I have nothing good to wear. It's all work clothes and mom clothes. Nothing for going out with a celebrity."

"You could go shopping." The doorbell rang, and Jackson bolted to answer it.

Marie walked back into the closet; she had to find something worthy of lunch with a celebrity. Parker would arrive in less than an hour. "He's so out of my league," she whined as she crumpled to the floor. "I should've never gone to the gym this morning."

Seth had been in the gym when she had arrived at seven that morning. For the next thirty minutes she watched him in the mirror, lifting weights and working out with cables, which explained his massive biceps. Then he talked while Marie ran on the treadmill, his biceps taunting her all the while. Though it was hard to concentrate on his words, she did learn he was from northern California, an electrical engineer and divorced with three kids. He had a set of twenty-year-old twin boys, Connor and Cooper, who were in college, and a sixteen-year-old girl, Aimee.

Guilt plagued her for judging him by his physical appearance the first day they had met. She had been sure he was a player searching for his next conquest. The tall, muscular pillar was nothing like what she expected; he was sweet and open about himself. So, when he asked her out for coffee following her run, she said, "Sure." They walked to a coffee shop up the road from the complex, and for an hour they talked. It was just before ten when she returned home and jumped in the shower. Now she was staring at her horrid wardrobe without a clue as to what to wear for her lunch date.

"Knock, knock… Your fairy godmother has arrived with a garment bag full of clothes," Ann announced.

Marie ran out of the closet and hugged her.

"Yes, I love you too, dearie. Enough of this mushy shit. We need to get Cinderella ready for her celebrity." Ann grinned.

"I don't know what I'd ever do without you."

"You'll feel different when I'm a pushy bitch again."

"Yeah, you're right. So, what should I wear? I don't know where we're going or what we're doing. And he said to plan on being home late. What does that mean? Crap, I don't think I can do this." She slumped on the bed.

"Breathe. You're doing this. I knew you'd fall apart. Who wouldn't with your shameful closet," she teased Marie to lighten the mood. "Listen, last night Parker was the most charming man I've ever met. And he's interested in you, babe. Do you know how awesome it is *you* said yes to him? He's one lucky man for scoring a date with the best girl in the world."

"I'm the lucky one for having such a terrific best friend. Let's do this. Make me beautiful, sexy, and presentable for any situation."

"Your wish is my command. Let's start with sexy panties and bra."

Marie's eyes widened. "I'm not having sex with him," she gasped.

"Oh, honey I know, but sexy undergarments make you *feel* sexy. It's not about the sex. Unless you want it to be…?" Ann nudged her.

Marie rolled her eyes. Typical Ann. "That's a relief. The thought of sex is too much pressure." To admit she wasn't ready to think about sex with Parker in real life lifted a weight off her shoulders. She'd leave the thoughts of sex in her bathtub.

"No pressure, babe. When you're ready, Parker will be too."
Ann's sinful laugh meant dirty thoughts ran rampant in her
head.

"I have to confess something."

Ann looked at her with concern.

"I had coffee with Seth this morning." Her face soured. "I
saw him at the gym, and we talked. Then he asked me to have
coffee with him, so I said, 'sure.'" She sighed and plopped on
the bed. "I feel like I did something wrong knowing I was having lunch with Parker."

"It was just coffee. Big whoop. My question is, do you like
Seth more than Parker?"

"No, Parker makes me melt. Seth seems nice, and he's not
bad-looking. He has amazing biceps, and he's like me. You
know, ordinary. He's divorced and has three kids. It's like we
understand each other. He's new to the area and doesn't know
anyone. I kinda feel bad for him."

"Don't feel bad for him. He's a grown man. He can find
someone else to be his friend or therapist. If you're getting involved with Parker, it needs to be just Parker. No man wants to
share his woman with another guy."

"You're right. Parker's my focus."

"Perfect. How about this cute little number?" She held up a
dress for Marie to consider. "It works for day or night, casual or
fancy. We'll bling you up with the right accessories, spritz you
with that intoxicating Chanel perfume of yours and add a little
makeup. Parker Nichols won't be able to resist you."

"The red background is gorgeous, and I love the floral print,
but is it off the shoulders?"

"Yes, a little trashy, but also trendy and classy." Ann snorted
when Marie's mouth gaped open. "Now go put it on. He'll be

here soon." Ann pushed Marie into the bathroom before her flighty girlfriend changed her mind about Parker Nichols.

Jackson opened the front door with a cheesy grin on his face. "Parker, this is awesome!" He gave Parker a high-five. "I can't believe you're picking my mom up…for a date! It is a date, right?"

"It's a date." He smiled as he walked into the entryway. "So, what are your plans while your mom is out today?"

"Ann is here helping Mom. We'll have lunch and see a movie. Then Lexi and Isaac will spend the evening with me." He rolled his eyes. "But I don't need a babysitter."

"I'm sure you don't. But it's nice to have someone to spend time with, right?"

"Yeah, I guess. So where are you and Mom going? She's frustrated because she didn't know what to wear."

"Is that right?"

"She was in her closet griping about having nothing to wear. Girls are weird. Her closet is full of clothes." He shook his head, and Parker just smiled.

So, Marie was worked up about their date. It mattered to her.

"I'll go tell her you're here."

"Okay, but there's no rush. If she needs more time, I'll wait."

Jackson nodded and ran up the stairs.

"Mom!" Jackson blew through the door. "Parker's here."

"Oh man. How do I look?" She looked at Ann and Jackson.

"Gorgeous," Ann said.

"Pretty!" Jackson smiled.

She stroked his hair. "Thanks, buddy. I don't know if I'm ready to do this." She sighed, gripping her stomach.

"Well, if you need more time, Parker said he wasn't in a rush," Jackson informed her.

"He did?"

"Mhmm."

"What a man." Ann winked.

"Okay, let's do this." Marie pursed her lips, nervous with anticipation. They walked out of her room, Ann and Jackson following behind her. When her eyes met Parker's, a smile appeared on his face that said he liked what he saw. This was happening and she had the goosebumps to prove it.

"Hi..."

"Hi. You look amazing," he said as he gazed at her.

"Thanks." She blushed, then turned her attention to Jackson. "If you need anything call me, okay?"

"He won't need anything," Ann answered for him. Marie frowned at her.

"She's right, Mom. I'll be fine," Jackson agreed.

"Well still, if you need me, call me." She kissed the top of his head and then turned toward Parker. "Let's go."

He nodded, then turned to Ann and Jackson. "Jackson, you have a good day, and we'll see you later. Ann, always a pleasure."

They both smiled and waved as Marie and Parker walked out the front door.

From the moment they stepped out of the townhouse Parker was the epitome of chivalry. His hand went on Marie's lower back, guiding her to his SUV. The way he gazed at her in admiration when he helped her into the vehicle warmed her. The flutters within her danced delightfully. She couldn't remember the last time a man made her feel sweet, romantic feelings. It was nice, but it also scared her. It wasn't hard to see how different their lives were as she sat in his luxury Range Rover. Her car was a five-year-old Toyota Camry.

The longer they were together, the faster her heart beat. Would she be surrounded by other celebrities, or worse, mobbed by fans and paparazzi? Seeing her face plastered all over social media would be mortifying, not to mention the gazillion tagline possibilities: *Who's the older woman? NOT a designer dress. Has Parker Nichols lost his mind?* The humiliation would be crushing. Worse, she would have to stop seeing him, to protect herself and her privacy. For the hundredth time, she questioned her sanity.

Parker took her hand in his just then, rousing her from her reverie. How she loved the feel of her fingers in his hand and the way he enticed a deep yearning inside her. She diverted her focus to the music playing in the background. It was a welcome distraction from her worries, and it gave her a glimpse into Parker Nichols, the man. *Classic oldies*...she loved it.

"So where are we going?" she asked.

"Santa Barbara."

"Santa Barbara? That's an hour and a half away." Her mouth gaped open.

"Yes, is that okay?"

"Sure...I guess. It seems far to go for lunch."

"You can decide after you've experienced the ranch."

"Ranch? I'm intrigued now. I've never eaten with livestock," she joked.

He roared with laughter. "It'll be an experience you'll never forget...I promise."

The drive to the "ranch" was pleasant. Marie loved to hear Parker talk. His calming voice put her at ease. There was a genuineness in his eyes, not the fake "I'm tolerating you" look she often got from Craig. Everything about Parker was non-threatening. Comfortable. How was that possible? She didn't know him and yet she felt safe and content.

As she listened to him talk about his show, *Pierce*, she wondered, *why her?* Why a "ranch" an hour away? What was he after…sex? No, that couldn't be it, she reasoned. Her gut said he was a complete gentleman. None of this was about sex and it made her want him even more.

They pulled into the parking lot, and it wasn't a ranch. It was a beautiful stone resort with gardens and spectacular views of the hills. Parker walked around to her side, opened her door, and put his hand out to help her.

"Thank you."

"You bet," he said taking her hand, and they walked up to the restaurant.

The hostess was waiting to greet them. "Good afternoon, Mr. Nichols." She smiled. The woman didn't appear to be an awestruck fan, which Marie appreciated. "Your table is ready. Please follow me."

"Thank you," Parker replied.

They followed the hostess to a stone patio. Lavender and California poppies danced in the gentle breeze with the unkempt sea of green grasses. Mature olive trees graced the border of the gardens with their wild trunks and crooked branches, creating a canopy framing the azure sky. In the center of the whimsical garden stood a single round table and two chairs next to a water fountain—the focal point of the courtyard. Marie beamed as she scanned her surroundings. They were alone in the natural beauty of the terrace with the Santa Ynez Mountains as a backdrop. No celebrities, no fans, no paparazzi.

Parker pulled out her chair with care.

"Thank you," she whispered. Chivalry was not something she was familiar with, and she liked it.

"Mr. Nichols, your waiter will be with you in a moment. Enjoy your meal," the hostess said.

"This place…I have no words," she said, drinking in the magical splendor surrounding them.

"That's good I hope."

"It's fantastic. I wasn't expecting private dining. Is this preferential treatment because you're a celebrity?"

"Well, anyone can request this if they want to pay for the privacy. I wanted no distractions. Not when I have you all to myself." He stared at her with a small smile in the corner of his mouth. "I wanted to show you we can have privacy when we're out together."

"I appreciate that. I worried about your encroaching fans."

"I knew you would. I respect your need for privacy, and I'll do my best to protect you," Parker said with sincerity in his voice. "I don't like my life flaunted on the internet and tabloids. There are times I go out, expecting to engage with fans. But it's not always like that. But *it is* the fans that make me who I am—it comes with the job."

"Don't you want a normal life?"

"Yes, but what is normal?"

She cocked her head to the side. He grinned.

"My life is normal," she returned. Fans don't hound me everywhere I go, and I don't have to pay top dollar for privacy."

"There are ways around the fans and plenty of restaurants that serve celebrities. My life isn't always chaotic," he assured her as their server approached.

"Good afternoon, Mr. Nichols. My name is Francisco, and I will be your server today."

The afternoon unfolded beneath the bright blue sky. The waiter, Francisco, was professional just like the hostess. It helped Marie to relax at the ranch. The food was delicious, the atmosphere enchanting with the encircling gardens and fountain. She enjoyed the privacy, and the best part was that Parker focused on her and her needs. It made her feel cared for and respected.

"I know I said you looked amazing earlier, but I have to tell you...you're stunning." He reached across the table for her hand and played with the tips of her fingers. Her cheeks warmed as he slipped her fingers between his. "Despite your griping, you chose well for our date."

"'Griping?' What are you talking about?"

"Jackson told me you had been griping in your closet because you had nothing to wear. I like your choice."

"That little stinker. I must talk to him about not telling you everything." She softly laughed. "This isn't my dress. It's Ann's. My wardrobe is horrible. I have work clothes and mom clothes, not 'going out on a date with a celebrity' clothes."

"Hmm, then we should fix that problem."

"Fix it? No. There's no problem to fix. I need to expand my wardrobe. You're the first man I've gone on a date with since my divorce. I've been 'herm-ing,' as Tessa calls it, for two years now." Marie blushed. "That night at the club, Ann had forced me out of my house. She's bossy like that."

"I'm glad she's bossy. If she wasn't, we wouldn't be together right now. I owe Ann big."

"I'm glad she did, too. Today has been…" She paused a few beats drinking in the gardens, then she said, "Enchanting."

"I'm pleased you think so. Let's take a stroll around the property before we leave."

After lunch, they made the hour-long drive southward toward Sherman Oaks, except Parker didn't take her home. He took her to his house in Malibu. He drove up to a private gate, entered the passcode, and the gate opened. The vast ocean anchored his estate while the Mediterranean home welcomed its guests with its elegant splendor. The tour alone took half an hour to see the almost nine thousand square-foot villa. The luxurious backyard felt like a tropical oasis with a view of her ocean. It all overwhelmed Marie. She could live alone in the outdoor escape for the rest of her life. Between the endless pool, outdoor patio, covered veranda, and a fire pit surrounded by built-in seating with attractive cushions and pillows, she was in heaven. Inside was even more spectacular.

"This backyard is breathtaking," she said in awe. "And you live here alone? It's a huge house for one person."

"Yes, alone. When I saw it, I knew it was the one. I'm decisive when I know what I want." Parker took her hand and led her inside to the kitchen. "What can I get you to drink?"

"What are you having?"

"Just water. But you can have anything your heart desires."

Marie's heart fluttered, wondering if he truly meant, *anything*. Throughout lunch he would look at her with sweet, tender longing and then at times with a sinful glint in his eyes, seducing her, and now they were alone.

"Water works for me too," she said.

He nodded and took two bottles out of the refrigerator, and they went out to the veranda.

"So why are we here?"

"Well, I like being here. And I wanted more time with you. I wanted you to see my life isn't always crazy."

"I'm glad you brought me here, and your home is gorgeous." Marie took a moment to stare out at the ocean. She sighed deeply and seemed to release every bit of tension that had occupied her body for the last two years. "I envy your view," she said without taking her eyes off the vast blue water. "Every day you get to cleanse your soul, breathing in the salt air."

"You have an open invitation to cleanse your soul here anytime you want," Parker said with sincerity in his voice.

Marie's eyes darted to his. "You don't know me. How can you say that so blatantly?"

"That's why you're here. So we can get to know each other." He reached out his hand, and she met him halfway, letting him take hers. They walked to the veranda and sat down on the outdoor sofa.

The next few hours Marie and Parker talked while enjoying the views. There wasn't a topic they didn't discuss. Sports, music, their childhoods, her divorce, his career, and Latin dancing were all topics they covered. Parker spoke so candidly about himself, Marie wondered if he was like that with everyone, or just her. She hoped it was just her. The impression he gave was that everything he said was for her ears only.

"So, you learned to Latin dance for a movie you did several years ago? And you remember how to salsa?"

"Yes, after we finished filming, I've made it a point to visit Latin clubs as a refresher several times a year. Immersing myself in the Latin culture during filming grew my love and appreciation for the food, the music, the dancing, and the…." His voice trailed, and he stopped himself.

Marie waited for him to finish but he didn't.

"Are you getting hungry? I thought we could order Chinese or a pizza or anything else you might want," Parker offered.

"Do you do that with everyone?"

"Do what?"

"Offer them anything they want."

He leaned toward her and looked her straight in the eyes. "Only with those that matter, and right now that's you and my mother."

"Hmm, that's sweet…for 'right now.' Warn me when someone else comes into the picture that matters to you, so I can move aside." Her dark, piercing eyes drew him in.

Parker moved closer to Marie just inches away with smoldering eyes. He touched the tips of her fingers, then entwining his, she inhaled as her hand met his lips. Softly he kissed the top of her hand, and then the palm, sending chills down her spine. She swallowed hard, watching him, then licked her lower lip, desperate to feel his mouth on hers. *Was this happening?*

As if he read her mind Parker scooted even closer and, like in a movie, she cupped his face without thinking. The heart-pounding anticipation of tasting his lips made her dizzy. Would it feel like she imagined in her bathtub? Desperate to realize her own superhero fantasy of being kissed by Parker Nichols, she stroked his cheek with her thumb.

As if commanded by her magnetic lure, he moved in for the kiss. Warm and tender, his lips covered hers. Parker took his time discovering her for the first time. As he nibbled and kneaded, she parted her lips, wanting more of him. He accepted the invite, parting them further, and she trembled. Then a hum of musical pleasure filled the air as her tongue met his in a heated tango.

Marie could feel his desire as he gripped her nape, pulling her closer. The feel of him against her sent an electric current through her body, and when he groaned against her mouth she knew it flowed through him too. She shivered from the sensations as she kissed Parker with abandon and melted into him.

Marie and Parker remained lost in each other for some time, until Marie's phone startled them, forcing their entwined limbs and lips to break. She pulled back, flushed and hungry for more. Then in the next breath, she composed herself and answered the phone.

Parker welcomed the break, needing to regain control of his arousal. He didn't want to take things too fast; Marie mattered to him. So, the call had come at a perfect time. Now he could regroup and adjust his focus. But the desire to touch Marie again overpowered him, and he surrendered, taking her hand.

"Hi buddy, how's it going?" Marie smiled as Parker fooled around with her fingers, doing his best not to let the flame subside and it was working.

"Where are you? Are you having fun?" Jackson asked.

Her eyes smoldered when her finger entered Parker's mouth. His tongue swirled around the tip, then he drew it in and slowly pulled it out. Marie's breathing deepened each time he repeated the titillating dance between finger and tongue.

"Mom are you there?"

"Sorry! Yes, I'm having fun," she said, squirming on the sofa. "I'm at Parker's house. Is everything going okay?"

Parker smiled, watching her hand tremble as she struggled to hold onto the phone. He stroked the inside of her knee and then proceeded up her thigh. Marie's eyes widened, and she sucked in her lower lip. He loved how she tried with all her might to maintain control, and driving her wild, became a challenge.

"Yeah, just curious and Ann said it would be okay if I called," Jackson explained.

"Did she? That Ann's a keeper. A nosey keeper."

Parker laughed.

"Look, buddy, I need to go," Marie said, as she struggled to sound normal and not breathy. All the while, Parker was on the cusp of winning his self-imposed challenge. "But I'll see you later tonight."

Parker cleared his throat and shook his head no.

"Or maybe in the morning if I get home late."

Parker nodded, putting the tips of her fingers to his lips.

"Okay, be careful. Oh, and Ann said, 'Make good choices.'"

"Right, I will. Bye, buddy."

"Bye, Mom."

The instant the call ended, their mouths crashed together as they fell into each other's arms, entangled on the sofa, their passionate intensity reignited.

"Marie?" Parker said through his hungry kisses.

"Hmm?"

"There won't be anyone else. Only you."

Her eyes opened, and she could see he meant it. Parker slowed down, and each sweet, tender kiss that followed made her want more of him. Everything in her said this wasn't just a date, but the start of something. Then doubt set in, and her mind raced as he kissed her. How could he be sure there'd be no one else? Just words? A script? Promises he makes to all the women he brings home? *This has to be a dream.*

Chapter 10

The Double Date

Marie had taken up residence on cloud nine after her date with Parker; she was walking on air and smiling like a fool. On Monday afternoon flowers were delivered to her work, and when Natalie brought them into her office, she had a huge grin on her face. She said, "These are from Parker Nichols." The tropical arrangement matched Marie's style to a T. Every time she looked at them her insides warmed, recalling his kisses and the way he touched her.

In the evening he'd call her, and they'd talk for a while before calling it a night. The hardest part was going to bed with his voice in her head. It made sleeping difficult. No man ever turned her on the way Parker Nichols did. When she closed her eyes, his face would be right there. And now she knew the feel of his lips, his touch, and the taste of him. As much as she had wanted him to make love to her that night, they hadn't. Parker held back and didn't push further than passionate kissing and sensual caresses. It made her wet just thinking about him.

Lost in her thoughts, staring at the flowers he sent, she heard her phone ping. A text from Ann…a typical Wednesday occurrence.

Ann: Happy Hump Day! Will you be humping to-
day?
Marie: Do you have to be so crude?
Ann: Don't deflect, you know I do. So are you?
When do you see Parker again?

Just then Natalie knocked. "Marie, Mr. Nichols is here to see
you."

Marie stood from her chair, and Natalie held the door open.
Parker walked in with a brown paper bag and his heart-stopping
smile. Marie's eyes brightened, and her mouth instantly wanted
his.

"Hi, beautiful. I brought you lunch."

Marie walked toward him in a trance, her insides screaming
for his touch and Parker delivered. He took her fingers, entwining them with his, just the way she loved.

"Um, if you need anything just call me," Natalie said, closing
the door.

Neither Parker nor Marie paid attention to Natalie. It had
only been days since they were last together, but each time they
spoke, they were longing to see each other. Parker set the bag on
the desk, then pulled her into a searing kiss. Her arms wrapped
around his neck, and his went around her waist. Parker lifted her
off the ground, devouring her delicious mouth. The intensity of
their attraction held them captive in the embrace.

Parker reluctantly pulled back. He was desperate to see her,
and distract her with kisses and lunch, but it *was* her place of
work. They could only go so far. He kissed Marie's hand and

ushered her to the sofa. He'd brought them gourmet salads from a nearby bistro and a brownie to share. She couldn't stop smiling at him.

"I'm glad you look pleasantly surprised. I missed you. I know it's a little late to ask, but is it okay if I stop by?"

"My schedule is usually open from eleven to one. Just for future reference," she said, biting the corner of her lower lip. Her phone pinged again. "Ugh, Ann." Marie read the message and sighed.

Parker's brows raised. "Something wrong?"

"No, just Ann being her nosey, bossy self. She's a bully." Marie shook her head and laughed.

"Why, what's she saying?"

"She asked when I'll see you again. It looks like, right now." She batted her lashes.

"Yes, you are." He leaned toward her for a peck on the lips. "What are you going to tell her?"

"That you're here now."

> Marie: Stop being a bully. He's here now and surprised me with lunch.
>
> Ann: I don't believe you! Send me a pic.

"I can't believe her! She doesn't believe me and wants a picture."

"Well, let's send her one."

Marie laughed. "You know that's just feeding her controlling ego."

"Eh, maybe." He shrugged.

Marie snapped a photo of them sitting close and sent it to Ann.

Marie: Now leave me alone!
Ann: I love it. Now get humping!!!!!

Marie giggled, and her face turned red. Parker looked at her, intrigued, and took the phone. With a steamy gaze, he pulled Marie into another passionate kiss. Against her lips, he said, "Whenever you're ready."

She hummed as she pulled back, keeping her hand on his cheek. "Thank you for all of this."

"You matter to me. But, I'm also here to ask you a question."

"Oh?"

"Do you have plans Saturday night?"

"Hmm, nothing at this point. Jackson will be with Craig for the weekend if he doesn't cancel. Why?"

"My friend Dave, the guy I was at the club with, has four tickets for a show in Vegas and asked if we'd like to go."

She frowned at him.

"What? Not your kinda thing?"

"He asked if *we* would like to go? What does he know about me?"

"Just that you're an amazing woman. He knew I was interested in you the moment I saw you. And he's my best friend. We talk. What do you say? Do you want to go?"

"To Vegas? How would that work?" She tilted her head, pursing her lips.

"How do you want it to work?"

She raised her brows.

"Well, we'll fly out late in the afternoon and then have dinner before the show. We could stay there overnight or fly back after the show. Whatever you want."

She laughed. "There's that 'whatever you want.' So, who is he bringing?"

"Yeah, when he bought the tickets he was seeing a woman. But they ended it two months ago. He has no one to bring."

"Won't that be awkward, him with us? I don't even know him. There must be a friend or some other girl he can bring?"

"No, there's nobody. Do you want to bring one of your friends?"

"Bring one of my friends? For Dave, or for me?"

"For whomever. Dave is a liberal man; he wouldn't mind being set up."

"Huh, you know I think Brooke would love to go. I'll talk to her after work. And I think we should return Saturday. I shouldn't be staying in Vegas overnight with you," she said.

"Okay, whatever you want." And he kissed her, rousing her carnal side. Best lunch she'd ever had.

Marie wasn't surprised by Brooke's enthusiastic response to Vegas. She squealed, clapped her hands, and about had a heart attack while on the phone with Marie, who laughed at Brooke's excitement. Nobody made her giggle as much as Brooke. She was the most animated of the four friends, and her antics were adorable. Marie told her she'd call her back with the details after she spoke to Parker.

After getting Jackson off to bed, Marie called Parker. It was crazy, calling a man. She had to laugh. Dating, double-date, blind dates, and Vegas were not terms she's used or thought of in a long time. How her life had changed overnight…or so it felt. She couldn't help but smile as she dialed Parker, eager to hear his velvety, crooner voice.

"Hi, beautiful." He answered the phone the same way every time she called. And each time, she melted. Now, whenever she went to bed, the memory of his voice filled her dreams with his essence.

"Hi…So I talked to Brooke, and she'd love to go. Not that I'm surprised."

"That's great. I'm looking forward to this weekend."

"Me too. What do I need to plan for?"

"Well, I took a chance and chartered a plane. We'll pick you and Brooke up at three Saturday afternoon and then we'll have dinner at five before the show. Unless you want to do some gambling or sightseeing? Whatever you want," he said.

"Wow, a chartered plane…fancy. But why?"

"So, we can leave Vegas when we're ready and not when the airlines tell us."

"Oh, makes sense. I think what you have planned sounds fine." The truth be told, it was more than fine. Marie was being swept off her feet by the charming and sexy Parker Nichols.

"One more thing," he paused.

"Yes?"

"I'd like you to spend the night. We'll get in late, and I thought it might be nice to have more time together. Dave is staying with me through the fifth; he lives in San Francisco. We could make a weekend of it. Have brunch Sunday morning and whatever afterward. What time will Craig bring Jackson home? I can have you home before he returns."

Marie's stomach knotted up. Spend the night?

"Marie?"

"Sorry, you want me to spend the night? Parker, I don't know."

"Don't worry. You can have your own room. I don't have expectations, Marie. We can take this as slow or fast as you want. What…"

"Whatever I want," she finished his sentence. "Yes, I'm learning that." She giggled. "How about this—I'll pack a bag and Brooke will too. Then we'll see what happens."

"Sounds perfect. I'll let you go so you can call Brooke. Goodnight, beautiful."

"Goodnight, Parker."

After the call, Marie was on the phone with Brooke, giving her all the details for the weekend. As Marie expected, Brooke didn't think twice about staying at Parker's. They talked about what to wear for the show, and the whole call was filled with Brooke's happy squeals and clapping until Marie said goodnight to her "Brookie."

Friday afternoon was busier than usual for Marie. Her morning was jam-packed with meetings, and it was the monthly work lunch. Through it all, thoughts about the weekend preoccupied her. All she kept thinking about was spending the night with Parker. Part of her wanted to be open to taking the next step with him. The way she felt Sunday night was out of this world. Even so, she was afraid of disappointing him with her body and sex. What did she know about sex? Craig had always taken the lead, which wasn't saying much. As long as he got his, he didn't give a damn about her. Then she remembered Ann saying, "You just need to get laid, or that man will show you a thing—or ten." Thankfully it was just lunch, and she could fake her way through the meeting while lost in her thoughts. After she returned to her office, she checked her email. In her inbox was an email from Craig. Her stomach soured.

```
Marie  below  is  the  summer  schedule
Sasha  and  I  want  with  Jackson.  Look
it  over  and  get  back  to  me  by  the  end
of  the  day.  I  need  to  buy  his  plane
ticket  to  Orlando.  I'm  making  plans
and  don't  want  to  be  waiting  on  you.
Craig

7/2-7/10  (WDW),  8/5-8/14  (new  house),
8/19-8/28  (Hawaii  wedding)
```

Marie sat stunned. He wants Jackson for a whole week starting tomorrow? Tomorrow!

Her heart raced, reading the email for the second time. WDW. New House. Wedding in Hawaii. It was so typical of Craig to be demanding and last minute. She shook her head. Walt Disney World and Hawaii… Her heart sank. She couldn't even afford Disneyland. What a loser. And Craig, still the winner—the best, the top dog, taking Jackson on two fun trips. Do I agree?

She called Ann at work.

"Hey girl, to what do I owe the honor of this mid-afternoon call?"

"Ann," her voice cracked.

"What happened?"

"Check your email. I don't know what to do. Do I agree or not? One day's notice he gives me. He will give Jackson an amazing summer." She sniffled.

"That jackass! A dick to the end," Ann spewed.

"What do I do? I can't say no; Jackson will miss out on the fun. Ann…"

"I'm here babe. Listen, maybe the timing is perfect while you and Parker are developing your relationship. You could spend more time with him during the week while Jackson is with Craig," Ann suggested.

"I always do the fireworks with him on the Fourth of July. Parker's friend Dave will be out until the fifth. Then he'll be working. It doesn't matter, I guess. I've gotten used to being alone, but now Lexi won't even be home." Two large tears rolled down Marie's face onto the keyboard.

"Oh honey, this is just part of the adjusting. Don't let this bring you down. You're going to Vegas with Parker Nichols tomorrow and spending the night with him. Make him give you what you need—oral sex and his big dick."

Marie gasped. "You're unbelievable! Can't you ever have a serious conversation with me? I think I'll cancel Vegas. I'll ruin the trip for everyone."

"Like hell you are! You're not canceling the trip. You need this. You need Parker. Plus, it would crush Brooke. Do you want to crush your Brookie?"

"Ann…"

"That's it. I'm coming over tomorrow to make sure you leave with Parker."

"Fine."

Marie replied to Craig's email. All she could muster up was, "Okay."

She was off during her goodnight call with Parker and knew he sensed it after he asked her twice if everything was all right. But she didn't want to talk about Craig's email or his demands, or Jackson leaving tomorrow for a whole week. She tried to keep the call short, so she didn't get emotional on the phone. Most of all, Marie didn't want to burden Parker with her problems. Dealing with divorce and visitation issues wasn't something she'd wish on her worst enemy, let alone Parker, who had been wonderful to her. It would be selfish and cruel to bring him into her messy life. The frustration and pain were often too difficult for her most times. She didn't want that for Parker.

In the morning, Marie was up at five o'clock. She had slept like shit, waking multiple times during the night. There was no way she could go back to sleep, no matter how tired she was. *I need to run*, she thought.

She put on workout clothes, pulled her hair into a ponytail, and headed for the gym. Ten minutes into her run, Seth walked in.

"Morning, neighbor. I hoped I'd see you here."

She nodded and concentrated on her run.

"Everything all right?"

"I need to run."

"Okay." Seth shrugged and started his workout routine.

Marie ran for forty-five minutes at a faster speed than what was normal for her, trying to make the pain disappear, which pushed her to run faster and faster and faster. Her heart pounded, and she felt her pulse beating in her head, ready to explode any second. As she slowed, her labored breathing weakened her ability to hold back the tears that fought to be released. Marie stepped off the treadmill. Her legs wobbled, then buckled, and she collapsed. Seth ran over as her tears broke free. He pulled her into his arms, and she cried right there on the gym floor. Seth didn't say a word as she sobbed. The five minutes felt like a lifetime to Marie, but as she quieted the realization that Seth's arms cradled her protectively made her pull back hard.

"I'm sorry," she said, trying to compose herself.

"Don't worry about it. I'm glad I was here. What happened?"

She shook her head no.

"Talk, Marie. Let me help you. Is it your ex?"

She knew she was in a vulnerable position and she hated it. But she needed to talk—she needed a friend. Someone who'd understand. She nodded, with a tear rolling down her face.

They wound up at the same coffee house as before, and over a cup of coffee, Marie told Seth about Craig's email. Just getting it off her chest helped. She shared a little more about his controlling nature and how Craig always tried to make her life miserable.

"Marie, can I take you to dinner tonight?"

"That's sweet, but I can't."

"Why not? Jackson won't be home, and Lexi doesn't live with you. I don't see the problem."

"Wow, you paid attention."

"I'm an engineer. It's my job to pay attention to details. So how about dinner?"

"I can't. I'm going to Vegas with friends later this afternoon."

"Oh, so you *really* can't have dinner with me? I thought you were giving me the brush off." He chuckled.

Marie stared at him. It was easy to see that Seth liked her. And she liked him. He was a nice guy who had also had a difficult marriage, and like her, he tried to make it work for the kids. It wasn't until his wife Erika had had an affair that Seth was done trying. It was a hard blow, and when he retold the story of finding his wife in their bed with her lover, Marie couldn't help but feel deep compassion for him. A nervous twinge in her stomach told her to tread with caution so she didn't hurt Seth.

"Seth, I think you're a nice guy," she began.

"Uh-oh, here it comes," he teased.

"I'm seeing someone, and I don't want to lead you on."

He frowned. "You are? Is it serious?"

"We're just starting out. But..."

"Then I have a chance," he interrupted. Seth's icy-blue eyes had hope in them. But, he didn't stand a chance. Marie didn't have the same feelings with him as she did with Parker.

"Seth, I'll be straight with you. He's a terrific guy, and I think I want it to work out with him. I'm just nervous after my divorce."

"Hey, I understand. We'll be friends. And if it doesn't work out with the guy, I'd like a chance," he said with a sweet sincerity that made her smile.

"Friends would be great."

Ann arrived to help Marie pack and with Jackson. He never liked going with Craig for a whole week, and it killed Marie to force him to go. In classic Craig form, he was running late and wouldn't be over until three. Marie was out-of-her-mind angry.

"Dammit. Why does he do this? And Parker will be here at three. I knew I should've canceled Vegas."

"Stop it. It will be fine," Ann assured her.

"Ugh, I don't want Parker meeting Craig yet. I don't even know where things are going with him," she said, exasperated.

"Hon, just let life happen and let Parker be part of it."

Marie stared at Ann. In her mind, it was cruel to bring him into her mess. Why didn't Ann see that?

Her stomach twisted into knots while she waited for Parker to arrive. Brooke had come at two and in true form was bouncing off the walls with excitement and totally open to meeting Dave, whom she knew nothing about. Marie envied her and her free-spirited nature.

The doorbell rang at three and Marie knew it was Parker. Craig was never punctual. She left the living room to answer the door.

"Hi, beautiful." He kissed her on the cheek. "This is Dave Sumner."

"It's nice to meet you, Dave. Please come in."

"Marie, it's a pleasure." Dave shook her hand.

"Parker!!" Jackson came running down the stairs. "I'm so glad I got to see you before I left."

"Well, I would have seen you Sunday."

"No." Jackson shook his head. But before he could explain, the door opened and Craig walked in.

"Hey, Jackson." Craig acted as if he owned the place. He stopped short, surprised to see two men in the entry. Marie's heart jumped into her throat.

"Dad. You're here," Jackson said.

"Yeah, you ready? We're gonna have a great time," he said. "Marie, do you have his things ready?"

"Yes," she answered, as Ann appeared from the living room.

"Craig, it's been a long time," Ann said.

"Wow, a full house today, huh?" he said, looking at Marie.

The hairs on her neck stood like quills on a porcupine. She shot a glance at Parker who looked irritated with a furrowed brow. She could see him sizing up Craig as any competitive man would. Craig was five foot ten, a trim one hundred eighty pounds, semi-muscular, with dark-brown cropped hair, haunting black eyes, and a mustache to make him look "macho." There was one word everyone seemed to agree upon to describe Craig—douche.

"Dad, meet Parker Nichols. He's Professor Pierce on the show, *Pierce*," Jackson said.

"Hey, how's it going?" Though it was a question, Craig didn't wait for an answer, turning his attention back to Marie.

Parker nodded but didn't appear to like Craig. Marie couldn't blame him. Nobody liked Craig, and most people thought he looked familiar. Like someone on *America's Most Wanted*.

"Are you ready, Jackson?" Craig said firmly.

"Dad, isn't it cool? Parker's Mom's boyfriend and my friend. All my friends are jealous of me because I'm friends with my favorite superhero." Jackson grinned at Parker. Craig's harden gaze bore into Marie's.

"Let's get you on your way." Marie abruptly handed Jackson his duffle. "Call me if you need anything."

"I will. Love you, Mom," Jackson said, hugging Marie tight around the waist. Her eyes glossed over. Parker smiled at the warm embrace but frowned at Craig, who looked angry.

"All right, get in the truck," Craig said.

"I'll see you when I get back, Parker." Jackson waved good-bye.

"You betcha, buddy. Have a good time." Parker waved in return.

"Marie, I need to talk to you." Craig grabbed her by the wrist and gave it a firm jerk to follow him outside. She tensed, seeing Parker's eyes darken like he wanted to protect her, but Ann stopped him, shaking her head no.

"You gonna let him treat her that way?" Marie heard Dave goad Parker, and his teasing appeared to work. Parker looked as if he wanted to pummel Craig.

"No, I won't let him treat her that way!" Parker pushed forward, following Marie and Craig, and she was sure hell was about to break loose. But relief washed over her when she heard Ann step in to stop him.

"Parker, she'll handle him. It's no secret he's a fucking asshole. But you can't interfere," Ann said in a commanding voice. "Stay put while I show Dave, the trouble-maker, to the living room."

"I'll try," he said, watching from the door like he was ready to act in a split second. Marie could see Parker with Craig facing her.

"What the hell is going on here? Are they your posse? And how in the hell are you dating a celebrity?" His mocking and snarled lip she had experienced a million times. "He's not really your boyfriend, is he?"

"What do you care? It's none of your business," she shot back but tremored inside. Just knowing Parker was watching gave her the courage to speak more freely.

"It won't last. Mr. Celebrity—superhero—whatever the fuck he's called will drop you the second a younger woman catches his eye. He's way out of your league."

"Parker is his name!"

Craig ground his teeth and his nostrils flared. "He'll run after one look at your body. You might look good in clothes, but it's a mirage. Enjoy the fantasy while it lasts. You couldn't satisfy him or any other man in bed. I should know. Just keep your damn clothes on," he warned.

"Do you always have to be a dick? Maybe you do since you can't do anything beyond five minutes with the one you have."

Craig's eyes filled with contempt and as his mouth opened to set her straight, Marie saw Parker step out of the house

"Everything all right?" Parker said as he approached. He took Marie's hand and she squeezed it. Parker was about four inches taller than Craig with a larger muscular build. Craig wouldn't stand a chance against him if it came to blows.

"It's fine," Craig said. "Don't forget what I said. Keep 'em on."

Marie waved at Jackson as the truck drove off. She turned to Parker. "Sorry about that. I hope I haven't made us late." She frowned. He pulled her into his arms, kissing her deeply and her stressed body relaxed.

"You have done nothing wrong. We aren't late. That's the beauty of a chartered plane." He smiled down at her. "Your ex is a fucking asshole."

Marie giggled. "I heard Ann bossing you around."

"Yeah, she stopped me from coming out and pounding him into the ground."

"I'm glad she stopped you, it might have gotten ugly. But I'm flattered."

The foursome arrived at Parker's mansion just before midnight. Dave and Brooke cuddled in the backseat, while Marie sat quietly in the front, staring out the window on the drive. In fact, the whole evening she was quieter than usual. She had tried her best to have a good time, but whenever she remembered what Craig said, she'd tense up and fell into herself. The entire evening dozens of thoughts swirled in her head, making her question everything. Parker had asked her several times throughout the night if she was okay. She admitted to him Craig had rubbed her wrong, but it was no big deal because she was used to it. Her attitude would perk up for a while, and then she would sink back down into herself. Her constant thought was that Parker didn't deserve to be mixed up in her messy life.

Was Craig right? Was she living a fantasy with Parker? Him, a celebrity. Her, a paralegal. They were leagues apart. The whole night she had watched younger women gawk at him with their firm, perky breasts and tight asses. Once he saw her body, would he gasp in horror? It scared her to think about having sex with him. With her lack of experience and soft body, she would surely disappoint him. Maybe she *was* a fool thinking she could have something meaningful with him...with anyone.

As the night had progressed, anxiety and sadness had consumed her, even though Parker showered her with a tender affection. She adored him—wanted him. But she didn't deserve him. *Damn Craig.*

The second Brooke entered the estate it was as if she had died and gone to heaven. Marie watched her scan each room at top speed, taking it all in, determined not to miss anything. Since it was Brooke's first time in a mansion, her wonderment was understandable. It was not only beautiful with the highest quality of materials and decor, but it was also warm and inviting. It reflected its owner to a T. Marie smiled as she marveled at its luxurious beauty, remembering her awe the first time on the property.

As she continued to watch Brooke, she admired how comfortable she and Dave were together. It hadn't taken them long to act on their mutual attraction in Vegas. The change occurred during dinner after Parker took selfies with some "adoring" fans. Dave had laughed, saying, "It's part of the job, but I'm glad I can live life without being asked for pictures." Then he leaned towards Brooke and kissed her. From that moment, they had stayed connected by hands, lips, or wrapped in each other's arms. The sight of them spurred Marie's envy. Such laissez-faire…what limitless boundaries, being able to start a new relationship without baggage. How glorious. To add insult to injury, Brooke had an amazingly fit body. Dave was in for a treat. It was salt in an open wound. Marie sunk further into herself, and a fortress went up around her heart. The decision made, she'd stop dating Parker.

"This place is spectacular, Parker." Brooke beamed.

"Thank you. I'll take your things to your room," he offered.

"That's okay, I've got it." Dave winked, and Parker's brows shot up.

"Sure, man."

Brooke shot Marie a cheeky grin, followed by a shimmy when the guys weren't looking.

Well then, not sure why I'm surprised.

"We'll see you two in the morning," Dave said.

"Yes, goodnight Marie," Brooke said. "Parker."

"Goodnight, sweetie," Marie said.

"Well, I guess that leaves only you and me. Let's take your things to your room." Parker took her hand and led her upstairs.

Marie's heart galloped, fearful of the finish line. She knew the room he was taking her to, the one next to his. She would have been fine in the south wing with Brooke and Dave. Apparently, that wasn't where he wanted her. It thrilled her to know he wanted her close, but it also terrified her. What were his expectations? Before they got to the door, she stopped. Parker looked down at her, expectant.

"Wait. I'm not sure what I want." She frowned, looking at the guest room and down the hall, past the second-floor office toward his room. She took a deep breath, thinking.

"You know, we don't have to do anything except sleep," he assured her.

"Is that right? You can just sleep in a bed with me?"

"Yes. I can hold you through the night."

"That's some restraint," she said. Parker tilted his head down, staring into her eyes and stomach twisted.

To be held through the night sounded lovely, but she lost her nerve. She had to stick to her plan. Besides, what if he tried for more? "I'll stay here," she said, walking into the room without looking at him. Had she seen the disappointment on his face, she wouldn't have been able to refuse him.

"Okay." He put her bag down and pulled her into his arms. "I know something's been bothering you today. What is it? Craig?" He pressed his lips to her forehead. And she leaned into him. This genuine man acted as though he cared about her. She loved it.

"Yes. He knows how to ruin my day. I'll be better in the morning," she said, forcing a smile.

"Are you sure you don't want me to hold you tonight?"

"I'm not ready for that but thank you for everything." *Lies.* She didn't have to be a martyr anymore. There was no need to deny herself. He'd fulfill her every need and want, all night long. Or so that's what Ann told her. But Marie believed she was saving him from her complicated life...and herself from mortal embarrassment.

"If you need anything, I'm a few yards down the hall." He cupped her face and kissed her with a tenderness she had been craving her whole life. She gripped his waist, not wanting to let him go...not wanting the kiss to end...burning the feel of his lips and the taste into her memory. Mere seconds later, it ended.

"Goodnight, beautiful." He lifted her hand and brushed his lips across her palm, leaving behind his essence, and the realization that tomorrow it would be over.

Marie savored the moment and would keep it close to her heart...even when it was all over. "Goodnight, Parker." She closed the door behind him and traced her lips with her finger as her eyes welled with tears.

This won't work. It can't work. It has to end before I...she wouldn't let herself think it.

In the bathroom, Marie undressed in front of the large mirror that spanned the length of the luxurious bath, giving her a full view of her body. Above the ivory marble counter with grey veins and the onyx faucet, her eyes traveled to her satin bikini underwear. They were nothing special...three years old, and the nicest pair she owned. She remembered the day she bought them at Victoria's Secret...the day she signed the divorce papers. Ann had insisted she treat herself to new panties and perfume, after the hell she had been through before and after the divorce. Marie turned to look at her ass. "Nothing impressive there," she said disdain in her voice, and a glare full of contempt. It was laughable, wearing them on the off chance they might have sex. That was Marie trying to be prepared for every situation, but deep down, it was only her wild fantasy of being ravaged by Parker Nichols...like in her bathtub.

And there were her breasts. If they were firm, they'd be a respectable C-cup and desired by men. But soft with a pillow-y bounce didn't cut it. It didn't matter what Ann said about soft breasts fitting in their mouths easier. Two words came to mind: *horrific* and *embarrassing*. "Why didn't I get that boob job?" The fact of the matter was, breasts mattered to men. Big or small, size didn't matter. Firm and perky was where it was at…that is, according to Craig.

The lighting in the bathroom provided full illumination of her naked body; this wasn't a positive. In some ways, having tan skin was a blessing, as it was forgiving of minor imperfections. If she could have seen past Craig's negativity, she would have seen that her body wasn't horrible like she believed. Sure, she didn't have rock hard abs, and her breasts weren't like they were pre-kids. Still, she had a fabulous body. Her thoughts were a product of Craig's lies. They controlled her in a way that made her believe she was hideous—gross—disgusting.

Marie pulled her nightshirt over her head and crawled into bed, beat up after her self-deprecating tongue lashing. It was as if Craig had been there. She could regurgitate his putdowns, word for word. And yet, knowing Parker was steps away made her yearn for him. The way he had stepped between her and Craig earlier, ready to protect her made her feel valued. Other than Ann and the girls, no one stood up for her. But she couldn't do this with Parker. It wasn't fair to him. He deserved a woman who could match his youthfulness and sexual experience. Not her. Not the divorced mother of two with breasts falling south, and who'd never had a sexual experience last beyond ten minutes. Parker deserved so much better than what she could give him. There was nobody more wonderful, funny, sexy, and sweeter than him. And she was none of that. Plus, she was older than him by a few years. *Oh crap, what if he wants chil-*

dren? No, no, no… I need to stop this before we get in too deep. Before I…
fall in love with him.

The morning light streamed onto Marie's face from the glass
French doors, waking her with its warm radiance. She stretched,
reaching for her phone to see what time it was—6 am. Like
clockwork, she always awoke before six, no matter what time
she went to bed. And just like that, she rolled out of bed, ready
to start the day.

"Okay Marie, today's the day you pull back from whatever
this is," she rallied herself. "You gotta let him go. He'll find
someone new…*younger*. And you can look for someone *normal*."
She paused when Seth entered her mind. A divorced man with
three kids. Should she consider him? He was older than Parker.
And he wanted a chance. "If you don't want to be alone, you'll
consider him," she told herself, looking at her reflection in the
bathroom mirror. "Do we want to be alone?" *No.*

After she indulged herself in the expensive marble shower
with a phenomenal waterfall shower head, she dressed for the
day. The French doors beckoned her to open them. And when
she did, the fresh, salty ocean air enveloped her, and its deep
blue waters calmed her nervous angst. There was a private balcony off the guestroom adorned with a lovely bistro table and
chairs. It made for a perfect spot to sit and savor the view while
inhaling the morning sea air. This was her last time there, after
all.

The elegant Mediterranean estate was quiet and peaceful at
seven in the morning. She wondered if Parker might be awake,
but the quiet grounds told her no one was up yet. Was it safe to
venture downstairs? Perhaps it was too early? After all, they had

arrived after midnight. She'd wait a little longer before going downstairs. The fear of being rude or offending kept her in place.

Across the courtyard, the balcony of one of three additional guest rooms on the south end of the mansion caught her eye. The iron railing was like hers but smaller, with clay pots filled with orange flowers. She guessed they were California poppies. French doors mirrored hers with sheer drapes covering them. The room was dark. Was it Brooke and Dave's? She laughed, guessing it was, confident it had seen more action than she had…by her own choice, of course.

That Brooke… I'm sure she had a good night's sleep.

At 7:30 am, she couldn't stand being secluded in the posh suite any longer. No matter how pampered she felt inside the well-appointed room, she had to go downstairs. If no one was up, she'd go out by the pool and relish the peaceful view of the Pacific Ocean in the solitude of Parker's tropical oasis. The halls, his private office, the movie room…all were quiet. Then her ears dialed into a soft clinking from the kitchen. To her delight, someone was awake, and she hoped it wasn't Parker. The dread of ending it with him and never seeing him again already tormented her.

Marie followed the noise and tiptoed to the entrance of the kitchen, and peeked in. An older woman was at the island preparing food.

"Good morning," Marie said to the woman as she entered the kitchen.

"Good morning. You must be one of Mr. Nichols' guests. I'm Vicky, his housekeeper. Can I get you a cup of coffee?"

"It's nice to meet you, Vicky. I'd love a cup. Point me in the right direction, and I'll help myself."

Vicky smiled. "I'll get it for you, dear. It's my job." Vicky looked at her closely, examining her like Marie's mother would. However uneasy she felt, she would endure Vicky's inspection as she did her mother's. It was easy to see her assessment of Marie was thorough, but when she smiled warmly, her eyes said it all. They were kindred spirits. Marie was not intimidating like royalty or the Hollywood elite; she was more like the help.

"Okay…I appreciate it. I'll have cream; no sugar, please." Marie watched, mesmerized by Vicky's graceful movements pouring the coffee and cream into a lovely ocean blue mug.

When she handed her the cup, Marie inhaled the comforting aroma. "Thank you so much. I've been up since six. I gotta have my coffee first thing in the morning." She took a sip. "Mmm," she hummed, sitting down on a barstool at the island.

"Well, in the future I'm here at six. Just come on down; the coffee will be ready." Her voice was pleasant with a soft and airy quality that appealed to Marie.

A sinking feeling in the pit of her stomach jostled her when Vicky's words finally registered. There would not be "in-the-future" visits. The painful reminder crushed her. Marie shook the sad thoughts out of her head and relaxed on the barstool, observing Vicky doing her job.

Vicky prepared a fruit tray and made fresh whipped cream. Next, she mixed up waffle batter and laid some pastries on a platter. The two chatted casually. Each time Marie asked if there was something she could help with, Vicky declined her offer in a sweet, respectful manner. Marie didn't know why Vicky wouldn't let her help. It seemed over-the-top as far as she was concerned.

"Which do you prefer, bacon or sausage?" Vicky asked. Her question caught Marie by surprise. "Mr. Nichols didn't specify. Whatever you select will be fine."

"I'd love bacon, but if he likes sausage, do the sausage."

"Bacon it is. He would want to please his guest." Vicky nodded.

"How long have you worked for Mr. Nichols?"

"Three years now, since he bought the mansion. He's one of the best employers I've ever had," Vicky replied in a plummy voice. With her refined manners and graceful gestures, she had to be English, but in California? That's rare…or perhaps socialites and celebrities preferred English servants waiting on them. It was odd that Parker had an English housekeeper, considering most of "the help" in Southern California were Mexicans. It wasn't what she expected.

"Wow, that's saying a lot." Though she wasn't surprised at all. Parker had shown himself to be a kind and generous man, and the more she learned about him, the more she respected him. It was heartbreaking really, as he was everything she wanted and more.

"I'm not exaggerating. I assure you, Mr. Nichols is wonderful. Have you known him long?"

"No, but I agree, he's wonderful." Marie smiled. Vicky smiled back, studying her again. Just as quickly, she redirected herself back to preparing the food.

Marie sat spellbound as Vicky cut an assortment of fruit into fun shapes. Vicky displayed her artistic talents well with a paring knife. In her trance, Marie didn't hear Parker come up behind her. He sat down, wrapping his arm around her back, and pulled her close, kissing her cheek.

"Good morning, beautiful." Her eyes brightened, seeing him. "Have you been up long? You could've come to my room and woke me."

Those blue eyes... The longing in them...she was sure they mirrored her own. "I've been up for a little while, enjoying your lovely home."

He rubbed her back, drinking her in.

She had never felt more desired than she did with him, nor did she ever feel more tormented. "I've also enjoyed sitting here with Vicky. Her coffee is the best." She smiled up at him. He leaned down and kissed her on the lips this time, sensually. It was clear he didn't care that Vicky was in the kitchen—she was the help, after all. Vicky understood her place, turning away. Marie laid her hand against his cheek, savoring the kiss. "Mmm," she hummed, pulling back. She couldn't let herself get lost in him.

"So what time do you need to be back for Jackson?" Parker accepted a cup of coffee from Vicky, and he nodded in appreciation. Marie pondered the question. If Parker knew she was going to be alone, she was sure he'd asked her to stay, and she couldn't do that.

"After brunch, if possible?" she asked, sipping her coffee to hide her dishonesty. Vicky looked at her for a moment. Marie stiffened, wondering if she sensed her apprehension and lies. A "woman's intuition" sort of thing. Either way, she didn't want Vicky dialing into her or reading her mind. Her remorse regarding Parker was more than she could take and adding Vicky into the mix would break her.

"That's earlier than I was expecting. Vicky, does that give you enough time to prepare the rest of the food?"

"Oh, please don't rush on my behalf," Marie interrupted. "Let's plan for noon." She faked a smile.

"Well that's better," Parker said leaning into her. "Now I can have you longer." A twinge in her stomach diverted her attention. She had missed her fluttery friends.

Stay the course, Marie. It won't be long now.

Vicky set up the food on the veranda next to the pool. It had already become Marie's favorite spot on the entire estate. The sweet memories of their first date and the passionate kisses they had shared made it special to her. Parker sat next to her, relaxed, as if they had spent a lifetime together, content and secure in each other. She loved the way he doted on her, but it also made pulling back complicated.

"Did you sleep well?" he asked, touching the tips of her fingers. "Were you lonely at all? I was only a few yards away," he teased.

"The bed was like sleeping on a cloud...but, of course, I was lonely." She paused. *Stupid.* She was flirting. "But it was too soon."

"Next time," he said, sounding confident there'd be a next time. Parker kissed her palm as if he knew how much she loved when he did that. Her defenses weakened with each painful kiss—another burning reminder of what she was giving up.

The screen door closed from the kitchen. Her eyes shot over to the patio. Brooke and Dave walked out holding hands, looking refreshed and satisfied.

"Good morning." Marie smiled. The biting realities of her decision replaced an ache for Parker's lips on her hand.

"It is a good morning." Brooke grinned and yet, it was Marie who blushed. She shook her head, Brooke was never one to hide her feelings, good or bad.

"Let's go get mimosas." Parker jerked his chin toward Dave. "I'll be right back." He kissed Marie on the cheek. The man simply could not get enough of her. It tortured her knowing she was giving him up.

"Okay." No sooner were the guys gone that Marie had huddled close to Brooke, startling her. "Listen to me," she said, squeezing Brooke's hand.

"Ow, Marie!"

"Sorry…" she whispered. "Just listen to me. Parker doesn't know Jackson's in Florida for the week, and I don't want him to, okay?"

"Why? What are you doing, Marie?"

"I've asked him to have me home by noon. He thinks it's so I'll be home when Jackson returns."

Brooke's face soured.

"Don't judge me. Just be my friend and keep your mouth shut."

"Marie, can't you see he adores you? Don't do this, babe. It's Craig, isn't it? He's screwing with your head." Brooke touched her hand. "Parker really likes you. Even Dave said so."

"I've thought about this. It's for the best. Please, Brooke," she begged. "Don't say anything."

"Fine, but I don't like this. I'll have Dave drive me to get my car later. But I wish you'd reconsider." The scene was familiar, and it was during times like this that Ann could ease her mind. She just had a way with her that neither Brooke nor Tessa had.

"Here you go, babe. Did I interrupt your girl-talk?" Dave handed Brooke a glass.

"Something like that." Brooke smiled. "Thank you."

Parker handed Marie a glass and sat down beside her. "I'd like to make a toast," he said as he put his arm around her. Everybody raised their glasses at once. "To new beginnings and good friends."

Marie clinked her glass to his, immobilized by the weight of his words, *new beginnings*. Parker kissed her lips softly after the crystal champagne glass left them.

Thank you for a taste of your magical life. I'll never forget you.

Chapter 11

Letting Go

The buzzing of Marie's phone woke her. Eight o'clock! She popped up and answered Ann's call. "Hello."

"Did I wake you? Good. Now tell me what the hell you're doing?"

"I guess you've spoken to Brooke?" Marie yawned. "It's my life. Just leave me alone."

"Leave you alone? So you can fuck up your life? No, thank you. What do I look like, an idiot? If I let you do that, I'll have no life of my own because I'll be wiping your tears and your ass."

"I see the bossy bitch is back. Great," Marie shot back. "I gotta go." Marie ended the call and pulled the covers over her head. *Happy Fourth of July.*

Marie milled about her bland, boring townhouse. Everywhere she looked she saw Jackson; on the stairs putting his shoes on, at the breakfast table eating his cereal, and sprawled out on the sofa. She wandered into the living room and turned on the TV, as if he was home. An episode of *Pierce* appeared along with the man who had her stirred up inside. The gravity of her decision on the screen looked at her, talked to her...but his lips and hands she'd never feel again. She turned off the TV and left the room.

Nothing appealed to her—not food, not music, and not people. Sliding open the glass door she inhaled the warm California air. The patio table where Parker had told stories and touched her knee sat deprived of entertainment and flirty looks. The patio had always been a place of peace and comfort when she was alone. It took her away from her problems. It was an escape...her hideaway. A knock at the door broke her trance. She tiptoed to the door and peered in the peephole. *Seth*. She cracked the door open.

"Hey there, neighbor," he greeted, a plastic bowl cradled in the crook of his arm and a Whole Foods canvas bag hung from the other.

"Um, it isn't a good time."

"Is *he* here?"

"No, I..."

"Then it's a perfect time." Seth pushed the door open. Floored by his bad manners, Marie followed. She didn't care much for his cheeky bluntness, and neither would her *abuelita*. That was the thing with Latinos, respect and manners prevailed above all else...after loyalty.

"What are you doing here?" she huffed loudly with her hands on her hips. She didn't need this right now.

He smiled at her annoyance. "Well, I have this recurring problem... Since the divorce, I cook too much damn food every time I'm in the kitchen. And today, I could feed a small army." He laughed.

Marie didn't see the humor, still fixated on the fact that he barged into her home.

"Look, I remembered your kids weren't going to be around. I wanted to see how you were." When Seth wasn't trying so hard to be funny, Marie actually liked him better. "So tell me, how are you?"

She sighed, putting the containers of potato salad and baked beans in the refrigerator and leaving the bags of chips on the counter. "Thank you for this." She forced a smile. There wasn't a rude or disrespectful bone in her body. And like now, Marie was poised despite her woeful mood. It was second nature to put others above herself, and Seth had been kind; this was just another self-sacrificing moment for her. It didn't matter if she missed her kids or Parker, she had a guest in her house, and she would be a gracious hostess.

Marie motioned to the patio with a subtle jerk of her chin, and he followed. They each took a seat at the patio table, and she talked. It was easy to talk to Seth about her problems because he'd been there, done that. So she let her guard down about her insecurities and about Craig. Marie told him the awful things Craig said to her when he picked up Jackson and her cheeks blushed with embarrassment.

"Marie, you're a beautiful woman. Any man who rejects you is a fool, like your ex. From where I sit, I assure you, you don't have to worry about your body." He took her hand, and she flinched but didn't pull back. She didn't notice the same intense desire coursing through her body that she had when Parker held her hand. But it also wasn't off-putting. Still, warning bells blared. Then confusion about what she wanted.

"Seth, I appreciate you stopping over and lending me your ear, but I'd really like to be alone. I have a lot to sort out in my head." She stood, and so did he. He followed her to the front door. When she turned around the pain she fought to mask won the battle. Any second, she'd break down.

"Marie, I'm not comfortable leaving you like this. You haven't mentioned the guy you're seeing. Why isn't he here with you?"

She looked away.

"He should be here supporting you through this if he cares about you."

"I don't want to bring him into my messy life. He deserves better." A glossy sheen of heartache covered her eyes. The strength she tried to project had weakened during their talk on the patio. To open herself up and talk about personal matters with anyone, let alone Seth, sent an internal earthquake through her body. All her courage caved into the pit of her stomach. Her heart raced. Each breath she took became more labored, Marie bent over while gripping her stomach.

"Just let it go. I'm here," Seth said, as he cupped her face. It unnerved her as she struggled through each gasping breath. She wanted him gone so she could fall apart. Despite her feelings, she couldn't move away as he stroked her cheek.

"Your life won't always be messy. It will get better. Your guy should decide if he wants to be in your life." He gripped her nape, giving it a gentle massage. In her neediness, she allowed herself to relax and take comfort in his hands. "I understand your fears. I've had them too. It's why I try to avoid women who haven't been married. They wouldn't understand the complexities of my ex or my kids, or the divorce."

She saw regret and compassion in his eyes for what she was dealing with.

"Marie, any man would be lucky to be with you."

His hands moved to her waist, pulling her to him. A shocked blink later, he was kissing her tenderly. Marie felt the firmness of his chest against her...the strength of his muscular arms around her, holding her defenseless body. The warmth of his kiss ignited a fiery passion that jolted her, and in the next beat of her heart, she melted into the large hand that cupped her ass. To have a man touch her, want her... She let go of her inhibitions. The possibility of Seth overtook her. Could she find comfort with him and his understanding? Maybe. Only one way to find out.

The tension in her arms relaxed, allowing her hands to venture over his hard biceps up to his neck. Gripped in the moment, she pulled his head to her. And she slipped her tongue into his mouth in a desperate need for affection, and Seth groaned against her mouth. Just hearing him thrilled her. A newfound satisfaction overcame her knowing she turned him on and it empowered her.

Seth pushed her against the door and kissed down her neck nibble by nibble with hot desire. Hungry for more, he lifted her leg up, and she followed, wrapping it around his thigh. She gasped, shocked by his arousal against her pelvis. His firm, elongated bulge intensified her kisses, her wanting, needing, and yearning for Parker. No, she made her choice and was confident it was the right choice. She dismissed his beautiful face, his name, and her need for him. Parker was too good for her, and she needed to let him go. Seth was like her. Average. Divorced. Normal. Parker deserved better.

Seth's hands moved under her shirt, stimulating her breasts—a thumb on each nipple. It didn't take much for her mindless moans to echo in her entryway. They were just the encouragement Seth needed to move a hand down over her flat stomach to her soft mound. As if stoking a fire, her moans grew louder as he lingered in place before continuing down.

"Oh... My!" Marie's body trembled like a rickety roller coaster. The only hands to delve between her legs in the last several years were her own. A rage of desperate desire took over her kisses, turning them frantic and wild...and desperate to forget Parker.

In one deft move Seth lifted her up, sending her legs around his waist as he carried her upstairs while she kissed him vigorously. She wasn't thinking. She wasn't talking sense to herself. The battle of confusion going on inside her didn't matter when her desperate need to be wanted took over. All she desired was to be worthy of a man—any man. It was impetuous, but she had needs and didn't want to be alone forever. And she would not live in a fantasy like Craig had said she would. Seth was real. Strong. Attractive. *Real.*

He laid her on the bed, then pulled off his shirt. The sight of his massive chest and arms excited her. But the sound of him unzipping his shorts made her tingle. As they dropped to the floor a gush between her legs rocked her and she held her breath. Beneath his boxers, a huge bulge reached out for her. She flinched at the sight of him.

"Are you okay? Do you want to stop?" he asked. However, Seth stood straight, unconcerned by his intimidating escapee. Marie didn't think, consumed by her pleas to forget. She shook her head no. That was enough for him to unleash his hungry kisses on her.

It was as if time stopped. First her shirt came off, tossed to the floor. Next, he freed her breasts, taking one in his mouth. The slickness of his tongue made her squirm on the bed in heated passion. In the next breath, her shorts and panties magically joined her shirt, the event of their removal had gone unnoticed.

She felt the intensity of his eyes staring at her body. "You are *perfect.*"

The word lingered in her head, as he kissed her again, but she wasn't responding with the same energy as before.

"Marie, are you okay?"

A casual nod was all she could produce as she stared up at her white popcorn ceiling. Parker's face appeared while Seth groped and suckled in ways she had craved, if only Parker's face would disappear, then she might enjoy the attention Seth freely supplied.

Everything happened so fast. Foggy with confusion, Marie blinked to erase the face of the man who had stolen her heart. A cloud of clarity brushed the fog aside as she refocused. Did Seth say she was perfect? Was he lying? If he found her attractive, desirable and wanted to have sex with her, wouldn't Parker also? Not possible. Parker deserved better than being burdened with her mess. And she would only disappoint him in bed. "Aaahh…" A pleasing release swept through her when Seth's fingers filled her. The surprise jolted her out of her reverie. Her nails bore into his shoulders at the friction of his fingers, in and out with ease from her slick insides.

"You feel amazing…so fucking wet," he groaned against her neck, then sucked on her skin while stimulating her with his fingers. The dual action overwhelmed her, but she also welcomed it. "Oh yeah, damn, you're amazing. So fucking amazing," he mumbled, licking her neck.

What was she doing? What was she doing??? Her panting increased with her arousal. Was she having sex with Seth…? She was doing something, all right. Something she'd never done before, but it was Parker she saw...that she wanted... *Parker.* On the brink of her climax, the weighted rue of Seth fingering her unleashed a panic within her.

"Seth, stop," she cried out gasping. "I'm sorry, I can't."

He abruptly pulled back, leaving her body. He stared at her, concerned

"Not like this." She covered herself with her comforter. "Sorry. I lost my mind for a second. I was..."

"Trying to forget him?" He looked at her, disappointed. "I understand. Don't forget what it's like with me. When you're lonely, or sad and hurting, or just *wanting,* call me. I'll help you move forward." He kissed her forehead.

"I'm sorry." She grimaced, watching him put his clothes on. He tossed her clothes on the bed, and she dressed quickly beneath the covers. They walked downstairs, and it was more than a little awkward, but she needed to walk him out. Seth turned to face her at the door, and she hoped like hell he didn't try his luck at round two.

"You're amazing. Don't believe what Craig says. He's lying." He stroked her cheek and kissed her again, and she stiffened. "Now, figure out your heart. Don't fear disappointing anyone. I assure you, you won't." Seth walked out of the townhouse, and Marie pushed the door closed, locking the deadbolt. She crumpled to the floor, curling into a tight ball, as her sobs filled the empty foyer.

After Marie had let it all go, she grabbed a bottle of wine and headed out to the patio to drink away her pain. A smutty romance novel on the small mosaic table taunted her. Any other day, she'd take pleasure in reading about what she lacked, but now she glared down at it. "Life isn't a freaking romance novel," she growled under her breath. With her glass of wine in hand, she curled up on the chaise beneath the bright haze that appeared daily at noon.

By four o'clock Ann had called twice and messaged half a dozen times. Parker had called and left her a message. Tessa stopped by, but Marie ignored the knocking out on the patio. The locked front door prevented anyone from just walking in. She had also turned off the volume on her phone so that she wouldn't hear the calls. All she wanted was to be alone.

Marie's behavior wouldn't be a cause of worry for Ann and the girls. It was typical Marie, but it pissed Ann off just the same. Since grade school, Marie had always shut down to cope. Nobody could ignore people better than her. She could be a shell that passed through life with not a care in the world. Weeks would dissipate into thin air. She talked to no one, not even Ann. After a while, she would be over it like nothing had happened. Ann always believed it was Marie's ability to shut down and ignore her surroundings that carried her through the seventeen years of marriage with Craig.

First and foremost, the girls worried she'd shut Parker out to avoid falling in love with him. They knew that fear drove her actions—the fear of being hurt. And they were right. Marie plummeted into self-protection mode, and she needed to snap out of it fast before she turned her emotions off.

The pop and crackle of fireworks sounded off in the distance among the haze of clouds and city lights. *Jackson…* Marie thought, cleaning up her mess and headed inside. Her gait was staggered, courtesy of the bottle of wine and three tequila sunrises she had consumed on an empty stomach. In her drunken state, Marie glared at the romance novel on the table beside the chaise. "Romance sucks," she spat.

All her grit from a week ago had vaporized in twenty-four hours. Marie wobbled through the house, locking doors and turning off the lights. Her dark, lifeless dwelling mirrored her inner self. She climbed up the stairs, pulling on the railing as she dragged her sorry, pathetic self to the bed where she dropped into unconsciousness.

Marie jerked from the pounding in her head. No, the pounding on the door? A violent, chorus of ringing commenced, followed by more pounding. Her first thought was that juvenile delinquents were having a post-fireworks heyday on her doorbell. *Little turds.* She gripped her head; there was a definite pounding it. In the three years, she'd lived in the complex she had never had a problem with obnoxious, disrespectful kids disturbing her, never.

No amount of pressure her hands provided covering her ears helped muffle the ringing and pounding. And then it hit her… "Shit." She glanced over at the clock…*ten o'clock!*

In a careful, methodical motion she rolled off the bed, and as she stood, she paused in place to get her bearings. All the signs were present spotlighting her drink-fest; fuzzy mouth, scratchy eyes, gurgling stomach doing flips, and the excruciating pain that pounded in her head. *Oh, the pounding.* Slowly she walked down the stairs, pausing every third step. The pounding on the door and the ringing of the doorbell infuriated her…*that bitch.* As she opened the door, a powerful punch came from the brilliant sunlight, smacking her in the face. She stumbled back, covering her eyes.

"What do you want?!" she cried out in agony. Ann and Tessa walked in, closing the door behind them.

"Holy shit Marie, stop this now!" Ann rebuked. "I called you over a dozen times, sent you twenty freakin' texts, and you haven't even so much as sent an emoji flipping me off."

Marie leaned against the stair railing, eyes downcast, taking Ann's tongue lashing. The humiliation of the entire scene compounded her grief and feelings of worthlessness. If she had had an ounce of strength or care in her, she might have tossed Ann out on her creamy white ass and would never speak to her again. Of course, those were just the foul musings of a self-loathing woman, post-inebriation.

"Come on, babe," Tessa said, touching her shoulder. Marie swayed forward letting Tessa help her walk back up the stairs. Without saying a word, Marie went with her and Ann followed them.

"Don't coddle her!" Ann shouted at Tessa. "She's a grown woman who needs to act like a freakin' grown woman. So she has a hangover, let her suffer like the rest of us have to."

At the top of the stairs, Tessa turned to face Ann with disgust on her face. "If all you're going to do is bitch, then leave. I have no patience for your mouth today. If you stay, shut the hell up and help me take care of our best friend." She glared at Ann, who was stunned speechless.

Tessa helped Marie into the shower while Ann sat on the bed, crossing her arms with her lips pursed. Her eyes burned into Tessa when she walked out of the bathroom.

"What in the hell was that? Are we playing good cop/bad cop?"

"No, we aren't. Sometimes you take it too far with your mouth. Marie is spiraling down into her black hole. If you think being a pushy bitch will help, you're wrong. She will cut you out of her life if you push too hard. Even she has a limit with you." Tessa inhaled deeply to calm herself. "She needs us, Ann. She's hurting. Are you going to help or not?"

"And here we always thought you were the nice, gentle one, but you turned out to be a badass," Ann teased. "I'm sorry I lost control. Her loser ex did this to her, and it pisses me off! Whatever it was he told her Saturday put her in this place. I want her happy, and she was getting there. Being firm usually works to bring her out of the abyss."

"I know, but there's more going on with her. She never gets drunk. So, be pissed, but not at her. She's all alone, Ann. Her marriage is over, which isn't bad, but Lexi's gone, and so is Jackson. She's alone. And she doesn't do 'alone' well. Those kids have been her world. Do you have any idea how hard this is for her? Cut her a break for Christ's sake."

"I'll go make some strong coffee and toast for when you come down," Ann said, hugging Tessa.

Marie was better after her shower and two cups of coffee, but she wasn't in the mood for talking. The three women sat out on the patio in silence for the next hour.

"Where's your phone?" Ann asked, breaking the silence.

Marie looked at her blankly.

"Where's your phone? We need to check it to make sure there aren't messages from the kids."

"In the junk drawer," Marie whispered.

Tessa looked at her with compassion. It had been a year since the last time Marie spiraled into nothingness. Everyone had hoped she'd never go there again.

Ann returned with the phone, which sounded, ping after ping as notifications loaded. "Huh."

Marie's eyes shot up with worry.

"Looks like some bitch named Ann was blowing up your phone," she snickered.

Marie exhaled in relief.

"Nothing from the kids. You have two missed calls and a text from Parker."

The mention of Parker didn't do anything to Marie. Not a flinch, a gasp, or a tear rolled down her face. The walls had gone up.

"I'm gonna fix us something to eat," Ann announced.

Another hour had passed, and Marie was still unresponsive and lost in herself.

In her sweet, gentle voice Tessa talked as she watered the plants. She looked like the brunette version of Tinker Bell. It was her peaceful, whimsical side Marie adored. "Brooke told me what an amazing time you had in Vegas. She really likes Dave. What do you think of him? Is he good enough for our *Brookie*?" Tessa's questions didn't even draw a blink from Marie. "She also said Parker doted on you like a love-struck puppy." She giggled softly. "I bet that made you feel cared about and wanted." Tessa paused, looking at the lemon tree. Marie remained unfazed, but she didn't usually snap out of the funk quickly.

And then Tess continued. "Did you hear Brooke and Dave had sex that night and in the morning at Parker's? Our Brookie doesn't waste time when she likes a man does she? She said she thought you might have slept with Parker too. Did you?"

Marie's eyes filled with tears.

"I hear the mansion is to die for and you appeared right at home there with him. Brooke said his eyes were constantly on you and his hands never left you, not even for a second. I love that for you, honey. It's about time you had a man in your life who treats you the way you deserve, because you're a treasure."

Marie's chest rose and fell hard with every word. Miraculously, Tessa was getting close.

"I bet Parker's worried about you. He's probably wondering why you haven't called him or replied to his messages. Do you think he'll come by check on you?"

Marie's eyes shot to hers; blinking hard she covered her face, then the sobs ensued.

"Oh honey, let it out," Tessa said, taking Marie into her arms. She held her for the next several minutes while Marie fell apart. The pain she had been holding back broke free in earth-shattering wailing, and forceful gasps. Tessa held Marie's shaking body firmly as she had many times before. "Let it out Marie, let all out." And Marie did, she let out every ounce of grief, pain, and regret.

Marie gasped as she tried to get control of herself, her ragged breathing winning the battle. "I... I can't be with him. He deserves better than me," she sobbed.

"What do you mean he deserves better than you? Honey, you are the best," Tessa comforted.

Marie shook her head. "No, I'm not. I can't be with him. I'm too afraid." She sniffled as she wiped her tears away.

"Afraid of what? Was he mean to you?"

Marie saw Ann standing at the sliding glass door eavesdropping. She knew it was never easy for Ann to watch her fall apart. Even a hard ass has a soft spot and she was Ann's. The coward had hidden inside while Tessa took care of Marie. But now, she ventured out, guardedly.

"No. He doesn't have a mean bone in his body," she defended. "I'm afraid of disappointing him. Jesus, I'm older than him…what if he wants children? Could you imagine it? I already have two kids…I have baggage. He shouldn't have to deal with it. He deserves to find someone younger. Someone pretty, sexy, and who will satisfy him in bed. I'm not that person and he deserves someone like that." She choked back tears, wiping the running snot off her lip, and Tessa handed her a tissue. "Thank you," she said as she hiccupped.

Ann sat next to Marie with a rare look of hesitation on her face and embraced her. "Whatever you want, we'll do. No more bossy bitch from me. I'm here for you, and we'll help you no matter what."

"Then help me walk away from him," Marie whimpered, her voice thick with emotion. "Please."

"Marie, we all have baggage. You're not the only one. Parker isn't a fool, he knows this, and he wants you, honey. You're an incredible, fun and sexy woman. That's why you caught his eye. You can learn about sex with Parker." Ann snickered, trying to lighten the mood.

"No, I have to do this. It's for the best," Marie said, digging in her heels. She was not going to let them change her mind.

"Okay, babe. Are you sure?" Ann asked.

"I am, and I think I'll go out with Seth."

"What?!" Ann said as Tessa's eyes widened.

"He's a regular guy. He's the real deal, not the fantasy. He's walked the road I have. It just makes sense," Marie said. She was numb, trying to convince herself that Seth was the right thing.

"Yeah, but are you attracted to him? You light up like a fucking beacon when you're with Parker. You even said he melts you when he touches your fingertips," Ann remind her.

"It has to be lust...or the fantasy of him. I was pretty swept away by it all—the whole actor, mansion... everything," Marie said.

"What makes you think Seth is the guy? Are you going to ask him out?" Tessa asked.

"I already know he wants me."

Their mouths gaped open, and their eyes bulged.

"Why are you looking at me like that? Are you disgusted a man might want me? Well, he does. He was here yesterday, and we almost had sex."

Ann and Tessa gasped simultaneously.

"What do you mean you *almost* had sex?!" Ann asked.

"He stopped over to bring me food, and we talked right here on the patio for a while. He's sweet and understands what I'm going through. When I walked him to the door, I'm not sure what happened." She shrugged. "He kissed me, and I didn't stop him. I was in a bad place; sad and hurting. And he wanted me. But not in a gross, 'I'm using you for a piece of ass' kind of way.' He carried me up to my bed."

The girls were hanging on her every word.

"He has a magnificent body. I liked his hands and mouth on me...but all I could see was Parker. And I wanted to forget him." She hung her head and inhaled before continuing her tale of yesterday's activities that didn't include fireworks. "Just before we, uh, did it, I stopped Seth. I told him it wouldn't be right in the state of mind I was in. I was just using him." A few tears of regret rolled down her face, and she dabbed them quickly with a fresh tissue.

"You didn't go all the way?" Tessa asked for clarification.

"Did he stick his dick in me, no."

Both Tessa and Ann gasped again, shocked by Marie's choice of words.

"What? I'm frustrated with myself. Angry! So, I drank myself into the toilet after he left. Guilt swallowed me whole for screwing around with him and with Parker. I've thought about it, and I'm giving Seth a chance and setting Parker free. It's not like we're an official couple or anything. He's already free. We've only been seeing each other two weeks. I'm just going to stop."

"Wow, I'm not sure what to say," Tessa said.

"Parker isn't a fantasy. He is the real deal, and he *really* likes you," Ann said.

"No, he won't stick around because my life is messy. He doesn't understand what getting involved with me will be like. At least Seth knows divorce, and he'll be able to deal with it. My mind's made up. Do you support me?"

"Yes. I don't agree, but I support you," Tessa said.

"I think you've lost your mind, but I'll support you," Ann said.

Chapter 12

Yes

Wednesday was a subpar day compared to the previous week when Parker had brought her lunch and she floated on cloud nine. Marie hadn't responded to any of his texts or calls. She figured she'd just let whatever was going on between them die off. And it wasn't easy at all. She missed him, but in the long run, she believed it was for the best. After her talk with Ann and Tessa, she called Seth and agreed to dinner with him. Dinner with Seth was her focus for Wednesday. Her phone buzzed.

> Ann: Happy Hump Day! Want to go out to dinner tonight?
> Marie: Sorry, I can't. I'm having dinner with Seth.
> Ann: That was fast. Let me know how it goes.
> Marie: Sure. Just remember we're grown-ups.
> TTYL

A knock on the door diverted her attention away from texting, Natalie peeked her head in. "Hey Marie, the office is ordering Thai, do you want anything?"

"That won't be necessary, I've brought her lunch," Parker said from behind Natalie.

"Oh, Mr. Nichols," Natalie said, surprised.

"You weren't at your desk, so I just walked back. I hope that's okay?" His eyes connected with Marie, who was more than a little unnerved to see him.

"Nope, not a problem," Natalie said as Parker walked past her. She promptly closed the door behind her.

"Hi beautiful. I've been worried about you. Is your cell phone broken? Did you drop it in the ocean?" he teased, but she didn't laugh.

Her eyes darted around the room; she didn't so much as say *hi*.

"When you didn't call or respond to my texts I just figured you were having fun with Jackson and I didn't want to interrupt your time with him." Parker walked closer to her desk and she stiffened. Marie didn't flash him a flirty smile. Only a panicked tension filled the air. "Marie…what's going on?" He set the bag down on the table near the sofa. "Talk to me. Please." He walked over to her and turned her chair to face him. Crouching down before her, he cupped her face, forcing her to look at him. "Talk to me. What happened? Were you avoiding me?"

"Stop," she said, moving his hands away. Then she pushed her chair back and stood. "I thought if I didn't respond to your calls or texts you'd get the hint."

He furrowed his brow.

"I think you're a great guy, but we're not going to work."

"What?"

Marie inhaled, holding her breath.

Parker stood from his crouching position and walked to the middle of the room, then turned to face her. "What happened?

Everything was magnificent and don't tell me it wasn't. I've felt your feelings for me every time our eyes connect, when I touch you and kiss you. I see it. I *feel* it." His words rolled off his tongue, tender and poetic, and pained with confusion.

"Parker, I like you. But…"

"No buts," he interrupted her. "Stop at; 'I like you.'" He pulled her into his arms and kissed her. She squirmed to get away, but he didn't stop, moving over her mouth resolutely like he needed to prove her wrong.

Just like the other times they had kissed, the passion enveloped her, but she fought the feelings that wailed inside to surrender.

"No, we can't do this." She pushed him back hard, and with the astonished look on his face, she could swear she heard his heart shatter.

"Is this about Craig? What did he say to you Saturday?"

"Parker, my life is a mess, and I don't want to bring you into this…"

"I'm a grown man. I can take care of myself," he shot back.

"Right, and when it gets too rough, you'll walk out of my life." She turned and walked away from him. "We'll never work. Try to understand. I don't want to hurt you."

"Marie, no estar solo," her dear *Abuelita's* words spoke to her heart. However, she banished them just as fast as they appeared.

"Then don't," Parker choked out. The pain in his voice stung, but she held strong. "I really like you, Marie. I understand your life is complicated and I still want to be with you. You matter to me." He took her hand, touching the tips of her fingers softly. She'd cave any second.

"I'm going out to dinner tonight with another man." There, she had said it. Now he'd hate her and walk away.

"Who?" he asked guardedly.

"I don't think it's any of your business."

"There's another guy?"

"I'm not lying. He lives in my complex. I met him in the gym the day of the barbecue."

"And you like him? You want to go out with him?"

"Seth understands me and what I'm going through with Craig and Jackson. And he's divorced like me with three kids. He's real."

His mouth fell open. "Real? What does that mean? Shit, Marie! I can't even believe what I'm hearing! He gets you. I get you. He understands you? I would understand you better if you'd let me in." His brooding blue eyes burned into hers.

Marie walked into his path, forcing him to stop. "Parker, I'm sorry. I really do think it's for the best." She swallowed hard trying to keep control of herself.

"You're afraid, aren't you? But afraid of what?"

"Parker, are you hearing me?"

"Don't push me away. We belong together."

"No, we don't. We're different. Night and day. Can't you see that?"

"You're telling me you don't want me? And you want *him*?" It was senseless to lie. He could probably read her mind with his superhero powers. Or more like she was a horrible liar. So, she remained silent as her labored breathing answered for her.

He cupped her face, "Tell me you don't want me." He stared fiercely into her eyes. "Say it, if that's how you feel."

"I can't be with you." A tear broke free, then another. She might as well admit her heart's desire because Parker was no fool. Stubborn in her resolve though, she remained unyielding to him despite the tears that gave away her true feelings.

"'Can't' and 'don't want to' are different things." Then her imprisoned desires got their wish—his mouth smashed hard against hers, and his arms wrapped around her tightly. Slowly his hands traveled down her back to her ass, where he caressed her until she weakened. Lost in him, his touch, his lips…his mouth on her neck, her body yielded as he licked a path up to her earlobe. Nibble after delicious nibble, powerful tingles erupted when he pulled her body even tighter against his.

Her breath caught, and she was instantly wet. "We can't do this." She pushed him back. "I'm having dinner with another man tonight."

"Cancel."

"No, I can't."

"Why are you doing this? None of this makes sense. You want me, but you're holding back. Why?"

"Parker…" She took an exasperated breath.

"No… I am not giving up on us."

"Please, in the long run, you'll see it was the right decision."

"I can't even believe this!" He threw up his hands, turned on his heel and walked out of her office, defeated.

In his Range Rover, Parker's heart pounded against his chest while Marie's words whirled around in his head. Her taste still on his lips. He had to call the one person who could help. But first, he called Dave. He needed him to ask Brooke for Ann's number. Five minutes later he called Ann on his way home.

"Hello."

"Ann, it's Parker."

"Oh, what can I do for you?"

"Don't pretend like you have no idea why I'm calling. You're her best friend. Why is she doing this? She said she's going out tonight with some guy."

"Parker, I'm sorry. But you know I can't tell you anything. I can't risk losing her trust."

He hit the steering wheel. "Dammit! Please help me. I need her, Ann. And she needs me. What is she afraid of? Why is she pushing me away?"

"I can't tell you anything. But if you asked me questions, I could answer yes or no," she offered.

"Okay. I'll take it, thank you. First question, Marie wants to be with me, doesn't she?" He held his breath waiting for her response.

"Yes."

He knew it and sighed, releasing his tension and fear.

"Does this have to do with what Craig said on Saturday?"

"Yes."

"Ann, this will take all day. Please."

She sighed and grumbled under her breath. Parker knew Ann would be risking her friendship with Marie if she told him anything. But he was desperate.

"I better not regret this. She believes she's doing you a favor ending it before it gets started. In her mind, she's beneath you and you deserve better than her. She doesn't want to complicate your life with her mess. And she believes you'll leave her for a younger woman and break her heart. Basically, she's afraid. She thinks if she stops now, she won't fall in love with you."

"Can you believe this? What about the guy? Who is he? She said he's divorced, and he understands her. And he's a real guy. Whatever that means."

"You're the 'fantasy' guy. The 'out of her league' guy. This other guy is a distraction to help her forget about you. He's nice and attractive, but he's not you. But, he wants her. And she's insecure and very vulnerable. I'll be straight with you, that's a dangerous combination in a woman. It makes us weak, and we don't think straight. We need affection and to feel desired. Read that as *sex.*"

"Shit, and she's having dinner with him tonight."

"Yes. I hope you can get through to her. She cares for you. It's why she's giving you up. Just remember, she's scared. Her pathetic ex did a number on her their whole marriage and he's still controlling her."

"I hate that guy. Thanks for your help, Ann."

"You bet…good luck."

Marie prepared for her date with Seth and in the process worked herself up into a nervous frenzy. Parker stayed on her mind after he had left her office. The pain in his eyes tormented her, while his words played over and over in her head, *"Tell me you don't want me."* The knock at the door rattled her. It would be Seth, and she was having second thoughts about their date after seeing Parker. But alas, there was no turning back now.

"Hi." She smiled as she opened the door. Seth looked handsome in a blue button-down oxford shirt and khakis.

"Marie, you're gorgeous." A sweet compliment to be sure, however, the taupe sheath dress and black wedge heels were her standard work clothes. There was nothing special about them. Marie had carefully selected her clothes, so as not to tempt him. Unfortunately, by the look on his face, she had failed.

"Thank you."

"Shall we go?" She nodded.

They walked out to Seth's charcoal grey Ford Explorer. The evening was off to an average, non-intimidating start.

Dinner was pleasant and typical as it was before Parker. Just everyday, ordinary Marie who flew under the radar and whom no one cared about. Why would she want to change it? It was a stark contrast to her dates with Parker and worrying about fans or the paparazzi.

This was fine, other than one fundamental fact—she wasn't with Parker. As much as she tried to open herself up to Seth, it wasn't easy. Seated across from him comfortably, she enjoyed his company. But comfortable didn't mean much, now that her head had cleared, and she wasn't coming apart at the seams. Through their entire meal, she couldn't dismiss the shame residing within her for what she did with him. Even though she had lost her mind, she felt she owed him a do-over, to make up for using him, and to see if something would develop. The thought had entered her mind earlier that her feelings toward Seth might change after she got over Parker.

They arrived back at Marie's, and she invited him in for a cup of coffee. They had been talking about custody issues on the drive, and she was curious about his experiences. His wife hadn't cooperated with his kids, and Marie could relate. Craig was never cooperative. Now Seth's kids were adults, and his ex-wife didn't have control over when they visited him.

"So, when will you see them again?" Marie asked as she sipped her coffee.

"I'm planning a week with them before they go back to college. I'd like you to meet them." Seth ran his hand down the length of her hair. A sweet display of affection that didn't light her fire. Perhaps she needed to try harder.

"Seth, that might be premature." There was no *might* about it. It was crazy.

"I'm here with you now, and you've given me hope." Seth kissed Marie, probing her tight lips actively and it became clear he was trying to stir her up like the other day. But, she quickly realized, it was futile. With Seth, she remained detached and unemotional. It wasn't natural like it was with Parker.

He pulled back. "It's him, isn't it?"

"What do you mean?"

"When we kissed the other day... Oh, I get it. That was your pain and neediness. You wanted to forget him. It wasn't about me, was it?"

"I'm sorry. I was in a bad place. I told you that, but I'm trying now." She leaned forward and kissed him, in a friendly, benign sort of way.

"I don't want to compete with another guy. If it didn't work out, that's one thing. If you still want him, then I'm the distraction." He held her hands. "I like you, and I want a chance with you, but only when you're ready. I want you to kiss me with passion like the other day, but not because you're thinking of *him*."

"Seth, you're right. Let's try one more time." It was her turn to take charge of the kiss. She pulled him close, and with a passionate intent pressed her lips to his. Then she touched his arms, enjoying the strength within them as she tried to turn him on. It worked. In one swift move, she was on her back, and he was on her. The kiss, his hands touching her hips—nothing. No arousal. Just a blank emptiness. No matter how hard she tried, she couldn't muster up the passion. The heat. A rapid knock at the door startled her, and she froze. Three more rhythmic beats echoed.

"Are you expecting anyone?" Seth asked, from atop her with a firm package pressed against her thigh.

"No, but I should answer the door," she said with relief.

He climbed off her reluctantly and helped her up. Before she could leave, he kissed her once more. Still nothing. On her way to the door, she took a deep breath...grateful for the Good Samaritan's interruption. She fixed her dress, then ran her fingers through her tousled hair. Marie opened the door, and her eyes widened.

"Hi, beautiful."

"Parker," she whispered, pushing him backward. She fumbled for the doorknob and managed to close the door. "What are you doing here? I told you." He pressed his fingers to her lips silencing her, and familiar tingles coursed through her body as he held her gaze.

"Yeah, I heard what you told me, and I told you I wasn't giving up on us. I assume your date is still here by the looks of your messy hair, flushed face and the fact that you didn't invite me in?" Parker didn't hide the tension in his jaw or his disappointment, and it broke her heart. "I've interrupted *something*, so I'll leave." He turned around to walk to his car.

"Wait!" She covered her mouth, shocked by her panicked tone. Parker stopped and looked back at her. "I..." The door opened, causing Marie to stumble back into the house, right into Seth. His hand gripped her waist and Parker glared.

"What are you doing out on the doorstep with," —he paused— "Parker Nichols?"

Parker nodded.

"Wow, please come in."

As Parker stepped inside, he winked at Marie. Even as he teased her during an uncomfortable situation, she still found him intoxicating. She closed the door, then leaned against it for support. This couldn't be happening. They stared at each other...the worst kind of awkward moment.

"Seth, this is Parker Nichols. Parker, this is Seth Gibson." The two men shook hands. Could she crawl under a rock? Parker didn't take his eyes off her, and neither did Seth. Just weeks ago, she didn't have a man and now she had two men in her foyer. Was she getting punked by life?

"Is he the guy?" Seth asked.

Marie nodded.

"Holy shit!"

She looked at him, insulted. "Holy shit? What's that supposed to mean?"

"I just mean he's a celebrity."

"And?" She crossed her arms over her chest but when she pushed her hip out, a small curve formed in the corner of Parker's mouth and she glared at him.

"Look, I'll leave you to your evening," Parker announced, then promptly took Marie's hand and pulled her outside, closing the door behind him. "We aren't done. I don't care about this guy. I'm not giving up on us," he declared, turning to leave. "I'll call you."

"Parker," she called, following him down the cement walkway, "Why did you come? I told you this afternoon we wouldn't work." The door opened and before he could say anything. Seth walked out towards them, a determined expression on his face.

"Marie, I'm leaving. I can't stay when you want him, *Parker Nichols!*" he said in disbelief. "If things don't work out, you know where I live." He kissed her on the cheek. "Nice to meet you, Mr. Nichols."

"Yeah, and Seth…"

Seth stopped and turned around.

"We *will* work out."

Seth nodded and threw up a dismissive wave. Parker looked at Marie, whose mouth was ajar.

"How can you say that? You don't know if we'll work out!" She pushed her hip out and crossed her arms. He smiled, taking her hand, and they walked back inside. Marie's reluctance as she tried to pull back didn't dissuade him. Parker stopped at the sofa, motioning for her to sit. Once she did, he sat beside her, thighs touching and shoulder to shoulder. And tingles sparked.

"Yes, I know we'll work out. I feel it in my bones. You need me and I sure as hell need you." He played with the tips of her fingers, a seemingly benign gesture that melted her every time. She knew that the power within his fingers was the same power that filled every inch of his body; she couldn't help but fall under his spell.

"Now talk to me. I'm not going anywhere until we work this out."

"You barged into my home like you're a damn celebrity. And Seth gushed over you!" She paused, staring at his handsome face and million-dollar smile. But Marie had to keep her wits about her before she crumbled to his charms. It would be so easy to succumb to the fantasy of him and taking a stroll, albeit a short one, into the vortex that was the *Rich and Famous*. Then Jackson entered her mind, and she knew she had to be stronger than Parker's sensual fingers. "I mean really, I had a guest, and it was after nine. You can't do that! You knew I had a date tonight."

Marie suddenly realized that with the tension in his jaw and the hard stare that bore through her, even he couldn't maintain control at all times. He was *real*.

"I don't want you dating other men," he said abruptly.

"You don't control me! We take a quick trip to Vegas and what, now you own me?"

"It's not like that and you know it. Why do you continue to push me away when I'm here pouring my heart out to you? Damn it, Marie! Don't you think it's fucking killing me that that guy Seth was kissing you before I arrived, and I don't want to know what else." He shuddered, squeezing his eyes tight as if blocking the image of her with Seth out of his head. The glossy sheen blanketing his eyes when they opened gripped her. "Shit, I'm not made of steel!"

"I guess you're not, Professor Pierce," she whispered, looking down at her lap. "Did you see the look on Seth's face when he said, 'he's a celebrity'? You're out of my league, Parker. You deserve better than me."

"No, you're out of *my* league." He held her hands, and she met his distressed gaze. "You're the most incredible woman, don't you see that? It's only you, baby… Only you." His sincerity was more than she could take. With every fiber of her being she wanted to believe him…she wanted…*him*.

Quiet, tension-filled seconds passed between them. Parker's words hung in the air. The moment she leaned toward him as if knowing her thoughts, he engulfed her lips, kissing her with a passion that was, well, *real*. Parker never hid his emotions as he kissed her. It was just how she loved it, since their first kiss. Every nerve in her body awakened. It was *only him* too.

Time stood still for them, filled with warm and tender kisses. With their dance of tongues, they were desperate for the song to never to end. Overcome by the sensations triggered by his mouth, her body trembled, and a soft moan flowed out of her. Painful yet pleasure-filled, the melody unleashed his desire for more; he pulled her onto him, splayed his hands over her ass and their bodies molded into one. The desperation of her kisses took off when he cupped her breast. The gentle, tantalizing way he kneaded and pressed his thumb over her nipple sent tremors through her. Even through the barrier of her clothes, his touch elicited arousal.

"I need you, Marie," he said through his kisses. "You matter to me more than I can express. Spend the weekend with me?"

She shook her head.

"Spend the night with me, and I'll show you how much you matter to me." To further entice, his hand moved down between her legs.

"Oh, Parker!" She quaked while he tempted her one stroke at a time. Each thoughtful glide of his fingers intended to rouse her craving for more. It worked, and she about came apart right there in his hands. The force of his touch intensified her kisses, increasing her thirst for him while she held him tight, pressing against him.

"Say yes," he coaxed as wetness seeped through her satiny undergarment. "Say...yes."

"Yes."

Chapter 13

Making Love

Friday afternoon, Marie left work early to prepare for her weekend with Parker. Ann planned to meet her at home for moral support, and because Marie likely would come unhinged. But it was a call from Lexi that unhinged her.

"What do you mean you won't be home this weekend? Isaac and I were going to stop by. Where are you going?" Lexi asked. Marie collapsed on her bed. She couldn't tell her she'd be spending the weekend with Parker. That would be inappropriate, and *Abuelita* would surely turn in her grave, or worse, return from the dead to scold her for her lack of virtue and chastity in person.

"I'm spending the weekend with Brooke," she blurted.

I'm a liar.

"Ha! Not true. I saw on Twitter that Brooke and her hunky boyfriend Dave will be in San Francisco this weekend. Why are you lying to me?"

"Oh, I meant to say, Ann. Did I say Brooke?"

"Mom, if you're spending the weekend with Parker, you can be honest with me. I'm not a kid, and it's not like I haven't had sex before."

"Lexi!"

"Mom relax, I'm an adult." She laughed.

"No, you're my little girl. Are you using protection?" The second the words left her lips she cringed. How could she ask such a question when she wasn't even on birth control and had plans for a sex-filled weekend? Well, she hoped it would be a sex-filled weekend.

"Seriously, that's the question you're going to ask me? After all the talks you gave me about unplanned pregnancy and condoms failing. 'Take control of your fertility, Lexi,' you chanted. In case you didn't know, I actually listened, Mom. I've been on birth control for two years now. After taking the pill for a year I forgot to take it two days in a row and freaked, so I got an IUD put in. I'm good as gold. Or more like copper." She laughed. "Now fess up."

"Two years...dear God." Marie crossed herself the way her *abuelita* and mother would do. She might even have to go to the nearest Catholic church and light a candle for Lexi. This call had taken a turn she didn't like.

"Mom?"

"I'm sorry Lexi. I was just saying a silent prayer for my unchaste daughter."

"Okay, so not funny. You're avoiding the issue; fess up!" Lexi repeated.

"I don't know how to talk about stuff or even if I should with my precious daughter."

"We don't have to talk about *stuff;* just knowing you'll be with Parker for the weekend is all I need to know. I'm happy for you, truly," she said in her comforting voice that reminded Marie of her *abuelita.*

"You sound just like *Abuelita*. So wise, understanding and loving. Have I told you lately how proud I am of you?" Marie sniffled. The emotions of the previous week had weakened her fight to hold them in. Lexi had always been a wonderful child— her 'dream child.' It was moments like this that she missed having her in the house, and the long talks they'd have, even if Lexi called them 'chanting.' During some of Marie's darkest days, it was Lexi that held her hand, so she didn't fall into the pit of hell. Marie always said Lexi was her priceless gift from heaven.

"I know Mom, and I love hearing how I sound like *Abuelita*," she said with a smile in her voice. After a reflective pause, Lexi sighed in the way that put Marie on alert. "Have you heard from Jackson?" Marie's stomach jumped into her chest.

"No…why?!"

"I've seen a lot of tweets from him on Twitter. I think he's lonely."

"Really? What makes you say that? Should I text him or call him?"

"No, I'll text him. If he hears from you, he'll just miss you, and then Dad will get pissed about his mopey attitude. You know what an ass he can be."

"Lexi! Don't be disrespectful. He's your father, and you need to show him respect. I know he hasn't shown himself worthy of respect from you or Jackson, but you're better than him. Don't forget that."

"Sorry. He just aggravates me. And I hate how he treats Jackson. I'm glad Parker is in his life now," Lexi said, which surprised Marie.

"You're glad Parker is in his life?"

"And in yours. Why do you sound so surprised? He seems like a great guy. And Jackson has a total man-crush on him. It so cute." She giggled. "They've gotten pretty close over the last month. And I haven't seen you so happy and relaxed like you were for the BBQ in forever. It was Parker that made you glow, and did you ever look gorgeous."

That did it, Marie's tears rolled down her face faster than she could wipe them away. "Oh Lexi, you need to stop now. My eyes are going to swell, and my face is going to get blotchy before Parker arrives to pick me up. I'll look hideous."

"Not a chance Mom, you're the most beautiful woman I know. But I'll stop. I have to go anyway. Have a great time and make him treat you like a queen. You used to tell me that, remember?"

"I do. Does that mean Isaac treats you like a queen?"

"He does, and he's the most respectful guy I know. And so damn loving." She sighed dreamily. Marie smiled. That was exactly how she wanted her daughter to sound about a guy. "Parker better do the same for you."

"I have a feeling he will. Love you, sweetie."

"Love you too Mom."

Marie looked at the clock. Ann was due to arrive any minute and Parker within an hour. Lexi's call was just what she needed to take her mind off Parker. However, Jackson was now on her mind. If he was lonely in the *Happiest Place On Earth*, it would only be because Craig was ignoring him. That thought enraged Marie, and she grabbed her phone to call Jackson at the same time the doorbell chimed. Ann's impeccable timing likely saved Jackson from being mopey following an impulsive call from Marie.

"Hey there, come on in." Marie smiled as she opened the door. "How is it you always walk through my door just when I need you?"

"It's a gift," Ann said. "So, what's the problem?"

"Do you have a Twitter account?"

"I do…Why?"

"Bring it up so I can see Jackson's page. Lexi said she thinks he's having a hard time, and I have to see for myself why she said that."

"I don't think that's a good idea. It might affect your mood for tonight with Parker. What time will he be here?"

"Five. Please, I don't know if I can do this with Parker anyway. Not after everything. I must be losing my mind," Marie said, walking up the stairs to her room. Ann followed, leaving deep frustrated sighs in the air. "If Jackson is on my mind nothing will happen for sure."

"Listen to me. You fell apart because you want Parker. You were afraid," Ann said. "That said, I'll let you see what Jackson's been tweeting if you promise to not back out of the magical weekend I am certain Parker has planned for you."

"Fine, I promise."

"Okay, here you go." Ann relinquished her iPhone to Marie.

"Thank you."

As Marie scrolled through Jackson's tweets, sadness overwhelmed her. All his tweets showed him alone—a picture of him eating a Mickey ice cream bar with a vacant expression— him alone on Splash Mountain surrounded by grinning strangers. Tweet after tweet began with, "Just me…" *Just me at the pool while my dad naps. Just me playing video games against myself. Just me and room service in my room.* Marie crumpled onto her bed.

"Shit, I was afraid this was going to happen," Ann growled, taking her phone back. "These tweets can just be random boredom; he's eleven ya know."

"You know that isn't true. We both know how Craig is. God, I miss my boy."

"Pull yourself together. Parker will be here soon, and Jackson is fine. Even if Craig is a douche, he won't let anything happen to him. In two days he'll be home, and all will be right in your world."

Marie sat quietly for a few beats. "What if I fall in love with him and he leaves me for a younger woman?" Her distress wasn't only about Jackson; she had other fears inside her.

"Parker isn't Craig," Ann said firmly. "You and Craig were never right for each other. I know you would have moved mountains to save your marriage, but don't you want real love and passion?"

"Yes...yes, I do. And that's why I'm afraid. I don't want to fall in love with him and then lose him. I don't think my heart can take it. Why do you think I used poor Seth?"

"You need to talk to Parker about this. Give him a chance to reassure you. He needs to know what he's up against...*after* he's made love to you." Ann elbowed her playfully. "Seth knew you were vulnerable and used that to his advantage. I wouldn't feel bad for a second. As for Jackson, you and Parker can give him a fabulous summer. It will *all* be OK."

Marie paced in the kitchen while she waited for Parker to arrive; it was minutes before five, and her nerves were off the charts. As she thought of the sexy lingerie beneath her dress and the expectations for the weekend, she couldn't help but be edgy. After one night with her, Parker was sure to shorten the weekend and drive her home first thing in the morning. The knock at the door startled her.

"Your prince has arrived." Ann grinned as Marie left to answer the door.

She opened the door slowly, and there was her prince looking as handsome...and sexy...as ever with a bouquet of tropical flowers in hand. Before she could say a word, he pulled her into an embrace and his kiss was so possessive and sensual she thought she might just die right there. Ann watched with a stupid grin, shaking her head. No question Parker had it bad for Marie.

The peacefulness she felt entering the mansion with her hand in Parker's was like nothing she'd ever experienced. How was this possible after such a short period of time? She released the thoughts from her head. *No doubting.* He put her bag down and wrapped his arms around her again.

"I'm so glad you came." He kissed the tip of her nose. "I'm going to put your bags in my room, and I'll join you out on the veranda."

"Okay." She watched him walk up the double-wide stairs in the center of the house. In awe that she was even there again, she looked down the long, arched hall that led to the back the estate. Sounds echoed from the kitchen, and she wondered if she'd see Vicky. The aroma guided her to the kitchen, but Vicky was nowhere in sight. However, a man dashed around the kitchen, cooking.

"Hi there," Marie said smiling brightly.

"Good evening," he returned. His eyes smiled as he glanced over at her.

"It smells wonderful in here. What are you making?"

"It's a surprise."

"Oh. Well, can I help you with anything?"

The short, stocky Latino man laughed. "No, no, I have it covered." He grinned. Now she was even more intrigued.

"Hmm, I smell ancho chiles and lime. Are you making a Southwestern dish?"

"Ah, the beautiful woman knows her chiles. I'm impressed. Mr. Nichols is a lucky man."

"The luckiest, Héctor," Parker interrupted. "Marie, this is Héctor, my chef. Héctor, this is my Marie."

Marie looked at Parker in awe. The depth of his earnest declaration astounded her. Every time they were together he claimed her proudly. And not once did she think he was dishonest or fake in his regard for her.

"Marie, it's an honor." Héctor nodded his head respectfully.

"Thank you, Héctor. It's a pleasure to meet you as well."

After the introductions, Parker took Marie by the hand out to the veranda. "You didn't get far," he teased.

"How could I? It smelled amazing in there. Do you always go all out for your ladies?"

"Are you implying I'm a womanizer, 'cause I'm not." He furrowed his brow.

"No, I'm sorry. I was just teasing." She grimaced. Apparently her teasing wasn't well received. What a horrible way to start off their romantic evening, with her foot shoved into her mouth. Here Parker was hard at work trying to prove his regard for her, and she poked fun at him. That was going to change, now.

"No worries, but I do go all out for the one that matters." He pressed her hand to his lips.

"Mmm." She inhaled deeply.

Marie stopped, stunned. The covered veranda had been transformed into a romantic tropical oasis with floral arrangements and candles. It wasn't like this the other times she was there. A man of his word, he had gone all out, indeed.

"Parker...it's beautiful," she said as she took it all in. The birds of paradise, lilies, orchids, and plumerias were all breathtaking. The candles in tall wrought iron holders surrounded the space with their warm glow, adding to the enchantment.

"One thing is missing." He picked up a remote, and a Latin song played at the press of a button. The instrumental intro spoke to Marie's soul, and she closed her eyes, absorbing the violins. This man didn't waste a second wooing her, and she loved it. She opened her eyes to him drinking her in.

"May I have this dance?"

"Mhmm," was all she could muster while her heart overflowed with... love?

They swayed to the heartfelt song, "No Sé Tú" (I Don't Know About You). The warmth of his body sent goosebumps up and down her while his muscular arms enveloped her protectively. She adored how he nuzzled his head against hers.

Marie's Spanish might have been rusty, but she could still make out the gist of the song. The lyrics as she understood them told the story of a man describing his feelings to the woman he cared about, and he wondered if she felt the same as him. Had Parker picked this song specifically? If he also wondered if she felt the same, the answer was *yes*.

Oh yes...yes, I feel the same.

Following the dance, Parker held Marie's hand, kissing it often while they were entwined in each other's arms on the outdoor sofa. Their fingers laced together, while he playfully ran the tips of her fingers between his. The sensations swept her away. No man had ever made her feel so desired, nor had she ever felt the desires that coursed through her body for any other man.

Héctor brought dinner out at 6:30 on the dot. The presentation of the food was artistically assembled—a chicken breast with an ancho chile lime sauce served with black beans, Spanish rice, and a colorful medley of peppers, and garnishment of lime slices and cilantro leaves.

"Mmm… Héctor, it looks delicious and smells amazing." She smiled up at him warmly.

"I really like her," he said to Parker.

"That makes two of us," Parker returned, with his gaze locked on Marie. "Everything looks great. Thank you, Héctor."

"Very good, enjoy your evening." Héctor nodded and made a quick retreat.

After dinner, they enjoyed more dancing, tender kisses, and cuddling. Marie had never had such a romantic evening before, and knew it wasn't over yet. Parker Nichols was definitely on a mission to capture her heart, and she never wanted it to end.

As the evening progressed, her fears slowly diminished. Just being with him felt natural to her. And it was so easy. Was that how it was supposed to be? The years in a high-stress marriage had made her believe *all this* was not possible for her.

The evening air turned cold as the ocean breeze suddenly picked up. Marie shivered against Parker, and goosebumps covered her body.

"Baby, you're cold. Would you like me to start a fire in the fire pit? Or I could grab a blanket?" he asked, rubbing his hands over her arms to warm them.

"Or…we could go inside?"

Enough said. Parker stood with his hand out to her. They walked into the house, stopping in the kitchen first. From the fridge, he grabbed a bottle of Prosecco and a covered silver tray. Next, he took two champagne glasses out of the cabinet. Marie smiled as she watched him; it was clear he wasn't done romancing her.

"I'll take these," she said, taking the glasses from him. He leaned down and gave her a gentle, sweet kiss.

"Thank you, baby."

The anticipation of what was to come amped-up her heart rate. She wondered if she should talk to him about her fears before or after…after…after they—what? Had sex? Or would he make love to her? She nervously bit her lower lip when his bedroom door came into sight. Did she even know the difference between having sex and making love?

In his room, there were more flowers, and he started lighting candles that had been placed around the room. With the press of a button, he turned music on…*was it Motown?* Her heart soared as his arms wrapped around her.

"How are you feeling?" He swayed with her to the rhythm of the music, but she didn't answer. "Marie, are you okay?"

"Honestly, I'm scared out of mind."

He pulled back with a look of concern.

Embarrassed, she put her face in his chest.

"I don't want you to be afraid," he comforted, rubbing her back. "We don't have to do anything except be together."

She popped her head up to search his eyes.

"Really, I can wait. I don't want to do anything you're not ready for." He cupped the back of her head, pressing his lips to her forehead.

This man was amazing. Never had she felt so cared for…so adored. He'd wait for her? His patience meant everything. How did she get so lucky? "Can we talk first?"

"Absolutely." He took her to the loveseat in his room, poured them a glass of Prosecco and raised his glass. "*Salúd.*" She smiled, clinking her glass to his. "Mmm, this is good."

"There's more." He lifted the silver lid to reveal strawberries, whipped cream, and truffles.

"Wow. That looks amazing."

"Help yourself." He moved the tray to her.

"Maybe later."

"Whatever you want." He kissed her hand. There was a calming peace in his slate-blue eyes. Just like her beloved ocean, she didn't need to worry with him.

How did he know what to say or what to do to make her feel good? It was official: Parker Nichols was a top-notch, first class *prince* and romancing a woman was his specialty. Little did she know that the amount of effort he had put into "romancing her" was not something he ever did for anyone else. It was only her he wanted to be romantic for. Marie had captured his attention from day one, and he planned to win her heart *forever.* Just like in storybooks and romance novels, he was confident there was a *happily ever after* in their future.

"Parker, I want you to know what you're getting with me. Before we go any further or feelings get too deep." He nodded. "I had Lexi when I was nineteen. Craig is the only man I've ever been with. I don't know anything about sex." She blushed, lowering her eyes to her glass.

He lifted her chin, "It's okay, go on."

"I've had two kids. Pregnancy does things to a woman's body." She took another drink. "I'm not, I'm not…well, whatever your expectation is…I'm not. Women with firm, perky breasts fall at your feet…that's not me. And I have emotional baggage from my marriage. You should be running away from me, not wanting to be with me." Her eyes teared up as she took another drink. "I don't want to disappoint you. I think we should stop this now."

Parker scooted closer, not saying a word, and held her for a while. In his arms, she relaxed as he kissed the top of her head and rubbed her side. All the while Marie wondered what he was thinking. Despite her curiosity, she didn't think he would run for the hills, or conjure up an excuse to end their romantic evening, and that relieved her.

"Marie, I'm blown away by everything you said. Do you realize women only want me for my money and because I'm a celebrity?" She sat up. "I'm not superficial and I don't want an artificial woman. I want real. Genuine. I want you. Let me in. Let me be part of your life."

She tenderly stroked the side of his handsome face.

"You're not going to disappoint me. Maybe I'll disappoint you," he joked.

She laughed heartily. That wasn't likely. "Promise me something?"

He stiffened when her tone turned serious. "Depends on what you're asking me to promise."

"Don't stay with me out of obligation. If you find me repulsive or a joke in bed, all you have to say is, '*I can't.*' Or if a younger woman comes along, I'll set you free. Just say, '*I can't.*'"

He shook his head, aghast. "Marie, *I can't*…take much more of this talk. You obviously don't know how incredible you are." He kissed her with a neediness that she hadn't felt before. He pushed her against the arm of the loveseat and covered her with his broad chest, possessing her with a passionate, searing kiss.

Music played in the background, adding another well-planned layer of stimulation. Marie tingled from her head down to her toes, losing her mind with every kiss and touch Parker gave her. No doubt he knew exactly what he was doing in orchestrating a perfect evening. And she, the lucky recipient. Marie unbuttoned his shirt, and he helped slip it off. Staring at his muscular, sexy physique, she wanted him…needed him. Tonight, she would have him.

Parker stood and extended his hand. This was it. In her core, she knew what was to come next. Such a simple gesture produced goosebumps on her arms as she accepted his hand and stood. Face to face he gazed at her, drinking in every inch of her. She exhaled deeply from holding her breath, and he smiled. Then he splayed his hands on her hips turning her around and brushing the tips of his fingers across her lower back. The sound of the zipper slowly moving down her dress accelerated her pulse. The cool air on her bare back roused her senses as the dress dropped to the floor. Frozen in place, she held her breath, awaiting his reaction to her near naked body.

In new sexy black lingerie, Marie was poised for the taking, but Parker was not in a rush. He brushed her long, black hair to the side sensually kissing her shoulders, while his caressed her stomach. Marvin Gaye's voice filled her ears, "Sexual Healing." Was there ever a more perfect song? Marie's head rolled back weakly against his chest, feeling his strong, warm hands on her skin. They glided across her pelvis to the beat of her heart, down her thighs, and between her legs. She trembled and whipped around.

"My turn," she whispered, looking into his lustful eyes. A small nod of approval released her to undress him.

She started with the belt, giving it a playful tug. Feeling his intense gaze, she looked up, locking her eyes to his. In a long, drawn-out move, Marie unzipped his pants then undid the button. A mischievous grin formed on her face as she slid his pants off his hips, letting them fall to the floor like her dress. She stopped breathing. Was it shock? No. Embarrassment? No. Desire? *Yes*.

Parker sported a full erection that caused her heart to pound. Did she dare touch him? *Yes*. She needed to touch him, wanted to feel him. Her small, delicate hand rubbed over his boxers, and he didn't so much as flinch. And he felt so good…

"My turn again." He gripped Marie's ass, pressing her into him. The firmness of his erection on her stomach drove her wild. She wanted him inside her…now. He unhooked her bra, and she let it fall to the ground. Feeling exposed and vulnerable, fearing what he would think as he saw her, she closed her eyes. She nervously bit her lower lip, imagining him studying her disgusting body.

Not a single word was spoken.

The silence killed her. Was he stunned speechless at the sight of her horrid body? Lou Rawls interrupted her thoughts singing one of her favorite songs, "You'll Never Find Another Love Like Mine." The timing was impeccable. How did he know which songs to select? Did he have a view into her mind…her soul?

Parker took her hand and kissed the tips of her fingers. She opened her eyes as he guided her to the bed. On the side of the king size bed, he sat down on the luxurious white linens, pulling her in front of him.

"You take my breath away." His eyes traveled over her body as his hands discovered her. "Perfect, absolutely perfect."

Relief filled her, then desire. Parker stroked her legs, then softly pressed the palms of his hands over her hips, making his way up to her breasts. He took possession of each one, fondling and teasing. She watched as he licked his lips, stimulating her nipples into firm pebbles. A look of mouthwatering thirst covered Parker's face while her soft gasps of enjoyment urged him further. He pulled her onto the bed as his hot mouth took in her soft, luscious breast.

"Oh…Parker…"

Marie weaved her fingers through his hair while she arched her back into him. The seductive music continued as her body danced on the bed, and a sensual wave of pleasure filled her. When he moved to the other breast to give it equal attention, she tightly gripped his shoulders. The flood of electric sparks between her legs surprised her and increased her need for him.

"So far so good?"

She nodded with her mouth slightly open. By the rise and fall of her chest and her sweet panting, all was better than good.

"You can stop me at any time."

Stop him? Never.

Parker resumed where he left off. He kissed her neck, bringing his tongue into play, licking a tantalizing trail down between her breasts. The way her body moved beneath him, it seemed to urge him to give her more, like a silent request he was more than happy to fulfill.

The sounds of their mutual enjoyment filled the room. If this was just 'foreplay,' Marie could go all night. Abruptly he stopped, a sly grin on his face as he slid her panties off; she thought she would die. Seconds later, he kissed a trail down her torso. She flinched when he stopped at her soft stomach. Would he notice the small stretch marks?

He lifted his head, "Are you okay?"

"Mhmm...yes," she gasped.

He continued his journey downward, and she gripped the comforter tightly. If he was heading down south, she was going to lose her mind. And God help her, he continued down. He kneeled on the floor and looked at her with a willfulness in his eyes, fully intent on giving her everything she'd never experienced. Their eyes connected as he spread her legs apart. *Breathe Marie.* She trembled with desire for the undiscovered. Parker caressed her inner thighs, moving closer to the one place that would take her to an unknown pleasure. The tips of his fingers brushed across her center, and she held her breath. Before she could think twice, his face was buried in her.

"Oooh Parker..." The way his tongue discovered her was like nothing she'd felt before. Delicious, indecent sensations swept through her body. To feel him taking pleasure in her in such a provocative way was inconceivable to her. But it was happening, it was real, and she loved it.

The awareness of his hands lifting her pelvis up to him was erotic. She couldn't believe he was down *there*. What he was doing between her legs took her to a place she didn't know existed. The slickness of his tongue moving in her and the pressure of his lips tantalized every inch of her.

Her moans ignited as a roll of unadulterated ecstasy traveled through her body from her toes up to her face. Marie grabbed the comforter tighter while her whole body clenched. "Parker...oooh, Parker..." Naturally, she wanted to thrust into his mouth, but she fought the urge, uncertain of what to do with herself. The shock of how her orgasm was reached blew her mind. She could hardly believe it. It was so mind-blowing she craved more.

Parker kissed his way up to her, taking his time while enjoying the sight of her aroused body on the bed. Eager to be one with her, he slid off his boxers and grabbed a condom out of his bedside drawer. Within seconds he had the package ripped open, and the condom rolled on.

Marie forcefully pulled him to her, covering his mouth with an intensity that made his groin tighten. It surprised him, but also thrilled him.

This was a side of Marie that didn't exist before now—to control, rather than be controlled... to be empowered. On fire, Marie playfully taunted him, caressing his firm backside. The scent of her on his face seemed to arouse her in unimaginable ways. This rousing moment was more than he had hoped it would be. It was erotic. Intoxicating. Delicious.

"Parker, please," she begged. "I want you... please," she panted.

His name on her lips brought a smile to his face as he moved into position. "Okay, baby." In one long, firm thrust he entered her. A deep groan flowed out of him...he was inside her...joined as one.

"Marie, you feel amazing. So warm and soft." He kissed her passionately as he gently rocked in her.

She gripped his biceps, held her breath and took all of him in. "Oh...oh Parker..."

Parker put his hand down between them. The move startled her, and her eyes widened in surprise. While still rocking in her, he found her erotic knot and went to work caressing and strok-

ing her into an unhinged, lusty state. Marie cried out as her nails
bored into his back and she bucked against him as another orgasm took form. It only took a brief moment being devoured by
him when she suddenly bit down on his bottom lip in her ecstasy. He flinched but didn't stop.

Through another powerful orgasm, she came apart beneath
him. Controlled by the ravenous pulses charging through her
body, she could only yield, having no control. The flood of her
warmth sent Parker over, and he struggled to not explode in her
just yet. She held tightly to him, trying to regain control, but he
didn't want her to come down from her high. No, he would take
her over the edge once more. The oneness he shared with her
was everything to him…he wanted to make her his forever.

The strong connection he felt with Marie was like nothing
he'd ever had with anyone. It drove him to give her the most
passionate, explosively intimate experience she'd ever had.

Her body joined him in the rhythmic dance, while another
orgasm quickly took shape. She wrapped her legs around him,
pulling him closer like she needed him deeper.

"Oh Marie…yes baby," he groaned against her mouth. His
kisses turned desperate as he pumped into her faster and faster.
Then he shot off like a rocket at the same time her orgasm
reached its peak. They tensed together through an explosive
climax as Parker braced himself above her, but she pulled him
onto her.

"I like the weight of you on me." A tear rolled down into her
hair.

"Sweetheart, did I hurt you?"

She shook her head *no* and kissed him with love and tenderness. Finally, she pulled back with a satisfied glint in her eyes. "I

don't know what to say...thank you seems so trite," she said with a contented smile.

"No, that was amazing. I should be thanking you. The way your body responded to me, mmm, I loved every bit of it."

"That's just it, my body has never responded like that before. I had three orgasms. Do you know how crazy that is?"

"I know, I was there...you were incredible." He kissed the tip of her nose.

"Parker, it's never been like that for me before," she whispered.

"How's that possible? You were married for a long time."

"Craig was all about himself. If I didn't enjoy sex or have an orgasm, it was my own fault. He did his job, sticking his dick in me as if that should have been enough."

Parker's expression soured.

"And foreplay—we didn't need it for the five minutes it took him to get his. It's so embarrassing. That's why I was worried about disappointing you. I wasn't sure I'd know what I was do-ing."

"Marie, that breaks my heart. And you didn't disappoint at all. But I'm curious, how did you get yours?"

"In the bathtub," she admitted. "What just happened be-tween us...I'm without words. I didn't know sex could be like that. But then Ann always told me I was missing out on mind-blowing sex with Craig. I just thought she was giving me a bad time. Parker, this *was* a mind-blowing experience. And I can't believe you're still here with me...in me."

"I don't want to leave you." He nuzzled his face in her neck. "But Marie you should know, this wasn't just sex for me."

She looked at him, perplexed. "What do you mean?"

"I made love to you. I didn't have sex with you. It was emotional for me. Every touch, kiss…taste. I wanted to connect with you and create an unbreakable bond." He stared into her eyes. "You matter to me. More than anyone has ever mattered."

"Oh, come on," she teased. "You were so good, you've obviously had a lot of experience."

"I've been with women, yes. But, I don't do everything with every woman. I took my time with you, and the night isn't over, baby."

Her eyes widened.

"I'm going to run to the bathroom then I'm coming back to you…for round two."

The morning light warmed her face, and her eyes blinked open. Parker was next to her, sound asleep. The clock said 8:15 am…*wow*. She was naked beneath the sheets, and so was he. A smile came to her face. *This can't be real.*

It was well after midnight when they had finally quenched their desires, contentedly exhausted. Hours. They pleasured each other for…hours. He made love to her…*love*. She was convinced he had the stamina of a hundred men. The way he had guided her in experimenting with positions to create a new experience for her every time was fiery and sensual.

The entire night Parker had treated her with love and tenderness, but the way he craved her drove her wild. Never for a second did she feel used for her body the way Craig made her feel. With Parker she felt adored, cherished, and loved.

It was an unforgettable night. So amazing that her feelings for him deepened and she knew she was falling in love with him.

And the icing on the cake, she still had one more day and night with him.

Feeling his body heat on her skin aroused her. The smell of his hair…his musk…she tingled, he was so intoxicating. Marie rolled toward him, running her thumb gently across his cheek. "You're so handsome," she whispered. His eyes slowly opened. There was no resisting him. Marie pressed her lips to his and kissed him softly. To her surprise, his hand moved over her hips. "Mmm."

Parker pulled her to him closer and she felt the tip of his erection against her leg, and a lustful yearning filled her.

"Really…now?" She smiled at her blithe assumption. He nodded and pulled her onto him. She had just died and gone to heaven.

Chapter 14

Taking Time To Process

It had been the most spectacular, orgasmic weekend of Marie's life and she was enthralled with Parker. The direction they were heading together was one of love and commitment. The raw and vulnerable intimacy they shared created a strong foundation for their relationship to be built upon. They were blissfully happy when they arrived at her townhouse an hour before Jackson was to come home; neither could keep their hands off the other.

"Parker…Jackson could blast through the door any second. Control yourself." She giggled.

"Na-uh, I haven't had enough of you yet. And tomorrow, I'm leaving for a couple of weeks." He kissed her with his hands under her blouse.

"How is it possible you haven't gotten enough? Since Friday night we've been locked in your bedroom having…"

"Making love," he interrupted her with his intense, amorous gaze. "We made love for twenty-four hours." He resumed fondling her. "Have you had enough?" He reached under her skirt, slipping two fingers into her panties. "Uh-huh, just as I suspected…wet." He groaned.

Marie rocked into his fingers, and it didn't take long before she covered him in her hot juices. As she clenched around him, she pulled him into a lustful kiss.

"I don't want you to leave me for two weeks," she said through her kisses. "I'll have to start taking baths again." She pouted, stroking his cheek with her thumb.

"Just as long as you think of me in the tub." And she started to laugh. "What? What's so funny?"

"I have thought of you in the tub. You're better in person."

His brows shot up. "Now I'm curious."

"Later. We need to clean up before Jackson gets home."

Marie was trying to make lemonade in the kitchen, but Parker was doing an excellent job of distracting her when Jackson yelled for them.

"Moooom…Parker!!! I'm hooome!" Together they went into the entry and Jackson ran into Marie's arms. "I missed you, Mom." He hugged her tightly. Parker came alongside her and briskly rubbed the top of Jackson's head. Jackson flashed him a broad grin.

Craig walked through the door and frowned at the happy reunion. "Jackson, here's your duffle bag and souvenirs." His brash tone startled Marie, and Parker stiffened. He gripped her shoulder, reassuring her that he was with her.

"Did you have a good time buddy?" Marie asked, just as Sasha ran into the house.

"Jackson, you left your cell phone in the truck." She smiled at him, giving him the phone. Then her eyes connected with Parker's and they beamed. "Parker, oh my God. Parker!" She wrapped her arms around him, giggled as if reunited with a long lost friend or was it long lost lover? Marie's mouth went slack. Craig's eyes bored into her, his irritation equal to hers.

"Sasha, wow, this is a surprise." Parker stepped back nervously.

"More like a small world. I can't believe you're the celebrity Jackson's mom is dating. I can't believe I didn't connect the dots when Jackson would talk about you. I have to say, I'm surprised." Sasha didn't think much of Marie; her own conceited nature matched Craig's. Marie glared. Her biting words hurt.

Parker reached for her hand. "I know right? I'm the luckiest guy. It was a miracle she said *yes* to a date with me." He kissed Marie on the cheek, but she was squeezing the hell out of his hand. Craig glowered as if she had just screwed up his life.

"Well, who would have thought that our paths would cross this way. I'm mean, after we broke up, you know." She shrugged her shoulders and leaned into him. "And here we are once again in each other's lives. With people who were once married. It's just the craziest thing ever." Her ridiculously high-pitched cackle that made both Jackson and Marie cringe with annoyance filled the room.

"Sasha, we need to go," Craig interrupted. "Jackson, we'll see you in a couple of weeks when we move into the new house."

"That's right!" Sasha smiled. "I'm looking forward to decorating your room with you, sweetie." She bent down and kissed his cheek and he hugged her back. Marie's hand went limp in Parker's. "I'll be seeing you around, Parker." Sasha stroked his arm, grinning wide, and then she followed Craig out the door.

The front door closed, and Marie jerked her hand away from Parker.

"Mom, what's for dinner?"

"We'll order a pizza," Parker answered. She shook her head and glowered at him.

"Jackson, I'm gonna put your duffle away. You decide what kind of pizza you want, okay?" Marie stomped up the stairs, mumbling under her breath.

"Oh-oh, Mom's mad. Is it because Sasha's your ex-girlfriend?"

"Buddy, go in the living room while I go talk to her. Then you can tell me about Disney World during dinner."

"Okay," Jackson said, with his shoulders slumped as if he knew this wasn't good.

Marie fumed in Jackson's room. "Sasha... Sasha!!!" Just when her life was taking a positive turn...Sasha.

"Marie," Parker said as he entered Jackson's room.

"No! I don't want to hear it. And I don't want you here for dinner," she said, leaving the room. Parker grabbed her hand and pulled her into her bedroom and shut the door behind him.

Marie whipped her hand away from him and started pacing the room with her hands on her hips.

"We need to talk about this. We both had lives before each other. You were married for seventeen years and have two kids with another man. That's huge."

She paced, shaking her head.

"Marie, we were only together a few months, and I haven't seen her in three years."

She stopped and stared at him. It was taking everything in her to not fall apart. She could only shake her head, "no."

"Please talk to me. Don't let this come between us. You matter to me, baby." And her eyes shot to his.

"Did Sasha matter to you?" He stared at her. "Did you break up or did she break up with you?"

"She ended it," he admitted. "But it has been the best thing to happen to me." He stopped her. The distress in his eyes reminded her of the day he had gone to her office. It had broken her heart that day because she had ended it with him. But not now. Not after their glorious weekend, now she only felt betrayed. "Let's talk this out and fix it. I leave tomorrow, and I don't want us to be in a bad place. Please baby."

Her hand went on top of her head as she turned away from him to continue pacing. "I don't think I can do this."

"Do what? Us? Talk? What?"

"Everything." Did he honestly think him being with Sasha wouldn't be a big deal to her? It was a huge deal. It was just another blow to her self-esteem and pride.

"Na-uh. I'm not leaving here until we fix this. Please don't shut me out." There was a knock at the door and they both stopped.

"Mom, can I come in?" Parker opened the door, and Jackson's eyes went wide. "Are you guys fighting? Mom, don't break up with Parker," he begged her. "Mom, please."

"Jackson, what do you need?" Her voice was flat.

"Just that I wanted Sonny's Meat-Sa-Rio pizza," he answered in a small voice.

"Okay. Give me a minute, and I'll be down." Marie lovingly stroked his hair to reassure him.

"Don't make Parker leave." Her eyes welled with tears at his plea. He still believed she drove Craig away and now he believed she was going to do the same with Parker. "Parker is a good guy."

"It will all be okay, buddy," Parker assured him. "Just give us a little time, okay?"

Jackson nodded and left the room.

"How can you tell him it's going to be okay? You're just giving him false hope!"

"Because I believe we'll be okay." He pulled her into his arms, and she tried to pull away, but he wouldn't let her go. Marie stiffened, trying to hold back her tears. She just kept shaking her head, and he wouldn't release her.

"Parker, Sasha is…who Craig left me for. If you were with her for a few months, I know you made love to her." She blinked back her tears. "I can't deal with knowing you touched her, kissed her and …and …well, look at her! She's a swimsuit model for Christ's sake!"

"The feelings I have for you are stronger than I've had for anyone else. The last twenty-four hours with you have blown my mind. I don't want to lose you. In fact, I want you to come with me on location."

"You know I can't," she sighed.

"I don't want to be without you." He kissed her tenderly, and she responded to him with a neediness she wasn't accustomed to feeling. "You're the only person I want, and I'll do whatever it takes to prove it to you."

She looked into his genuine eyes. Was she a fool to believe him? She desperately wanted to.

Marie dropped the topic of Sasha for the evening. They ordered the pizza from Sonny's and listened to Jackson talk about his trip. She loved seeing his face light up with Parker—his favorite superhero. The next couple of weeks she'd have a lot to think about and process while Parker was away filming on location in Budapest.

After tucking Jackson into bed, she walked downstairs to the living room, and Parker put his hand out to her. She took it and sat beside him. "Is he asleep?" She nodded. "Good." He kissed her with the same passion and love that melted her, but this time it made her chest tighten. *Did it have to be Sasha?*

Sasha monopolized Marie's every waking thought as well as her dreams. No matter what she did, she couldn't get Sasha out of her head. The last three days, post-discovery of Parker and *Sasha*, Marie was lower than low. Yet she tried to hold her own. The black hole that she often lobbed herself into was nowhere on the radar.

There was a new strength in her; she was in control this time. With Parker in Budapest for two weeks, she would have time to process. Unfortunately for Parker, the only way Marie could deal with her jealousy, pain, and insecurity was by avoiding him. She didn't take his calls or text messages. She worked late, took Jackson out and she begged Lexi to come home for dinner. It had been weeks since she had last seen her, and she missed her terribly. To her surprise, Lexi agreed to dinner Thursday night, and that was what Marie focused on for the day.

"Jackson, please come into the kitchen," Marie hollered. She had just put a pork shoulder in the crockpot.

"Yeah?" Jackson yawned, shuffling into the kitchen. It was early, and he had just gotten up. He was taking full advantage of his leisurely summer mornings.

"Look, when I text you to turn the crock pot to 'low,' you turn this dial right here," she said, pointing to the knob. He nodded. "Do you understand?"

"Yes. What are you making?"

"Pork tacos, like street tacos. Lexi loves them."

"You were supposed to make those for Parker when he gets back," Jackson reminded her. "Are you still angry with him?"

"I can make tacos anytime. Do you want me to pick up ice cream on the way home?" She dodged his question to avoid additional questions about Parker.

"Sure, cookie dough. Why does Parker have to be in Budapest for filming?"

"He said it's because it doesn't cost as much for the alley and warehouse scenes. I don't know. You should ask him." Her answer was unemotional, and she didn't look at him. If she did, she might break down, knowing how much he loved Parker. "Okay, I need to go to work. I'll text you later." She kissed the top of his head and was out the door.

When the copyright for a song stares back at you for hours on end, it's likely your day has stalled out. And Marie's day dragged on at a snail's pace. The moment she arrived at the office, Parker's name was mentioned, and it continued to be mentioned several more times before lunch. It was all Natalie, who followed Parker on Instagram and Twitter. It was no secret Marie wasn't on social media, so Natalie showed her Parker's posts as if doing Marie a favor. Marie knew Natalie meant well, but it put her in a funk.

Her office phone rang, breaking her trance. "Yes, Natalie."

"Hi. Um… I have a Seth Gibson holding for you." Her voice was leery and curious. "He says he's your neighbor friend." It wasn't a question, just Natalie being a nosey receptionist.

Marie's stomach lurched. "Oh, okay, put him through." Marie waited the two seconds to be connected to Seth. "Hello, Seth?"

"Hi, how are you?"

"Good. How are you?" Marie nervously doodled on a paper.

"I'm good, thanks." There was silence. "I haven't seen you in the gym since last week, and I was worried about you."

"Oh, that's sweet. But there's nothing to worry about."

"Have you been avoiding me because of Mr. Nichols? Does he not want us being friends?"

"Seth, it isn't anything like that. I just haven't made it to the gym. And his name is Parker." She rolled her eyes. So much for not thinking about him.

"Well, I'm glad to hear you're not avoiding me. I can't afford to lose any of the two friends I have here in SoCal."

She laughed.

"Why are you laughing? It's true. There's you and Mr. Bushner."

"What?" Marie started giggling. "Your other friend is Mr. Bushner, the crabby old man who lives across from the gym?" She continued to giggle.

"Stop laughing at me, he likes to play poker, if I let him win. I don't have the heart to turn down his dinner invitations. So, I say yes because I have nothing else better to do."

"Oh Seth, that's very sweet. But Mr. Bushner will never let you go now. You're stuck with him forever." She giggled some more.

"Yeah, that's what I'm afraid of. I need to take up a hobby or find Mr. Bushner a lady-friend by six o'clock before he comes looking for me."

"Aww, you sound so pathetic. You need to learn boundaries. How did you get hooked up with him anyway?"

"Shoot, don't make it sound like I'm dating him. All I did was take over a bowl of pasta salad to him on the Fourth of July. I told you I had made enough food to feed a small army."

"Oh my, and you've been with him ever since?" She giggled.

"Okay, now I'm getting frustrated, and you need to stop sounding so damn cute. It's all your fault, you know."

"What?!"

"Yeah, if you didn't pick the superhero over me, I'd have somewhere to be every evening. Mr. Bushner would just have to find another poor sap to latch onto." His tone was teasing, but his words stung.

"Seth, that's not fair."

"Yeah, you're telling me. No worries, I'm just giving you a bad time. I'm glad you're not avoiding me. I'll let you get back to work."

"Wait." She paused a few beats. Should she invite him to dinner or would it be a bad idea? No, she should. "Would you like to come over for dinner tonight? I'm making pork tacos."

"Wow, that's an offer I can't refuse. And not just because I want to have a night without Mr. Bushner. I love pork tacos. You'll have to show me how you make them."

"You got it. Dinner will be at six. Don't be late."

"I wouldn't dream of it. Bye…friend."

Marie sat at her desk, stunned.

What just happened? It's just dinner with a friend and Lexi will be there along with Jackson, and maybe even Isaac. No biggie. So why did she suddenly feel weird, like she was doing something wrong?

Marie rushed home after work and saw that Lexi's Jetta was parked out front. Her face lit up; she was really looking forward to seeing her. "Hello, I'm home."

"Hey, we're in the living room," Lexi returned.

"Hi everybody." Marie smiled. Lexi stood to give her mom a hug. To Marie's relief, Isaac was able to make it for dinner. "I've missed you," Marie said, hugging Lexi. "It's good to see you, Isaac."

"Hi Marie, thanks for inviting me to dinner."

"Seth will also be joining us for dinner," Marie said matter-of-factly. Jackson's head whipped around to look at her.

"Who's Seth?" Lexi asked.

"Just a friend. He lives in the complex. I'm going to get dinner finished."

While Marie was getting all the accompaniments arranged for the street tacos, Lexi joined her in the kitchen. Marie was chopping up onions, cilantro, jalapeños, and limes.

"Can I help with anything?" Lexi asked.

"Nope, this is it. I figured we'll eat outside, so if you want to grab some paper plates, that would be great."

"Sure, so tell me about Seth."

"There isn't anything to tell. He lives in the complex."

"Well, Jackson seems upset about him coming to dinner." Marie's eyes shot up from her cutting board. "He said you and Parker argued and that you weren't talking to him anymore."

"He doesn't understand what's going on."

"Did you break up with him?"

"No." Marie stopped wiping the counter and turned to Lexi. "Parker dated Sasha a few years ago."

Lexi's eyes bulged.

"Yeah, seriously."

"Wow, that's huge."

"I know. So I'm taking some time to figure it all out. I don't know if I can handle being with him knowing he's been with Sasha too. This isn't something Jackson would understand, so don't talk about it, okay?"

"I won't. But what does Seth have to do with anything? You've never had men over before. Well, except Parker."

"I went out to dinner with Seth last week. He's nice and he's also divorced."

"Holy crap, you're dating two men?!" Lexi's mouth gaped open.

"No! I went out with Seth when I thought I wasn't going to date Parker. But then…Lex, I can't talk about this with you. Sorry, you're my kid. It just feels wrong talking to you about this kind of stuff."

"I get it." Just then there was a knock at the door.

"That must be Seth." Marie dried her hands on a towel and went to answer the door.

Marie opened the door to Seth holding a pitcher and flowers. "What's this?" She furrowed her brow as he handed her the flowers.

"It's customary to bring the hostess a gift when you're invited to dinner. So I brought you flowers and a pitcher of margaritas." He grinned, as she stared at him. "Margaritas go with street tacos, right?"

"Yeah, perfectly. Please come in."

"You look like you've seen a ghost. Relax...friend." Seth planted a friendly kiss on her temple. "Hi. Jackson, right?"

Marie whipped around to see Jackson scowling at her. She knew he saw Seth kiss her and now his arms were crossed over his chest. "Jackson, this is our neighbor Seth. He lives over by the pool." She smiled. Jackson didn't say anything. He just pushed his chin out and marched upstairs. "Jackson, dinner is almost ready."

"I'm not hungry," he said dejectedly, stomping up the stairs.

"I'm sorry, Seth. He can be a little moody sometimes."

"It's because of Parker, isn't it?" She nodded. "His superhero?"

She nodded again.

"Well, where is the superhero? I would have thought he'd be here."

"He's filming in Budapest." Marie led him into the kitchen.

"Oh. Am I missing something?"

"Glasses for the margaritas." She smiled reaching into the cabinet. "Serve it up."

"Right, it's none of my business. It smells great in here."

"Thanks, everything is ready. Let's eat."

Jackson brooded in his room the whole evening. He didn't understand what was going on, but one thing he did understand— kissing. And when a man kissed a woman, it meant something. Unless it was a parent or a grandparent. On his iPad, he looked up the time difference for Budapest—seven hours. If Budapest was seven hours ahead of Pacific time, that meant it was after midnight. He wanted to talk to Parker, but he didn't feel right calling him, so he sent him a text.

Jackson: Hi. How's filming?

Jackson waited for a reply, hoping Parker was still up. He remembered Parker telling him he'd stay up late while filming for nighttime scenes. He hoped tonight was one of those times and to his relief, his phone buzzed.

Parker: Hey buddy, filming is ok. What's going on? Did you like today's episode?

Jackson: It was ok. When are you coming back?

Parker: Not for eleven more days. Is everything ok?

Jackson: Mom's friend came to dinner. She made pork tacos. Lexi and Isaac are here.

Parker: Sounds great. How's your mom doing? Tell Ann I said hi.

Jackson: It's not Ann. It's Seth. Is Mom still mad at you?

Parker's reply took longer than the others, and it made Jackson anxious. As he waited, he paced back and forth in his room. Finally, he decided to send another text.

Jackson: Parker are you still there?

Parker: Sorry buddy, I'm here.

Jackson: Did you and Mom break up? You can tell me the truth. I saw Seth kiss her. Can we still be friends?

Parker: I'll always be your friend. I'll text you tomorrow. I need to get some sleep ok?

Jackson: Ok.

The rest of the evening Jackson stayed in his room. Marie
checked on him a couple of times, but he gave her the cold
shoulder, wanting to be left alone. He was just like before…before Parker had come into their lives. She left a plate of
food on his dresser and later brought him up a bowl of ice
cream. The tacos were still on the plate, so she removed them
and tossed them into the trash. At nine o'clock Lexi and Isaac
announced they needed to leave.

"Thank you for coming." Marie hugged Isaac.

"The food was awesome. The best pork tacos I've ever had,"
Isaac said.

"Aww, that's sweet. And Lex, you two come anytime okay? I
miss you when I don't see you for weeks at a time," she hugged
her tightly.

"We will, Mom. I love you."

After Lexi and Isaac left, there was an awkwardness that
filled the space. Marie fidgeted with the hem of her blouse, and
she tried not to make eye contact with Seth. The evening had
been pleasant, and the margaritas were terrific in calming Marie's
nerves. She had watched as Lexi and Isaac had interacted with
Seth, and they seemed to get along nicely. But it was Jackson's
painful avoidance that occupied her mind. Even though she
would never let her child call the shots in her romantic life, his
feelings mattered to her. He loved Parker. And so did she.

"I'm going to head out too," Seth said. "Thank you for a
great evening with excellent tacos."

She smiled and nodded.

"I won't push, but I want you to remember that I'm here. And if it never happens between us, I still want to be your friend."

"I appreciate that Seth. I don't know what's going to happen, but I do know I care about Parker a lot. I want things to work with him. I want to be with him." She wanted to be honest with Seth. And the truth was, Parker mattered to her more than even she realized. It's why knowing he had been with Sasha pained her as much as it did.

Chapter 15

Trying

Friday morning Marie somberly walked into the office. Jackson had ignored her just like he used to. It made leaving him all the more difficult. They needed to talk. She wanted to explain what was going on, but she couldn't miss work. Jackson's hurt and anger only added to Marie's pain. All she was trying to do was deal with her emotions—to get past Parker being with Sasha. Now she had to also worry about her relationship with Jackson. Then Parker entered her mind for the millionth time. She knew he had to be worried and going out of his mind, not knowing what was going on with her. But if they talked, Marie would miss him, and the pain of knowing he'd been with Sasha would consume her. She had to keep her head clear, more than ever.

The day progressed quickly, and it pleased Marie. After a late, working lunch she sat at her desk, rocking in her chair. Thoughts of Parker, Jackson, and Seth filled her mind. The way she felt when she was with Parker...finally after two years she had gotten Jackson back...Seth was a nice guy who she enjoyed talking to. So many thoughts and not one of them helped her deal with *Sasha.*

Natalie knocked on Marie's door.

"Come in."

"I gotta say you're the luckiest woman to be dating Mr. Nichols. Look at these flowers." Natalie grinned as she carried a large tropical arrangement and placed it on Marie's desk. "He sure likes you. I'm so jealous."

"Thank you, Natalie."

"Is everything okay? You don't look very happy about getting flowers from Mr. Nichols. To be honest, you've been 'off' all week."

"Yeah, relationships aren't always easy." Marie turned her attention to her computer screen, disengaging Natalie.

"Oh…well, if you need anything you know where to find me." Natalie frowned, as she closed the door and walked back to her desk.

Marie took a deep breath once the door was closed and removed the card from the arrangement.

Hi Beautiful, please answer the phone @ 4. You matter to me, Parker.

She plopped down in her chair and looked at the clock— 3:55. Instantly, her heart raced. Parker would be calling in five minutes. How did he do that? It's like he was right there with her and he wasn't going to let her shut him out, even if he was in Budapest. A sudden flood of emotions overwhelmed her. She missed him terribly. If they could run away and stop time, she would spend the rest of her life with him. But reality wasn't that simple. What was she going to do? What would she say to him? For the next five minutes, she stared at the flowers until her phone rang.

"Yes, Natalie."

"Mr. Nichols on line two."

"Thank you." Marie paused a few beats before answering. "Hello…"

"Marie…thank you for taking my call. What's going on? I thought we weren't going to do this." He sounded tired, sad, and panicked.

"I'm taking time to process, so I can't talk to you."

"Then listen to me. I'm going out of my mind over here. I haven't been worth shit since Monday when you didn't answer my call or texts. I knew you were shutting me out. But then when I heard Seth was over for dinner and kissed you, Jesus, Marie! Every time we have an issue are you going to turn to Seth?"

"No! It isn't like that." Her voice broke. "How do you even know?" She paused and then she knew. "Jackson!"

"Yeah Jackson," he shot back. "Did you think he wouldn't say something to me? I'm his friend. He texted me last night and told me. He asked if I would still be his friend if we broke up. I was up the rest of the night driving myself crazy thinking about you with Seth," he growled, then she heard a crash come through the line, like breaking glass. The noise made Marie jump in her chair.

"What was that sound?"

"My beer bottle hitting the wall." Marie took a deep breath with her hand on her chest.

"Listen to me, I'm not with Seth. He's just a friend."

"Jackson said he kissed you. Why did he come to dinner?"

"I didn't plan it, it just happened. He kissed my temple like a friend would."

"Except he doesn't want to be your friend. Shit! I can't do this. I'm pulling the plug on this project and flying back."

"Don't do that. It's your job; you need to stay."

"I don't give a shit about this job. Not if while I'm here, you're breaking up with me and turning to Seth. You're shutting me out when I'm not there to fight for us. Don't you know you're more important to me?"

"Parker…"

"Talk to me, baby, please," he begged her, his voice thick with emotion.

Marie took a deep breath to gather herself. She couldn't lose it on the phone with him. "I see you with her when I close my eyes." Her voice caught.

"Marie…"

"No, you listen to me. I imagine you touching her the way you touch me." She paused. "I hear you talking to her like you talk to me and making… I can't even say it. Do you know how that makes me feel? It makes me want to throw up." She inhaled deeply, choking back her tears. "Why did it have to be her?"

"I'm coming home tomorrow. With the time change I'll be on your doorstep by nine," Parker said, clearly panicked. "Please don't cry."

"Parker, be sensible. You can't."

"I need to hold you, Marie. You're breaking my heart. I don't want you hurting like this."

"Please don't leave your job. I'll feel horrible if I'm the reason you're leaving."

"I can't focus, so it doesn't even matter. And there's Seth."

"Seth is just a friend, nothing happened between us. What if I promise to answer every time you call? Please don't stop the project."

"You need me and God knows I need you."

"I know." Her voice shook. "That's why it hurts so much."
She could hear him rustling around. "What are you doing? I can
hear you doing something."

"I'm packing."

"Parker, stop! You'll be back in ten days. And…"

"And what?"

"And…I'll still be here."

"I'll compromise with you. I won't call you every day so you
can process, but when I do call, please answer. I won't text you
either. And please don't do anything with Seth."

"Don't worry about Seth. He's just my friend."

He exhaled like he had been holding his breath.

"I'll answer when you call, every time."

"When I get back, spend the weekend with me?"

"I don't know if I can do that."

"Marie, I'm so sorry. Please don't give up on us."

"I'm trying not to."

Marie took every one of Parker's calls. He did as he said he
would and only called a few times so she could process. He
sounded tired and worried every time she answered the phone,
and she felt bad knowing he was stressed out while filming. She
hated that her insecurities about them, and about him and Sasha,
caused friction between them. It took everything in her to work
through her feelings, but it was Sasha. And it didn't matter that
she didn't know Parker back then, or that they had lives before
each other. It was *Sasha*. As much as she tried to reason it in her
head, she struggled to get passed it.

Parker always asked about Jackson. After finding out about Seth, he had told her he worried Jackson would shut her out again. He did his best to reassure him, and each day Jackson opened up a little more with Marie. Parker even asked about Lexi, which Marie appreciated; she knew he cared about both of her kids. His genuine interest in her children meant everything to her.

Several times he invited her and the kids—along with her girlfriends—to his place to swim, but she declined. Mixing her personal life with her family life seemed like a bad idea. But by the fourth time he asked, she relented and agreed to bring the kids over, which was a huge step for her. It was a defining moment in her relationship with him. It would no longer be just him and her, but it would include her kids and her friends. It also meant the most important people in her life could form an attachment to him, the most important man in her life. She wasn't sure she was ready or if it was even a good idea, but she agreed to take everyone over Saturday afternoon to enjoy his pool and hoped she wasn't making a huge mistake.

"Wow, this is Parker's house?" Jackson asked, gawking out the window. Seeing the awe on his face warmed Marie's heart. "And he said we could come? You guys didn't break up?"

"Jackson, for the tenth time we did not break up." She sighed. "And yes, Parker said we could come over. He wants everybody to enjoy his pool." Marie smiled.

"This is the coolest day ever," Jackson said. "I just wish he was here." And so did she.

"Be on your best behavior inside, okay? And don't touch anything."

"Geez. Mom, we're not toddlers." Lexi snorted as she looked at Isaac. Marie glared at her, her sarcasm was not appreciated.

"To your mother, you'll always be babies," Ann teased. Tessa nodded in agreement.

"I can't believe this place," Tessa said as everyone piled out of Ann's SUV.

"I know, it's amazing," Marie agreed.

Marie led her clan up to the entry and she rang the doorbell and Vicky answered moments later.

"Well good afternoon, Marie." Vicky greeted with a sweet smile. "Come in everyone." She held open the door, pleasantly nodding to each person that passed.

"Thank you, Vicky. I'll just take everybody to the back so we won't be in the way."

"Oh dear, you could never be in the way. I have snacks set up on the veranda and Héctor will be over in an hour to grill."

Marie stared at her, stunned. "Oh, that's not necessary. We'll order pizza or something."

Vicky put her arm around her as they walked to the back. "Dear, Mr. Nichols gave me a list of items to have for your gathering. Even from another country, he's going to take care of you. Let him," she urged.

"Oh, I like you, Vicky." Ann smiled. "Listen to her Marie; let him take care of you."

Vicky smiled brightly, nodding.

Watching everyone "ooh" and "ahh" over the backyard was fun for Marie. It also made her miss Parker. It just wasn't the same being there without him. For the next hour she sat on the edge of the pool watching the kids, and everywhere she looked, she saw Parker.

The activity around Héctor made Marie laugh. Everybody took a turn talking to him as he demonstrated his grill master skills. The savory smell of tri-tip seasoned Santa Maria style filled the air, and she couldn't wait to try it. Marie wasn't the only one anxious for the dinner bell to sound. Everyone waited with bated breath to sink their teeth into Héctor's barbecue.

Marie observed Héctor with a keen eye and could see why Parker liked him. It wasn't only about his culinary skills, which were outstanding, but Héctor was genuine and personable. He had a relaxed, friendly demeanor, told jokes and stories about his cooking disasters. And his hearty laugh kept the spectators in stitches. Like with Vicky, Marie could easily be friends with Héctor.

The peace Marie felt being at Parker's amazed her. She felt like he was with her in some magical way and it made her yearn to be with him for real.

"Okay, everybody. Scooch together. I want to take a picture of you in the pool," Marie said. "One more." She snapped another shot. "Perfect."

Ann walked out of the pool, wrapped a towel around her and joined Marie on the veranda.

"This is some sweet living out here. How can you stand to not be here all the time?" Ann asked, taking a drink of her cocktail. This was her first time at the mansion. Like Brooke, Ann and Tessa were very impressed with Parker's estate.

Marie looked around and smiled. "It's breathtaking, isn't it? There, I just sent Parker the picture with a big thank you." She looked at Ann and frowned.

"He's a keeper you know. You gotta cut him a break. When will he be home?"

"Monday, if filming wraps up on schedule. You have no idea how much I want him. Why did it have to be Sasha?" Her phone buzzed just then, a text from Parker.

> Parker: Jackson looks crazy happy. LOL I'm glad everyone's having a good time. Why weren't you in the picture? Send me a pic of my beautiful girl...I miss her.

A dreamy sigh swirled out of her. "Can you take a picture of me? He wants me to send him one."

"Okay, take your clothes off."

Marie started giggling.

"What, you think I'm joking?"

Marie stuck her hip out and crossed her arms.

"Fine. Smile pretty."

"Thank you." Marie giggled some more as she sent him the picture. "How am I supposed to get over him being with Sasha?"

"The same way you got over Craig's affair and the divorce. You give it time. And while you're doing that, you can have the best sex you've ever had with the dashing Parker Nichols. You know he loves you."

"No, I don't know that." Her phone buzzed again.

> Parker: You're gorgeous. I can't wait until I can kiss you and make love to you.
> Marie: Me too.
> Parker: Really??? I'll be there in an hour!
> Marie: Ha-ha, funny. But really, I miss you too.

> Parker: I'll seriously be there in an hour. I have to
> strike when the fire is hot!

She took a deep breath and showed Ann the text.

"He made you tingle and get wet, didn't he?" She winked.

Marie giggled again. "He's crazy, but yeah."

"He's crazy about you, girlfriend."

Marie had to agree. Ever since they were in communication again, she had felt better, though it was still hard. Could she really get past him being with Sasha? She wanted to, desperately.

A year ago, at this time, Marie's relationship with Jackson wasn't typical for a mother and son. She was his cook, maid, and driver. A caretaker. There weren't hugs and kisses. Playful giggles. Or in-depth talks about superheroes. Now as he smiled back at her, her heart melted. Her little boy had returned. It didn't take long for him to turn into a water baby in Parker's pool, having the best time swimming with Lexi and Isaac. His squeals and laughter kept a grin on her face. But he wasn't the only person having a grand old time. Even Ann and Tessa got in on the fun. While her people were in the water, Marie relished the sun and the ocean breeze on a chaise. Feeling relaxed, her eyes closed, and she nodded off.

Dreams about Parker were a common occurrence these days. The scene always the same—he was making love to her. His hand glided up her leg, his fingers entwined with hers, and then he kissed the tips. She sighed, enjoying his touch. Then he spoke to her. "Nothing matters more to me than you," he whispered. And then he kissed her softly, running his tongue along the top of her lip and stirring her up inside. She hummed enjoying the taste of him. It felt so real... Wait. She tried to wake herself, but it wasn't a dream. It *was* real. Her eyes flashed open, and Parker kissed her nose.

"Hi, beautiful."

"Parker! I thought I was dreaming. You're not supposed to be back until Monday."

He laughed. "I texted you that I'd be here in an hour," he teased. "We wrapped up early after I pushed everybody to get the final scenes done in two days. I needed to see you…I needed to be with you. I like that I'm in your dreams."

She wrapped her arms around his neck and pulled him in for a hot, desire filled kiss. Overwhelmed with passion, she didn't even care that they had an audience. When clapping ensued, she giggled against his mouth, but she wouldn't let go of him.

For the next couple of hours, Parker played with Jackson in the pool and Marie watched him with longing. The sight of his bare chest made her tremble with the remembrance of their weekend together. It had been two weeks, and she was wanting… needing.

"Hey you, horny woman. I'll stay with Jackson tonight so you can stay here," Ann offered.

"Really?!" Marie's face brightened with excitement. No way would she deny being horny, she so totally was, and she'd never pass up a generous offer of babysitting.

"Of course. You need this, and so does Parker. It's disgusting really, to see him look at you like he wants to take you right here on the patio. He's an animal."

Marie giggled and then sighed deeply. She knew the look.

"Then to see him kiss you and whisper in your ear, like what the fuck is that?" Ann threw her hand up in the air and laughed.

Marie wrapped her arms around her. "You're the very best friend a girl can have." Marie smiled at Parker, watching from the pool. The devilish look in his eyes and bare chest made her want to run upstairs with him for a repeat of their first time.

"Well, shit. You just might make me tear up, seeing you so happy because you won the 'I get to fuck' lottery."

"See, I'm so happy, your filthy mouth doesn't bother me. That F-word is growing on me."

Ann's mouth gaped open, and the giggles followed.

"What's going on over here?" Parker came up behind her, snaking his hands around her waist. She leaned against him and looked up; she definitely *had* won the lottery.

"Ann has offered to stay with Jackson tonight, so I can stay here…if you want?"

"I want." He kissed the side of her head. "Thanks, Ann. Name your price and it's yours."

"It's a gift." She raised her glass of wine to him. "Nothing makes me happier than to see her grinning like a fool. So, don't fuck it up," she said sternly.

"Okay…got it."

Nine o'clock rolled around, and Jackson had collapsed from a full day of fun in the sun. He kept saying he wasn't tired, but as soon as he got in the car and buckled into his seat, he drifted off to dreamland.

Marie and Parker waved goodbye and watched the car leave the estate. He wrapped her in his arms and kissed her long and passionately under the stars. When they went inside he grabbed a bottle of wine and two glasses, then he followed Marie up to his bedroom. They had some making up to do, not to mention the two weeks' worth of lovemaking to catch up on.

The peace and contentment Marie felt in Parker's arms was perfect. As she lay on his chest, he stroked her back gently, and she never wanted to leave him.

"Marie, we need to talk about what happened while I was in Budapest."

She had suspected he'd wanted to resolve their issues as soon as possible so they could move forward. It wasn't a conversation she looked forward to. "Now, when we're both happy?"

"Baby, I want us to be happy forever, not just immediately after making love. What can I do to reassure you? I don't want you insecure. I'm not going anywhere, and I don't want anyone else, but you can't shut me out like that, especially not when I'm in another country. It was torture. And then there was Seth."

"I'm sorry. You don't have to worry about Seth. But I do have to protect myself. Craig was awful to me, and the very woman he left me for was once your girlfriend." She shook in disgust in his arms.

He held her tighter. "I know. And believe me, I'm not fond of Craig being with you either."

"It's not even the same. You're a million times better lover than him. But, Sasha, she's a swimsuit model and twenty-nine."

"No, your body is amazing. I love it. Your breasts are larger than hers, and they fit perfectly in my mouth." He groaned. "The way you come alive for me, nothing turns me on more and I never want to be apart from you."

"Really?"

He rolled her onto her back and stared into her eyes. "Really. Promise me you won't shut me out again. If any problems arise, we'll work through them together. Let's make us official, you know, a committed relationship."

"Okay…I promise." Parker looked at her with so much love, and it was at that moment Marie fully opened herself up to him. This was the happiest she had been in the last two years, and quite possibly in her entire adult life.

Chapter 16

Growing Stronger

Following her reunion with Parker, Marie and Jackson spent most of their free time at Parker's estate, lounging by the pool. At Parker's suggestion, she invited Ricky, Jackson's best friend, to join them a few times. It was a genius idea. Having Ricky with Jackson gave them free time to be together while the boys swam in the pool, watched movies, and played video games in Parker's state-of-the-art movie room. They took the boys to Disneyland, San Diego Zoo, and the Santa Monica Pier. It was turning out to be the best summer for all of them.

During their outings, Parker stayed incognito with a baseball cap and sunglasses. It bummed the boys that they didn't get mobbed by fans or the paparazzi. They wanted their pictures floating around on all the social media outlets with celebrity Parker Nichols. But Marie loved having a typical day with Parker the man, not the actor. To please the boys, Parker took pictures with them to post on their Snapchat and Instagram. The two no-name kids suddenly became the "cool kids" among their peers, and of course, they were thrilled.

One afternoon in August while the boys splashed around in the pool, Marie and Parker sat on the veranda discussing Jackson's visitation schedule with Craig. The new school year started in a couple of weeks, and they wanted to head off an email from Craig demanding specific dates. After all, Marie had full custody, so she should be the one laying out the plan. With Parker's support and encouragement, she felt for the first time she was in control. Just knowing someone had her back, like her family did for one another, wiped away her fear of Craig bullying her. The last couple of years Craig would dictate when he wanted Jackson, and she had given in to him every time. The scared, easily intimidated Marie was becoming stronger and more self-assured with Parker in her life, and he wasn't going to let Craig control her anymore.

Parker cleared his throat to get Marie's attention. "I have something I want to discuss."

"You do?"

"I do." He took Marie's hand and kissed it.

She tilted her head towards him with a curious expression.

"My parents are coming out for a visit in October. I'd like you and the kids to meet them."

"They know about me? And the kids?"

"Of course, they do." He laughed, kissing her hand again. "They know how much you matter to me—you *and* your kids."

She looked out at the pool. Jackson was having the time of his life. The constant smile on his face the past several weeks was the highlight of her day. In fact, she'd had a ridiculous grin on her face since Parker had returned from Budapest. Jackson was happy, and so was she.

"Wow, I haven't even told my parents about you."

"Why not?"

"I don't know." She shrugged. "So much has happened since we met that I've kind of been afraid to mention you. My parents are old-fashioned Latinos. They were disappointed when I got pregnant with Lexi and again when Craig and I divorced. I guess I was waiting to be sure about us."

"Okay, but what about now? We're in a committed relationship." The tone in his voice was one of firm conviction when he said "committed relationship." One thing about Parker she'd learned over the last two months was he could be steadfast and resolved when he'd made his mind up, and sometimes even unyielding, but always kind. And he never once tried to control her. Right now, if he said he was committed to her—to them— that meant he was all in. And so was she.

"You're right. The next time I talk to my mom, I'll tell her. The fact that you can salsa dance will instantly win her over." Marie gazed warmly into his eyes. "So, when in October are your parents coming?"

"My parents are retired. They picked the month, and now you pick the day. Whatever works for you will work for them."

She gripped his face and stared at him. She wanted to tell him *I love you*, but instead, she said, "You're the best." She kissed him deeply until a trail of 'ews' echoed from the pool, making her giggle. "One day you're going to like kissing," she hollered over to the boys. They made gagging faces, and then went back to playing. "Okay, back to business. How does October 15th sound?"

"I'm putting it on my calendar now. And what about Thanksgiving and Christmas? How do you usually do the holidays with Craig?"

"I always have Jackson for Thanksgiving. It's my favorite holiday."

"Is that right? It's my favorite too. The last few years I've hosted my parents, Dave, and a few random friends at my lake house in Idaho. I like having everyone around during the holiday to enjoy good food, drinks, laughter, and skiing. Does that sound like something you and the kids would like to do this year?"

"YES!" Jackson yelled. "Can we Mom? Can we go to Parker's Idaho house?"

"Are you eavesdropping on us?" Marie teased. "I think it sounds like a lot of fun."

"Awesome! Can I grab two bottles of water for Ricky and me?"

"Help yourself, buddy, whatever you guys want," Parker answered.

"Thanks!"

"I love seeing him happy." Marie smiled, watching Jackson. Parker's hand crept up her leg and into her shorts. "Mmm, I love when you touch me." She leaned in for a kiss.

"I love seeing *you* so happy. It does things to me," he said against her lips. Just as their kiss started to deepen the 'ews' returned, so they stopped. "One day I'm going to do this to him when he's kissing his girl." Parker sighed with frustration, his telltale sign that he needed some alone time with her.

"Aww, you'll have me for a whole week in six days, handsome. Now, let's talk Christmas." She looked down at her calendar.

"You know you're teasing me?"

She blew him a kiss.

"Aren't you cute." Parker laughed out loud. "Okay, let's talk Christmas. Whatever you want to do is fine with me. If you want to take a trip or stay home, it's up to you."

"Really? There isn't anything you want to do?"

"Nope. I only want to be with you."

Again, she wanted to say *I love you*, but she held back. "Well, my parents usually fly out, and we do Christmas Eve, and then Jackson goes to Craig's on Christmas Day."

"Okay, let's do Christmas Eve here at my place."

"Are you sure?"

"Yes, I'm sure. We can host as many people as you want. I'd love it if you and the kids stayed here. Even your parents or whoever else. You're all welcome to stay."

She wrapped her arms around his neck and hugged him. She was happy...and in love.

With each passing day, Marie's feelings deepened for Parker. Not only was her relationship with him strengthening, but so was her relationship with Jackson. A unity had developed between the three of them, and Jackson's attachment to Parker became more than just idol worship. They were bonding. However, his attitude regarding Craig remained the same. He never wanted to go to his dad's, and Marie would have to coax him into going every time. The second he returned, his attitude would change back, thrilled to see her and Parker. The three of them spent their evenings swimming, watching movies, and playing video games or board games together. They were feeling more and more like a family and Marie was utterly delighted.

One afternoon Parker surprised them with a tour of the studio where *Pierce* was filming. Jackson was over-the-moon ecstatic. His little superhero fantasy had just come to life. He met several actors from the show, and Marie was introduced to everyone too. Most knew of her and treated her like family. Later that evening, Jackson posted pictures on Instagram with

Parker and other actors with the taglines *#professorpierce #best-dayever #meandparker #myheromyfriend*

The month of August was quickly becoming Marie's favorite month. Her confidence was at an all-time high, along with her vitality and libido. Jackson was on cloud nine, and Parker was in love, though he hadn't revealed it yet.

But Marie's spectacular month soured one day at work when she received an angry email from Craig. She could always count on him to stomp on her joy, and his timing was impeccable, just two days before Jackson was leaving with him to Hawaii. In a numb state, she stared at her computer screen after reading the email.

Goddamn you Marie! What the fuck is going on with you and that celebrity SOB??? How dare you let him fill my son's head with promises of ski trips to his lake house in Idaho and going to Budapest!! You're trying to steal my son away from me by using his superhero against me!! This isn't happening, Marie. I don't want my son spending the night at your fucking boyfriend's mansion and I sure as hell don't want my son posting pics with him all over Snapchat and Instagram. Who the hell do you think you are?? You're a nobody, that's who you are! Parker Nichols is just using you for a piece of ass, a lousy piece at that!!!!! He'll drop your tan ass as soon as the seasons change. You're stupider than I thought if you think he takes you seriously. Stop this

```
shit right now, or I'm taking you
back to court and suing you for FULL
custody, on the grounds of Parental
Alienation and Parental Substitution—
you pathetic slut.
```

Marie read the email half a dozen times. Why did he hate her? Reaching for her cell phone, she paused; who did she call? She always called Ann for everything, but Parker was becoming everything to her. Not that either of them could do anything at the moment. But she needed support, someone she could trust, and she needed someone who would understand. The only person who would understand was Ann, so she called her at work.

"What happened?" Ann answered in a knowing tone.

"Check your email," Marie replied in a quiet voice. She waited while Ann read it.

"Son-of-a-bitch, don't let anything he said scare you. Don't shut down honey. You have support, you have me, and you have Parker. Have you showed him the email?"

Marie didn't say anything.

"Marie... Marie, are you listening to me?"

"He'll sue me for custody if I don't end it with Parker. Ann, I can't lose Jackson. He's all I have left. But Parker..." Her voice thickened with emotion.

"Marie, don't freak out. Call Parker right now and tell him what's going on. Let him help you. He knows people. Big, important people. He's a celebrity with a name in L.A. I'm sure he knows top-notch lawyers."

Marie sat silently again.

"Marie... Marie?"

"He said such awful things about me. It's embarrassing. How can I let Parker read that, or anyone else?" She sniffled as the first tear rolled down her face.

"Are you joking? Nobody would believe anything Craig says. He's a moron, a liar, and a bully. Call Parker right now!"

"He's working. I don't want to bother him," Marie whispered. She felt so small and fragile.

"He would want you to call him. This will all be okay. I promise."

"Okay...bye." She hung the phone up, dazed, as she stared at the email, unable to move. "I can't lose Jackson."

An hour had passed and Marie hadn't moved. The email stared at her, still pulled up on her monitor. She had read it over and over again, burning the words into her memory. Her phone buzzed, and she hesitated, looking at it. Her gut told her it was Ann, but it could also be from one of the kids or, Parker. She looked and immediately was filled with dread. "Crap... Ann..."

> Ann: What did Parker say?
> Marie: I haven't told him.
> Ann: Shit, I knew you wouldn't. I'm calling him.
> Marie: DON'T!!! I'll tell him.
> Ann: Then do it now. Or I will call him. And I want proof that you called him.
> Marie: You're a bossy bitch!
> Ann: Yes.

Marie took a deep breath. She didn't have a clue how to tell Parker about the email, but she had promised not to shut him out. He mattered to her, and she loved him.

Five minutes passed, and she hadn't dialed his number. What was she afraid of? Did she really think he'd walk away from her, especially now that they were in a committed relationship? Maybe she needed to Google what a committed relationship was. *Stop stalling, you big chicken!*

True to form, Marie tried to talk herself out of calling Parker. If she couldn't call him when she needed him out of fear of, God knows what, then what was the point of being in a relationship with him? Sex? It was so much more than sex, and she knew it. She needed him...needed...*him.* She nervously pushed the call button and waited for him to answer. It rang—one-two-three...*I'm going to voicemail...*

"Hi, beautiful. Is everything okay?"

"Parker, are you busy? Did I interrupt something important?"

"Marie, you're important. What's going on?"

"I did interrupt you, I'm so sorry. Just call me tonight." She ended the call quickly, and he called right back.

"Parker."

"Why did you hang up on me? I know you're upset, what happened?"

She blurted it out, "Craig is threatening to sue me for full custody of Jackson."

"What? Did he come to see you?"

"No, he emailed me. I can't lose Jackson. I just can't."

"You won't, I promise. Send me the email."

"No...I can't," she said, her voice trembling with fear.

"Why not? I've got a friend who's a lawyer."

"It's awful. Embarrassing. I'm sitting here, stunned. I'm scared."

"I'm coming, baby." The tenderness in his voice was what she needed to hear. She needed him.

Parker was in her office within the hour. A fire raged inside him while he held a distressed Marie. It astonished him a person could be so ugly and hateful. Marie was a kind and compassionate woman, a fantastic mother and a sweet, friendly person. It didn't make any sense. Why was Craig doing all this? What kind of man treats his ex-wife this way? It had to be about control. But then he was the one who cheated and left. However, that didn't mean he wanted to give up his control over Marie. Parker had never hated anyone so much until now.

Chapter 17

Finding Peace

Marie busied herself cleaning the house while she waited for Craig to pick up Jackson. The last two days had been hell. Her head overflowed with horrible thoughts of court battles—of Jackson moving in with Craig—of Parker leaving her because the custody battle was too much, and she would be alone...forever. At the same time as her mind filled with the worst-case scenarios, Parker had remained by her side. After she let him read the email, he was more than angry. He was irate, with a clearer picture of the way Craig had treated her while they were married and how he had continued after the divorce. The same day Marie received the email, Parker had called his lawyer friend and was assured Craig was only harassing her. The email was saved as evidence, should they need it. Of course, Marie wasn't convinced, no matter how many times Parker tried to reassure her. She believed Craig had the power to take Jackson away from her.

Parker was seated at the kitchen table watching Marie zip around the house. Counters were wiped down, the fronts of the appliances sparkled after a firm cleaning, and she swept the floors. Marie didn't stop there; she cleaned the sliding glass door and dusted the light fixture above the table. Everything was already clean, but her nervous energy drove her cleaning frenzy.

"Marie, Neil said Craig doesn't have a snowball's chance in hell of changing the custody agreement. Try not to worry. Come here." Parker reached his hand out to her.

She went to him and sat on his lap.

"Everything will be okay, I promise." He kissed her softly until the shuffling of a certain eleven-year-old's feet was heard.

"Mom, do I really have to go?" Jackson grumbled as he walked into the kitchen, startling Marie off Parker's lap.

Parker winked at him.

"I want to stay here with you and Parker. Pleeease."

"Jackson, you'll have a great time in Hawaii and Lexi will be there too." She forced a smile. "You'll be so busy the week will fly by."

"You're not going to do anything fun while I'm gone, right?"

Parker laughed.

"No, buddy. We'll be hanging out with Brooke and Ann this weekend. Just grown-up stuff and then we both work," Marie said as she rubbed his back. "I want you to have a good time and try not to talk about Parker and me, okay? Our lives are private from your dad's and Sasha's." She glanced over at Parker and frowned.

"Yeah, okay."

The knock at the door made Marie and Jackson flinch.

"He's here." Jackson's shoulders slumped. "Bye Parker," Jackson said as he hugged him. It melted Marie's heart to see them so close.

"See ya buddy. Have a great time." Jackson nodded and went to answer the door. Parker took Marie's hand. "I'm right here, and I'll be listening."

"Thank you." She leaned down and gave him a peck on the lips.

Marie felt it was best for Parker to stay out of sight when Craig picked up Jackson. He didn't like the idea, but he respected her wishes. She knew what he really wanted to do was give Craig a piece of his mind…and a mouth full of his fist.

Jackson opened the door, and Marie had his backpack and suitcase ready for the handoff. "Hi, Dad." Jackson forced a smile.

"Hey, Jackson. Marie." He jerked his chin up at her. "Are you ready? I see the black Range Rover is here, so we'll get you out of your mom's hair. We don't want to keep her man waiting."

Her mouth fell open.

"He's not her man!" Jackson snapped. "Parker is her boyfriend, and he's great," Jackson defended with a tight fist of attitude. The anger in his tone and eyes filled the entryway.

"It's okay, buddy. Your dad's just teasing." She bent down and kissed him. He grabbed onto her, hugging her tightly. "I want you to have a good time. Maybe you and Lexi can snorkel together."

"He'll have a great time. We'll be one big happy family," Craig interrupted, ending Marie's encouraging words with Jackson. "Let's go, Jackson."

The house fell silent once they left. She closed the door, pressing her forehead to it like she often did. Parker walked up behind her and wrapped his arms around her. She wasn't alone.

In the truck, Craig fumed beside Jackson. His little heart raced. He had seen that look on his dad's face dozens of times.

Stopped at an intersection, Craig turned towards Jackson. "If you ever take that tone with me again, I'll make sure you never see your superhero again. Do you understand me?"

Jackson stared ahead, unmoving.

"Answer me!"

"Yes, I understand," Jackson answered. He pulled his phone out to text Ricky, but Craig snatched it out of his hands. "Hey!"

"Watch your tone. It's my time now. You'll get the phone back in a couple of days when you call your mom." Jackson crossed his arms over his chest, pursed his lips and tried not to cry. The Hawaiian vacation was off to a terrible start.

Marie was staring out at the ocean, breathing in the salt air. With each breath she took the more relaxed she became. The ocean was her comfort. Its full vastness, multiple shades of blue, the sounds of waves crashing, and the smell of the salt air filled her with peace and breathed life into her. His arms engulfed her, and she rolled her head back against his chest. Now she was safe.

"How are you doing, baby? Can I get you anything?"

"I'm doing better, thank you. You can kiss me." She turned to face him, and Parker kissed her with a warm tenderness. But kissing didn't seem to be the only thing on his mind. His hands moved down her back, over her bottom and he pressed her against him.

"Mmm… so much better," she whispered against his lips. She pulled back. "Brooke and Dave will be here any minute." She made a pouty face.

"Yes, but they aren't sleeping in our room tonight." He kissed the tip of her nose. Her phone buzzed, jolting her, and she quickly grabbed it off the table.

"Oh, just a text from Ann." She exhaled with relief. "Huh, she says, 'FYI I'm bringing a friend.'" She looked at Parker, perplexed. "She's bringing a friend? It's not Tessa; she's in Maine visiting relatives."

"Maybe she has a male friend," Parker said, making his best Groucho Marx impression.

Marie nudged him playfully. "I guess we'll just have to wait and see."

Brooke and Dave arrived, and the women hugged while whispering and giggling. It had been several weeks since Marie had last seen Brooke. Her relationship with Dave had taken off fast after Vegas. In fact, she was rarely around and spent every weekend in San Francisco with him. The only thing Marie knew was Brooke had met the man of her dreams and was seeing him exclusively. It shocked all the girls. Brooke was committed to a man, and she had never been committed to anyone before. Marie was thrilled for her and seeing Brooke so happy made her happy. It had appeared her *Brookie* might be in love for the first time.

"So, you said Ann's bringing a friend?" Brooke's eyes sparked with intrigue.

"That's what her text said. Has she mentioned seeing anyone?"

"No. But then I've hardly spoken to anybody these days. I've been a little preoccupied." Her gaze moved to Dave, who had the same contentment in his eyes.

"H-e-l-l-o." Ann's voice carried to the veranda where they were seated. Marie jumped up as did Brooke. They looked at each other with wide eyes. Ann's friend was a handsome, bearded ginger. The girls all hugged and bounced excitedly.

"Oh, he's sexy," Brooke whispered. Marie giggled.

"Quite handsome, and we need details." Marie nudged her playfully.

"Of course you do." Ann snorted. "But after the introductions."

Parker and Dave stood to greet Ann and her friend. "It's good to see you, Ann," Parker said, giving her a friendly embrace, and Dave followed suit. Marie moved to Parker's side, and he put his arm around her waist.

"Now, I know you are all curious about this gorgeous man," Ann said, rubbing his chest. "This is Troy Hughes, my boyfriend."

Marie and Brooke's mouths fell open.

"Girls, you look surprised." Ann laughed out loud.

"How? But when? Why haven't we heard about him until now?" Marie asked.

"I was taking a line out of your book and keeping my life private," Ann teased. Marie cocked her head and put her hands on her hips. "We met at a jazz club the weekend you girls went to Vegas with your men."

"Ann! That was over six weeks ago," Brooke scolded.

"Yes, well, if you recall, Marie fell apart after that trip." She wrinkled her nose at Marie, who lowered her head in embarrassment. "Don't worry hon; it's okay. I guess I decided after that to keep Troy all to myself for a while." Ann smiled up at him. "But he's here now, and I'm the happiest I've been in a long time."

"I'm very happy for you." Marie hugged Ann. "Troy, I'm glad you're here."

"Thank you. Mr. Nichols, I'm in shock that I'm here. I'm a big fan, and I watch your show all the time." He eagerly shook Parker's hand.

"Thank you. Please call me Parker."

A bell softly rang, and Parker looked over to the patio. Héctor nodded, indicating dinner was ready.

The three couples joyfully and often animatedly talked the evening away. They had finished several bottles of wine, and when the ocean breeze picked up, they moved their small party indoors.

In the morning they gathered on the patio for a lovely brunch prepared by Vicky. Parker made plans to take the guys golfing while the ladies stayed behind, reconnecting and gushing about their men. *Their men*—it was crazy, they all agreed. How was it they were all in relationships at the same time after all these years? All but Tessa, who they decided needed to find a man *asap*.

Later that evening over dinner, Brooke made the shocking announcement that she was moving in with Dave, and the table fell silent.

"I don't believe it. You're moving in together?" Ann asked. Marie sat lost for words.

"We're in love. We don't want to be apart." Brooke looked at Dave, and he nodded, pulling her closer.

"Wow, I'm happy for you honey," Marie finally said. "But I'm gonna miss you."

"I'm sure we'll be down to visit often. Parker is Dave's best friend." Brooke smiled.

"Right, and we'll go visit them often too," Parker added. "I'm happy for both of you."

After the shock wore off, the table came alive, and everyone resumed their conversation, talking until well after midnight. Parker invited everyone to his lake house for Thanksgiving, and his invitation was enthusiastically accepted. Laughter filled the mansion as the group made plans for the holiday and talked about skiing.

The weekend was one of the best Marie had had since the divorce. It was also exactly what she needed after Craig's email. All that was missing was Tessa. Having her with them would have made it perfect, especially if she had a man of her own. Still, Marie loved how everyone got along and genuinely enjoyed being together. There wasn't any tension or fake smiles. She didn't walk on eggshells trying not to offend or anger anyone. It meant the world to her, having authentic people in her life.

After a spectacular luau with roasted pig and all the trimmings, Lexi sat with Jackson on the patio of their hotel room. Jackson had been unusually quiet the last couple of days. His funk concerned her. Even when they played in the ocean, he was less than thrilled about it. His behavior was off from the moment they boarded the plane. Lexi hadn't seen him like this in a while or since Parker had entered the picture. Then again, it had been almost a year since Lexi had spent more than a couple of hours with Craig and Sasha.

"Everything all right buddy?" Lexi touched his hand.

He nodded.

"You've been super quiet."

He shrugged.

"Come on, talk to me. What's going on?" she coaxed.

"Nothing, I just miss Mom and Parker."

"Well, give them a call. You know Mom says to call if you need anything."

"I can't! Dad took my phone." He pushed out his lower lip, on the verge of tears.

"Oh, I didn't know. You can use mine," Lexi offered. He shook his head. "But if you want to talk to Mom or Parker, just use my phone."

"Will you stop," he huffed. "I'll get in trouble, and then Dad won't let me see Parker."

"Jackson, that isn't true." He looked up at her. "Dad can't keep you from seeing Parker. I promise you. Mom would never let that happen." Lexi pulled out her phone. "Let's call Mom right now." Even though it was after ten o'clock, she knew her mom would want Jackson to call. She handed him the phone, and the relief on Jackson's face spoke volumes.

"Lexi, how's it going?" Marie answered.

"Hi, Mom."

"Oh Jackson, why are calling me on Lexi's phone?" She shot a glance at Parker who was working on his iPad. "Did you break your phone?"

"No. Dad took it away. He said he'd give back when it was my day to call you, but I missed you now." Marie stood up and started pacing. Parker stopped what he was doing the second Marie popped up from the sofa. She could see he dialed into the conversation with interest.

"I'm glad Lexi had you use her phone. Why did he take yours away?"

"Because it's his time and I think because of the way I talked to him in the house. He was angry in the truck."

"Listen to me, Jackson. I want you to have a good time with Lexi. Use her phone whenever you want. I miss you too, buddy, but I want you to mind your mouth, okay?"

"Okay, Mom, I will." He was silent a few beats. "I ate roasted pig tonight and watched a man put fire in his mouth. It was pretty cool," he said with a smile in his voice.

"Yeah, that does sound pretty cool. Now don't get any ideas about putting fire in your mouth." They broke out in a chorus of laughs.

"I knew you'd say that."

Marie talked with Jackson for a little bit longer and then handed the phone over to Parker. Smiling, she watched Parker laugh, and then she giggled along with him while he teased Jackson about getting kissed after he departed the plane. Parker masterfully changed the mood, putting everyone in good spirits. She treasured him. Once Parker finished talking to Jackson, he handed the phone back to Marie while Jackson put Lexi on.

"Lex, thank you for having him call me."

"Mom, he was really in a funk. He looks a lot better now."

"Good. I'm glad you're there with him. Is everything else okay?"

Lexi was silent.

"Lex?"

"Sorry, I was waiting for him to leave to take a shower. He told me he had to be good or Dad wouldn't let him see Parker again."

"What?! That son of…" She stopped herself. "I can't believe he would say that to him. Then again, I don't know why I'm so surprised. Poor Jackson."

"I told him you wouldn't let that happen. But Mom, can Dad stop him from seeing Parker?"

"No! He's just bullying him, to control him." Marie started pacing again.

"This is a prime example of why I don't like to be around Dad. Don't worry. I'm with Jackson all the time," Lexi assured Marie.

"Thanks, Lex."

"No problem. Tell Parker I said hi, and try not to worry. I'll have him call you again tomorrow night."

"That would be great. Goodnight, hon." Marie ended the call and turned on her heel to face Parker. She was furious. So much so, she could spew fire out of her mouth and join the show Jackson had mentioned. By the time she filled Parker in on Craig's threats, he was equally livid.

"Why does he have to be such a jerk? Always bullying and making threats," she said, pacing the room with her hands balled up in tight fists.

"Insecurity?" Parker said. "I hate that he is using me as the pawn to keep Jackson in line. Man, I hate that guy."

"I hate it too, but it's classic Craig."

The mansion was quiet after their guests departed. Ann and Brooke had returned to their homes with their men. Vicky and Héctor were gone for the day. Parker was seated beside her on the sofa, reading his lines for the week's filming, and Marie was happy. With her romance novel in hand, she thought about her life while she relaxed next to Parker. There was a rightness to it all, a rightness that was unfamiliar to her. Her eyes scanned the beautifully decorated room filled with only the finest materials

and furnishings, and she sighed. Was it wrong to feel so comfortable and at home in Parker's villa, or to know his
housekeeper on a personal level, as well as his favorite chef? She
came and went as she pleased like it all belonged to her. Was any
of it wrong? Her life had dramatically changed over the last
couple of months because of Parker Nichols. Was it wrong for
her to think of a future with him, to *want* a future with him? Or
was Craig right and she'd end up alone? At this very moment in
the still quiet of the mansion, she had a sense of peace that was
indescribable, and it told her everything would be okay.

Chapter 18

I Love You

September came and went, mercifully uneventful. There weren't any ugly emails from Craig, and he didn't harass her when he picked up Jackson on his scheduled weekends. Marie believed it was because Parker was always present when he came to the house and Craig could see Parker was ready to defend her the instant he became belligerent. Still, there was the daily worry of a hostile email from Craig, but her fears wouldn't control her.

Her relationship with Parker continued to deepen, and they had found their groove together. They lived their lives without fear of Craig getting custody of Jackson, trusting Neil's experience and knowledge that Craig didn't stand a chance. His assurances were just what Marie needed to relax...at least until October when she'd meet Parker's parents, which would be a new stress. To say she was nervous was the understatement of the year. What would they think of the 'divorced mother of two?' She wanted them to like her as well as the kids. She wanted their approval, so moving forward with Parker wouldn't be strained. And if they didn't give their support, she worried what it would mean for her and Parker.

The night before Parker's parents arrived, Marie was uneasy. She had put Jackson to bed, said goodnight to Lexi, and joined Parker in his bedroom. It was the first time Jackson and Lexi had stayed overnight in the mansion, and there was a rightness to it, a wave of peace Marie hadn't felt in a long time. It was wonderful to have everyone she loved under one roof. But, her nerves spoiled her joy. She desperately wanted Parker's parents to like her and could think of nothing else. She paced back and forth; her worry was written all over her face.

"Marie, stop pacing. You're making me dizzy," Parker teased. "Come to bed. We have a big day tomorrow. They should be here around noon."

"I'm trying, but I'm just a ball of nerves." She continued to pace. "I thought I'd take the guest room next to Lexi during the visit."

He laughed out loud. "Why would you do that?"

She stopped pacing to face him, hands on her hips. "Parker, we can't sleep together while your parents are here. That's inappropriate. We probably shouldn't be doing it while the kids are in the house either." She resumed pacing and wrung her hands into a ball.

"Marie, you're staying in our room." Parker hopped off the bed and stopped her.

"Our room? No, this is *your* room."

"No, it's *our* room, and you're staying here. I don't want you to worry, baby. Everything will be fine. My parents will love you and the kids because I love you."

She stared at him, speechless. What did he mean, *I love you*?

"Did you hear me?" He cupped her face. "*I-love-you.*"

She inhaled, and he kissed her.

Did he say he loved her? The words swirled around in her head, *Parker loves me?*

"You love me?" She needed clarification; he had mentioned loving the kids, too. Maybe he just meant it in a general, as-a-friend sort of way. "Like, love me how?"

He laughed heartily. "I love you, Marie. I want forever with you."

She wrapped her arms around his neck, pulling him in for a passionate kiss. Every worry and fear for the present and future melted away.

Parker eased her into the bathroom, not breaking their kiss. He undressed her in a slow, sensual manner, placing soft kisses on her bare skin. The feel of his lips on her sent a wave of electric pulses through her body, elevating every nerve to a higher state. Her quiet moans filled the room. She was aware of how her entire body responded to his touch from the tingles within her, to the unhindered sounds she made. She smiled at how incredible her life had become.

He turned the shower on, and she looked at him with sultry eyes as he took off his boxers. He was already hard and ready for her. The sight of him—his beautiful body, and the love in his eyes, aroused her. She stepped into the shower, excited for what she knew was to come. Their showers together were always loving with an X-rated twist. Parker enjoyed pleasuring her, and she received his advances openly. The pure carnal acts she enjoyed also gave Parker an immense satisfaction.

He pressed her up against the stone wall, his hands protecting her from the cold stone tile. "Let me show you how much *I love you*," he whispered into her ear. The 'showing' started with a passionate kiss as their wet, slick bodies pressed into each other.

His lips traveled down her chest while his hands roamed over her, kneading and stroking.

The wanton between her legs was building—oh, how she craved him. Never had she been so lascivious until Parker. He lit a fire in her only he could quench, and she could never get enough of him, his addictive talents her drug of choice.

She buried her fingers into his wet wavy hair as he kissed his way down her thigh, stimulating her skin with his tongue. Marie lifted her leg over his shoulder, welcoming his hungry mouth. Now experienced from previous encounters, she knew how to get the most out of his titillating treatment. Feeling his mouth on her, she pressed into him, then lost herself in his tongue. His strong, wet hands held her in place, gripping her ass while she rocked into him. Her speed increased, and she arched her back, rubbing her head against the wall as she came apart from the explosive climax that shot through her.

"Oh, Parker!" She held his head in place until the wave of ecstasy traveled through her and had calmed.

To hear him say "I love you" and that he wanted forever with her had released feelings she had been holding protectively in her heart. The timing of his declaration was perfect. She loved him too. Now, confident and assured of his feelings for her, she wanted to love him completely.

Ready and poised to take control, she pushed him against the shower wall, and his eyes widened in surprise. Her fingers danced over his chest, teasing him down to his cut abs, and she took him in her hand. She knew he always enjoyed the feel of her delicate fingers stroking him. She flicked his nipple with the tip of her tongue, then kissed a trail down his stomach. What she was about to do, she'd never wanted to do before. In a slow, dramatic motion she lowered herself to her knees, holding onto his hips. The rise and fall of his chest told her he was yielding to her touch.

"Sweetheart, you don't have to do this."

"I know, but I want to." She stared up at him, feeling all the love in her heart crying out to be released.

In his next breath, he melted into her hand as she caressed the tip. She pulled him gently to her mouth, and he weakened right before her eyes.

The feel of his soft skin and firm erection against her lips made her quiver nervously. All she wanted was to please him in the same manner he'd always pleasured her. She inhaled and in a methodical motion, she licked him from the base of his shaft up to the tip, and she could feel the tremors inside his legs. Parker was a pillar of strength and didn't flinch as she played with him, using her tongue and fingers to discover all his sensitive spots. She wanted to fulfill his every desire, and she was succeeding. So much so, he pressed his body to the stone wall for support. Marie smiled mischievously, watching Parker brace himself. It was obvious he didn't want to fall on her and ruin the moment. She could see and *hear* his enjoyment, but what she loved most was the empowerment she felt as he squirmed in her hand…no, in her mouth. It made her lust for him more.

"Baby…what you're doing to me," he said through labored breaths. "Holy shit." He inhaled, as her mouth took him in, then slowly pulled him out. She wanted to provoke erotic sensations in him that would send his mind spinning. And she could see his heightened state of arousal was overtaking him. "Marie…baby…please. I don't know if I can hold on," he begged. The struggle to control himself was real, and she loved it. She knew he didn't want to explode in her mouth, but she didn't care if he lost the battle.

Marie watched him with a racy satisfaction that drove her forward. The risqué act she performed was once lewd to her. It was something she never wanted to do while married to Craig, and she didn't...ever. It amazed her how she felt completely different with Parker. She loved him deeply and wanted everything with him. Nothing was more important to her than giving to him as he had given to her.

Cupping his balls, she fondled them gently. The tremors in his legs increased when she took him in further. "Holy fuck, Marie!!!" She looked up and could see he was losing his mind in her mouth.

Parker was on the fast track to exploding. The desire and love he felt overwhelmed him. His ache for her consumed him as he fought hard to hold himself together, but he had to stop her before he lost all control.

"Baby, I need you...badly," he begged, pulling her up. He covered her mouth in a searing kiss of gratitude. Overcome with rapture, his emotions took over and drove his actions. He lifted her up against the wall and lowered her down onto him in one swift move. She was open and yielding like he'd never experienced before. Her slick, wet entry evoked a deep groan from him.

"Parker...yes!" She gasped as he filled her.

Transfixed, feeling her warm, supple insides, he was in heaven. He pumped into her rhythmically, watching her lose herself in his eager, desperate kisses. Driven by her salacious moaning his pace quickened, leading him into a powerful climax as he pressed her against the wall. Seconds after his final, forceful thrust her, legs cinched his waist tighter. Marie clenched around

him, boring her nails into his back as her body quaked. He filled
her with his hot passion at the same time she covered him in her
warmth. His head went numb, feeling her barrier-free. It was
intoxicating, raw and natural, exactly how he dreamed it would
be. To be inside her, connected to her and one with her meant
everything to him.

"Parker…" Her soft gasps made him smile. "That was amazing. No, it was mind-blowing." She kissed his neck as he carried
her to the bench in the shower.

"Marie, *I love you,*" he said, sitting with her legs wrapped
around him, still joined as one. He exhaled. "There may be a
problem."

"What?"

"Baby, I was so lost in the moment I forgot about a condom.
We've never made love in the shower before. We've always
moved to the bed. The condoms are in the bedside table. I'm
sorry."

She stared at him, processing what he had said. Condoms
had been their only form of birth control. "I'm sure it's okay
this one time." She stroked his cheek and kissed him softly. "If
I'm honest, this time was so much better than all the other times
because I felt *you.* I liked it this way."

"I did too. I think that's why I lost my mind. Sliding into you
without a condom was…well, there's nothing better." As soon
as the words left his lips, he grew hard inside her again.

How Parker knew what Marie needed, when she needed it, was
one of the many things she loved about him. She also liked how
she was confident with him. Taking charge in the shower and
pleasuring him was new to her, but she craved the undiscovered

sexual encounters they shared. Intimacy with him was always fresh and exciting. It was because *he loved her* and that night he loved her deeply. Marie knew nothing in the world mattered more to him than she did.

It was eight o'clock in the morning when they finally woke. Gone were the days when Marie would wake at six in the morning. Every time she stayed with Parker they slept in. Their late-night lovemaking sessions and morning interludes altered her schedule in a welcomed and satisfying way. Snuggled against him, she had the biggest smile on her face. He loved her. Down deep she knew it, but hearing him say it, and then the passionate night they had shared, validated what she knew in her heart.

"Parker…" she whispered. His hands pulled her close in response. "I love you too." She looked up at him with a sweet smile and stared into his ocean-blue eyes that flowed with adoration.

"Marie, I wish my parents weren't coming today, and the kids weren't here so I could keep you locked in this room for the weekend." He pressed his lips to her temple, his hands feeling their way over her body. She giggled and pulled him onto her. "Say it again," he said kissing her.

"I love you…"

Marie was out by the pool with Jackson when her phone buzzed. It was Brooke. She hadn't talked to her in quite a while and sensed something was up, so she answered, promising herself to keep the call brief. It was just before noon and Parker's parents would be arriving at any moment.

"Hi Brookie, how are you, hon?"

"Marie, I'm beyond happy. How are you?"

"I'm…in love…!"

"In love? As in *love* love? Does Parker know?"

Marie giggled, "He does know…as of this morning. But he told me first last night."

"Marie, I'm so happy for you. I'm *really* happy for you…both of you."

"Thank you; I feel like I'm going to melt into a puddle of love. His parents should be arriving any time. Was there a specific reason you were calling? Or just 'cause?"

"Oh, I definitely have a reason. What are you guys up to on the twenty-second…next weekend?"

"Gosh, nothing I guess. Parker's parents will still be here. They'll be out for two weeks. I can ask him. I don't think he has anything work-related. Why, are you guys coming down?"

"Nope, we'd like you guys to meet us in Vegas." Brooke giggled. "You know, where it all began."

"Really? For a show?"

"Marie, will you be my matron of honor?"

Marie's mouth fell open just as Parker walked out of the house with his parents. She put her hand up and pointed to her phone.

"Marie…I know you're shocked so let me shock you more— I'm pregnant."

Marie's hand covered her mouth and Parker walked over quickly, leaving his parents on the patio.

"Brooke, you're pregnant? Oh honey…I'm so happy for you. How far along are you?" Parker's eyes widened.

"I'm eight weeks. Do you think you guys can make it? I know Dave will be calling Parker, but I had to tell you first. Marie, I'm so happy."

"October 22nd. I'll be there for sure and I'll check with Parker. Listen, Parker's parents just arrived. Call me later with the details okay. I'm so happy for you. Tell Dave I said congratulations."

"Okay, I'll be in touch."

"Wow, she's pregnant and they're getting married in Vegas, 'where it all began' she says."

"That's fantastic. I'm sure I can make it. There is no way I'm letting you go to Sin City without me." He winked. "Now, let's go introduce you to my parents." Her eyes widened and she took a deep breath.

To Marie's delight, Peter and Nancy Nichols were just as sweet and charming as their son. It was like they welcomed her into their lives and hearts the minute they hugged her. Like Parker, they were down to earth and easy to talk to. Nancy had been a stay-at-home mom while Parker and his two older siblings, Chad and Hillary, were young. Peter was a realtor in Tennessee and she learned that Parker used to show horses and had competed in riding competitions before he started acting.

"Wow, I had no idea he was in riding competitions," Marie said.

"I want to learn how to ride a horse!" Jackson blurted excitedly.

"Well, we have four horses on our property," Nancy said. "Y'all need to come out for a visit."

"That would be awesome!" Jackson exclaimed.

Marie giggled, surprised by his interest in learning to ride a horse.

The stories about Parker continued into the evening while they gathered around the fire-pit, roasting marshmallows and making s'mores. If it weren't for the spectacular setting at the mansion overlooking the Pacific Ocean, it could be mistaken for a good old fashioned campout, telling stories around the camp-fire. Marie loved how everyone seemed relaxed and happy.

Parker was his usual attentive self, but he had stepped it up a notch with his open display of affection for her, nor was he holding back anymore around the kids. He kissed Marie freely and teased in a playful way, which sometimes included tickling. He loved to hear her laugh heartily, and the way she molded her body against him. Life was beautiful, and he would show the world he was in love with Marie.

Later that night after Jackson went to bed and Lexi retired to her room, it was just the four adults in the living room.

"Marie, you're more beautiful than Parker described," Nancy said. "And Lexi and Jackson are the spitting image of you—both gorgeous. We couldn't be happier for both of you." Marie blushed as Parker pulled her closer.

"That's very sweet of you to say, thank you. Now I know where Parker gets his charm." She looked up at him, and he kissed her. His parents smiled. Apparently, they approved.

The more time Marie spent with Parker's parents, the more she liked them. They were just the kind of people she wanted in her life, and in her kids' lives. They were honest, caring, funny, and family was very important to them. *Familia es todo* popped into her head. In the fifteen years she was married to Craig not once did she feel accepted into his family. In less than twelve hours with Parker's parents, not only was *she* accepted, but so were her children. The Nichols family were wonderful and re-vealed another layer of Parker that made loving him so easy.

Sunday evening when Marie and the kids prepared to leave, Jackson didn't hide his disappointment. They could always count on him to express his feelings through his hunched-over gait and dragging feet. Marie felt guilty. Jackson had had so much fun with 'Papa' (Parker's dad) playing poker and pool volleyball that he didn't want to go home.

And Peter and Nancy returned the sentiment and looked smitten with Jackson. They took him into their hearts as if he was their grandchild. That morning they had doted on him like any adoring grandparent would while Marie and Parker took their time leaving their bedroom. There was no doubt in Marie's mind she would be happy being part of the Nichols family.

Out at the car, while everyone said their goodbyes, Parker wrapped her up in his arms. "I don't want you to go. I think we need to talk about this living arrangement because it's not working for me."

It wasn't working for her either, but was he talking about moving in together? There was no way she could do that, so rather than tell him right then and there, she deflected. "I'll miss you. Enjoy your parents this week. Oh, and the awards show. Jackson and I will be watching. Good luck."

"You know I want you there with me. Won't you reconsider going?"

"I can't. I'm not ready for being in the public eye as Parker Nichols' girlfriend. And I have a lot to do as Matron of Honor for next weekend, but I'll be there in spirit."

"You're more than a girlfriend. You're the woman I love." He kissed her with abandon as everyone watched. When Jackson's 'ews' flowed from the car they pulled back and laughed.

"I better go. I love you."

"The sweetest words ever." He gave her a little peck. "I love you too, baby."

Chapter 19

Social Media Outlets

Marie arrived at work Wednesday morning just like any other day. Her routine was always the same. She would walk through the large smoked-glass door with her travel mug of coffee in hand and would be greeted by Natalie's smiling face. Except for this morning, Natalie wasn't smiling. She looked ill...or worried.

"Natalie, is everything all right?"

"Marie, I know you're not on social media, so I printed these out for you. I thought you should know." She handed her a few sheets of paper with pictures on them. As Marie's eyes scanned each photo over and over again, her mouth fell open. A flood of emotions took her heart hostage, and she swallowed hard, fighting the savage fears that threatened her. The pictures were of Parker kissing an attractive, younger woman on the red carpet at the awards show. Acid crept up her throat. She gripped her stomach as she stared at the photos.

"Thank you, Natalie," she whispered so softly her words were barely understood as she walked to her office in complete disbelief.

Sitting in her executive chair, she was numb. She had talked to Parker just before the awards show and again right after. Did he decide to kiss another woman for the sake of publicity? The acid burning her throat would not retreat no matter how many times she swallowed. Were these photos real?

But he loved her...right? She turned on her computer and searched the internet. The pictures were everywhere. The tagline read: Who's Parker Nichols' Sexy Love Interest? Her phone buzzed— a text from Jackson.

> Jackson: Mom, who's the woman Parker's kissing on Instagram? Did you break up with him?

Her heart plummeted into the depths of the unknown. Tears welled in her eyes and her stomach turned. This couldn't be happening. Her phone buzzed again, and it was Lexi.

> Lexi: Mom, did you see this?

She attached the same photo Natalie had printed out for her. The lump in her throat grew by the second. Her office phone rang. She didn't want to answer it but had to.

"Yes Natalie," her voice croaked.

"Marie, Ann's on line two," Natalie anxiously announced.

"Thank you." She took a deep breath before answering the call. "Ann."

"Marie, don't freak out. I know you've seen the pictures. They can't be real. They're fakes, I'm sure of it. Have you heard from Parker?" Ann talked at top speed as if she instinctively knew Marie was likely losing it.

"No, I haven't. Maybe this is his way of dumping me?"

"No! Stop that! Those pictures are not real. I am certain of it," Ann tried to reassure her.

"The kids have already texted me. I feel like I'm going to throw up. I gotta go." She hung the phone up, grabbed her bag, and left her office. On her way out of the office, she told Natalie to call her if anything urgent came up. She started driving home and then changed her mind. She didn't want to go to her bland, depressing house. She needed to process. She needed to drive. She hopped onto the 405, destination...unknown.

Parker flew into the law office, and Natalie's eyes widened. When he had left the estate, his hair was a mess, and he was wild with worry. He didn't look at all put together, poised, and confident.

"She's not here," she blurted before he could speak.

"Where is she? She saw the pictures." It wasn't a question. He was sure she had. He bent at the waist, taking deep breaths as Natalie nodded her head, confirming his fear. "They aren't real. I swear. They're fabricated." Natalie just stared at him as he paced.

"They're everywhere, Mr. Nichols. Ann already called. Marie left shortly after. She didn't say where she was going, but she looked pretty upset. She did say to call if anything important came up. Do you want me to call her?"

"No, thanks. Natalie, they're not real, the photos," he repeated. "I love her. I wouldn't cheat on her, ever."

She nodded her head.

He knew what seeing those pictures would do to Marie— they'd crush her. He had assumed she would have refused his call, so he went to her work to explain, but he was too late.

On his way to Marie's house, he called her, but she didn't answer, and dread filled him. He was sure she was ignoring his call, so he called Ann next.

"Parker, oh man. You calling me isn't good."

"Ann, she left work, and she isn't answering her phone. I'm driving to her house now. Those pictures aren't real. I swear."

"I believe you, but they are all over the internet and social media. They look real, and this is Marie we're talking about here. The tagline to the photos called the woman your 'sexy love interest.'"

He inhaled deeply.

"Worse yet, the kids have seen them all over social media."

"Dammit." He slammed his hand against the steering wheel. "I wanted her to go with me to the awards show and she said she wasn't ready. Now this. Ann, I can't lose her."

"It's going to take her time to adjust to being with you and in the public eye. But I think it needs to come out that you're off the market and who snagged you. I know she won't go for it, but if she's going to be with you, she'd better get used to this. And she'd better grow a thick skin because this is only the beginning."

"This isn't fair to her." He sighed regretfully. "Okay, I'm here." He had pulled up to her house, jumped out of his car and ran to the door. He knocked and then pounded on the door. "Shit, she isn't answering."

"Look in the clay flower pot with the pink flowers. I made her put a spare key in there after the Fourth of July fiasco." He found the key and seconds later was in the house. Everything was just as she had left it in the morning. He went up to her bedroom—nothing.

"She's not here!" he said frantically. "Where do you think she went?"

"I have no idea. I think it's best if you go back to your place and wait for her. I'm hoping she'll come to you when she's ready. Parker, she loves you and needs you."

"I need to know she's okay. Just when we thought our lives were settling into a routine, this shit happens. Please call or text me if you hear from her."

"I will. Try not to freak out. Marie may meltdown at times, but she's smart and sensible."

"Thanks, Ann."

Parker drove home as Ann suggested. His parents were waiting for him on the patio. When he walked out looking deflated, their faces sank, disappointed for him.

"You didn't find her," his mother said. "I'm sorry."

"No, I didn't. I called her best friend, Ann, and she said the kids know about the photos."

Nancy and Peter shook their heads.

"Is it fair to ask her to deal with this crap?" Parker said, throwing up his hands. "She once lived a quiet, private life and now she's been thrown into the celebrity jungle. How is she supposed to protect herself and the kids?"

"Parker, this is your life. If she loves you, she'll stick by you. But you need to support her and do your best to protect her. Scale back your public appearances for a while, and when you have them, she needs to be by your side," his mother advised.

"Your mother's right. She needs to support you, and you do the same. It's not like you floated those pictures out there yourself. This happened to you too. Stick together and be a force in Hollywood."

"Thank you, both. I'm going to call my agent. I need to occupy my mind."

Marie was heading on the 405 towards Santa Monica. The ocean called to her, but when she saw the CA-1N exit for Malibu, she took it. For the last hour she had been driving around, all she could think was, *I need Parker.* Every fiber in her being told her those photos weren't real. How could they be after she just spent a wonderful weekend with him and his parents? They had declared their love to each other. Everything about the weekend had felt natural…meant-to-be.

Dozens of times he had asked her to go to the awards show with him. If she had gone, would this have happened? If he had someone on the side, surely she'd know about it, just like she did with Craig.

The azure water blended into the sky, reminding her of Parker's adoring eyes. This was ridiculous. Parker had proved himself reliable and was always on time. He left work for her and had motivated the crew in Budapest to wrap up two days early, so he could come home to her. Parker even mentioned her moving in, so they could be together every day and night. The way he made love to her filled her with the kind of love that was genuine and real. And he told her he wanted "forever" with her. The pictures were a lie.

The smell of the salt air filled her with strength and clarity as her hair beat across her face from having the window down. The closer she got to Parker's estate, the more her confidence grew in the two of them. If she was going to be with him, she'd better toughen up. Running away and hiding every time something happened was stupid and she'd only hurt him. Frustrated with herself, she shook her head. She was cutting and running way too frequently, even for her.

"Geez Marie, if you can't stand the heat, then you'd better get out of the damn kitchen," she scolded herself. The depth of her love for him negated that as an option. Unless he did something truly horrible, like cheat on her, she would be with him forever. She *wanted* to be with him forever, through the good, the bad, and the ugly. This was the ugly.

After she pinned the passcode, and the security gate to his estate opened, she took a deep breath. What would she say to him? There were too many 'what ifs' in her head. She didn't even know if he was home. All she knew was she couldn't lose him. Before Craig had screwed with her head, she had been strong. Now, she was getting strong again with Parker in her life. Her handsome, kind, loving, and passionate man believed in her. She nodded her head, resolved. She wasn't afraid anymore, and it was all because of him. He would fight for her and support her through any situation. It was her turn to fight for him…for them. *Parker's the one that matters.*

Marie confidently walked into the mansion where Vicky was busy preparing what she assumed was lunch. "Hi Vicky, is Parker around?"

Vicky looked up, surprised. Before she could say anything, Nancy walked in from the patio. Marie forced a smile, but it was easy to see she was embarrassed. "Hi, Nancy. I'm just looking…"

"For Parker." Nancy opened her arms to her and Marie willing walked into them. "Marie, I'm so glad you're here. It must have been awful seeing those photos."

Marie was without words.

Nancy pulled back to look at her. "If there's anything you need, we're here for you."

"Marie."

She whipped around at the sound of his voice and saw the torment in his eyes. He had disheveled hair like he had just woken up, not styled and perfect like she was used to seeing him. His grieved eyes were drinking her in as he walked to her. "I'm so sorry." He touched the tips of her fingers. "Are you okay? I went to the office, but you had left. Then I went to your house, and you weren't there." He shook his head, "Marie, you have to believe me."

She placed two fingers over his lips. "Shhh, I know. I freaked. I'm sorry."

He pulled her into his arms and held on to her for dear life. Nancy and Vicky left the kitchen just as Parker kissed Marie.

"I'm going to fight for you...for us," she said against his mouth.

Marie and Parker met Tessa, Ann, and Troy at the airport Friday evening. The wedding was being held Saturday afternoon at the Four Seasons. They boarded the chartered jet and Marie had to giggle at Troy's excitement. It was her second time on a private plane, but even she wasn't as excited as he was, and Ann ate it up.

"So, you're doing better?" Ann asked Marie.

"Yes, I'm better."

"She's been a trooper. Thankfully I'm not the top story anymore. These things usually blow over in a couple of days. They're up just long enough to stir up interest, and then they fade," Parker said.

"So, when are you coming out as a couple?" Ann asked.

Marie looked at Parker and shrugged her shoulders. "I don't know. Soon, I guess."

"My publicist has mixed feelings about it. It's a toss-up on whether the fans will receive it well or not. I don't care how they take it, but Marie cares."

"I don't want his career to take a hit because of me," Marie said.

"Are you kidding? Professor Pierce fans love him," Troy interrupted. "You have to give it to them in small doses. Make them fall in love with Marie. And then your career as a family guy will take on a whole new platform."

Parker looked at him curiously.

"How do you suggest we make them 'fall in love' with me and what exactly does that mean?" Marie asked.

"Well, I think easing the fans into your lives is the way to go. Do teaser photos with great taglines that get them talking. Like, Parker tweets something about you but doesn't mention your name. And then he can post a picture on Instagram where they can't see your face. It stirs up interest. He slowly reveals you. After a couple of months, they can see your face. I think, if we do this right, you'll have the fans eating out of your hand by the new year." Troy proudly nodded his head. "But you'll have to be willing to go public and get your picture taken."

"I like this," Parker said. "Let's try it now, here on the plane." Marie's eyes widened. "Yes baby, I'm serious. Let's tease my fans." He grinned. "We can get them primed and ready to see your beautiful face at the next awards show." Marie took a deep breath and looked at Ann who, surprisingly, was silent through the whole conversation. Tessa looked intrigued herself.

"Ann, you haven't said a single word. What's wrong with you?" Marie teased.

"It's this man. I love to hear him talk. He's so damn smart. But I think you should go for it. Be bold, be a badass." Ann winked at her.

"She's right Marie, you need to be a badass," Tessa agreed. "Don't let the fans and media ruin your relationship with Parker. You're the happiest I've ever seen you. Fight for it. Join the celebrity circus and perform your little heart out like the Kardashians," Tessa encouraged.

"Okay Troy, what do you suggest we do?" Marie asked.

"Parker is in the perfect setting, on a luxury private jet and taking you on a trip. He teases that he's taking his...well, whatever Parker wants to call you, on a secret getaway. And then he can do something with your hand and one of his sexy looks. The girls eat that shit up and they'll think he's the most romantic man alive." Troy laughed, rubbing his beard.

"He *is* the most romantic man alive," Marie said, squeezing Parker's hand.

The photoshoot of Parker and Marie commenced while they were on the hour-long flight. Parker posted the photos on Instagram first. It didn't take long before the likes flooded in by the dozen. The pictures only showed Marie's hands. The first picture was of him playing with her fingertips with the hashtags *#lovethesefingers #loveofmylife #weekendgetaway*. In the next photo, he was kissing the same hand with the hashtags *#justgettingstarted #mylove*. Then he shared those Instagram posts on Twitter. Last, he tweeted: *I'd fly anywhere with my beautiful woman. Our weekend is just getting started baby! #myforever #secretgetaway*

By the time they arrived in Vegas, Parker's numbers were pushing one-hundred thousand, and the chatter was all positive.

The fans were intrigued. Mission accomplished. His publicist sent him a text: *Nice work.*

Marie and Parker entered their suite, which was perfect and romantic with flowers and champagne. Parker was always on top of all the details. They had no aspirations to venture out of the room. They weren't in Vegas for gambling, shows, or dining. No, they were there for Brooke and Dave's wedding, and to be alone. They ordered room service and focused on each other for the rest of the night.

Brooke was a beautiful bride. Her giddiness was contagious, and the girls followed suit. They visited the hotel spa for a little wedding-day pampering. Giggles kicked off the fun, followed by stories. The whole time they watched Parker's accounts to see the numbers continue to rise, and the buzz from the fans on each media outlet. It was awesome, and the common question among fans was, *"Who is the mystery woman Parker Nichols is calling the love of his life?"*

"I can't believe I'm doing this," Marie admitted.

"Well, you're doing it like a pro. And that man loves you so much." Ann smiled.

"He completely does," Tessa agreed. "Now I need to find me a man so I can join the party."

"You guys are great, but we should be focusing on our bride-to-be," Marie redirected.

"No, I love this talk. Our Marie, finding real love after all this time. I'm so happy for you," Brooke said, her eyes sparkled with love. "Dave said he's never seen Parker like this. He believes you guys will get married one day."

"Married? Um…" Marie shrugged, she had no words.

"Now don't go freaking out, honey," Ann ordered. "Let's stay focused on one wedding at a time."

Marie nodded in agreement. But the girls weren't blind, and Marie knew she couldn't hide the uneasiness that filled her with the mention of marriage. The truth was, Marie had been dreaming about marrying Parker. Her dilemma was the fear of losing what she most wanted—a life with Parker that would last forever. If she let her hopes and dreams be known, she would be devastated if they were never realized.

The ceremony was simple yet elegant. It was just close friends and the bride and groom's parents. During the ceremony, Parker held Marie's gaze as he stood beside Dave and she was beside Brooke. He looked at her with adoration, like she'd imagine him if they were getting married. Marriage would be so different with Parker.

Through the entire, short ceremony Marie watched Parker, who looked like he was listening intently to the vows. And so was she. She couldn't remember for the life of her the vows she had said when she married Craig in City Hall. They didn't have a wedding, just a reception her family had supplied. It was a day she hardly remembered, except for the puking, which she did a lot of on her wedding day. She had been three months pregnant with Lexi.

At dinner after the ceremony, Parker leaned into her and whispered, "Wanna be next?"

She just stared at him.

"Don't worry, that wasn't the proposal. I'm just fishing for an idea when you'll be ready. I'm ready...but no pressure." He kissed her, and she loved him for it. He had never hidden his feelings or intentions. But marriage, would that mean family too? Did he want a baby of his own? Wasn't she too old to have a baby? After all, her kids were already grown. It would be like starting over, except her do-over would be with the most amazing and loving man she had ever known.

Chapter 20

Reassurances

Listen to me—the time will go by fast. I know you don't want to go, but it's just ten days this time, and it's your job," Marie reassured Parker.

"You sound like you're trying to get rid of me. What do you have planned while I'm gone? Baths?"

"Maybe. But I promise you're better than baths." She kissed him softly.

"Glad you think so, baby. The whole time I'm gone I'll be thinking about our trip to Idaho and having you in my bed." He held her tightly. "Remember, you mean everything to me. I love you." He kissed her deeply, then reluctantly pulled away. He needed to go. On this trip he traveled with the cast and crew, so he wasn't on his own time.

"Be safe and let me know when you arrive. I'll be expecting a call tomorrow afternoon."

"Absolutely." He sighed heavily.

"I love you."

"I love you so much, baby." He gave her one more fierce hug, and then he was gone.

Marie breezed through her workday uneventfully and had plans to cook lasagna for dinner as a special treat for Jackson. On her way home, she listened to the radio and enjoyed the beautiful November day. The countdown to Parker's return was on. She would do everything possible to keep herself busy and she hoped the next ten days would fly by uneventfully. In the meantime, she wanted to plan a wonderful Thanksgiving for her family, friends, and for Parker. She sighed contentedly at the thought of him. She loved him more than anything, unlike the feelings she had had for Craig, which were borne out of circumstances. The love she felt for Parker was far beyond what she had experienced with Craig, and there was no comparison. Did she ever really love Craig? It didn't matter. She knew she really loved Parker and that was all that mattered.

Marie arrived home and went straight to work preparing dinner. It did her heart good to hear Jackson raving over how good it smelled in the house. It had been way too long since she'd made lasagna.

They were seated at the small dining table and Marie laughed as Jackson devoured half the pan. She relished seeing him happy, and their relationship was the strongest it had been since before the divorce.

"Mom, that was the best lasagna ever." Jackson smacked his lips loudly, and then in an exaggerated motion wiped his mouth with a napkin. "Mmm, that was delicious!"

She laughed out loud. "Thank you. I think you say that every time I make it." She tousled his hair playfully as she removed his plate.

"Ha-ha, maybe you're right. Are you going to watch *Pierce* with me?"

"I'll join you after I clean up these dishes, okay?"

He nodded and was off to watch his favorite superhero.

While Marie cleaned up, she hummed a little tune, daydreaming about marrying Parker. Life would be very different as his wife and she'd had a small taste of it staying with him on his estate. When he mentioned getting married during Brooke's reception, she thought it was spurred by being at someone else's wedding. But then he brought it up several days later and presented her with having the option to work or not work. He preferred she didn't work so she could go on location with him. Not having to work appealed to her, as it would allow her to volunteer at Jackson's school. But then his school would be forty-five minutes away, and that's not counting traffic. The commute back and forth, twice a day sounded awful. Parker also suggested a private school or getting Jackson a tutor so he could go with them. There was no question Jackson would jump at the chance to travel with them, but what about socialization? She wasn't convinced getting him a tutor was the best option for him, since he was already antisocial. And there was Craig. Then again, she had sole custody so why did it matter what he thought?

Marie also resented missing so much of the kids' childhood because she worked. Early on in her marriage, she needed to work to make ends meet. She went to school full time and worked part-time...spending little time with Lexi. When Craig's family business started to grow, his salary increased, and Marie hoped she could quit her job to be home for the kids. To her disappointment, Craig never supported her in being a stay-at-home mom. He wanted her working for the extra money. He was always about the money.

The ache in her heart after taking Jackson to daycare still haunted her. She had learned he cried for hours after she left him and he never adjusted. Every day she felt like the worst mother in the world and Craig didn't seem to care. All she wanted was to take care of her baby and cuddle him all day long. But, what she wanted didn't matter to Craig, and begging and crying were futile, as his word was final.

"Mooom," Jackson hollered. "Mom…come here!!!"

She walked into the living room with her hands on her hips. "What's the emergency? I told you I'd join you after I cleaned the kitchen."

"There's a new person on the show…she's Professor Pierce's new girlfriend."

Marie furrowed her brow, walking closer to view 'the new girlfriend.' "What makes you think she's his girlfriend?"

"Because he introduced her to the team as his girlfriend and they just made out on his sofa."

"Did you record it so I can see?"

"No, but I might be able to find it online. Let me get my iPad." Jackson ran upstairs to his bedroom and Marie stared at the TV. Why didn't he mention a love interest on the show? Jackson returned in a flash while she was thinking of the possible explanations. "Okay, I got it. Watch." He handed the iPad to her.

The blonde love interest was young and beautiful with a fit, curvy body…*great*. Marie was fighting hard not to let her imagination get the best of her.

"I'll ask Parker about her when I talk to him. It's just acting, you know. It's not real."

"I guess. It sure looks real to me. It's like when I see you guys kissing. Bleh! I can't tell what's real and what's not," Jackson admitted, taking the iPad back.

"Yeah, me either. But there's nothing to worry about. Parker and I are together. It's just acting," she reassured him, although she needed some reassurance too. "I need to finish cleaning the kitchen. You watch your show."

Marie wiped down the table in slow motion, then the counters, and finally the stove, while she ran hot water on the dishes in the sink. No way did she want to watch *Pierce* now, so, she took her time cleaning the kitchen.

At nine o'clock, Jackson was in bed and Marie had turned off all the lights downstairs. Marie was glad to call it a night after viewing the cute blonde Parker, er, Professor Pierce, had kissed. It was earlier than usual but what else was she to do. She was alone. Climbing into bed, she fell back on her pillow and let out a deep, slow breath. A buzz came from her phone on her bedside table—a text from Parker.

> Parker: Hi beautiful, my body is shot. Jetlag is always hard for me. I'll call you @ 4:00 your time. Gotta get to work. Luv you.
> Marie: I'm glad you made it in one piece. I'll talk to you later. I love you.

The morning unfolded as it did most days at Malcolm-Bower, slow and steady. Most of Marie's busy hours were after lunch. The relaxed nature of her bosses made the working conditions ideal for everyone. They had been surfers in their youth, hence all the black and white photos of waves throughout the office. The attitude they upheld was, "Hang loose," which they chanted daily. It was a great place to work as a single parent, and they had been more than gracious and merciful during the year of her divorce. If she was late to work, or had to leave early or called in sick, she heard, "Hey no prob, just *hang loose.*"

This past May was her tenth anniversary working for *MalBow*, a nickname the bosses came up with during their college days at UCLA. The dynamic duo was a riot most days and never serious any day. Today was definitely a *hang loose* day.

Mentally, Marie was stable considering her worrisome news, which was a massive improvement over her previous freak-outs. She had made it to lunch, and over a bowl of Thai noodles, she casually chatted with Natalie. She only needed to listen because Natalie was talking her ear off about a guy she had started dating. It was nice to get lost in someone else's life while a young, curvy blonde bombshell had rattled your own.

After lunch, she was anxious as she watched the clock. Four o'clock couldn't come soon enough and her nervous energy was proof as she paced in her office. Her gait slowly began to slump as 4:15 neared, and by 4:30 she was in her chair, deflated. Did Parker forget to call her? Were they working late into the night? Was he with his female co-star? *No, stop Marie. You're working yourself up again.*

During her mental scolding, her office phone rang and she picked it up on the first ring.

"Natalie?"

"Wow, that was fast. Mr. Nichols on line two."

"Thanks!" She quickly clicked over. "Parker!" she said with relief.

"Hi, beautiful," he said in a quiet voice. "Sorry, I'm late calling."

"It's okay, but I was worried you weren't going to call. You've spoiled me by always being punctual. You sound tired. Are you okay?"

"Just tired. The crew went out for a late dinner and we just got back. I'm not going with them anymore. They're crazy. How are you, baby?"

"Well, I don't want to keep you. You need your rest."

"Why are you trying to get off the phone with me? How are you?"

Marie took a deep breath.

"What's wrong? Talk to me."

"Okay... Jackson was watching your show last night. He was concerned about your blonde love interest. It looked like you had good chemistry together." She sighed.

"Marie, I'm not cheating on you. That was filmed last spring before I met you. It's just acting."

"You're saying you didn't enjoy kissing her and touching her? As Jackson said, it looked real. I even thought it looked real. Is she still your love interest on the show? Did you kiss her today?"

"Marie, you have nothing to worry about. I promise. You're the only person I want and I love you more than anything."

"So, you did kiss her today."

"Marie..."

"Will you be kissing her every day?"

"Yes. But I've spoken to the writers and the scenes are short. By the end of filming, she'll meet her demise, so it's not going to be a long-term situation. Please don't worry."

She was silent.

"Marie, I don't want you to feel insecure. This is why I want you with me, so I can hold you during these moments and go to bed with you in my arms every night. Instead, I'm alone, and I hate it." She remained silent. "Marie please..."

"I'm here." Her voice was soft. "I don't like it. I can let go of what I saw because we weren't together, but now, how would you feel if I kissed another guy?"

"Well, you have, and I hated it. Don't go looking to get even baby. This is work with twenty people around me. There is nothing romantic or private about it. It's more like turn this way, put your hand there, your eyes were open, tilt your head more—it's work. I'm not attracted to her at all. She has the worst body odor. I'm not sure what it is, but it's gross."

She laughed a little.

"She's nice enough and a pretty woman, but there isn't an ounce of real chemistry. Now if we're talking about you, I love everything about you, from the feel of you to the taste of you...mmm, I love all of you. Now I'm getting turned on just thinking about tasting you." So was Marie. "The smell of your skin and your hair...you do things to me no other woman has ever done. You're IT for me," he said as a yawn took hold of him.

"I should let you go. You need your rest. Don't worry about me. I'm okay."

"Are you sure? I'll call you at the end of my day...every day. I love you, so much. Please trust me." He sounded exhausted but the sincerity in his voice was strong.

"I do trust you. I'm still trying to get a handle on having a boyfriend who's an actor. I love you, now get some rest."

"Okay. Bye, beautiful."

Marie ended the call, relieved by Parker's quiet assurance. The way he wiped away her fears and reassured her in a brief call was incredible. *He* was incredible and she missed him terribly. It would be the longest nine days of her life waiting for him to return to her.

Friday arrived and Parker had called her every day at four like he said he would. She loved how he sounded like he was feeling worse than she was when he'd call. It gave her satisfaction, but Marie also felt sorry for him. The connection they had was intense, she loved that he needed her, and he wasn't the same when he wasn't with her. It did wonders for her ego.

She took a deep breath before she entered her house, anticipating Jackson's unsavory mood. This was his weekend at Craig's, and she would have some coaxing to do to get him out the door, like every other time he'd go to his dad's. As if that wasn't enough, she was on edge seeing Craig. She hadn't been alone with him in a long time, and she worried it wouldn't go so well with Parker not present.

"Jackson, I'm home."

"I'm in the living room," he hollered back. Marie entered the room and he was sprawled out on the sofa. It was already starting.

"Are you ready to go? Your dad will be here in less than an hour."

"I guess. You're going to make me go, so I don't really have a choice," he grumbled.

She took a deep breath. "He's your dad and loves you. I'm sure you'll have a great time."

"He doesn't even talk to me. He does nothing with me. It's all Sasha. She plays games with me, but then Dad calls her away every time."

Marie frowned. She knew it was true. Craig was the same way when they were married. "Well, at least Sasha's there. Maybe she'll help bridge the gap between you and your dad."

He scrunched his face at her. "I'd rather be with you."

"I know, and you will. You'll be with Parker and me when we go to Idaho for a week. Let's get this visit out of the way with your dad and then we'll focus on our trip." She tousled his hair. "But Jackson, don't talk about Parker to your dad, okay? Men don't like to hear about other men. He'll always be your dad no matter what, so be respectful to him. You can have both men in your life and you can care about Parker, even love him if that's how you feel. But you have only one dad. Got it?"

"Yeah…I got it."

"Okay, let's get your bag ready. He'll be here soon."

"Are you and Parker going to get married someday?" His question stopped her in her tracks. He looked at her expectantly.

"Um, I don't know. How would you feel if I married Parker?"

"Well, do you love him? I heard him tell you he loves you."

"Yes, I do love him." She smiled at him.

"Well, if you love him, you should marry him. He's the greatest guy ever and not just because he's an actor," Jackson said. "I think he's good for you and you should marry him."

It turned out to be quite the interesting conversation with Jackson while packing his weekend bag to take to Craig's. If she felt she needed approval from him to marry Parker, she had it. The doorbell rang and Jackson looked at Marie, so she gestured to answer the door. His shoulders slumped, and she cleared her throat. He knew that sound, so he straightened up and answered the door.

"Hi, Dad."

"Hey Jackson, are you ready?" Craig peered around Jackson and saw Marie. He did a double take. In the last couple of months, there had been gradual changes in her from the way she dressed, to her hair, to the amount of makeup she wore. She had always been an attractive woman who turned heads wherever she went. But now, she had a confidence about her that showed in the way she carried herself and it made her alluring. He made eye contact with her. "Marie."

"Craig," she returned. "Give me a hug, buddy." Jackson wrapped his arms around her tightly.

"I don't see the black SUV. Did Mr. Hollywood finally come to his senses and dump you?" He smirked.

"No!" Jackson shot back. "Parker's in Budapest and he'd never dump Mom! He loves her." Craig's gaze on Marie hardened. "Bye, Mom." Jackson threw his hand up and waved.

"Bye, buddy" She waved back, then went to close the door but Craig just stood there, looking her up and down. Her heart raced at his overt delight in looking at her. "Goodbye Craig." She tried to move him along, but he didn't budge.

"Now that Mr. Hollywood is out of the country you're all alone." He laughed. "My lawyer is putting together a petition for shared custody. We want Jackson half the time, starting with Thanksgiving. You've had him the last two years, and I want him this year."

Marie's mouth fell open. "No. I'm the custodial parent. You gave up your rights on your own. I've already made plans for this year. You can have him next year for Thanksgiving" Her voice cracked there at the end, and she was shaking inside. Standing up to Craig wasn't something she often did, but things needed to change. Parker couldn't always be around to keep Craig in check. She needed to be able to stand up to him.

"You bitch!" Marie flinched when he lunged toward her. "How dare you talk to me that way." He sneered as his black eyes narrowed. "He's my son goddammit, and you won't tell me when I can see him!"

"Is everything okay here?" Seth interrupted.

Craig turned around to see a huge, towering man standing behind him.

"Marie, is this Craig?" His gaze was hard on Craig.

"He was just leaving. Craig, be sure to look over the schedule I sent you. If there are additional days you'd like with Jackson, email me your request."

Craig stared at her with disdain, and his jaw clenched hard. "My request? You have some nerve. You'll be hearing from my lawyer. The way you seem to have men in and out of your house might make some think you're taking on extracurricular activities to pay for your new look. No child should have to live this way." He fumed, as he walked out of the house.

"Wow, you had described him perfectly. What an asshole." Seth huffed. "Are you okay?"

"Yeah, but I'm shaking inside."

He moved to hug her, but she put her hand to his chest stopping him.

"No." He stepped back.

"Friends can hug, you know?"

"I know, but you want to be more than friends and I'm in love with Parker. Thank you for coming when you did." She took a deep breath. "It feels good to stand up to him, but as you could see, he didn't like it."

"No kidding. I was out taking a walk when I saw him at your door. Figured I should stop by just in case." He smiled. "Do you want to go for a walk?"

"No, but thanks. I have stuff to do around here. Maybe I'll see you in the gym tomorrow morning."

"Sure thing. Have a good evening."

Marie closed the door and leaned against it. She inhaled, then exhaled holding her stomach and locked the door. Craig was definitely pissed and there was no doubt in her mind he would be calling his lawyer. Extracurricular activities? What in the hell was he talking about, paying for her new look? And what does he mean, 'no child should have to live this way?' Was he calling her a prostitute?? "Is he going to lie to his lawyer and the judge?" She wished more than anything Parker was home.

Marie anticipated another lonely Friday night. She poured herself a glass of wine and went out onto her patio. The romance novel she had yet to start reading stared up at her. She picked it up and opened the book, then immediately tossed it back on the table. She had her own romance going on and didn't need a book to get her through the night anymore. It was going to be a long forty-eight hours.

Their trip to Idaho couldn't come soon enough so she could have a full week with Parker. Just thinking about what that meant caused her to tingle. She lifted the glass to her lips and paused. Then she put down the glass and grabbed her phone. Opening the calendar on her phone, she began counting the days when the phone rang.

"Parker! I wasn't expecting to hear from you again today."

"Hi, baby. I wanted to know how it went with Craig."

She smiled. "You're the sweetest. Unfortunately, he was as awful as he was before you were around."

"What did he say?"

She paused. "Craig thinks Jackson is suffering being with me because I have 'extracurricular activities' going on in my life, so I can afford my new look."

"What?"

"He basically called me a prostitute. He didn't say prostitute, but implied it."

"That son-of-a-bitch! Are you okay?"

"Yeah, Seth stepped in when he was getting hot under the collar."

"Seth? Why was he there?" There was a sudden tone of irritation in Parker's voice.

"He wasn't here. He was walking by and saw Craig up in my face. As soon as Craig left, so did Seth. You don't have anything to worry about."

"I'm not worried, but I hate that I wasn't there for you."

"I have to be able to handle Craig without you because you can't always be my protector...although I love it when you are."

"I want nothing more than to protect you, baby. Did anything else happen?"

"He also demanded to have Jackson for Thanksgiving and I told him 'no,' and that he could have him next year because we already have plans this year."

"You stood up to him! I'm so proud of you!"

"Yeah well, he called me a bitch and that's when he brought up the lawyer."

"He's a piece of work. I hate him!" Parker snapped. "Are you going to be okay? I'll be home in six days. Damn, that's a long time still." His voice fell.

"I'll be okay. I'm missing you a ton. I think I may take a bath tonight...I need you." He groaned. She smiled, loving the effect she had on him.

"You have no idea how much I want to join you."

"Mmm, I want you to join me too. In my imagination, you'll be there. I'll feel your hands on my body, your lips on mine and your fingers in me…yes, it will be you, handsome."

"Damn baby, you have me hard just listening to you. I can't wait to have you for a whole week. And I seriously want to talk about our living arrangements."

"You're amazing. We'll talk after you get back. I should let you go. I love you."

"I love you too."

Marie ended the call and the calendar was on her screen again. *Unbelievable.*

Shaking her head, she took her glass of wine inside and locked the sliding glass door. She poured the wine into the sink, washed the glass, dried it, and put it away in the cabinet.

Chapter 21

Life-Changing

When Jackson returned from his weekend with Craig, he wasn't himself. It surprised Marie when Craig didn't follow Jackson through the door like he did every other time. The unusual occurrence piqued her interest, prompting her to question Jackson about the visit.

"Did you have fun with your dad and Sasha?"

"It was fine." Jackson avoided eye contact with her. It was clear he was bothered by something, given his quiet and slightly detached behavior. If this were before Parker entered their lives, she wouldn't have thought twice about it. Jackson was always in a dumpy mood back then, but now, this was not normal and it concerned Marie.

"Wanna tell me about it?" she prodded.

"No." He carried his duffle up to his room, leaving Marie confused.

On her daily call with Parker, she filled him in on Jackson's solemn mood. Her mother's intuition told her something had happened at Craig's. She asked Parker to text Jackson to see what he could find out. To her disappointment, Parker came back empty handed. Whatever happened, Jackson wasn't telling anybody. Parker reassured her they would, in due time, find out. But she didn't like that answer. Short of calling Craig, what could she do?

During the remainder of the week, Marie busied herself preparing for Idaho. It helped the week fly by, but it also wore her out. There was no way she could ignore the extreme exhaustion that plagued her. She hoped it was just a fluke, like her late period.

If this was perimenopause, the timing couldn't be worse. Nothing like shining a big light on her age when she was finally feeling vibrant and alive. Rather than overthink the situation, she'd wait for Parker to return from Budapest, or for 'Aunt Flo' to show up. The latter would be ideal, wouldn't it? She was conflicted. They hadn't talked about kids. What if Parker didn't want children?

For now, Parker's return was her highest priority. Today's four o'clock call was the last one from Budapest, then he'd be coming home. Marie's excitement had kept her preoccupied all day, and she could hardly focus on work.

"Parker, it's driving me crazy not knowing what happened at Craig's. What if Jackson never opens up about it?"

"We'll find out. Maybe he's like his mom and needs time to process," he teased.

"Ha-ha, very funny. God, I miss you."

"Soon, baby, just one more day. Are you sure you don't want me to sneak into your house when I get into town?"

"You know I do. But I have to work Friday and Jackson has school, and you'd be a wonderful distraction I wouldn't be able to ignore."

"Yeah, I knew you'd say that, but I had to try. We can handle one more day. Then I never want to be apart from you again. A week with you in Idaho is just a tease. I'd like you to consider staying with me during Jackson's winter break."

"For two weeks? You know, I still have to work."

"I know, and Jackson can stay with Vicky and me. I'll have a lot of time off and we'll hang out while you're at work."

"Hmm, I'll consider it. I know Jackson would love to hang out with you. And I'd love to go to bed with you every night," she said with a wistful hum.

"We can make that happen permanently. Just say the word."

"What are you saying? Is this your proposal or are you asking me to move in?" she teased.

"No, this is not my proposal. But, are you saying you'd say, yes?" Parker asked, sounding hopeful.

She giggled.

"I'll take that as a yes." His voice melted her.

"We haven't even talked about kids, like if you want them? Or if I'm too old? Or what we'd do with Jackson if I go on location with you."

"Baby, you're not too old. I'd love to have a baby with you. Do you want another baby?"

She touched her stomach knowing she was late. "I want it all with you."

"Okay, I think one more day is going to be too long. I want to kiss you so bad and I want to get planning right away. I want you and Jackson on location with me the next time I come to Budapest."

"That sounds wonderful. I can't wait to see you."

"I'll text you when I arrive. I love you, baby."

"I love you too. Bye." Marie sat at her desk smiling. If she was indeed pregnant she knew Parker would want to get married right away. Christmas would be a perfect time, with her parents out for a visit. She sighed dreamily... *just one more day.*

Later that evening while Marie packed she heard Jackson talking in his room rather loudly. She quietly crept to his door to eavesdrop on his conversation.

"No Ricky, when a person has a miscarriage, the baby died. I'm not getting a little brother or sister." He went silent.

A miscarriage? Was he talking about Sasha? She couldn't believe what she was hearing.

Jackson continued, "It was a crappy visit, with Sasha crying the whole weekend. My dad kept promising her they could adopt and that I'll live with them full-time so she could be a mother to me." He was silent again, likely listening to Ricky.

Marie rubbed her stomach. She was stunned, as she continued to listen with her ear pressed against the door.

"No, I don't want to live with them. I want to stay with my mom and Parker. My dad doesn't really want me. He only wants to make Sasha happy. He's always about Sasha. At least my mom and Parker love me." Jackson was silent again. "Yeah, I'd like a baby brother or sister." Marie backed away from the door, utterly shocked by the one-sided conversation.

Sasha had a miscarriage? They want Jackson full-time?

Back in her room, she paced, not knowing what to think or who to call. No, there was no one to call. She'd wait for Parker and they'd figure it out together. No panicking this time. Craig would not get Jackson full-time. She resumed packing her things but the fact that she was *twenty days late* occupied her mind until her phone rang. It was an unknown number, but she answered anyway.

"Hello."

"Marie, it's Nancy. How are you?" Parker's mother asked.

"Nancy, so nice to hear from you. I'm good. How are you and Peter?"

"We're both fantastic and looking forward to seeing you and the kids for Thanksgiving, which is what I'm calling about."

"Oh?"

"Yes, the last couple of years Parker has hired a chef to cook our meals. I know he does it so we can spend time together and no one is stuck in the kitchen, but I want to cook the meal like I always have. So, I'm calling to ask you to be my ally." Nancy and Marie both laughed. "See, if you're on board with preparing the Thanksgiving meal, he'll listen to you. What do you say?"

"Well, I've always cooked the meal too, so I'm on board. I love how he tries to take care of everyone, but sometimes he needs to be taken care of."

"I couldn't agree more. So, when does Parker get home?"

"Late tonight. I'll see him tomorrow afternoon." They chatted for a while and planned the Thanksgiving menu together. Nancy volunteered to do all the shopping. Marie's excitement grew with the phone call. It was going to be a great week.

By nine o'clock, Marie was done for the day. The last several days she had been asleep by nine. This night was proving to be no different, except she wanted to stay up to hear from Parker that he had arrived safely. Once she kissed Jackson goodnight, she waited anxiously in bed for his text.

At midnight, Marie woke, startled after nodding off. She reached for her phone on the nightstand and was surprised there wasn't a message from Parker. It wasn't like him not to text, so she texted him.

> Marie: Hi handsome, you didn't text me. Is every-
> thing ok? Or did you forget?

She waited for a reply and fell asleep.

Marie popped up in bed and looked at the clock—7am. "Oh my gosh, I overslept." She rushed into Jackson's room. He was still asleep. "Jackson, wake up honey. It's Friday. After today we get a week-long vacation." She stroked his head.

As he stirred, she noticed a peculiar smell. She walked around his room in search of the foul odor and found a cereal bowl with curdled milk on the desk among his school books. She bolted for the bathroom. Into the toilet, she heaved and gagged…and she knew.

"Mom, are you okay? You're not getting sick, are you? Our trip!"

"I'll be fine. Go get ready for school. We're going to be late," she urged him. Marie rinsed her mouth and quickly gathered her clothes to shower.

In the shower, she touched her breasts. They had been ten-der, but she thought it was because of her impending period. They also felt heavier. Her body had changed over the last two weeks ridiculously fast. Parker was sure to notice, the second he had her stripped down. He loved her breasts and probably knew them better than she did; she giggled, thinking about how he might react.

Mere minutes later, she dried off and examined her breasts in the mirror. Yup, there were definite changes. The prominent green veins she'd gotten with both kids were present and her areolas were darkening.

She shook her head in disbelief as she threw on her clothes as quickly as possible. *A baby.* A smile stretched across her face while she fixed her hair and applied a little bit of makeup. Were they really going to have a baby? It was hard to believe.

"Jackson, are you ready?" she called to him from the bathroom. It was 7:40 and they had to get out the door quickly. She had a morning meeting first thing; it was such a bad day to be late.

"Yeah, are you?" he hollered back.

"Almost. Meet me downstairs!"

"Okay!"

Now that she had acknowledged the changes, she noticed she was not her typical zippy self. The facts she couldn't ignore—she was late, her breasts were changing, she threw up and she was exhausted. Parker was sure to notice. *Parker!* She picked up her phone, but there was no text.

She grabbed her handbag and rushed downstairs. "Let's go, buddy." She ushered Jackson into the car. She called Parker from the car and it went straight to voicemail. "Shit!"

Jackson looked at her, shocked.

"Sorry." She grimaced. "I'm just trying to get ahold of Parker."

Jackson's wide eyes softened, and he went back to whatever he was doing on his phone.

Why hadn't Parker texted her when he arrived? And why didn't he answer his phone? Did his flight get delayed? Jackson would be so disappointed if their trip to Idaho were pushed out or shortened. An uneasiness came over her then, turning her stomach queasy. Something was wrong.

Marie pulled up to the curb in front of the school and Jackson hopped out. "Have a good day buddy," she said as she waved. He was five minutes late, which meant she'd be fifteen minutes late with only minutes to dash into her office and gather the documents she'd need for the morning appointment.

Marie called Parker again and it went straight voicemail. She didn't know who to call that would know his whereabouts or any problems he might have with his flight. This could be an emergency and Marie didn't have anyone's phone number. Why didn't she have anyone's phone number?

"Oh my gosh, Brooke! I could call Brooke! Hopefully, Dave knows how to get in touch with him." She called Brooke, trying to keep control and not panic.

"Hi Marie, what a surprise."

"Brooke, I need your help," she blurted out. So much for maintaining control and not panicking.

"Marie, what's wrong?"

"I haven't heard from Parker. It's not like him not to message me or call, especially when he said he would. He was supposed to arrive from Budapest last night at ten. Brooke, he hasn't texted me. When I woke up this morning there was still nothing from him."

"Oh honey, that doesn't sound like him at all."

"I know. I called him this morning and it went straight to voicemail. I don't know who to contact and I'm starting to worry. Can you ask Dave to help me? Please, Brooke, something is wrong. I just know it!"

"Of course, we'll help you, but Marie, you need to stay calm. I can hear you getting worked up. Don't overreact, honey. Let me call Dave at work and I'll call you right back, okay?"

"Mhmm, please hurry. I don't know if I'll be able to work until I know Parker's okay."

"Yes, I'll hurry."

Marie tried her best to stay in control, but she struggled. It wasn't like Parker to go so long without talking to her. Something was wrong, and she felt it in her bones. The weight of the large smoked-glass door overpowered her as she pushed it open like it was a solid steel wall. As each second passed the fears she carried within her made her weak.

Natalie wasn't at her desk, so she went straight to her office. She threw her handbag on her desk and began pacing the floor with her phone in hand, waiting for Brooke to call back. Five minutes passed and Marie was growing more anxious as she kept looking down at her phone.

"Call—Me—Brooke!" She continued to pace, with her hand on her stomach. Her phone buzzed—Brooke.

> Brooke: Dave is calling around to see what he can find out. I'll call you as soon as I know something.
> Marie: Ok, on the verge of falling apart here. Please hurry.
> Brooke: Please don't worry, honey.

It was impossible for Marie to not worry at this point. The more she thought about the possibility of something awful happening to Parker, the more her chest tightened. If something happened to him, she didn't know what she'd do. She couldn't lose him. She needed him more than anything, especially now, with their baby growing inside of her. Her eyes watered and her heart raced. Until Parker, she had never known real love. She sat on her sofa and put her face in her hands. "Please let him be okay."

Time had stopped, or so that's how it felt while she waited for Brooke to call. What she didn't know was her best friends were assembling a plan to support her through whatever was coming. Brooke had learned from Dave that there was an accident, but he didn't have details. The last thing anyone wanted was for Marie to hear any fabricated news. They needed to protect her, so Brooke called Ann and then Tessa.

Ann promptly called the law office and told Natalie what was going on. She asked her to keep Marie away from the news and all social media outlets. Ann was on her way to the office and Tessa was on the phone with Lexi, who was to pick Jackson up after school. She was told to bring him to Parker's estate, which was where Marie would be. Through all their planning, Marie waited anxiously for Brooke to call. She was doing everything possible not to think the worst.

Ann walked through the large smoked-glass door and walked straight to Natalie's desk. Natalie stared up at her. "Have you seen the news?"

"No, but I just got off the phone with Brooke and it isn't good. How is she?"

"She hasn't come out of her office, but I've been peeking in the window. She's been pacing and sitting on the sofa with her phone in hand." Ann nodded as she walked back to Marie's office. She took a deep breath, then opened the door.

Marie's head popped up and they made eye contact. "Why are you here?"

"Brooke called me. I'm…"

"Brooke called you? She was supposed to call me back."

"Marie…" Ann's voice was uncharacteristically soft.

Marie stiffened and shook her head. "No, don't say another word. I don't want to hear it. I'm waiting for Brooke to call. Dave will get in contact with Parker. I know he's okay."

"Marie…" Ann sat down beside her. She reached for Marie's hand and was startled when she forcefully pulled it away and popped up from the sofa.

"Whatever you're thinking is wrong, I don't want to hear it. Parker is okay." Marie paced back and forth several laps as Ann watched her. "I think you should leave."

"No. I'm here to take you to Parker's." Marie stopped and glared at her. "There was an accident Marie." Marie shook her head. "We don't know the state of anyone's condition. Dave and Parker's agent are trying to find him or at least information about him. Dave wants us to wait at Parker's place." The blood drained out of Marie's face. "Marie, did you hear what I said?" Marie nodded, pressing her lips tightly together. A tear rolled down her face, then another and another. Ann stood and Marie grabbed her purse, walking out of the office without saying a word to anyone.

Ann drove through the security gate onto Parker's estate. Marie's breathing increased as she stepped out of the car. Just being at his place comforted her, but it also brought it home that he wasn't there, and Marie had no idea where he was or if he was okay. They walked inside, and Marie set her bag down on the entry table, aimlessly, she walked around. She was exhausted, both emotionally and physically. When Vicky saw her, she hugged Marie as a mother would.

"Can I get you a cup of coffee or something to eat?" Vicky offered. Marie shook her head and took a bottle of water out of the refrigerator.

"I'm going upstairs to our room. If you hear anything, please come to get me." Marie walked out of the kitchen as Ann and Vicky exchanged worried looks.

"The media is in a frenzy with this. Has she seen any of it?" Vicky asked.

"No, she hasn't seen anything. I told her there was an accident. She seems different to me. She hasn't fallen apart like I expected her to. I'm kind of worried. I think I'll go up and check on her."

"That's a good idea. I'm going to stay here in the kitchen and cook. And make Jackson the marble cake with ganache he loves." Her eyes misted.

"He will love that." Ann smiled, touching Vicky's arm.

Marie was seated on the loveseat in Parker's room—in *her* room. She remembered the first time he had made love to her, how he caressed her lovingly and took his time giving her an unforgettable experience. His brazen hunger for her had opened up a whole new sexual world that was sinfully gratifying. The level they connected on, filled with respect and adoration; it was beautiful, and it bonded them. Now, sitting in their room alone surrounded by his essence, her heart filled with painful longing. She needed him, desperately. He had to be okay.

She walked over to Parker's side of the bed and grabbed his pillow and hugged it. There wasn't the faintest hint of his scent due to the frequency the linens were changed, and it made her angry. She wanted to smell him, feel him…kiss him. Tears rolled down her face and her anger grew. "This isn't happening. No! This isn't happening." She threw his pillow down. "Not when I finally found my soulmate—the love of my life." She paced with her hand on her stomach. "Dammit Parker, I need you. Don't do this to me! You can't leave me…you can't leave me dammit! We need you. Do you hear me, we need you!"

Ann watched through a crack in the door with a lump in her throat. Marie was strong because of Parker. If she lost him now, it could be the one loss that would forever send her back into her lonely, dark hermit life. Marie climbed onto the bed to cuddle with his pillow as she quietly cried. Ann didn't dare disturb her during such an intimate moment. She would leave her alone for now and check on her in a little bit.

In Budapest, Parker was in the midst of utter chaos. He was going out of his mind trying to get out of the hospital and on a flight back to America. His phone had been left at the scene of the accident, and he didn't have Marie's number memorized, or anyone else's for that matter. The less than melodic obscenities that left his mouth was heard throughout the emergency room, he was going out of his mind. How could he not know her number by heart? By this time, he imagined she was thinking the worst, and he had to get word to her somehow. After hours of trying to persuade anyone who looked like hospital staff, he finally convinced a young nurse to search the internet for the phone number of Malcolm-Bower and Associates Law Office and once he had it in his hand, he called from his room.

"Malcolm-Bower and Associates, how may I help you," Natalie answered.

"Natalie, it's Parker."

"Mr. Nichols, you're alive!"

"Shit, is the media saying I'm dead? Let me talk to Marie."

"She left with Ann. Ann came to take her to your place," Natalie said.

"How was she?"

"Not so good, Mr. Nichols. How are you?"

"I'm alive with a splitting headache and some cuts and bruises. I'm trying to get on the first available flight home if I can get these people to release me. I need to talk to Marie. Call her and give her this number. She needs to know I'm okay. Are you ready?"

"Mhmm, go ahead."

Parker gave her the hospital number and his room number. Now, he would wait to hear from Marie.

An hour had passed since Parker had spoken to Natalie and he hadn't received a call from Marie. The stress he was under was making his concussion worse and he was out of patience. His only thought was to get home to Marie. After going back and forth with the doctors, he discharged himself and hoped to catch the first flight home. He called Natalie again.

"Good afternoon…"

"Natalie," he interrupted her. "Marie hasn't called me. Did you get in touch with her?"

"Mr. Nichols, she didn't answer, so I left a message."

"Shit!"

"I have our tech guy unlocking her computer to see if I can find Ann's phone number. But, Marie may not have her phone on her."

"You're right. She often leaves her phone lying around. Natalie, I have to talk to her soon. I'm going out of my mind trying to get on the first flight home in the morning. Call my house. I should have given you the number earlier. This damn concussion has my head screwed up."

"Okay, I'm ready for the number." Parker rattled the house number. "Got it."

"Please hurry, I'm about to blow a gasket."

"Yes, Mr. Nichols."

Vicky had just ended the call with Natalie when Ann entered the kitchen. "Ann, I have the number for the hospital where Parker is. Marie's secretary called. He's okay." She handed the slip of paper to Ann, who ran upstairs to Marie. Ann's rapid knock made Marie jump up from the bed as she walked in.

"Marie, Natalie called with the number to the hospital and Parker's room number. He called your office. He's okay honey." Tears welled in Marie's eyes and her lip quivered. "Okay, let's dial this number. He's waiting for you to call." Ann dialed and once transferred to Parker's room; she handed over the phone to Marie.

"Hello," Parker answered.

"Parker." Marie's voice was jagged as she tried to hold back her emotions, but there was nothing better than hearing his voice at that very moment, and the tears naturally fell. Ann rubbed her back and left the room to give her privacy.

"Baby…are you all right? I've been going out of my mind trying to talk to you."

"I've been crazy with worry." She sniffled, drying her eyes. "I'm so glad you're okay. I want you home…now. Use your superhero powers."

He chuckled. "I'm leaving first thing in the morning and I'll be home in time to go to bed with you. I'm going to hold you all night long, baby."

She smiled and touched her stomach. "That sounds wonderful. Now tell me, are you okay? What are your injuries?"

"I have a concussion and some cuts and bruises, but I'm okay. My phone is gone and I'm kicking myself for not having your number memorized. We are definitely going to make sure this never happens again."

"Yes. I'm going with you next time. I love you so much."

"That's what I needed to hear. We'll talk about it when I get home. I love you… more than anything."

Marie and Parker talked until he had to get off the phone. Gratitude and relief swept over her, he was alive and coming home to her. Though, she wouldn't have real peace until she wrapped her arms around him.

Chapter 22

Holiday Traditions

If a person could ping off the walls, it would be Marie at this very moment as she anxiously waited for Parker to walk through the mansion doors. He had sent her a text from Dave's phone after they left the airport. The last twenty-four hours were the hardest she'd ever experienced. Parker occupied her mind: his safety, his concussion, and their future. The torture she was under not knowing the state of his condition after the accident had been dreadful. However, now Marie knew without a doubt a future with Parker was the only thing that matter. She wanted him, forever. The whole package, including a baby.

"Marie, do you want a piece of this delicious apple tart Vicky made?" Ann asked.

She shook her head.

"There's also Jackson's favorite marble cake with ganache. But if you want some, you'd better hurry up. He's eaten half of it already." She laughed.

"No, I'm not hungry. Thanks." Marie was doing what she did best, pace.

"You really should try the apple tart," Brooke interjected. "I've never had anything like it. The caramel gives it a wonderful depth. Oh my gosh, it's good."

"Maybe later." Marie paced, wringing her hands.

Ann and Brooke didn't seem to get her this time, offering her food, as if she could eat when Parker wasn't safely in her arms. No matter what they did to comfort and support her, they had to know she was an anxious ball of nerves. After all, they'd seen it before over the years, like when Craig cheated on her. During the divorce, when she was in escrow for the townhouse, and through the custody suit for Jackson. Her focus had always been unwavering, and she would not be distracted.

"Hey, how's it going in here?" Tessa asked, walking into the living room. "Have you heard if Parker landed yet?"

"Yes, he texted me from Dave's phone almost an hour ago. I hate Los Angeles traffic. I'm going nuts here. How's Jackson?" Marie asked.

"He's great. That is one awesome movie room. I'm going back. Just wanted an update and a couple of sodas," Tessa said.

"Sure, whatever you want." Marie brushed her off.

"Great, then I'd like to move in," Tessa teased. Marie continued pacing and ignored her. Tessa shrugged her shoulders, grabbed the sodas and left. For Marie, there was not time for nonsense despite Parker being okay.

"Marie seriously, stop pacing. You're driving me crazy," Ann snapped, as Marie continued. "Don't ignore me. This craziness can't be good. Just sit down for a freakin' minute," Ann demanded.

Marie turned towards her with the scariest scowl on her face. She was about to give Ann a piece of her mind when Parker entered the room.

"Cut her a break, Ann. It's been a rough forty-eight hours."

Marie spun around and she couldn't move. Tears rolled down her face as he walked to her.

Hi, baby." He wrapped her in his arms and held her tight. "You feel amazing in my arms."

"Oh Parker, I'm so glad you're okay. I don't know what I'd do if I lost you." Her voice trembled but her grip around his waist strong.

"Don't give it another thought. I'm here." He cupped her face and tenderly kissed her in front of everyone, including Jackson, who had just entered the room with Tessa. This time he didn't tease them with "ews."

For the next hour, everyone gathered around Parker as he told the scary, unthinkable story. They were all speechless and grateful for his safe return, and that none of the cast and crew had severe injuries.

"Okay, enough of all this. Parker needs his rest. Just look at him—he's exhausted." Marie stroked his cheek.

"I am wiped out. My head is pounding, but I'm so happy to be home. Thank you all for being here for my girl. We can talk more tomorrow and hammer out the details for Idaho."

"Um no. Idaho's canceled," Marie said, matter-of-factly. Parker gave her a puzzled look.

"Why?" he asked.

"Why?" You have to be kidding." She laughed. "Parker, you could have died, and then you checked yourself out early. You need to rest, and you need time to recover."

"But I really wanted to go to Idaho," Jackson whined.

"Jackson," Marie began firmly, but Parker patted her hand.

"We'll talk about this tomorrow," he said. Then he winked at Jackson to reassure him.

Marie inhaled deeply. She was emotionally spent but was beginning to notice her abruptness with everyone. "Fine, we'll talk about it tomorrow. Now, let's get you upstairs," she said to Parker. He nodded and stood, taking her hand.

"We'll lock up down here," Dave assured Parker.

"Yes, and we'll make sure Jackson gets to bed at a reasonable time," Tessa added.

"Thanks guys, I appreciate it." Parker smiled. Marie was quiet and only gave everyone a small wave.

When they got to their room, Marie grew nervous. She didn't want to delay telling Parker she might be pregnant, nor did she want to overwhelm him just hours after he had returned home. She had bought a pregnancy test earlier in the week and planned to take it with him present. Maybe she'd wait until the morning.

Parker stopped at the foot of the bed and pulled Marie to him. "Baby, what's going on? You've been tense and agitated since I returned."

"I've just been out of my mind worried about you. I don't want anything to happen to you. Idaho will still be there when you've recovered. We don't have to go so soon after your return."

"Yeah, but I want to go. Jackson will love it there and I don't want to disappoint him." Parker studied her. "You look wiped out, too. I bet we'll both feel better in the morning," he said before he gave her a gentle kiss. "Let's change and hit the sack."

Exhausted didn't begin to describe how she felt. It was after ten and she had gotten used to going to bed by nine. The pregnancy had drained her the last couple of weeks.

Marie walked out of the bathroom and Parker was already in bed waiting for her. She climbed in and they nestled in together, enjoying the feel of each other and sharing tender kisses. It didn't take much for them to drift off to sleep after their much needed, emotional connecting. Neither woke through the night while Parker held Marie close until morning.

Marie stirred, then popped up out of bed panicked. Parker wasn't in bed and she briefly feared she had only dreamed he returned home. The sound of the shower instantly made her relax. It wasn't a dream. She looked at the clock and it was after nine. She crawled back in bed to wait for him and fell back asleep.

Marie woke for the second time to the gentle brushing of her hair. Parker smiled down at her when she opened her eyes. He looked refreshed and a hundred times better than last night.

"Morning, handsome." She smiled.

"Morning, but it's almost noon," he said, kissing her cheek.

"Ha-ha, you must be feeling better teasing me like that."

"I'm not teasing. It is almost noon." She twisted to see the clock, which read 11:35 am.

"What?! I don't believe it. I woke earlier and heard you in the shower. I just meant to rest my eyes while I waited for you. I must've fallen back to sleep. And we have guests. I'm sorry."

"Relax baby, It's okay. I checked on Jackson and the others, and everyone is good," he assured her. "I had Vicky fix up a tray of food and a carafe of coffee. We can take our time going downstairs."

She grimaced at him.

"What's wrong?"

"Nothing," she said with a smile.

"Okay, do you want to sit on the loveseat? Or I can bring the tray to you."

"Um, let me go to the bathroom first and then we can sit."

"Okay."

In the bathroom, Marie pulled out the pregnancy test and peed on the stick. There was no better time than the present. While she waited for the test results, she brushed her teeth and fluffed her hair. The temptation to peek was stronger than her will to wait the three minutes. A quick glance would be okay, she reasoned, and it was just enough to see the double lines—she was pregnant. The test was only a formality. In her heart, she knew she was carrying Parker's baby and it thrilled her to the core. Leaving the test on the counter, she strolled out of the bathroom. Parker was seated on the loveseat waiting for her, and the tray of bacon and waffles was on the table. A small vase of roses completed the presentation. She smiled at him.

"You always take care of all the details, don't you?" She sat on his lap and kissed him passionately, and then she surveyed his injuries. His cuts and bruises were minor on his face, but his arms were pretty roughed up. She frowned, touching the small cuts on his face, then lightly kissed them. There was nothing but love as she gazed deeply into his.

He took a deep breath, staring back at her. "I want it all with you and I never want to be apart from you again."

His hand moved over her hips and up to her breast. He gently ran his finger over her nipple through her silk nightgown and she flinched, startling him. Before he could say anything, Marie kissed him to divert his attention and it worked. When their kiss momentarily ended, she pulled back and sat beside him. "You know, I'm not really hungry or anything. I'll go shower so we can go downstairs." She went to stand and he took her hand, pulling her back down.

"Wait. I want to talk to you."

"Okay."

"I love you so much, Marie. What happened in Budapest scared the shit out of me. When I woke with all the emergency personnel around me, and in the thick of an accident scene, all I could think of was you. That was too close of a call, baby."

She nodded in agreement.

"Then when I couldn't call you, with no way to tell you I was okay, and knowing you had no idea what happened to me, it twisted me up inside."

"Me too. You didn't text me like you said you would and I couldn't get in touch with you. I didn't know what was happening for over twelve hours." She shook her head.

"Right, and I never want either of us to go through that again. So, now's the time." He got down on one knee and she held her breath. He pulled a ring box out of his pocket, then took the tips of her fingers in his hand.

"Oh wow." She sucked in a deep breath.

"You are the most caring and loving woman I have ever known. The way you love me so completely with every fiber of your being, it blows my mind. Baby, you're everything to me. I've never wanted so desperately to ask this question before...until you." His eyes shone from the wetness in them and he swallowed. "Life is too short to not be with the woman I love. I need you like I need air. I want to grow old with you and love each other until our dying breath."

Marie wiped away a tear rolling down her cheek as Parker opened the ring box. Inside was the most exquisite four carat, emerald cut diamond ring. She gasped and covered her mouth.

"Marie, will you marry me and do me the greatest honor of becoming my wife?"

She leaned towards him and wrapped her arms around his neck. Marie's mind raced at the same time every emotion she ever dreamed of feeling swept through her as she kissed, her love. The last several days swirled around in her head—*the fear of losing him...the fear of having his baby without him... the fear of never feeling his lips or hands on her again...and him never making love to her again.*

Suddenly, every fear she had been holding captive drifted away while her mouth moved over his. Her tears were of love and adoration. Parker was her everything. She pulled back, beaming. "Yes, I will marry you. There is nothing in this world I want more than to be your wife."

"Marie, you've made me the happiest man alive." He smiled, removing the ring from the box and slid it onto her finger. The undeniable statement it represented overwhelmed her. She was going to be Parker Nichols' wife. He joined her on the loveseat and kissed her again, his unquenchable desires mirrored hers. Unfortunately, they had a house full of people and couldn't spend the entire day hidden away from the world. "Before we go downstairs, when do you want to make this official? You name the day and we'll make it happen."

"Well, how soon do you want to get married?" she asked him.

"Honestly? Tomorrow!" A grin stretched across his handsome face, and it touched her heart.

"How does December 23rd sound?"

"Next December?" he asked with a touch of disappointment. Butterflies woke from their slumber in her stomach—her moment had arrived.

"No, I want to get married before the baby is born." She gazed at him with a small curve to her mouth.

He nodded as if he understood, then he suddenly stopped.

"I meant this December, like in five weeks if you think we can pull it off. It would just be convenient since my parents will be out for Christmas." She smiled at Parker. Was he in shock? "I don't want anything big—just us, the kids, our closest friends and family…and our baby growing inside me, of course." She watched him process. His silence was a first. She couldn't help but softly giggle at her dashing, and usually eloquent Parker Nichols. "Are you going to say anything?"

His head fell forward, and when it popped up. The emotion on his face made her gasp. He took Marie in his arms and kissed her so passionately that it took her breath away.

"This is turning out to be the best day ever. December 23rd it is and anything you want, it's yours."

"I just want you."

"How far along are you? Did you see a doctor yet? Do you want a boy or girl?" Suddenly he was very talkative. And all she could do was giggle while he rambled on. "Baby, I am so happy! I want you and Jackson to move in right away."

"Slow down handsome. We have a lot to talk about, but we also have a house full of people. I should get ready."

"Nuh-uh, I don't want to let go of…the two of you." He kissed her temple.

"I love you so much," Marie said. By the way, I suspect I'm six weeks along…remember our shower? I guess one time was all it took." She smiled sheepishly. "That would make my due date in July. Are you okay with all this?"

"Are you kidding? I'm more than okay. I want a baby with you." He held her tightly to his chest. "You know, we need to go to Idaho so we can make the announcements in person for my parents." She looked up at him. The excitement in his eyes was adorable, and she couldn't deny him.

"Okay, you win. We'll still go but in a couple of days. I want you well rested before you travel again."

"Anything you say, beautiful."

Before they went downstairs, Parker had the idea to wait until everyone was in Idaho to announce the baby. He only wanted to indulge in the wedding excitement for now. The baby was its own exciting news. Marie agreed. She loved how he always made every moment and event special.

They walked downstairs hand and hand. Everyone was outside on the patio while Héctor grilled. The goofy smiles on their faces made everyone pause and stare at them.

"Afternoon all," Parker greeted the group. "Vicky, please join us outside for a moment," he hollered inside the house.

"Is this about not going to Idaho?" Jackson frowned.

"Shhh." Marie pressed her finger to her lips.

Vicky walked out and Héctor joined the crowd. Again, everyone turned their eyes to Parker and Marie.

"First, I want to tell you that we're so happy to have all of you here," Parker said. He couldn't help the grin on his face. "With Thanksgiving approaching, there is so much to be thankful for. We would like to meet you all in Idaho on Wednesday for a long relaxing weekend. My lovely Marie has ordered me to take a couple of days to recover before we head up north. She always knows what I need." He kissed the side of her head as she eyed Jackson wildly punch the air, mouthing 'yes-yes-yes.'

"There's more," Marie said to Jackson, waving her hand for him to settle down. He grimaced and nodded rapidly.

"Yes, I do have an announcement."

A trio of gasps filled the patio from Ann, Brooke, and Tessa's direction, their eyes were wide with anticipation.

"Wow ladies, you look excited," he teased.

Marie giggled, shaking her head.

"Well, maybe instinctively you already know what I'm about to say." Now the women were on the edge of their seats. "Instead of fumbling my words because I am so freakin' happy, I'm just going to cut to the chase. No sense in delaying or dragging it out, or putting off such fantastic news until dinner, which I did consider …"

"Parker! Stop screwing with us and spit it out for Christsake!" Ann demanded.

"Okay… okay." He raised his hands in surrender. "Earlier today I asked the beautiful Marie to marry me and she said, yes!"

"What?! For real?!" Jackson jumped off his seat. He ran over to Marie and hugged her and Parker at the same time. "I'm so happy! This is awesome! Woohoo!!"

"Let us see it…now," Ann said with her hands on her hips.

"See what?" Jackson asked.

"The ring." Tessa nudged him.

"I don't get it. What ring?" Jackson scratched his head.

Marie blushed as she presented her hand, with the giant diamond taking center stage.

"Holy shit, that is the biggest fucking rock I've ever seen." Ann let out a whoop and grabbed Marie's hand.

"It's real, isn't it?" Tessa teased. Marie rolled her eyes and leaned into Parker.

"Oh, it's real all right and insured." Parker laughed.

"When did you have time to shop for this?" Brooke asked.

"I didn't shop for it. It's custom made. I placed the ordered three days before my parents' visit."

Marie's mouth fell open. "What? Last month?"

"Yes, I've been in love with you since August, but it was in October that I knew you loved me too. So, I ordered the ring and picked it up the week before I left for Budapest. I've had it waiting in our room for the perfect moment, which happened to be today."

"Unbelievable. You're amazing." Marie cupped his cheeks and planted a big kiss on him. Laughter ensued.

The excitement in the mansion wiped away the last few days of fear and stress that plagued Marie and Parker. After a celebratory dinner with wedding plans in the works, Ann, Brooke, and Tessa went home. Everybody would reconvene in Idaho in a few days for the long weekend.

Wednesday morning Jackson bounced off the walls, anxious to ride on a private jet. Marie, on the other hand, woke exhausted, her new normal. The pregnancy hormones came at her full force after she peed on the stick and told Parker. The announcement couldn't come soon enough. She would not be able to hide it for much longer.

"Mom, when are we going?" Jackson asked while he chewed on a bagel.

"Jackson, I've told you three times already. We're leaving at ten. Now please don't ask me again."

His eyes widened at her stern tone.

Parker winked at him. "Can I get you anything baby?" Parker asked Marie.

She shook her head. "No, I'm fine. Thanks." She walked out of the kitchen and Jackson looked concerned.

"What's wrong with Mom?" Jackson whispered. "She sure is cranky."

"She's just tired, but she's okay. Let's try to help her as best we can," he whispered back.

Jackson nodded and finished off his bagel. "Okay, but it's better if we stay out of her way," he said matter-of-factly. Parker grinned. He was probably right.

The car service arrived at ten and all the luggage was loaded into the back of the SUV. They were soon off to the airport. Jackson sat in the third row with Lexi and Isaac and talked the entire time. Marie tried to hide her irritability, but her cranky vibe hung in the air. When they picked Tessa up, Marie wasn't her playful self.

"What's wrong with you, hon? You love Thanksgiving, so why the grumpy attitude?" Tessa asked.

"I don't know. Maybe it's just the letdown after everything that happened. And I'm just tired." Marie shrugged.

"Well, okay. It's reminiscent of when you were pregnant with Jackson," Tessa said.

Parker turned back to look at Marie whose mouth gaped open.

"Boy, you were a pill when you were pregnant," Tessa continued.

Parker winked at Marie.

"Tessa, that's not a nice thing to say." Marie frowned.

"Geez, it's not like you're pregnant, so don't act offended. You know how you were. That first trimester was a bitch for all of us." Tessa snorted and nudged Marie.

"Okay, enough! Let's just enjoy the car ride." Heads turned, they exchanged shocked expressions and not another word was spoken.

By the time everyone had arrived and boarded the plane, Marie was over it all. The animated chatter from everyone, was like nails on a chalkboard for her sensitive nerves. Troy, Ann and Tessa gushed over the luxury jet, while Jackson annoyed Lexi and Isaac non-stop. Parker did his best to settle the troops into their seats. Marie appreciated his take-charge nature. It wasn't ten minutes into the flight before she had nodded off on his shoulder. Ann and Tessa looked at Parker perplexed and suspicious.

"Is she okay?" Ann whispered.

"Yeah, she's fine. It's been a rough few days and it's taken a toll on her," Parker whispered back.

"It's probably the weight of that hunk of glass on her finger that's exhausting her," Ann teased.

"Now careful babe, I might think you're envious and there is no way in hell I can afford a rock like that," Troy said.

"Don't worry, I don't need mansions and jewels. I only need you." She blew him a kiss.

"Yeah, but a diamond like that would be nice." Tessa bobbed her eyebrows.

"Oh, I wouldn't complain if he gave me four carats to exhaust me like Marie," Ann agreed. "I'm just saying I don't need one."

Everyone quieted down for the next hour and Parker was glad. He hoped the short nap would be enough to help Marie make it through the rest of the day without biting off anyone's head. Jackson and Tessa had already gotten a tongue lashing. He smiled then. Marie could yell, cry, and complain as the mood struck her. She had his baby inside her. There was nothing she could do that would bother him.

"Parker, will there be snow in the mountains?" Lexi asked, interrupting his thoughts. "Isaac and I would like to play around in it, maybe ski or something."

"There won't be much at my house, but up in the mountains there should be a fair amount for everything you want to do. It'll be great."

"Cool," Isaac said. "This plane is awesome. Do you always fly this way?"

"Depends. When I go abroad I go commercial. But here in the States I like to charter a jet."

Marie started to stir. They would be landing in Coeur D'Alene in less than an hour. She snuggled closer into Parker and he kissed the top of her head. "Do you need anything, baby?"

"No." She kissed his cheek. "But I'm feeling queasy," she whispered.

Parker's lake house looked modest and ordinary from the front, compared to his Malibu mansion. Little did anyone suspect upon entering the house it would rival the estate with its warm, rustic charm. The breathtaking views of the lake and mountains were the very reason Parker purchased the property.

Peter and Nancy had arrived several days earlier and greeted everyone with open arms as they entered. Nancy noticed Marie's engagement ring right away, as if a little bird had chirped in her ear. The bags weren't even put away before the squeals ignited.

"This is wonderful. The ring is gorgeous!" Nancy complimented. "I'm so happy for both of you. So, have you set a date?"

"Yes, December 23rd, next month," Parker answered.

Nancy's eyes widened.

"We don't want to wait." He winked.

"No, that's good. We're free. We'll be there for sure." She hugged him.

"It's going to be a small gathering on the estate," Marie added. "I love the ocean view. Although, this view is equally beautiful." She looked out the large floor-to-ceiling windows, taking it all in.

"Let's get everyone settled into their rooms before dinner," Parker suggested.

"Yes, I'll get the kids squared away," Nancy offered.

"Thanks, Mom." Parker carried their luggage to the luxurious master bedroom. The room seduced Marie with its dark woods and wall of windows. She loved their bedroom in Malibu, but this bedroom rivaled it with its rustic elegance and a million-dollar view.

"You own this place too?"

Parker smiled at her. "Yes, but it's *ours*, not just mine."

She shook her head. "I can't wrap my brain around that notion. You've seen where I live." She frowned. "Next month when I become your wife my life will do a three-sixty. I'll go from the pauper to a princess."

He pulled her into his arms. "You'll be the *queen* and we're going to be the happiest we've ever been. When we get back, you can quit your job."

"I can't just quit."

"Yes, you can. It's not like you'll ever have to work again...unless you want to?"

"Parker, I have expenses I acquired before you and..."

He put his fingers to her lips and she stopped talking. "Marie, I want you home and now you're pregnant with our baby. You need to take care of yourself. Plus, I need you *all the time*. Let me take care of you...all of you."

"Wow, I love you so much."

They were the sweetest words to hear, words she wanted to hear. She was the luckiest woman in the world and Parker knew how to make her feel adored. She had never dreamed of having such a generous, loving man in her life. Not only was she hopeful for the future, but she also couldn't wait to announce the baby on Thanksgiving. Life was beautiful.

Marie woke early Thanksgiving morning with Parker by her side. Now that he was back to his usual, amorous self, they were making up for the twelve days they were apart. Their intimate life was back in full swing, despite Marie's queasy stomach and exhaustion. She needed Parker as much as he needed her. They took their time indulging in each other. After they made love, they showered together, extending their time.

Parker strutted into the bathroom dressed for the day's festivities and looking quite satisfied, with a ridiculous grin on his face. Marie was curling her hair when she noticed him gawking at her.

"What?" She put her hands on her hips, just the way he liked.

"Do you even have to ask?" Parker laughed out loud. "You know I can't get enough of you and now, with your changing body, I'm doomed."

"Doomed?"

"Yeah, 'cause I can't hide away with you for the rest of our lives." He wrapped his arms around her and kissed her neck.

"I think we'll be okay." She giggled, and the instant she felt him growing hard she pushed him back. "Parker! Seriously, it's Thanksgiving and we have guests."

"See, I'm doomed. I'm addicted to you."

"Well, it's time you learned self-control. After all, you're going to be a father." She grinned.

"A father...you're absolutely right, I'll go check on Jackson while you finish getting ready. But tonight, you're mine."

"Promise?" He cupped her face and kissed her until she moaned against his mouth. And then it ended. "Wow, glad to know I can count on you," she said as she fanned herself.

"You can always count on me. Now don't be too long." He winked and walked out of the bathroom, leaving her swept away as he often did.

Parker had plans to take the kids tubing with Troy, Dave, and Tessa while everybody else stayed behind preparing the meal. Marie heard Parker talking in the kitchen, so she followed his voice.

"Hi, baby." He nodded as he put his mug to his mouth.

"Hi." She gave him a flirty look. "Morning, Nancy. I see you're hard at work. What can I do to help?"

"Well, this bird is bigger than I thought," she said, looking in the sink. Marie walked over to take a look. The smell and sight of the raw poultry turned her stomach. She bolted out of the kitchen straight for the bathroom. "Marie, are you okay?" Nancy called. The commotion drew attention from Ann, Tessa and Brooke who were in the living room with Dave, Troy and Peter.

"I'm sure she's fine," Parker said, following after her. He closed the bathroom door behind him.

"What was that?" Ann asked, entering the kitchen.

"Oh dear, I think Marie may have the flu," Nancy said. "She just ran off to the bathroom and Parker followed after her."

"I'll go check on her," Ann said. "It would stink if she was down with the flu."

"Indeed, it would." Nancy nodded, staring at the turkey.

In the bathroom, Parker did his best to support Marie as she hovered over the toilet seat. But he honestly didn't know what he could do, other than be there for her. She stood up and flushed the toilet.

"This is the not-so-fun part." She took a deep breath, with her hand on her stomach. Parker studied her with compassion. What else could he do. It wasn't like he could take her queasy stomach away. "I'm not going to be able to help your mom," Marie said, rinsing out her mouth.

"Don't worry about helping. You need to take care of yourself."

"You're sweet, but I'm pregnant, not gravely ill." She smiled at him.

"Doesn't matter, I don't want you worrying or overdoing yourself."

A knock at the door caused Marie to jump.

"Yeah?" Parker asked.

"Parker, is everything okay in there?" Ann called through the door as Lexi and Isaac walked in from outside with Jackson.

"Yes, we'll be out in a minute," Marie hollered. "Shoot, Ann might be suspicious," Marie whispered.

"What's going on? Are Mom and Parker in the bathroom together?" Lexi asked.

"Why would they be in the bathroom together?" Jackson asked.

"Let's not worry about it." Ann ushered them into the living room. Marie stared at Parker with her brows pinched together.

"She knows. I know she knows," Marie whispered.

"Well, if now's the time to announce the baby, then let's do it." Parker grinned, rubbing his hands together. "I'm ready to shout it from the rooftops."

Marie took a deep breath. It wasn't exactly the way she wanted to announce the baby...after hurling into a toilet. "Let's just see how it goes," she suggested. "Maybe nobody will think anything of it. Then we can make a nice announcement during dinner as we planned."

"Okay." Parker smiled

They walked out of the bathroom and Ann appeared out of nowhere. "I hope you're not sick." Ann eyed Marie with care. Up and down her gaze followed the length of her.

"No, I'll be fine." Marie smiled, but inside she shook like an earthquake along the San Andreas Fault. "The raw turkey just turned my stomach is all." She gave Ann a dismissive wave walking into the great room.

"Right, turned your stomach. That's quite odd considering you cook the bird every year." Ann challenged.

"It is odd that you would suddenly have issues with raw meat," Tessa agreed.

Marie just glared at both of them. Then, Brooke raised her eyebrows, as if she wasn't buying Marie's story either. They were going to force the announcement out of her, instead of her and Parker deciding when the time was right. All eyes were on Marie with expectant expressions. Parker pulled her close. She looked up at him and he winked.

"Well, I don't know what the big deal is," Parker teased. "I thought a queasy stomach was a common symptom?"

"Common symptom for what?" Nancy asked.

"Well...pregnancy of course," he said matter-of-factly. Nancy stared at him.

"Pregnancy," Lexi said, staring at Marie.

"Holy shit, I knew it," Ann blurted out.

"Yes, she's pregnant and we are ecstatic," Parker said with a wide grin.

"Well, this is turning into quite the eventful holiday! Congratulations!" Nancy hugged Marie. "Don't worry about the bird, I've got it covered." She winked.

That year's Thanksgiving would go down in the books as one of the best for Marie. Not only was she engaged to be married to the love of her life, but she was also having a baby with him. There wasn't a single worry in her body. The day unfolded with those she loved all under one roof and there was nothing better than that. Once all the hugs were given and questions were asked, the day settled into a leisure day of tubing, games, and good food. It had been a perfect day and Marie was beyond thankful.

Chapter 23

He's My Son

December arrived sunny and bright, just like Marie loved. The night they returned from Idaho, she didn't want to leave Parker. It didn't take much for her to be convinced to stay at the mansion with the accident still fresh in her mind.

Before Marie knew it, she had spent the entire week with Parker. He was on a break from filming for the month, so the timing was perfect. This made him available to be her personal driver, a service he was happy to provide if it meant she would be with him every night. Each morning, Parker drove her and Jackson into Sherman Oaks. They'd first drop Jackson off at school and then he'd drop Marie off at work.

When she gave her two-week notice, Natalie cried, though she understood. After all, Marie was marrying Parker Nichols and he was the perfect reason to quit her job.

Marie had her first appointment Friday afternoon and it reminded her that she was engaged to a celebrity when they walked into the office. The looks and whispers were hard to ignore. Marie thought for sure Parker would be asked for a picture, but to her surprise and relief, no one bothered them. Her first appointment was routine, with the usual lab work, exam, and questions. Marie was in perfect health and had an estimated due date of July 8th. The ultrasound was the highlight of the appointment. There was nothing more endearing than watching Parker. The minute the tech turned the screen on, it captivated him watching the baby and listening to its heartbeat.

After the baby's appointment, they had another a meeting with Eve Manchester, an interior decorator. Parker had hired her when he first bought the mansion and now he wanted her to convert the second-floor office into a nursery. Marie was delighted by his surprise. The sweet gesture was another way to acknowledge the baby in a unique way. In addition to the nursery, Parker gave Marie free rein to make any changes to the mansion she wanted, as it was her home too.

"Parker, I love, love, *love* the idea of turning the office into a nursery for the baby. But I can't think of anything else I'd want change."

"What about our room? New furniture, linens, paint?"

"Hmm, well maybe a few changes to our room would be nice." She smiled.

Then it was settled. Renovations of the office-turned-nursery and their master bedroom would begin after the New Year. As Marie sat in the passenger seat, she glowed with her hand resting on her stomach.

"You know, we forgot Jackson's room. We'll need to call Eve and add his room to the list of projects," Parker said.

"No, that's not necessary. We can just move his stuff from the townhouse to the mansion. You don't have to spend any more money. You're already pay a ton on the nursery and wedding."

He laughed out loud. "Baby, I'm loaded and so are you. I don't want you to worry about money. Let's let Jackson decide what he wants in his room." Then he played with the tips of her fingers and she melted.

Back at the townhouse, Marie and Parker found Jackson sprawled out on the sofa watching *Pierce*. It was his weekend at Craig's and as usual, he wasn't going willingly.

"Hey, buddy, how was your day?" Marie asked.

"Why do I have to go to Dad's this weekend? I want to stay with you and Parker," Jackson whined.

"Jackson, be reasonable. You know the schedule is every other weekend. Parker and I won't be doing anything you'd find fun. We're just doing some wedding planning."

"Yeah buddy, next weekend we'll do something fun. Anything you want," Parker added.

"Ricky and I have been talking about Disneyland. Can we go?"

"Absolutely," Parker nodded.

Marie furrowed her brow. "But that will be just two weeks before the wedding. What about if you go after the wedding?" Jackson scrunched his face as if in pain.

"Oh, I think we can squeeze Disneyland in. Aren't you and your girls getting together next Saturday for dress shopping?" Parker reminded her.

"Yes, you're right. So then, you'll take the boys on your own?"

Parker laughed. "Yes. I think I can handle two twelve-year-old boys."

"Yes! Okay, I'll go to Dad's," Jackson agreed.

Marie shook her head and smiled at him.

"So how did your doctor's appointment go?" Jackson asked. "Is the baby okay?" His questions gave Marie pause, remembering how he felt about having a baby brother or sister.

"Yup, so far everything looks good. The baby will be born in July." She bent down and kissed the top of his head.

"Cool! Will you find out if it's a boy or girl?"

"Um, I don't know if we want to find out the gender of the baby." She looked at Parker.

"It might be fun if it were a surprise," Parker said.

"Yeah, I guess," Jackson agreed. The doorbell rang and without being told Jackson went to open the door. Marie looked at Parker with raised brows as they followed him to the entryway.

"Hi, Dad," Jackson said when he opened the door.

"Hey, Jackson. Are you ready?" Craig looked at Marie, who was standing next to Parker. "Marie…Parker." He nodded.

"Hi, Craig." Marie turned to Jackson. "Give me a hug, buddy." When she wrapped her arms around him, Craig saw the large diamond ring on her finger. The scowl on his face was juvenile.

"So, what? You two are getting married?"

"Yes, we are," Marie answered. "In fact, after this visit, we'll need to set up a new arrangement for your weekends with Jackson."

"What are you talking about?" Craig asked.

"Well, we won't be living here. We'll be living with my husband," she said matter-of-factly. She felt Parker's hand on her lower back. It was a comfort to her, and it strengthened her. "Rather than have you come to our home we'll just meet you somewhere convenient for both of us." She could see the tension in Craig's jaw. She knew there was nothing more he hated than to be told what to do, especially by her.

"Why after this weekend? I don't want my son living at his place when you're not married," he said, glaring at Marie.

"Craig, get over yourself," she snapped. "Parker and I are getting married this month. I don't see the problem with us moving into our new home a couple of weeks before the wedding." She shook her head at his ridiculous assumptions. His fair skin turned red as he filled with rage. Craig's eyes met Parker's intense gaze. If Craig were smart, he'd tread with caution.

"Well, I want more visitation," Craig demanded. "Sasha and I want shared custody."

Marie stiffened and Parker rubbed her back.

"What does that mean?" Jackson asked with a tone of worry and confusion.

"It means you'll live with Sasha and me for half the month and your mom the other half," Craig explained.

"What!? No," Jackson whined. He looked at Marie and Parker for assurance.

"Look, you're just a kid and you don't get to decide," Craig scolded.

"And neither do you, Craig," Marie interrupted. Craig glowered at her. "Have your lawyer contact mine if you want to discuss this further."

Jackson looked at her with a panicked expression. She winked at him and kissed his cheek, giving him the reassurance he needed. There was no way in hell she'd let Craig have Jackson for half of the month.

"My lawyer will be in touch. Let's go, Jackson," Craig said, waltzing out of the house.

Parker closed the door behind him.

"Man, he's an asshole," Parker said. He pulled Marie into his arms and kissed the tip of her nose. "You did good, baby. You're feisty when you're pregnant, and I like it."

"No, I'm stronger because of you. You'll need to call Neil. Craig will not get Jackson for half the month," she said decidedly.

"No, he won't. I'll call Neil."

It was all coming to a head with Craig, just as she knew it would. The moment she noticed him staring at her engagement ring, it was game on. He was no longer the 'big dog' free to control her, manipulate her, or hurt her. Parker would never allow it and she could see Craig knew it. The relief and comfort Marie felt with Parker by her side was indescribable. Everything would be okay, and she was no longer afraid, or alone.

"Okay, let's get busy. We have a lot to accomplish this weekend while Jackson is gone. First and foremost is the wedding."

Saturday evening, Parker walked out to the veranda where Marie had been camped out with a list of calls to make. She was focused and driven, and he loved it. Watching her talk about the wedding with her mother and then Lexi warmed his heart. They were both happy and in love, and nothing could spoil their excitement. Not even Craig. Parker would do everything in his power to make sure Craig didn't continue to be a problem, and Neil had reassured them Craig wouldn't get shared custody.

Parker's phone buzzed, interrupting him from his script. He stood up and walked out by the pool so he wouldn't disturb Marie's call. Glancing at the number, he was not thrilled about taking the call.

"Hello, Sasha."

"Hi, Parker. How are you? I hear congratulations are in order?"

"Yes, thanks." Dread filled him. What did she want? He didn't want Marie to know it was Sasha. It might ruin their weekend.

"Listen, I'm calling about Craig. I know we aren't on the best of terms, but our lives have reconnected in the craziest way. I do care about Jackson." Her tone had turned serious.

"All right, what about him?"

"When Craig got home yesterday from picking him up, he was furious. He said Marie was trying to replace him with you in Jackson's life. He told me the only reason she's marrying you was to steal Jackson away."

Parker laughed out loud and he noticed Marie had stood up, looking over at him.

"I can tell you that's not the case at all. Marie has to encourage Jackson to go with Craig every time. The boy doesn't want to go to your house. Why do you think that is, Sasha?"

She was silent.

He could only assume she didn't want to say anything that might make Craig look bad. "Marie marrying me has nothing to do with Jackson. We're in love."

"I know about the baby," she whispered. Parker was silent. Jackson must have told her, but did he also tell Craig? "I'm happy for you. Jackson is ecstatic about the baby and the wedding. He really loves you."

"And I really love him. He's a great kid. But Sasha, nobody is trying to alienate Craig from his son. The damage to their relationship happened over the course of Jackson's life. The only reason he wants Jackson around is that you want him around."

"I know," she admitted shamefully. "I love having Jackson at our house. But you're right, Craig never talks about him when he's not around. And when he is, Craig's irritated during the whole visit."

Parker didn't know what to say. He had heard the same thing from Jackson every time he returned from Craig's.

"Parker, I can't have kids."

"What? What do you mean you can't have kids?" His tone softened, and there was even a hint of concern.

"I won't give you all the sordid details, but I had a miscarriage and had to have a hysterectomy in early November." She sniffled.

"Sasha," Parker said in a stunned tone just as Marie approached him. She furrowed her brow at him and turned to walk away. He grabbed her arm and mouthed 'wait.' Then, he put Sasha on speaker. "I'm sorry for your loss Sasha."

"Thank you. I've had a tough time of it. Since then Craig and I haven't been good. He's different. I know he was hateful towards Marie, and he made her sound like a horrible person. I believed him. I thought she drove him into having an affair, but not anymore. He comes home late sometimes, and sex seems to be all about him."

Marie's eyes widened.

Parker recalled dozens of late night talks about Craig, and this sounded way too familiar. "Sasha, what are you saying?"

"I think now that I can't have a baby, it's driven Craig to find someone new. He really wanted a baby, 'a do-over' he would say. But honestly, I started suspecting there was someone else a month after our wedding. There was a change in him. Then he'd talk about Marie—how she's changed. I wasn't sure what he meant by that, but it's like he was intrigued. One night in bed he called out to her in his sleep. I know he was having sex with her in his dream." She sighed.

Marie put her hand to her stomach and covered her mouth, disgusted. She walked away and headed into the house.

"Sasha, I'm sorry to hear this. The mental and emotional damage he caused Marie was immense. The stories she's told me are awful. But, she's stronger now and finally happy. Just be careful."

"Parker, he hates her. Though, I'm not sure why. And now that she's marrying you, it's fueled a fire in him. He doesn't know about your baby yet, but when he does find out, he'll come unglued. It's always about him. His jealous rage controls him. I can't believe I didn't see it before. I thought he only directed it at Marie, but I was wrong. It's anyone who gets in his way. I'm so sorry for the way I treated her all these years."

"Thank you for saying that. Listen, I have to go. Marie needs me. I don't want to cross the line here, but if he tries to lie his way into taking Jackson away from Marie, the court battle will get ugly. I won't let him hurt her anymore."

Marie had returned and listened to Parker, her eyes filled with tears at his declaration.

"I know he's your husband, but Sasha, I will fight hard for Jackson and Marie. They mean everything to me and I only want what's best for Jackson. You know what goes on in your house. Think about the boy, not what you and Craig want. Think about Jackson and what's best for him. I know you love him."

"I do love him. And I do see what goes on here. He's better off with you and Marie," she said. "Whatever happens Parker, I'm happy for you. I know we would have never worked. And you never looked at me the way you look at Marie. You do really love her."

At that moment Marie touched his arm and he pulled her close, pressing his lips to her temple.

"I do. Take care of yourself, Sasha."

"I will. Thanks for taking my call and I wish you all the best."

Parker and Marie held tight to each other without saying a word. What was there to say? Sasha had just told them everything they already knew, but the validation gave Marie the peace she needed. She needed it confirmed that Craig was the awful guy she'd always known him to be and it wasn't her that drove him to be that way. Now Sasha had to deal with the Craig Marie knew, and it was unfortunate. Finally, after all these years, Marie could move forward with a clear conscience.

Chapter 24

Twists & Turns

The feel of tender, velvety kisses woke Marie. She opened her eyes to see Parker smiling down at her. He rolled her towards him and her leg entwined with his, her growing stomach rousing him. Everything about her was sexier and alluring. She wore pregnancy well with a glow that took his breath away. The increase in her libido took her to a level he didn't expect when she entered her second trimester. She was ready and wanting—all the time. So before he left the bed to get ready for a day of filming, he made sure he took care of his girl.

They had been in Budapest for a week now and would return to the states in two days. Having Marie with him was better than he had hoped and he looked forward to the next trip when they'd bring Jackson. But, this time it was just the two of them for a short mini-honeymoon while he worked. Marie would ogle him from behind the cameras during filming. She loved the sight of him working, and boy did it do things to her—risqué things that made her crave him more.

During Parker's daily breaks they'd sightsee, but it was going to bed every night together, that was perfect and how Parker had hoped it would be. His life was meaningful in ways he never imagined possible.

Making love to Marie was his greatest pleasure and she received him abundantly. They were in tune with each other, body and soul. Neither had known a love like theirs. Parker moved down her body, placing soft kisses over her, and she hummed, enjoying him. Parker pulled the sheet over his head and her eyes closed with soft, harmonious moans flowing out of her. What a glorious way to wake up.

"This has been the most relaxing week I've ever had," she said, curled against him. "I love watching you work. You're my hero."

"I've loved having you with me this time. My focus has been on point. In fact, having you here makes me better at my job."

"Aww, that's sweet, but you were great before me."

"No. I was good, but you make me great."

She giggled.

"Sweetheart, I'm not joking." He cuddled her close and was getting stirred up again when Marie's phone buzzed with a text message. "Dang it, horrible timing," he grumbled, reaching for the phone and then passed it to Marie.

"Dark forces are working against you, handsome," she giggled as she opened the message.

Lexi: Mom, call me asap!

Marie popped up in bed and read the text to Parker. "Something's happened."

"Calm down, baby. You don't know that." Marie shook her head and called Lexi.

"Mom, oh Mom!" Lexi started to cry.

"Lexi, what's wrong? Honey talk to me." Parker leaned in to listen.

"Mom, they were in a car accident. Jackson and Dad." Marie dropped the phone covering her mouth, her eyes filled with tears.

Parker picked up the phone. "Lex, we're coming home right now," he told her.

"Hurry. Jackson looks bad, Parker," she cried. He inhaled deeply.

"Okay sweetheart, can you give me the number for the hospital?" He paused and jotted down the number. "Who's there with you?"

"Just Sasha."

"Let me talk to her and I want you to call Ann. She'll know what to do. I don't want you alone." His tone was loving and protective toward *his daughter.*

"Okay, take care of Mom. Here's Sasha."

"Parker, oh god, Parker," she gasped.

"Sasha what happened, how's Jackson?"

At this point, Marie was beside herself. Parker watched her get dressed, with trembling hands and uncontrollable tears. He helped her gather up their things to catch the first flight out of Budapest while he talked on the phone. They needed information, but what he needed was to hold Marie.

"Parker, he's pretty mangled up, but he's alive and will recover."

"Jesus, what are his injuries?"

"A broken arm, and collapsed lung, cuts and bruises. Poor guy has been crying for Marie ever since he woke" She sniffled.

"Tell him we're coming." Marie stopped to look at Parker, then turned away and continued to rush around the room throwing their stuff into their luggage.

"Parker, Craig had been drinking and ran a red light. He's worse off. He wasn't wearing a seatbelt. They found him several yards away from the truck. Thank God the impact was on his side and not Jackson's." Her emotional, hoarse voice filled his ear.

Parker took a deep breath. "Okay, I gotta go so we can get out of here. I told Lexi to call Ann. Will you make sure she does? And please stay with her and Jackson until she gets there. Ann and Tessa can handle the kids so you can be with Craig, okay?"

"Yes, I've got it. Thank you.

"Okay, bye." Parker stopped Marie and held her.

"How is he?" she asked, her body shook in his arms.

"He's going to be okay baby. In the grand scheme of it all, his injuries are minor: broken arm, cuts and bruises, and a collapsed lung. But, they could have been so much worse."

She looked up at him with swollen eyes and a glimmer of hope.

"He's going to be demanding, you know. We'll have to hire a personal servant for him," he teased to lighten the mood. It worked like a charm making Marie giggle softly through her tears. "He's going to be just fine. Now let's get out of here and go home to *our* boy."

Marie and Parker briskly walked into the hospital. The second Lexi saw them she ran to Marie and wrapped her arms around her. Sasha slowly approached them and instantly stared at Marie's baby bump.

"Where is he?" Marie asked Lexi.

"I'll take you. Ann is with him right now," Lexi said. Marie looked at Parker.

"Go, I'll be right in." He kissed her temple. Marie nodded as Lexi led her away. Then he approached Sasha, who looked exhausted. "How are you doing?"

"I've been better. I'm glad you and Marie are here."

"Us too." They walked to Jackson's room just as Ann walked out and Tessa came around the corner with coffee and snacks.

"Hi, Parker." Ann greeted him with open arms.

"Ann, you look exhausted. Where's Troy?" he asked while hugging Tessa.

"He went to buy the little turd In and Out," she said with a grin. Parker laughed out loud.

"That's my boy. Being demanding, just like I predicted he would. That's good. It means he's on the mend."

"That he is. I think his emotional state was worse than his actual injuries." Ann shook her head.

"Yeah, he really needed her," Tessa added. "Poor guy was terrified."

"Thank you both for coming."

"Of course," Ann said. "How's Marie? I was worried when Lexi said she didn't melt down."

"No melting down. She was strong. Tired but strong. And she cried, but once we were on the plane she calmed down. We've been going back and forth with names, so that occupied our time." He smiled.

"Yeah, so what names are you considering?" Tessa asked.

"Nope, she said not to tell anybody. You know she's private like that," he teased.

"Aw shit, she would keep this a secret," Ann grumbled.

Parker laughed as he walked to the window of Jackson's room. Marie was lying on the bed holding him. He smiled, Jackson was patting her stomach. Then his eyes lit up brightly and he hugged Marie tighter. Parker wondered what Marie had told him.

"I think I'm going to go now," Sasha announced. Parker turned toward her. He had forgotten she was there.

"I'm sorry. It was insensitive of me to talk about the baby," he said, as Ann and Tessa looked on.

"No, it's okay. Be happy about your baby. I noticed Marie's baby bump. She looks beautiful pregnant." She forced a smile. "I'm gonna go check on Craig."

"Thank you for everything," he said, and to everyone's surprise, he hugged her. Then he felt a hand on his back. He pulled back, unsure of how to react.

"Thank you, Sasha," Marie said. "I'm glad you were here for the kids." Parker's arm went around her waist. Marie looked up at him, "He's asking for you."

He nodded and went into the room.

Marie looked back at Sasha. "How's Craig?"

"Not good. He's not awake yet. Did Parker tell you he was drunk and not wearing his seatbelt?"

Marie nodded.

"I should have known better than to let him take Jackson. He's been unpredictable the last couple of months. I'm so sorry."

"No, you can't control him. He's going to do whatever he wants. It's what he always does," Marie said. "I hope this straightens him out."

"Me too. I'll be back later to see Jackson before I leave."

"Okay." Marie smiled. Then she turned to Ann and Tessa. She rubbed her tummy as she sat down and slowly exhaled. "Once again, you girls are the very best. I could never survive this crazy life without you."

"Well, it's a good thing you don't have to." Ann patted her leg. "By the way, I'm gonna need you desperately for the next eighteen years."

Marie looked at her, confused.

"What? Is it longer than eighteen years?"

"Ann, what are you talking about?" Marie asked.

"Raising a baby. The kid is only my responsibility for eighteen years, right?"

Marie and Tessa both jumped up, and all three women hugged, and soft squeals of delight filled the air.

"Oh honey, congratulations! Now our kids can grow up together. With Brooke's!" Marie looked at Tessa. "Girl, you need to find a man ASAP, so you can join the party."

"I have." She smiled sheepishly as Marie and Ann's jaws dropped.

Marie eyed Parker in the doorway of Jackson's room. He was a real prince for letting them have their moment.

"You found a man? Does he know?" Ann snorted, but Marie's mouth hung open.

"Shit yeah he knows," Tessa snapped. "Why do you think I've gone to Maine so frequently when I usually only go once a year?"

"You found a man in Maine?" Marie frowned.

"Mhmm, and he's wonderful. I was waiting to tell you after you were back from Budapest. I'm moving to Maine at the end of the school year."

Marie's lip quivered and she shook her head no. Tessa hugged her.

"No honey, you can't move," Marie cried, with tears rolling down her face.

"Goddamn, these friggin' hormones." Ann sniffled.

Chapter 25

She Is Strong

Two months had passed since the accident, and life as Mrs. Parker Nichols had been exciting and beautiful. There was nothing better than having a marriage filled with love, respect, and tenderness, and a husband who adored her. Marie couldn't imagine her life without Parker. It was how she had always believed marriage should be, and now she finally had it. To know real love after all these years was well worth the wait. The alternative would have been tragic.

Despite the last couple of months and all the challenges that came with it, Marie was the strongest she'd ever been. After she and Parker rushed home from Budapest, the media broke out in a frenzy about the accident and their marriage. She was thrown into the spotlight overnight. Through it all, she held her own. There was no way she would crumble under the scrutiny, after finally getting everything she ever wanted. Now, she was making her first public appearance with him.

"Okay, this is ridiculous." Marie sighed. "I'm busting out of this dress. I look like one of those provocative celebrities with their tits hanging out."

"Nuh-uh, you look gorgeous," Ann said. "You're just nervous. This is your first public appearance with Parker."

"Of course I'm nervous. But I have to do this. The fans have been amazing the last couple of months. Parker's social media numbers have skyrocketed."

"Troy is totally addicted to watching the numbers," Ann said with a chuckle. "He said the wedding, the baby, and the accident drove the numbers up to the highest they've been. He says it's been great for his career."

"Oh, it's been great for his career all right. They also love me, apparently. When we took those teaser photos back in October, I had no clue how they'd benefit Parker. Now I get it. My own Twitter page is doing pretty well too." She giggled at the lunacy of having a Twitter account.

"No shit. The fans love you. You're freaking amazing. They're also anxious for the birth of your baby. This is exciting stuff. I even feel like I'm part of the celebrity world." Ann laughed heartily.

"Ugh, I still think I need a wrap or a parka to put over this dress," Marie said as she looked in the mirror.

"Not a chance," Parker said, walking into their bedroom. He looked sexy in his black tuxedo. "Oh baby, you look delicious in that dress." He placed his hands on her stomach and kissed her neck.

"That's my cue to leave." Ann snorted, then exited in a flash.

"Parker, my breasts are bulging out of this dress and so is my stomach. I look ridiculous." She put her hands on her hips and he guided her to the bed. "No! You've got to be kidding. We are not having sex an hour before we leave for the banquet," she said, aghast.

"First off, we never have just sex. Secondly, I want a taste of these beauties." He sat down pulling her to him and proceeded to kiss her breasts, making the cutest sounds that melted her.

"Stop it." She giggled like a silly love-struck teenager. "You're incorrigible. I suppose you'd better enjoy these while they're still yours."

He stopped and looked up at her. "What do you mean 'while they're still mine'?"

"When the baby comes I'm transferring ownership over to the baby." His head fell forward. "Aww, don't sulk, handsome. It won't be forever." She cupped his face and kissed him. Her seductive and slightly saucy charms turned him into putty against her lips.

After they returned from the banquet, despite her exhaustion Marie stirred with crazy, passionate love for Parker. The way he had held her close the entire night, introducing her as his 'beautiful wife,' and tenderly rubbing her stomach, made her gush all night long. The positive response she received from everyone boosted her confidence even more. All her worries melted away and she believed she could handle anything Hollywood threw her way.

She walked out of the bathroom in nothing more than a red silk robe that barely covered her growing stomach. Parker's mischievous grin sent shivers down her back. Now, they could make love.

Jackson had settled into the mansion—his new home—quite nicely and recovered completely from his injuries. He loved his superhero bedroom that was dominated by Professor Pierce memorabilia, and the sleepovers he had with Ricky twice a month were 'the bomb.' He was thriving, and so was his relationship with Marie. He was almost unrecognizable. Long gone was the angry, disconnected boy he was a year ago.

After the accident, he had clung to Marie and didn't want to be apart from her. As traumatic the accident was for Jackson and everyone else, it brought them all together. But that wasn't the case for Craig. His injuries were life-changing, both physically and mentally. His careless choice left him paralyzed from the waist down. He had tested at twice the legal alcohol limit for a DUI and had been charged with child endangerment. Between physical therapy and AA meetings, Craig hated life. On top of everything else, his ego took a hit when Sasha demanded marriage counseling as well as individual counseling for him.

Craig had been home for several weeks, but he wasn't accepting visitors, not even Jackson. That didn't bother Jackson one bit, but it bothered Marie. Craig was still his father and she didn't like him cutting his son out of his life. After several attempts at calling and emailing Craig, Marie felt it was time she went to see him. That would be the topic of discussion this morning. On her drive home from dropping Jackson off at school, she gathered her thoughts to present to Parker.

"Morning, handsome." Marie smiled as she walked out to the patio. Parker was sitting in the same spot he occupied every morning after his workout. She bent down to kiss him with her hand behind his neck and held him there.

"Mmm, morning, baby," he said against her lips. He gave her stomach a rub and kissed it. "Morning baby," he greeted the baby sweetly. She gazed at him fondly. Oh, how she adored him.

Their morning routine of breakfast together on the patio quickly became one of her favorite times with him. There were no interruptions from Jackson or anyone else for that matter. It was a splendid way to start the day, just the two of them. She served him and then herself.

Parker watched her, and her cheeks warmed. She was gorgeous at seven months pregnant and he told her so daily. She put his plate in front of him and he took her hand and kissed it.

"Thank you."

She stroked his hair and sat down adjacent to him, as she hummed along with the soft Latin music in the background. Every morning Parker had his playlist on during breakfast—a little romantic ambience to start their day. She loved how he enjoyed the Latin rhythms, as she did. It was one of her favorite things about him.

"I bet you'll be glad when school is out," he said, taking a sip of his coffee.

"Mhmm, it'll be glorious." She paused a few beats as she gazed out at the pool. "Um…I wanted to talk to you about Craig."

Parker slowly chewed his food, holding her gaze. "Okay, what did you want to talk about?"

"I think I should go see him about Jackson. He hasn't answered any of my calls or emails."

"That's not such a horrible thing," he said, taking a bite of his toast.

"Parker...he's still Jackson's father. If he cuts him out of his life now, the damage could be permanent. I feel like I have to do this, so I know I tried."

"Baby, I know you've tried. Jackson knows you've tried. Craig has made his choice."

"Yes but, I still need to do this. If he throws me out, then that's it. I won't try again. But Parker, *familia is todo.*"

"Family is everything."

"Yes! My family chanted that all the time. I have to do this for Jackson."

"Okay, I'll go with you. You're the most loving, and caring woman. Craig doesn't deserve your kindness."

"Thank you, that's sweet of you to say, but I think I should go alone," she cautiously said.

He leaned forward on the table and took her hand. "No, you won't go alone. I know you're stronger than you've ever been. But we're a team. We go into battle together."

She shook her head.

"Marie, I couldn't live with myself if something happened to you or the baby. I don't trust him, paralyzed or not."

"Okay, we'll go together."

Marie was anxious all day, knowing she would be seeing Craig. The last time she saw him was before the accident. Now, he refused to see anyone— or more likely he didn't want anyone to see him. The only updates on his condition would come from Sasha. After the accident, she would text Parker random updates on Craig. She never called, and he certainly never called her. However, six months ago, if Parker talked to Sasha, it would have sent Marie over the edge. But now, it didn't bother her.

She wasn't insecure anymore. What she had with Parker was real and unbreakable. She was confident in his love for her and trusted him completely.

On their way to Craig's, she wondered if she was making a mistake by going to see him. Life was finally quiet and stress-free with him incapacitated. She hoped she wasn't opening Pandora's box.

"I'm nervous," she admitted to Parker.

"It'll be okay. I'm with you."

"And I'm grateful you are." She smiled. "So, Sasha was okay with us stopping by?"

"Yes, but she's not telling Craig. I guess he stays in the great room mostly."

"Ugh, he's going to be pissed. Did you Google the house? You know I've never seen it. Not that I cared to. I knew it was better than my townhouse. The kids never talked about it and that told me it had to be great."

"Yeah, I mapped it. It's okay I guess."

"Better than my townhouse anyway."

"Yeah, but not better than your mansion." He winked.

"You know, I knew he was rubbing his new house in my face. He would go into debt for a big house. Why do you think I always had to work? None of that mattered to me. I just wanted to be home with the kids. And now, I'll get to be home with this little one." She affectionately rubbed her stomach. "I'll be able to hold the baby all day long and nurse for more than three months."

"You only nursed for three months?"

She nodded.

"Aww, baby, that stinks. All you've been talking about is nursing the baby for at least the first year. I assumed that's how long you nursed Jackson and Lexi."

"No, just a few months each. You have no idea how much I'm looking forward to doing everything with our baby the way I wish I could have with Lexi and Jackson." She sighed wistfully. Getting to be home full-time with their baby, that made her feel like she had won the lottery. She thought back to a time in her marriage with Craig when she had thought there might be hope for them. Craig had changed briefly, for the better.

"Are you okay, baby? You were zoning out."

"Yeah, I just remembered when I thought Craig and I would make it."

"Tell me about it."

"Well…"

It was the day we found out the gender of the baby. It was a boy—Jackson. Craig's whole attitude changed toward me. Suddenly he was treating me with kid gloves on. He was sweet and attentive…gentle and loving. He blew my mind and my heart started to soften towards him. I didn't love him when we married. My Latin culture was strict. If you got pregnant out of wedlock, you married the father. End of story. And so I did, even though I didn't love him. But I refused to believe I couldn't fall in love with him and have a happy, fulfilling marriage—one that would last a lifetime if I put in the effort to love him. But it was never meant to be.

For Craig, having a son was the ultimate. Like for all his buddies, a son would be his legacy, his pride and joy. He'd teach him to play football and baseball. They'd go to games together, fishing, and camping. All his dreams of having a son to follow in his footsteps were about to come true. The day Jackson was born was the happiest day of his life and mine. Craig couldn't stop smiling or kissing me. He doted on me as he'd never done before, brought me flowers and started calling me honey. I was stunned, the man had never been affectionate. But, the new Craig made me smile and he smiled back. It warmed my heart. I totally ate up the attention and affection, and I had renewed hope in our marriage.

That first year of Jackson's life was the happiest I had with Craig. I had finally done something right—I had given him a son. Unfortunately, after Jackson turned one, my 'happily ever after' went up in smoke. I went from blissfully happy to filled with sadness and shame.

Every year Jackson grew older the more Craig's dreams unraveled, along with his attitude towards the kids and me. Jackson wasn't an athlete. Jackson was clumsy—a nerd—an embarrassment, and so was I. Craig would rant on and on, 'Why isn't Jackson bigger? Why isn't he tougher? Why isn't he popular?' It broke my heart, listening to him putting my precious boy down, day in and day out.

I didn't understand him or his expectations. Jackson was perfect. He was funny, curious, smart, and sweet. He had a heart of gold. Video games and superheroes were his passion. Not the Raiders or Dodgers, like Craig. By the time Jackson was six, Craig had disconnected from the family. He started hanging out with his buddies and brothers more often and drinking. When he was home he was angry and unhappy, and so was everyone else. I'm not exactly sure when he started cheating on me. When he left us, I believed Sasha was the first woman he cheated with, but I think there were others before her. I'm sure there were clues I refused to see. I didn't want to believe I had failed.

Marie took a deep breath after telling Parker about the only time she was happy with Craig. He squeezed her thigh. Now her stomach was twisted in knots and she was so glad Parker was with her.

"Baby, if you've changed your mind we don't have to go."

She didn't answer.

"Damn I wish I could hold you. I hate that you had a crappy marriage, but I'm grateful our paths crossed."

"Me too." She smiled at him. "I'm ready to cut and run, but I honestly feel like I have to do this. I know he's awful, but he's still their father. Lexi already ignores him, unless I urge her to see him. I know I'll carry the guilt around with me if I don't try one more time. This way if he rejects us, it's on him."

"Well, we're here."

Marie took a deep breath then let it out. This was it.

Parker knocked on the door and Sasha opened it quickly. The look on her face when she saw Marie's pregnant belly humbled Marie. It was like Sasha had forgotten about Marie's pregnancy after her life imploded after the accident. Marie forced a smile, but she felt awkward. Poor Sasha.

"Hi," Parker said, breaking the silence.

"Hi. Please come in." Sasha smiled pleasantly.

Parker held Marie's hand, constantly stroking the top of her fingers.

"He's in the back and he doesn't know you're coming. Marie, you look beautiful."

"Thank you, Sasha." Marie was taken aback by the compliment.

They followed behind Sasha. Goosebumps covered Marie's body as she walked through the house. It was eerie how similar it was to the home she had when she was married to Craig. The same color palette and style of furniture, right down to their placement. Everything was in its place and meticulous. It was almost a replica of her old home and it made her nauseous. It was Craig getting what he wanted.

His back was to them as they entered the great room. Marie's heart raced. Craig was in a wheelchair watching TV. Parker wrapped his arm around her waist and it calmed her.

"Craig, we have visitors," Sasha announced. When he turned, his eyes traveled up the length of Marie, landing at her swollen stomach. She trembled and Parker pulled her even closer, protectively.

"What do you want?" There was that familiar tone of irritation she hated. It triggered something deep within Marie and suddenly, she wasn't afraid. With an air of confidence, she walked towards him.

"Now, that isn't any way to greet your guests," she said with sarcasm dripping from her voice. "We're here to talk about the kids. You haven't returned any of my calls or emails. If you think about it, our unannounced visit was brought on by you."

He stared at her, his jaw tense. "Maybe you should've gotten the hint. I don't want anything to do with you guys!" he shot back.

"Well that's perfectly fine with me, I don't want anything to do with you either. But this isn't about me or you, it's about the kids," she returned in a strong voice. "If you're cutting them out of your life, then have the balls to tell them. You owe them that much!"

Parker and Sasha's eyes widened in shock. Who was this woman?

"You bitch, how dare you talk to me that way!" Craig lunged forward in his chair, attempting his usual tactic to intimidate.

Marie didn't so much as flinch. She laughed.

"What the fuck are you laughing at?" he roared.

Marie saw Parker tense, but, she didn't need him to protect her.

"I'm laughing at you. Even in your condition, you'll still screw yourself over because your pride always gets in the way. And that's just fine with me. Be an arrogant ass. It's the only side I've ever known. But you will not be that way with our children!"

Craig's brow furrowed and he said nothing.

"Now you listen to me." She crossed her arms over her chest like a warrant officer. "Your visitation with Jackson resumes next weekend and you will enjoy him. You will play games with him and you will talk to him about *anything* he wants. If you don't, you'll never see him again." She stared at him and he held her gaze. "If my son comes home upset and not raving about what a great visit he had with his dad, it will all be over for you. Do you understand me?"

Craig only stared at her, speechless.

"Answer me dammit, I don't have time for your shit!"

"Fine," he grumbled. "But as you can see, I can't *do* shit."

"You don't have to. All Jackson wants is to be loved. All he's ever wanted is for you to respect him and his interests. Now's your chance."

Craig looked down at his legs. "But he doesn't want to see me, he never has. I know he doesn't like me."

"Have you ever given him a reason to like you? Put yourself in his shoes; would you like *you* for a father? Just because your blood is in him doesn't mean a damn thing. You never wanted a relationship with him. You pushed him away. And now you need him and that's why I'm here, to give you one last chance at being a father to your son. But after this, if you fuck it up, it's on you."

Craig's eyes shot to her. She had cursed several times and had everyone's attention. She was the one in control now.

"All right. Sasha will pick him up," he said.

"No. Parker and I will drop him off and pick him up. So, we'd better pick up a happy little boy, or I'll come back in here and lay into you the way I should have years ago."

He took a deep breath. "Okay."

"Okay then." Marie walked back to Parker and he took her hand. They walked out of the great room towards the front door. Sasha followed behind them.

At the door Parker turned to Marie and stared into her eyes. "Baby, you were amazing." He hugged her tightly and kissed her.

She smiled up at him, stroking his cheek. "It's all because of you."

"No, it's all because of *you*."

Chapter 26

Love You Forever

Summer was in full swing and proving to be eventful and filled with tears, both happy and sad. The day Marie, Ann, and Brooke said goodbye to Tessa, the sobs were heart-wrenching. How could they live without her? She had always been at Marie's side through every difficult situation. And most importantly, she would stand up to Ann in defense of her. Life wasn't going to be the same without her.

The next eventful moment was Lexi's twenty-first birthday. Parker and Marie wanted to host a small party to celebrate her, and they decided to extend an invitation to Craig and Sasha. It was a gesture to show Marie's support in restoring relationships. More than anything, she wanted her kids happy and having a relationship with Craig was the right thing to do.

Parker pulled the Range Rover into Craig and Sasha's driveway, and there was no whining coming from the backseat. Marie turned back to look at Jackson who was *smiling*.

"I can walk in by myself," Jackson declared. "After all, this is my house too, and Dad said I can come over whenever I want, plus you don't walk so good anymore. You kinda walk like a duck." He grimaced.

Parker roared, laughing.

"A duck?" Marie's mouth gaped open. "I'll have you know carrying around a ten-pound watermelon in your belly is no easy task, mister." She winked.

Jackson laughed, slapping his knee. "It does look like there's a watermelon under your shirt!"

"Okay, enough of this, your dad is waiting. Are you sure about going in alone?"

"Yes, I'm sure."

"Okay, we'll see you tomorrow for the party. Have fun buddy." She smiled warmly.

Jackson grabbed his backpack It was all he needed. He opened his door but paused before stepping out. "I love you both. See you tomorrow!" And he dashed out the door.

"He's the greatest kid ever," Parker said, waving to him.

"He's the best and I can't believe he went in alone. Just a year ago we had to coax him out the door and now he's going on his own. Wow."

The last couple of months Craig had made positive steps in improving his relationship with Jackson. The process was slow, but the change was happening. After Marie put him in his place, it was like a new Marie had been born. She opened her heart and her home (the mansion) to Sasha and formed a casual friendship with her. Together they would mother Jackson so he would thrive all around knowing everyone loved him. It was a turning point for Marie, who was not only thinking of Jackson but also Parker who treated Jackson like his son. In fact, he never referred to Jackson as his "step-son;" he was just his son. It was at that point Marie realized the more people Jackson had in his life who loved him, the better off he would be, and he was one lucky boy. The realization caused her to focus on restoring and building relationships. Because *familia is todo*, and it doesn't matter if it's a traditional family or blended. *Family is everything.*

Jackson walked through the front door without knocking. "Hello...Dad...Sasha? I'm here," he called.

"We're out back," Craig hollered.

"Hey, what are you guys doing?" Jackson kissed Sasha on the cheek and high fived Craig.

"Take a look at this," Craig said, pointing to his iPad. Jackson looked, but he didn't know what he was looking at. "It's an email from our adoption lawyer."

"How do you feel about a little sister?" Sasha asked grinning widely, her eyes sparkling with a glossy sheen.

"Are you kidding me?! That would be awesome! When is she coming? What's her name? How old is she?"

Sasha and Craig laughed.

"Slow down buddy." Craig patted his back. "These things take a little time. We don't know anything about the girl yet."

"Yes, it can take up to six months before the agency has a baby for us. But, I'm hoping to have her home by Christmas." Sasha wiped a tear off her cheek.

"This is awesome." Jackson smiled.

"It is but now that we've shared the news, I thought we could binge-watch *Pierce* today if you're not sick of the show?" Craig nudged Jackson playfully.

"Never! It's the best show ever!"

"Nah, I think you're biased. You do live with the star of the show." He laughed awkwardly.

"Yeah, and he's pretty great, but he isn't my dad."

Craig was silent for a few beats, and Jackson knew the look. Since the accident, he often choked up with emotion. "Well, you lucked out with him. Having someone in the business will help you after college with film production. Or has your interest changed since two months ago?"

"Still the same." Jackson waggled his eyebrows. There was a time when Craig didn't remember anything Jackson told him, and now he never forgot anything Jackson shared with him.

It was party day, and as always, Ann was the first guest to arrive. "Look at this place," Ann raved following Marie out to the patio. "I swear you guys have the most beautiful home in SoCal."

"Thanks, hon." Marie smiled as she wobbled around. "Do you think I overdid it with the decorations and food?"

"No way. Are you saying you did all this in your condition?" Ann teased.

"Stop it. You know I only directed. Such is the life of the rich and famous." She giggled. "We direct and the staff goes to work making it all happen. Except, I'm close friends with Vicky and Héctor. They're more than staff."

"I can't believe Craig is coming. Wow, have things changed since last year. I gotta hand it to you; you're one effing awesome woman…a true badass." Ann giggled, holding onto her pregnant belly.

"That she is," Parker agreed, walking out to the patio. He kissed Marie's temple and rubbed her stomach. "How's my girl? I think you need to sit for a bit. You've been on the go since seven this morning," he said, pulling a chair out.

Marie sat down, and her hands instantly went on top of her belly, as she exhaled. "Fine. I think everything is perfect now anyway. I'll sit here to please you. So, Ann, what's with *effing?* You're usually throwing f-bombs around left and right."

"Ugh, I know. I even felt weird saying effing when I really wanted to say fucking, but I promised Troy I'd work on curbing my cussing. For the baby." She rolled her eyes.

"Nothing wrong with that. You're just putting your baby first. Good for you," Marie encouraged.

"Oh shut up, you're just teasing me," Ann snapped, then fell into laughter with Marie. They always knew how to get a rise out of the other.

"You girls crack me up," Parker said as he handed both pregnant women a bottle of water. He was on baby watch and keeping a close eye on Marie. Once they entered July, he nagged her constantly to slow down. She was due any day and yet she acted as if she had weeks to go.

"Well here you are," Nancy said. Nancy and Peter had flown out for Lexi's birthday and the arrival of the baby. They had booked all of July for their visit to be sure they didn't miss the baby's birth. "I have something to show you." Nancy grinned, handing Marie a gift bag.

In the bag were the cutest little western boots. Marie gushed over them. "Oh my, were these Parker's?" she asked. "They're adorable."

Nancy and Peter's excitement over their fourth grandchild was precious. Marie loved them both very much. After the wedding, they hadn't skipped a beat treating her and the kids like they had always been part of the family. They were good people, just like her parents, who were equally ecstatic to be getting another grandchild. They would be out after the baby was born.

"Yes, they were Parker's. He loved these boots so much he'd even sleep in them." Nancy laughed. "He was the cutest little cowboy ever."

"Aww, I love them. Thank you." Marie hugged her.

Vicky walked onto the patio and everyone turned. Sasha was pushing Craig in his wheelchair. It was the first time Craig had been to the mansion. Parker helped Marie to stand so they could greet their guests.

"Hi, I'm happy you both could join us." Marie smiled and hugged Sasha.

"We wouldn't miss Lexi's twenty first birthday," Sasha said. "How are you feeling?"

"Big." Marie sighed, rubbing her tummy. "It won't be long now."

"Well, you look amazing. So where's the birthday girl? Jackson and Ricky ran upstairs. Before we picked Ricky up to bring him to the party, I took Jackson shopping to buy a gift for Lexi. He wanted to wrap it himself." Sasha winked.

"That's so sweet! I'm not sure where Lexi is." Marie looked at Parker.

"She's probably inside with Isaac. I'll let her know you guys have arrived," Parker offered.

To say the luxurious estate Marie called home humbled Craig was an understatement. His envy was evident, but Marie pressed on being her usual joyful self and refrained from rubbing it in his face. The change in dealing with each other was very different. Marie was outspoken and didn't take any crap, and that seemed to make Craig back off. It even looked like he respected her now, which was something Marie had never believed was possible.

Jackson and Ricky ran out of the house with Parker trailing behind them. Ricky was a regular attendee of all events at the mansion, on top of his monthly weekend visit they established after they had moved in last December. It did Marie's heart good to see Jackson carefree and loving life. She looked behind Parker for Lexi and Isaac, but they weren't anywhere in sight. She looked at Parker expectantly.

"Lexi and Isaac will be out shortly. I think they're having a little…disagreement." He winked. Marie's eyes widened. Over the last couple of months, their 'little disagreements' were occurring more frequently. Everyone liked Isaac, but they were young and growing into themselves as independent adults. Marie was cautiously optimistic they would last.

When Lexi and Isaac finally made an appearance, they were smiling and holding hands, crisis averted. Lexi hugged Sasha first and then Craig.

"Happy birthday, Lex," Craig said. His tone was genuine. The effort he was making to mend fences with both kids was noticeable. Craig was often slow as molasses with changes, but Marie hoped for the kids' sake the transformation would be positive and permanent.

"Thanks, Dad. I'm glad you and Sasha could make it." Lexi smiled.

The evening unfolded with Brooke and Dave arriving with their baby, Lucas. He had been born in May, and was the spitting image of Brooke. To everyone's surprise, Brooke fell into motherhood gracefully. She was a natural, and it blew them all away. Their *Brookie* went from living life on the edge with a different man each month to settled into all things domestic. She and Dave were already talking about baby number two.

Marie had laughed heartily when Parker and Jackson teamed up to convince Marie to have another baby shortly after *this* baby was born. All she could do was smile. The truth was, she wasn't against having another baby, and she would want them close in age.

"Mom, thank you for all this," Lexi said as she hugged her. "I know in your condition this couldn't have been easy, but I appreciate it."

"Oh honey, I love you. Just enjoy your twenties—they fly by fast."

"I'm in no rush." She rubbed Marie's stomach. "But, I am in a rush to meet this little one."

"You and me both kiddo."

The nursery renovations had been completed back in May, and the nursery was the most enchanting room in the house—fit for royalty. The dark stained furniture was warm and inviting, the creamy white linens were luxurious, and the art gallery themed room breathtaking. It had turned out better than Marie imagined and it was all Parker's idea. She had given him total control over the nursery and he didn't disappoint. The whimsical room had become her favorite room in the mansion.

Parker had hired a favorite local artist to paint original artwork for the baby's room. He asked everyone to select a childhood story for the artist to create original works out of each person's favorite scene. It was a beautiful and expressive way for everyone to take part in the baby's nursery.

Over the last several months as each new painting entered the room, Marie would spend hours in the rocking chair transfixed by the wall. The paintings created a gallery wall in the baby's suite that was surrounded by baby pictures of Marie, Parker, and both Lexi and Jackson. The sentimental value the wall held touched Marie deeply each time she entered the nursery. Sometimes there would be tears, which she blamed on hormones.

Scenes from Corduroy (Parker's favorite) to The Velveteen Rabbit (Marie's favorite) lined the walls. Lexi chose The Lorax and Jackson loved Goodnight Moon. The artist herself selected the fifth book. Parker had asked her to pick a book she felt would complement all the other books and their family. It was the last of the paintings to enter the room, and it didn't arrive until after Harrison Peter Nichols was born.

The day of the reveal once again brought Marie to tears. *Love You Forever* was a book Marie had forgotten about, though she had read it to Jackson dozens of times until he tired of it at about age six. It was the perfect story to complete the gallery wall.

Chapter 27

A Full Life

One August afternoon, Marie was in the nursery rocking Harrison. She had just finished feeding him, and he was in a milk-induced coma, comfortably snuggled against her chest. Six weeks had already passed since his birth and Marie cherished every second with him. The babymoon was still going strong. The constant foot traffic of visitors in and out of the estate Marie welcomed. Many were friends and most were celebrities bringing lavish gifts for baby Harrison. Being married to someone famous was anything but simple or practical, and she loved it. Not once did she feel alone after moving into the mansion. "Do you see this, Abuelita, I'm not alone."

Rocking softly, she smiled, staring at the gallery wall. The feel of his soft silky brown hair against her chin tickled, and his intoxicating scent drew a contented sigh from her. His fair skin made her smile every time. He looked just like Parker as a newborn, except with brown hair. When she stared at the picture on the wall, it was as if she was looking at Harrison. A giggle rolled out of her as she looked down at her fair-skinned baby against her tanned chest. It was hard to believe Harrison was hers. Her

Latin genes weren't dominant in him like they were in the older kids. This was a whole new experience for her.

"Tessa would eat you up, Harrison," she whispered against his little head. "Just like she did with your brother when he was born." The sweet memory produced a tear that rolled out the corner of her eye.

It had been over two months since Tessa moved to Maine and Marie missed her terribly. Thanksgiving couldn't come soon enough so she could see her dear friend and introduce her to Harrison. They had made the plans before Tessa moved away. Everyone would meet at Parker's lake house, like the previous year—their new Thanksgiving tradition. Then they could meet her boyfriend, Joe. But, three months seemed like a lifetime to wait. And Marie's sadness had a keen hold on her mood.

Everyday Marie would talk about Tessa and how she would smother Jackson's neck with kisses, or nibble on his fingers, or beg to change his diaper. Marie missed having her around to dote on Harrison. Tessa had been the only one of the girls who swooned over Jackson. Ann and Brooke loved him for sure, but when he was born, they weren't wanting to get bit with baby fever and kept him at a safe distance. But Tessa would have welcomed a baby anytime, and she relished every opportunity to love on Jackson.

"Hi, baby, how's the little man doing?" Parker asked, walking into the nursery. He bent down and kissed her, and then he kissed the baby's head.

"He's an angel. You're later than I was expecting you."

"Yeah, I had an errand to run. You look a little sad. What's wrong, baby?"

"Nothing, just hormones I guess. What errand?"

"I think your problem has a name." He squatted down and looked her in the eyes.

"What name?" She frowned at him.

"Tessa."

Marie blinked her eyes and swallowed her emotions back.

"I know you've been sad for the last few weeks. I don't like to see you sad," he said, with so much sincerity it put a lump in her throat. She inhaled and stroked his cheek.

"I miss her."

"I know, baby." He kissed her while rubbing the baby's back. "Do you know how much you matter to me? How much both of you matter to me? No, how much *all* of you matter to me?"

"Yes, I do. You show me dozens of times each day."

"Well, let me show you again." He stood and went to the door. "The reason I was late," he said in his best theatrical voice as he opened the door.

"Hey, momma." Tessa squealed and ran over to Marie for a hug. The floodgates blew open. "Look at you...you're beautiful." Tessa gushed.

"I can't believe it! You're here...you're really here! Why didn't you tell me you were coming? I've been crying for days...no, for weeks. If I had known you were coming, I could have saved a tree with all the tissue I've used."

"Parker wanted it to be a surprise. You know he's very convincing." She giggled, looking at him. "Now gimme that baby."

"Absolutely. I'll trade places with you." Marie stood from the rocking chair and Tessa sat down. First Marie kissed the baby's head and then placed him in her dear friend's arms. The joy Marie took in watching Tessa swoon over Harrison, drinking him in, and smelling the top of his head like he was a drug, was precious. A precious gift from the man she adored. Marie looked at Parker and walked into his arms.

"Are you happy, baby?" he asked wrapping his arms around her.

"Mhmm, I'm the luckiest woman in the world."

"There isn't anything I wouldn't do for you," he said, pressing his lips to her temple. She knew he meant every word. His unfailing love and support exceeded her highest expectations. She saw it the first time she met him. And over the course of the last year, he'd never let her down.

An hour later, Marie was surprised again when Ann and Brooke showed up. Parker wasn't done spoiling her. It was a mini-reunion for the four women whose laughter filled the air for the next several hours. They ate, they talked, and they all loved on Harrison and Lucas.

Marie excused herself, leaving Harrison with Tessa while she went to look for Parker. She needed to thank him for the fantastic evening he had planned for her and her friends. It didn't take her long to find him nestled in his study looking over his lines for the coming week. Her eyes smoldered as she walked over to him.

He swiveled toward her in his big leather chair and she sat on his lap. Immediately, his hands roamed over her body. Her little hums and moans of enjoyment excited him. So much so, she could feel him growing hard beneath her. Thrilled by the unspoken proposition, she kissed him deeply.

A wickedly playful smile took shape as she stroked him. His pleading, wanting eyes burned into hers. "Tonight I'm going to thank you properly," she promised. "What you did for me today, baby it will take me *hours* to show you how much I love and appreciate you."

"Wow…"

When Marie rejoined the girls, they had moved out onto the veranda. The dreamy smile on her face told all, and she knew they'd know Parker put it there. They made kissing sounds just to tease her.

"Ha-ha, you're all so cute. I just had to thank my husband for this sweet and thoughtful gift. And to promise him there would be more thank-yous tonight." She grinned with a slight shake and shimmy to her body. She collected Harrison from Tessa and sat down next to Ann. "So, did I miss anything?"

"Not a thing. Just lots of lovin' on these boys." Tessa smiled. "I have to say, Harrison doesn't look a thing like Jackson or Lexi. It's crazy how he's all Parker. The genes were strong with that one," Tessa teased.

"I know, when they put him on my stomach, he was so creamy white and pink. I almost didn't believe he was mine. But I love that he looks like Parker. Maybe the next one will look more like me."

"Ah, 'the next one.' Sounds very promising," Ann said.

"Yes, we want another one so Harrison will have a sibling close in age. And hopefully, it will be a girl. So far, Lexi is the only girl in our group of kids. We're all hoping you've got a little girl in there," Marie said giving Ann's swollen tummy a rub.

"Well, it's a good thing I love you all to pieces and would never let you down. Your wish is my command." Ann giggled holding her belly. The girls all squealed and clapped.

Parker happened to be walking out and his curiosity quickly led him to the veranda. He stood watching the four friends hug and laugh, admiring their friendship. These women would go to the ends to the earth for each other. "What's all the squeals about ladies?" he asked.

"Ann is having a girl!" Marie stood and handed the baby to him. Parker cradled the baby in his arms like a pro. In her excitement, Marie clapped and bounced. "This day couldn't get any better!"

"Congratulations, Ann." Parker smiled. "So, which one of the boys will get her hand in marriage?"

Marie and Brooke looked at each other. Serious expressions and silence filled the space.

"Well, Lucas was born first so he should have first dibs," Brooke plainly stated.

Ann laughed.

"Wait, Harrison will be around all the time. They're sure to fall in love," Marie returned with an arched brow.

"No, that doesn't mean anything. I'll bring Lucas down twice a month to spend time with her. So, he still gets first dibs," Brooke countered.

Parker and Tessa watched the girls go back and forth. There was a battle of wills going on right before them. Hopefully, an all-out war didn't ensue over what was to be a harmless, 'all in good fun' question.

"Seriously, with you in San Francisco, it just makes sense that Harrison will get the girl," Marie said with a firm tone. "Ann, do you have a name yet?"

"Well of course we do." She batted her eyelashes. "You know what a planner Troy is." Everyone looked at her expectantly. "Oh, you actually want to know the names?"

"Duh, yes we want to know the names." Brooke rolled her eyes.

"Names? As in plural?" Marie asked to verify.

"Yes, names." Ann laughed. "Skye and Brea...what do you think?" She looked at everyone with a cool, matter-of-fact air about her.

"I like Skye," Marie said.

"No. Brea sounds perfect with Sumner. *Brea Sumner*...," Brooke sang the name.

"Nuh-uh, Brea Nichols sounds better. But, *Skye Nichols* is my favorite," Marie said. "Which is your favorite?" she asked Ann.

"Both. Each one needs a name you know," Ann said nonchalantly.

"You're having twins? Twin girls?" Parker asked to clarify. They all stared at Ann, stunned.

"Mhmm, good job Parker." She winked. "Looks like we're going to have to tag-team these girls to resuscitate them."

"I don't believe it. Twins? Girls?" Marie repeated.

"Yes babe, now there will be a girl for each one of the boys. I'd never let you down." Ann smirked.

"Oh-my-gosh, I'm so happy for you!" Marie squealed as she hugged Ann. "Wait, why didn't you tell us sooner?" Marie pulled back with a scowl on her face.

"Because it's more fun this way. And truthfully, we only found out last month. It seems these girls were already trying to trick us." She laughed, rubbing her tummy.

"Well, we'll let it slide this time. But these secrets have to stop," Marie demanded. "If anyone else gets pregnant, married or whatever...fess up right away. Got it, girls?"

"*DEAL!*" all three women called out in unison.

Later that evening, once the house emptied, and Jackson and Harrison were down for the night, Marie was ready to make good on her promise to Parker. She walked out of the bathroom in her red silk robe that covered her body completely, unlike the last time she wore it over her pregnant silhouette. From the bed Parker watched her, his dreamy gaze lit a fire in her. She crawled onto the bed and cuddled up to him. Then she started to giggle.

"What's so funny?"

"I can't believe it. Twins. Four babies in one year." She sighed. "Last year at this time none of us would have ever imagined we'd all be having babies...like rabbits." She giggled again. "Well, except for Tessa." She made a sad face.

"I guess the timing was right. All it took was meeting the right men at the right time, and bam...we's raining babies."

"Seriously, it's crazy. I keep thinking how none of this would have happened if it weren't for Ann. She forced me out of my sad hermit life. That day I had my heels dug in deep, unwilling to open myself up to anyone. I didn't think anyone would want me."

"I remember you in that white dress with the pink on the bottom. Damn did you look sexy on the dance floor. The second I saw you, *I* wanted you." He snuggled her close.

"I was afraid of everything back then and unsure of myself." She looked up at him. "You helped to bring out the woman I am today. I'm strong and confident because of the love and support you gave me."

"Aww, baby." He kissed her head.

"No really, you believed in me...in us. If you hadn't fought for us when I walked away...into Seth's arms...we wouldn't be here right now." Her head popped up to look at him. "Harrison wouldn't be here right now, and Lucas either!"

"Now, don't get yourself worked up. This was all meant to be and that's why all of our lives are amazing. We each found the one that matters. I didn't do anything spectacular. I just acted on my gut feelings and I loved you—that's it."

"So, you're saying it was fate? Serendipity? That night in the Latin club changed all of our lives?"

"Mhmm, and our life is amazing. Sometimes I wake up in the morning thinking it was all a dream and then I see you lying beside me. I'm in awe of all that I have with you."

"Our life is amazing," she agreed. "Now, I want to show you how much I appreciate you, as I mentioned earlier. I haven't forgotten," she said as her hand moved over him. "I can feel you haven't forgotten either." She looked up into his wanting eyes. "Harrison will be waking up at midnight, so we should get this started now."

Marie took a little remote out of the pocket of her robe. She pushed a button and a Latin song started playing. With the same remote, she dimmed the lights. It thrilled her to have such power in her hand.

"This song. It's the song we danced to at the club, isn't it?"

"Yes." Marie smiled seductively at Parker. "It's called Me Enamoré. It means *I Fell In Love*." She sensually kissed a trail that began at his temple and ended at his lips. He held her there while his enjoyment grew beneath the sheets. In a slow, sultry manner, she pulled away from him. The yearning in his eyes sent a shiver down her spine. That's all she needed to turn into a fiery, passionate woman.

Marie rose to her knees before him and untied her robe, letting it fall off her. Parker's eyes gleamed with adoration, followed by desire as he drank in the sight of her body. There was no flinching, or closing her eyes from embarrassment. She wasn't unsure about her body anymore or her ability to satisfy him. Confidently, she straddled him.

"Damn, baby." He inhaled deeply and went to touch her, but she stopped him.

"No, not yet." Her control of the situation made him shudder beneath her. But he knew as well as she did that all he needed to do was touch her and she'd come apart in an instant. Lightly she kissed his neck, suppressing her ravenous desire for him while playfully torturing him, all to get him stirred up inside. A wicked, empowering smile stretched across her face. Next came a wave of warmth and wetness through her body. "Enough of this torture," she declared. With an approving look, his hands were all over her, and she loved it.

"About time," he said covering her in desperate kisses.

"In the morning, after the baby eats, I want to enjoy you in the shower like I did the night we conceived him."

Parker stared at her, his ocean-blue eyes turned red, hot with desire. He swiftly flipped her onto her back and filled her core with a heated passion only meant for her.

Dear Reader,

Thank you for being part of Marie's journey. Like Marie, you also matter. Marie took a chance. She stepped out of her comfort zone and her life changed course. So can yours, if you just take a chance, and your life's journey can also change. Marie's *abuelita* would tell her, *"No estar solo."* Do not be alone. I want to tell you, *"No estas solo."* You are not alone.

With much love to *you*.

XOXO, Elle